BIRD'S-EYE VIEW

Also by J. F. Freedman

Above the Law
The Disappearance
Key Witness
House of Smoke
The Obstacle Course
Against the Wind

J. F. FREEDMAN

BIRD'S-EYE VIEW

WARNER BOOKS

A Time Warner Company

This book is a work of fiction. Names, characters, places, and incidents are the product of the author's imagination or are used fictitiously. Any resemblance to actual events, locales, or persons, living or dead, is coincidental.

Warner Books, Inc.,
1271 Avenue of the Americas, New York, NY 10020
Visit our Web site at www.twbookmark.com.
For information on Time Warner Trade Publishing's online publishing program, visit www.ipublish.com.

For information on time Warner Trade Publishing's online program, visit www.publish.com.

A Time Warner Company

Printed in the United States of America
First Printing: August 2001
10 9 8 7 6 5 4 3 2 1

Library of Congress Cataloging-in-Publication Data
Freedman, J. F.
Bird's-eye view / J. F. Freedman.
p. cm.
ISBN 0-446-52823-4
1. Illegal arms transfers—Fiction. 2. Political corruption—Fiction. 3. Bird watching—Fiction. 4. Maryland—Fiction. I. Title.

PS3556.R3833 B57 2001
813'.54—dc21 00-054654

Text design by Stanley S. Drate/Folio Graphics Co. Inc.

For Markus Wilhelm

BIRD'S-EYE VIEW

"I have looked upon these brilliant creatures
And now my heart is sore.
All's changed since I, hearing at twilight
The first time on this shore,
The bell-beat of their wings above my head . . ."

W. B. Yeats, *The Wild Swans at Coole*

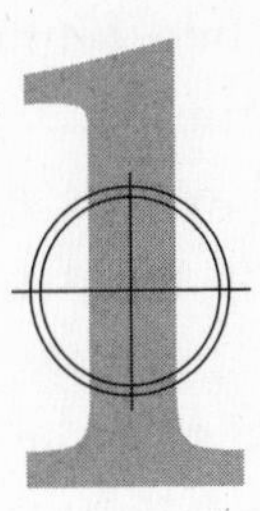

The bottle flies banging against the window screens wake me up. Not yet dawn and they're already out there, lying in wait, drawn by the ripe human odors wafting out of the open windows. Big green flies, the kind that when they bite you, you feel the sting for days, the welts rise and itch like crazy and neither calamine lotion nor rubbing alcohol nor the direct application of urine from a virgin can soothe the pain.

Although my windows are open, it already feels hot and muggy—in a couple of hours the heat will be of blast furnace intensity, particularly for the unfortunate souls, like me, who don't have air-conditioning. It's a bitch living around here without artificial cooling; those bereft of it suffer mightily from June until October. Air-conditioning in this region is like television—who doesn't own a TV? The answer is, very poor folk; struggling students in tomblike dorm rooms; alternate life-stylers who eschew modern conveniences altogether; and a handful of fall-through-the-cracks people, like me.

Along with the flies there is a swarm of mosquitoes, buzzing like a ripsaw. Cousins in kind, in intention. Vampires of the insect world, they want blood. They smell it, from the other side of the mesh. They have extremely keen senses of smell, these relentless little sons of bitches. Hundreds of eyes to see everywhere, and olfactory awareness way more evolved than ours. If the human sense of smell was as highly developed as that of these insects we could not stand to be near each other. We would have perished millennia ago.

I inspect my screens two or three times a week religiously, to make sure there are no holes, not one solitary pinprick. They are resourceful fuckers, these denizens of the insect world, they've been around much longer than we have, and will be here, buzzing and biting, long after all trace of our species has vanished.

The clock on my nightstand reads five o'clock straight up, the tail end of the wee small hours. First light is not yet on the horizon. Slipping out from under the thin cotton sheet, wet with a nighttime of sweat and other bodily fluids, I make my naked way through the house and out onto the back porch, taking care not to wake up my companion, who sleeps on her side, her back to me, snoring heavily, rhythmically. She has her own sets of unique bodily smells and effluence, some rather lovely, some distinctively funky. I checked them out last night with great pleasure, from a considerable number of positions, both hers and mine.

It was our first time together sexually, this particular woman and me. Whether she and I will have other such nights, I don't know; I doubt it. Commitments of any kind, especially mid- or long-term, aren't in the picture for me these days. I'm recuperating—I need space, lots of it.

If there is any marrow left in my bones this morning—there seems to be, since I am walking and breathing—it is because of the body's extraordinary ability to regenerate itself. The French call a great fuck "a little death"; the difference between that and the real thing is that in the little death you go to heaven *before* you die, and you feel better afterward, as opposed to feeling nothing at all. At least I assume that's the difference.

But I digress. I do that a lot these days. I'm good at avoiding, too, and I'd be at the top of the list of championship procrastinators as well. I'm excellent at not staying on the topic, especially when the topic is me or about me, about what I'm doing or how I'm behaving. Actually, avoiding myself takes up most of my time. Not looking at why I am where I am, and how I got here.

That's not quite true—I'm an academic by vocation, I should be precise with terminology. I know how I got here, I just don't like to think about what it is about me—environment, genetics, heredity, plain dumb luck, or some pathetic combination of those and other factors—that has made me such an expert about fucking up my life. My cock isn't all that long, but I've been stepping on it with great regularity the last couple of years.

I grab hold of it. Tilting up a screen panel, I lean over the porch railing and take a good long piss into the shallow, torpid water below, bracing myself against the edge post for support. The flies buzz over, but I shoo them away with my free hand. They hover and make angry noises. They are primitive creatures, they don't like waiting on a meal. But I don't want my body to be their meal, especially not the family jewels. I finish taking my leak, and go back inside.

I live in a shotgun shack. Front room, kitchen, bathroom, bedroom, back porch. Less than six hundred square feet, total, not counting the porch. An old sharecropper's shack that had been sitting empty and abandoned for decades.

Sharecropping is a defunct way of life now, at least in this region. The practice still exists in some of your deep South shitkicker states, where people are still living in the nineteenth century, not only philosophically but physically, but not in modern, enlightened societies such as mine.

My people were not sharecroppers—far from it. We were landowners and water people for almost three hundred years, from well before the Revolutionary War. An old, solid Maryland family. My mother and all my grandmothers going back forever were card-carrying members of the DAR. There are both Union and Confederate generals scattered throughout the family tree. My forebears owned slaves until the Civil War and they had sharecroppers after that, up until the late 1950s, when my father stopped the practice. He felt it was morally repugnant for people to live in a serflike situation. We had seven sharecropping families working our land when he decided not to do it anymore, and he deeded over forty acres to each family. Some of them still farm their sections to this day, and speak of my father with great reverence.

During this time, the first part of the century, my people were comfortably well off, and pretty much cut off from the larger world—theirs was an insular life. The Chesapeake Bay area away from the big cities, like Baltimore and Annapolis, was a rural, sparsely populated region. Even people with money, like my parents and their forebears, didn't travel much, didn't see much or know much of the world. Which suited them just fine.

That life-style began changing at the end of World War II, and the pace accelerated in the 1970s. The population boomed all over southern Maryland and northern Virginia. The new people moving into the outlying areas needed places to live, work, shop. Suburban sprawl was inevitable, unstoppable. The Maryland counties of Prince Georges, Calvert, Charles, and St. Mary's all underwent tremendous growth, which hasn't abated for fifty years.

This surge in population, however, didn't extend as far south as our county, King James, which is the southernmost county in the state on the Bay's west bank. It's too far away from Washington and Baltimore for people to commute. There's only one road, a four-lane highway connecting the county to the rest of the state. And the area's not suitable for casual recreation—much of the land is heavily wooded or semiswampy, the roads are narrow and scarce, the beach areas are not as hospitable as those north of here, or on the Eastern Shore, or the ocean. Our census is lower than it was a generation ago—for every new face that moves here, more than one departs for a life that's more promising—socially, culturally, financially. The young people, especially.

Those who have moved down here in the recent past have generally been older people who want a quiet place for their retirement. A sizable amount of the property that's been carved up for these ten-, fifty-, and hundred-acre parcels used to be in my family—we owned the best land in the county for having access to the waterways that feed into the Potomac River and the Bay. My father, the late Horace Tullis, who was a mover and shaker in local businesses and politics, started selling off bits and pieces of the farm during the 1970s and 1980s. The money was too good to say no to, and by then it was clear that none of his children were interested in living here and carrying on the family's affairs.

My little abode is on the southernmost edge of our family's still sizable holdings—we have over two thousand acres, although the greater portion of it is, as it's always been, uninhabitable swamp. By the time I came upon this ramshackle mess, which is at the end of an abandoned dirt-and-oyster-shell hardscrabble road that stops at the edge of St. Ambrose Creek, one of the many small uncharted tributaries that feed into larger rivers that eventually flow into the Chesapeake Bay, it was on the verge of collapsing completely—floorboards rotted out, holes in the roof bigger than cannonballs, walls sagging, the well gone dry. In a couple more years the vegetation would have reclaimed it, as if it had never been.

I rebuilt the place enough to make it livable—shored up the foundation, reframed most of the walls, put on a cheap plywood floor over which I laid surplus linoleum I got at a junkyard, dug new septic and water lines. For heat and electricity I put up some solar panels I found through a government surplus catalog and attached them to heavy-duty batteries for energy storage, for those extended periods in the winter when the sun is weak. I also bootlegged an electric line from a power cable about half a mile away. Probably my mother's, although it could be a through line to somewhere else. I only use it in emergencies, so whoever owns it isn't going to notice, because the power draw is minimal. (They haven't so far, anyway.) My stove and refrigerator run on bottled propane, and my shower is a gravity feed. Not the Plaza, but it works.

It took me four months to complete the job. Fortunately, the weather was mild this winter, so I wasn't held up all that much. I had nothing else to do except fuck off—smoke dope, drink beer and whiskey, read, shoot film. I camped out in the bones of my shack while I was working on it. Two or three times a month I went up to my mother's house for a proper shower and to do my laundry. If my mother was feeling charitable and not exceptionally pissed off at me she would invite me to eat dinner with her. Not that I was enjoying her culinary talents—she doesn't cook; she never has. Mattie, the family cook for the last forty years, handles that. She is a superb cook, specializing in dishes of the region. I have been eating her cooking since I was born. We Tullises are damn fine eaters.

Mary Bradshaw Tullis, my mother, is among the last of a bygone-era class: a genteel Southern woman of means. She was born in 1918, before the end of the First World War, less than twenty miles from the house in which she's now lived for the past sixty-one years, from the day she was married to my father. At that time, horse-drawn vehicles outnumbered gasoline-propelled ones fifty to one in King James County. Most of the local farming work was still horse-driven until after the Second World War. Even in Washington and Baltimore horses drew milk carts, bread wagons, junk wagons, up to the early 1950s. Both of those cities were dormant, sleepy burgs then, not today's booming metropolises. Air-conditioning was not yet common, particularly in private homes. People put pallets on the floor and slept with fans blowing across wet towels to alleviate the humid misery; or they flat-out suffered. When the history of the New South is written in centuries to come air-conditioning will be the defining characteristic, analogous to the pyramids in ancient Egypt or the Roman aqueducts.

There was no television, and radio was in its infancy. No computers, of course, no Internet. People of my mother's position had servants: maids, nursemaids, cooks, washerwomen, governesses, yard men, field men, chauffeurs. Two or three servants to each person in a family, man, woman, and child, was not uncommon. It was a languid, privileged life.

Those days are long gone. My mother, still spry and energetic at eighty-three, gets by fine now with Mattie, who will be with her until one of them dies, a woman who comes in three days a week to clean, and a gardener.

Anyway, getting back to my situation. Why am I, the son of rich parents, a man of intelligence and wit, with a powerful ego, a man who, until recently, was building a wonderful and exciting career, doing work that he loved, why is this man who is not yet forty living in a rebuilt sharecropper's shack on the edge of his family's property?

The answer is long and somewhat complicated. And difficult for me to confront. But the basic answer is that I am doing penance for having fucked up, big-time.

But where am I going? Which is what my mother asks me from time to time. Where is Fritz *going?* she will say, speaking of me in the third person, as if I'm not in the room. Will I ever marry and present her with grandchildren before she dies, which could be at any moment, given her age. (She says this, not me. I expect her to live past ninety; when people reach her age they usually keep going, they were strong enough to get to this point, they'll be strong enough to keep on trucking.) I remind her that she already has grandchildren, courtesy of my older brother and sister. *Your* children, she replies. As if all of us must continue the family line. Or else it's that there's something about me the other two don't have. Like thoughtlessness and willfulness; along with an almost pathological drive, it often seems, to self-destruct.

Maybe I'm being too hard on myself about my present circumstances. I'm probably no more interesting than your garden-variety fuckup. I'm not violent, or overly critical of others. And the truth is, most of my life has been quite different from the way it is at present. Much more productive, in the socially acceptable scheme of things. My curriculum vitae is most impressive. Until very recently, when the devil in me overwhelmed my better gods, I was a star in my own small firmament.

It's a long way from the top—or near enough to the top to see it—to the bottom. For someone like me, living in a rebuilt sharecropper's shack on my mother's property is the bottom. Despite my present lowly station, though, I'm at peace. Living low-key, taking it a day at a time. The way I see it, I have nowhere to go but up; at worst, my movement, in the short term, will be lateral.

I give myself a quick sponge bath and brush my teeth—using the toothbrush to scrape the caterpillar from my tongue—slip into a pair of shorts, T-shirt, Tevas. Going into the kitchen, I take a can of V8 juice and a Heineken out of the refrigerator, pop the tops, pour the two liquids in roughly equal amounts into a tall mug, and make myself a "red one." Some people call this drink a "tomato beer," and use plain tomato juice, although I prefer the tang of V8. Rock 'n' roll musicians have been quaffing this libation for decades—friends of mine in the country music business that I met in Austin told me that the King of the Road himself, the late, great Roger Miller, drank one about every morning of his life. It's the best way to start the day when you've been drinking to excess the night before. Add a dash of Worcestershire, a few drops of Tabasco sauce, and you're in business.

I finish my drink, rinse the glass and set it on the sideboard, and unlock my special cabinet. I have over ten thousand dollars' worth of equipment in this little space—cameras, a Nikon coolscan slide scanner, an Epson 3000 printer, as well as my Apple PowerBook, with Adobe Photoshop 5.5 for printing out pictures of my transparencies. All top-of-the-line stuff. Anything better than this, you'd have to go to a professional shop. My pictures in particular—thousands of slides, and prints I've made of them on the computer—can't be valued objectively: they're irreplaceable.

I select one of my cameras, a Canon EOS I bought last year. It's a good camera for shooting in the wild. My normal lens of choice, a 35–350 mm zoom, a nice all-around lens for nature photography, is attached to the camera body. In addition, I take a super-long lens, 800 mm. For my purposes, an ultralong lens is often the only way I get close-ups of my subjects. I take two rolls of 50 ASA Fuji Velvia film (a good fine-grain slide film) down from a shelf, plus a tripod and a pair of Nikon 8×23 power binoculars. I toss everything into a waterproof canvas camera bag, secure the locks, grab a plastic jug of ice water out of the refrigerator and a sack of grain from under the kitchen counter.

One last check of my houseguest. She's sleeping like a hibernating bear—she tried to keep up with me last night in the drinking department, not a recommended practice for a novice. My watch reads a quarter to six—time to be motivating, get some shooting done before the day heats up to unbearable. I leave her a note on the empty pillow next to her head. *Coffee and juice in fridge. Help yourself to anything.*

My small boat is wide-bottomed, good for navigating in shallow waters. I pole out from where I tie it up at the back of the house and fire up the outboard. I let the little engine run for a minute to warm up, then choke down the idle and point downstream.

This section is the most wild of all our land. To be more specific, it is located in one of the northernmost cypress swamps in the United States. Bald cypresses grow all along the river edges, their kneelike roots jutting out of the water. There's other vegetation, water lilies, sweet gum, various evergreens. It's very dense in here, not so dissimilar in feel to a South American rainforest. You can get away from civilization real fast in these small streams and tributaries.

For the past several months I've been coming to one particular area—a group of small, marshy islands at the southernmost part of our family's property that lies at the tip of a remote, narrow inlet that opens up out of the swamp. It takes me less than twenty minutes of easy putt-putting to get there. I cut my engine. The boat bobs in the water. The canopy of trees obscures the view into the perimeter unless you're right on top of it, as I am now.

There's no way to get here except the route I've taken. The waterway here, for miles in either direction, is a narrow channel—a larger boat wouldn't make it past all the twists and turns and shoals. Since I've been coming out here, I haven't seen a soul. Nobody's going to get to this place unless they're invited, and I'm not inviting anyone.

My family's always been very protective of our privacy. We've never allowed hunting or other trespass on our property. I don't hunt. My father wasn't a hunter, either, we never shared that particular male-bonding blood experience so common in these parts. That's an anomaly around here—bird hunting is a ritual of manhood, passed on down the generations. My father was a tough businessman and a tough man in general, but killing for sport did nothing but disgust him. Our land has always been off-limits to hunters; when Horace Tullis would catch a trespasser he would come down hard, marching down to the sheriff, pressing charges. It's been known in the county for decades that you don't hunt on Tullis land. Which doesn't make us popular with some of the locals, not that we give a shit.

I tie up my boat. Grabbing my duffel bag, tripod, the jug of water, and the grain sack, I wade ashore in bathtub-warm water, and walk inland.

The birds, dozens of varieties, are thick on the ground. They've come to expect me, because of the grain. It's like pigeon-feeding time in Central Park as I traverse the area, dropping piles of it here and there. They fly in and out, darting for position, crying and screeching their own particular bird cries. They're loud, they raise a hell of a racket.

An orthodox birder would decry my feeding these birds. You don't want to make a wild animal dependent on man, it softens them up, dulls their survival instincts. I know this, but my feeling is, it's not that big a deal. They were doing fine before I got here, and they'll be doing fine, too, when I don't feed them, which will be in the fall, when the migratory birds come back down here. That would be criminal, because it would leave them prey to hunters. It's illegal to seed flyover areas for that very reason.

I finish dumping my load, take my camera gear out of my bag, and wade through about a hundred yards of shallow water to another small knob of land. Although bird-watching is a huge leisure time activity—I read somewhere there may be as many as fifty million bird-watchers in this country—I am not one of them, in any traditional sense. I do not belong to the Audubon Society, I don't keep count of the different kinds of birds that I've seen, or catalog them, or take part in any organized activities regarding birds. I shy away from groups except in my work and normal social situations, like going to an Orioles game. I'm not a team player.

Until I moved back here I wasn't into birds at all. Except for working on my house and abusing myself with recreational drugs and alcohol I had nothing else to do and plenty of time to do it in. I've always been interested in photography, it's been a favorite hobby since I was a teenager; one day late last winter, sitting on my work-in-progress front porch with a Beck's in my paw and a half-eaten salami and Swiss-cheese sandwich in the other, I looked skyward and saw a great flock of Canadian geese flying in formation overhead, coming toward me. I hadn't been shooting much color, but luckily I had it in my camera that day. I grabbed the camera out of my bag, pointed it at the sky, and shot off the rest of the roll, about a dozen frames.

I'd been shooting black and white almost exclusively, knockoff Walker Evans kind of stuff, old houses and interesting-looking faces, rusted-out cars up on blocks, Amish women at the farmers' market, esoteric shit like that. I had never been interested in action stuff or pictures about nature. I appreciated them, I used to envy the photographers who did the spreads in magazines like *National Geographic.* But I didn't see the artistry in it.

These birds got to me, though, seeing them up close, so many of them, the enormous range of colors, the wonderful aerodynamic shapes, the great variety of types. I had stumbled into a new world.

Overhead I hear a loud birdsong, almost like a bugle call. Smiling, I look up. A small flock of extremely large birds is circling high in the air. They're stretched full-length, their long necks extended fully forward, their legs strung out behind them. As I watch, they come swooping in, a cloud of feathers landing in one of the shallow water marshy areas some distance from the other birds, at the edge of the little plot on which I'm standing.

These birds are sandhill cranes, *Grus canadensis,* a large, elegant species of bird. They roost in nearby shallow water at night, then spend their day here. They stay apart from the other birds—they're territorial, they don't like to share.

By rights, these birds shouldn't be here, they aren't native to the region. Occasionally, though, Mother Nature will throw a curveball, and a flock will go off course and wind up on the Eastern Seaboard.

These sandhill cranes are not why I'm here, though. I'm here to see Ollie.

Ollie is a whooping crane. *Grus americana.*

Whooping cranes are extremely rare, and highly endangered. There are only about two hundred of them in the wild; including captive birds, there are only four hundred in the world. They are beautiful birds, the tallest in North America, five feet in height, almost as tall as a man. In flight, their wingspan reaches nearly eight feet.

What makes this particular bird so extraordinary, beyond his exoticness, is that whooping cranes are never found in this area, not even close. Their natural breeding grounds are in the Canadian Northwest Territories, near the Alberta border. When winter's setting in they migrate south 2,500 miles, an incredible journey, to the Aransas National Wildlife Refuge, on the Texas coast, the only place they live in the wild.

Ollie is a lost bird. By fifteen hundred miles.

How he wound up on a small, isolated island in southern Maryland is a mystery. The most likely guess—which is only a guess, since I've kept him my personal secret—is that he lost touch with his flock and hooked up with this flock of sandhills, who are his close cousins. There are only two species of cranes in North America; I've done a bit of research on them. These are immature birds, less than two years old. They become independent in the spring following their birth, when parents cut them loose and they drift and explore and begin to flock together until they breed at about three to five years.

My best hypothesis as to what happened is that this flock of sandhills, plus the whooper, must have been driven off course, probably by a severe storm, and the adult sandhill that was guiding them to their breeding area was killed in flight (either accidentally, or by a jerkoff hunter). Leaderless, the flock drifted further off course until they found this isolated area, which is a perfect habitat for them—it's similar, in many ways, to the area in the Aransas Refuge. There are crabs, clams, other small mollusks for them to feed upon, as well as ample vegetation, and the predatory animals that live in these parts—bobcat, fox, other preying animals—can't get to them, because they stay out in the shallow water. So they're safe, and well-fed.

When I first saw Ollie I was in awe of his size and splendor and general regalness, and I still am; every time I see him my throat tightens, I feel a shortness of breath, like being in the presence of a power greater than the ordinary—the first time I saw Michelangelo's *David* invoked the same response in me; except that was a statue, this is a living creature. As I'm not a birder, however, I didn't know what a rare jewel I had on my hands. I didn't even know they were cranes, I thought they were great blue herons, *Ardea herodias,* another large, similar-looking fowl that is seen often around here. I shot several rolls of pictures of him and his mates, developed them, studied them. When I saw what he was, after looking him up in my *Petersons Field Guide* and comparing his characteristics to those of the sandhills, I didn't believe it—how could I? It would be like finding a unicorn grazing among a herd of zebras.

Ollie isn't a sandhill crane. He's a genuine whooping crane. He looks like a whooping crane and flies like a whooping crane. And most tellingly, he sounds like a whooping crane. Sandhill cranes have a shrill, rolling call: *Garooo-a-a-a.* Ollie's voice is different, a loud, brassy, trumpet call, a whoop!: *Ker-loo! Ker-lee-oo!* On some days, I can hear his whoop from over a mile away, it's that loud and piercing. It's like no other birdcall, or sound for that matter, that I've ever heard.

Once I understood what kind of bird Ollie is, and how rare, I had to figure out what to do. By lucky coincidence, there is a captive breeding program for whooping cranes at the U.S. Biological Service's Patuxent Wildlife Research Center near Laurel, Maryland, which is about a hundred miles north of here. I went up there and spent a day nosing around, chatting up experts and gathering information on whooping cranes, without revealing what I'd found. My initial thinking, of course, was that he was a stray from their program. If that had been the case I'd have turned him in, no second thoughts. But none of their birds had gone missing.

My next step was to get in touch, via the Web, with The International Crane Foundation and with a group called Operation Migration, which is spearheaded by some of the people who became famous in the 1980s, when they led an orphan flock of young sandhill cranes to their new home by disguising an ultra-light airplane as a mature sandhill crane, an incredible feat documented in the movie *Fly Away Home.* They're about to try the same unorthodox approach to teach new migration routes to whooping cranes; right now, there's only one migration path for whooping cranes, from Canada to Texas, and ornithologists are very concerned that if alternate routes aren't established, the tiny flock could be wiped out if a disease hit their population.

They were very helpful; but incredibly they, too, weren't missing any cranes.

So I've kept quiet about Ollie.

I have my reasons for doing this. They're selfish, but they're genuine and necessary. I need peace, quiet, serenity—I had my head handed to me in the not-distant past, I'm still in the recovery stage. If Ollie was discovered by the outside world he would become a cause célèbre, a national object of intense curiosity and scrutiny. Thousands of avid birders and scientists would flock to my private little corner. That would be disastrous for me—I can't handle invasion on that level. Privacy and space are my two most important needs right now.

So I kept quiet about my exotic discovery, although that's not a decision I take lightly. If I was a real birder, I would have sacrificed my own needs and turned him in, but I'm not, so I didn't. At some point soon, though, I will alert the proper authorities, because Ollie's too valuable to be left to nature's random capriciousness for long, particularly once hunting season starts around here—it would be catastrophic if a hunter shot him while he was flying over this small area. For the near future, however, I'm leaving him alone. It may be selfish in the infinite scheme of the universe, but he seems to be happy. I value happiness highly—I know from my own recent experience how fragile it can be, and how easily lost.

Observing Ollie, I've come to believe he has a sixth sense that this area is a safe haven for him, that the sandhills provide him cover, and protection. I know that Ollie can't stay here forever. He has to be returned to his flock. The survival of his species could depend on him. I'm just not ready to let him go yet.

I load a fresh roll of film in my camera and take some pictures of my pride and joy. With the ultralong lens I get vivid shots of his eye, his beak, the curve of his wings. He isn't afraid of me, we've gotten accustomed to each other over these past months, but I keep my distance from him anyway. I don't want him thinking of me as part of his extended family—when he is, ultimately, united with his own kind, he can't be dependent on man. Which is why I never feed him or the sandhills, as I do the other birds.

The drone of an airplane brings me out of my reverie. I look up. It's a jet, I don't know what kind. Not commercial. I watch as it flies low across the water and lands on a private strip a half-mile away, on the other side of the lagoon, taxiing to a stop on the tarmac.

The land that airstrip is on used to be part of our family holdings. It's changed hands a few times since we originally sold it thirty years ago. It's the only piece of real estate that's within five miles of my shack, which means it's the only property remotely near this area. The runway was built last year, shortly before I came back home, so I assume the property is under new ownership. I don't know who the present owner is—I've never seen anyone land here before. I suppose my mother knows—she knows everything that goes on in the county, nothing escapes her.

Back to the work at hand. I shoot some more stills of Ollie. If he misses other whooping cranes it doesn't show, he doesn't look like he's moping around and pining for like companionship—the sandhills provide that.

The sound of voices cuts through the air. Noises carry great distances out here—the water acts like an echo board, although specific words are indistinct. I glance at my waterproof Timex.

It's still early, well before seven. I turn and look again at the airfield across the channel, where the voices are coming from.

The airplane is parked on the runway. The entrance door is open, the steps extended to the tarmac. Three men are standing in front of the nose.

I swing my camera in their direction and stare through the lens, using it as a telescope, to get a better look. There's some coarse bunchgrass growing at the sides of the runway—through the distortion of the long lens it looks like a sea of grass, flowing in the wind like waves on the ocean.

One of the men I'm spying on appears to be a pilot, complete with epaulet shirt and MacArthur-style pilot's hat and shades. Of the other two, one is dressed casually, wearing a long-billed baseball-style cap and sunglasses, while the third man, who is smaller, is dressed more formally, in a coat and tie. He's bareheaded and is without glasses. Those two seem to be in animated, angry conversation—the smaller man paces back and forth, gesturing with his arms. The pilot-type is standing to the side, looking off into the distance.

I'm snooping on them; I shouldn't be, but I am. A private plane landing on a secluded airstrip at dawn's first light, a heated argument, who wouldn't? They don't know I'm here, they can't see me hidden on my island, nor can they espy my boat, tucked in amongst the reeds.

That used to be our property. I have the right to look.

I have them in full figure through the ultralong lens. I can't make out features—their faces are backlit, because the sun is rising directly behind them, silhouetting them against the milk-white sky—but I snap off a couple of pictures anyway. It's reflex—I see it, I shoot it. Besides, I'm almost finished with the roll. Might as well expose it.

I wonder who they are and what they're arguing about. My mind conjures up the most lurid possibility—criminal activity. That's not solely paranoia talking, although I've been accused of that. It's known that there is a lot of drug-running taking place here. This region, with its multitude of hidden waterways, has become an important drop-and-distribution point. It's commonly believed that some of the large farms in the area, including pieces of our old property, have been bought by international drug syndicates, using fictitious owners as fronts, and are being used as embarkation points. It's a good setup—this is a rural area, you can pretty much come and go without being noticed, via the Bay, and you're within a few hours of all the major Eastern cities, Washington, Baltimore, Philadelphia, New York. Large ships can go in and out of these waterways virtually undetected; they could be transporting hundreds of millions of dollars of drugs, guns, any kind of contraband you can imagine. There's over a thousand miles of shoreline in the southern Chesapeake Bay, and it's impossible to patrol and control it all. The Coast Guard's lucky if they interdict ten percent of the illegal stuff.

Which is not to say that the people I'm looking at are criminals. My imagination tends to run amok these days. Nevertheless, the owner of that property is my neighbor. I'd like to find out who it is who has his own airstrip, his own private airplane. One of these days, when I foray into town, I'll check county records and see what name is on the deed. Whether he's one of these men I'm looking at I have no idea.

The sun is scorching the morning like a hot fist. I'm feeling the aftereffects of last night. I don't want to be out here when the sun is high, which will be soon. I turn away from them and go back to my own business.

The gunshot is not loud—a pop that echoes across the water. I turn back.

The pilot is nowhere to be seen. The taller of the other two is now standing over the smaller one, who lies motionless at his feet. The standing man, the one wearing the long-billed cap and sunglasses, has a pistol in his hand. He extends his arm and delivers the coup de grâce. Through my lens I see the body on the ground jerk from the impact of the bullet as it hits him in the head.

The killer bends over and picks up the discharged bullet shells. Then he grabs the dead man under the arms, throws him over his shoulder as one would a sack of potatoes, and carries him onto the airplane. The stairs are pulled up. A moment later the airplane takes off down the runway, gathering speed as it ascends into the sky.

I watch, frozen and mesmerized, until the plane disappears from view. Then I put my equipment away, dump my gear in my boat, and wait for several more minutes until I'm sure they're gone. Using extreme caution, I pole out into the narrow channel, keeping as close to the shore as I can, and sneak away for home.

My houseguest is awake when I return. She's lounging at the kitchen table, bare-ass naked, sipping from a cup of steaming black coffee. "The early bird gets the worm?" She gives me a half-sleepy smile.

I'm shaky from what I've just seen, but I manage to hide my nervousness from her. "How do you feel?" I ask solicitously, the good host. Despite the traumatic episode I just witnessed I'm getting hard looking at her. There is a rich soft-earth fragrance wafting up from her nether regions.

"Kind of blurry," she admits. "And hot." She fans herself with a folded-up page from yesterday's *Washington Post,* holds up her coffee cup. "This helps—the blur, not the heat. And a Bromo. You don't drink that much all the time, do you?" We don't know each other well enough for her to know all my habits, especially the bad ones.

"I kind of got carried away."

"Didn't we both?" She shakes her head at the wonder of it. She shifts in the chair. Her pussy's staring at me. I look away from it, up to her face.

Dakota Chalmers. Named for Dakota Staton, the '50s jazz singer, her mother's favorite vocalist. This Dakota is a fine-looking woman. Robust. Pretty face, big luscious tits, bodacious ass, long muscular legs: storybook. I especially like her complexion: coffee with cream and a little peach thrown in the mix. There's a resemblance to another jazz singer, Billie Holiday, when the great diva of blues was young, before the drugs wasted her looks. This lady will never have that problem. She's smart. She's a lawyer for HUD.

Dakota and I were introduced at a party in Annapolis that was given by a mutual friend. We've dated casually a few times; I go up to her place for dinner and a movie or some music, she comes down here for some country relaxation. Last night we went to a party not far from here that was given by a friend of hers, and got relaxed enough to decide to have sex.

By mutual understanding, there will be no demands on either side. What more could you want in a nice noncommitted relationship? Nothing, except that she not linger too deeply into the morning. I've got shit to do. A lot more than I bargained for when I woke up.

She's on my wavelength—after we share a cup of coffee she showers and dresses, gathers her things.

"Drive safely," I advise her as I walk her outside to her Lexus. "Do you remember the way?"

"I can find my way," she says with easy assurance.

I stand there for a moment with the hot morning sun beating down on me, watching her disappear around the bend. Then I go back inside.

Now that she's gone I can indulge my emotions. I forage for anything in the liquor cupboard—Chopin vodka is the first thing to hit my hand, so I drink a shot of that, straight from the bottle. That helps; my heartbeat isn't as rapid as a hummingbird's anymore.

Here's what I'm thinking: what the fuck am I supposed to do? I just saw a murder being committed. I know what I'm *supposed* to do—go to the cops. But for several reasons, I don't know if that's what I'm going to do.

I don't want to get involved. If that makes me a bad citizen, so be it. I wasn't supposed to see that murder take place, it was pure coincidence. If I'd left ten minutes earlier, or had stayed in bed with my guest, like a good host should have, I would never have seen one damn thing. If a tree falls in the forest and no one hears it, does it make a sound? Not to me, if I don't hear it.

Besides that, there's my credibility, or lack thereof. The local constabulary, some of them friends from childhood, view me with a skeptical eye these days. College professor who throws it over and comes home to live in a piece-of-shit shack out in the boonies? Doing nothing except drinking too much, smoking weed, hitting on women? This is not a man to be trusted, not an upstanding citizen. I call in and report a murder, they're going to first want to know how much I drank last night, how much dope I've been smoking. Since the answers are too much and too much, they're going to drag their ass getting in gear. And if they do go check out the scene, what will they find? No bullet shells, I saw the killer pick them up. Will the body still be there? Of course not. That was a premeditated hit, most likely a contract killing. There isn't a shred of evidence lying around.

I take another hit of vodka to calm my nerves some more, and formulate a plan. I'll wait a day or two, see if anything turns up. A story on the news. If there is something, then I can go to the police. Otherwise, I'll clam up. The killer doesn't know I saw anything. Hell, the killer doesn't know I exist.

I hope nothing turns up. I don't want to get involved. Whoever that murderer is, he's not a remorseful person. I put my nose into this, that could be me staring down his gun barrel.

It's not my problem. And I'm not going to make it my problem.

I dump my gear on the kitchen table and unload my camera. I have to go into town for supplies later this morning. I'll drop the film at the community college film lab. King James Community College in Jamestown, the county seat, has a nice photography facility, and I've become friendly with the head instructor, a retired *Baltimore Sun* photographer named Pierce Wilcox. He lets me use the facilities.

I didn't check my phone messages when I got home last night; I had more important things to take care of. I dial up my service.

Sent yesterday at 8:15 P.M. A woman's southern Maryland drawl. The age doesn't show in her voice. *"This is your dear old mother, Fritz. Where are you, anyway, son, you never seem to be in when I need to talk to you. I have left you an e-mail. I'll need your answer by ten in the morning."* Click.

I glance at the wall clock—it isn't nine yet, ample time to reply to my mother. I continue listening.

Sent yesterday at 9:38 P.M. "Fritz. Sam. See you tomorrow night. Hope you're sober, for mother's sake. Wear clean clothes, if you have any." Click.

Lovely. This evening is going to be a hell of a lot of fun.

Sent this morning at 12:49 A.M. "Fritz? This is Marnie? Are you there, Fritz. If you are, pick up, please! . . ."

A few pregnant beats, then silence, end of message. I stare at the receiver in my hand like it's alive, a cobra that's going to rise up, spread its hood, and sink its teeth into my arm.

Twelve-forty-nine was minutes before I got home. That would've ripped it as far as Dakota and I were concerned. Thank God I missed the call. But in a perverse way, which has been my way these last months, it would have been something to hear Marnie's voice for real. Too late now.

Zap. Button pushed. Message gone. Marnie—the light of my life, and the ruination. I don't need to hear any more of that, I know where it was going. Straight to hell on a rocketship, with me riding shotgun, like Slim Pickens in *Dr. Strangelove.*

Is this a portent of some kind? What I saw on the landing strip across the water, and now this phone call? I hope not—I've been successful in avoiding the world, I want to continue to do so, for a while at least. They say troubles come in threes—already this morning, two bad episodes.

There are no more messages. I turn my Apple PowerBook on, check my e-mail. There isn't much. Four items, two of them porno come-ons. Does everybody get this garbage, or just people with bad reputations like me?

I delete the stroke stuff, open the one that isn't my mother's (I'll save that for last, because it will require an actual response). It's a missive from a friendly colleague at Stanford, a fellow I did graduate work with, wondering how I'm doing, if I'm planning on teaching again anytime soon, would I be interested in relocating to the West Coast, there might be an opening at UC Santa Cruz, or maybe even UCLA, a plum situation.

I don't know what to say. I don't want to *not* teach forever, but I don't feel I'm ready to get back into harness yet. I'm certainly not ready to undergo the rigors of a tough interview process, trying to respond to questions that have no explainable answers.

I type back a quick response. *"Thanks for thinking of me in my time of need, but I am currently on a project here that although not in my direct field is providing enjoyment and insight. If these are legitimate openings, rather than either fishing expeditions or an old friend trying to help out (which I appreciate, believe me), send me the info. Great hearing from you. Fritz."*

My mother's message is simple and to the point. *"Fritz: I am having a small dinner party tomorrow night."* (That's tonight.) *"Cocktails at seven, dinner at eight. Jacket and tie, preferably a suit. Your presence is requested."* (Meaning I'd better show up unless I'm in the hospital, and if I am, why haven't I called her?) *"There will be interesting and important people present, it would not hurt you to meet them. I'm sure that even you will find them charming and amusing. Please reply by tomorrow morning, so I can make the necessary seating and catering arrangements. Mother."* Then as a postscript: *"Do you have a presentable summer suit? You should. If you wish to go to any good men's clothing store in Washington, Baltimore, or Annapolis, you can put it on your charge card and I will reimburse you. Love, Mother."*

Thirty-eight years old and my mother's still offering to pay for my clothes? How low does she think I've fallen? Extremely low, apparently.

I write her back: *"Mommy dearest. I'll be there. I have a suit which I trust will be suitable, but thanks for the offer. Fritz."*

Seven o'clock tonight, the family manse, in mufti, plus my brother. Whoopdeedo.

Being out on the water gives me an appetite. I make myself a couple of fried egg sandwiches on white bread with garlic mayo, accompanied by bacon, lettuce, tomato, and onion. The vegetables are from the garden I've cultivated behind my house, the tomatoes so ripe the saliva drools down my chin as I'm slicing them. Iced tea to wash it all down; I'm not going to drink any more alcohol until dinner, there's a point where abusing my body stops, and I'm at that point now. Not that bacon and egg sandwiches are healthy, but I like them. I try to live in the present now, as much as possible, so I do as I like. Tomorrow I'll run four miles, sweat the garbage out.

It's a half-hour drive into Jamestown, the only town of any size in the county. I stop by the college and drop off my film. It'll take about three hours to process my transparencies—it's all done by machine. The technician, a male student in this case, doesn't even have to look at them. The images are there or they aren't, the developer can't create what the camera didn't capture.

If Pierce was around I'd spend some time bullshitting with him, but he isn't, so I go into town and do my weekly shopping. Then I go back to the college, hang out until my slides are ready, and drive home.

I put the groceries and other sundries away and scan the transparencies on my Nikon cool-scan and into my computer via Adobe Photoshop, tweaking the colors a little to cherry them up. There are some good shots of Ollie. I also have a nice one of a bald eagle—they've come back well from near-extinction in this area. I hope the same will be true about Ollie and his tribe someday.

After playing with those pictures for a while, I look at the images of the two men who were arguing by the airplane.

Their faces are indiscernible. I mess around with the pictures, trying to lighten the images, but it's impossible, they're directly backlit.

But those pictures aren't why I start shaking so violently.

The final two pictures on the roll were shots I didn't realize I'd taken. My finger must have been snapping them reflexively.

They're of the murder itself. The actual act. The killer is standing over his victim, his pistol pointing down.

I stare at them, shaking like a leaf in a hurricane. My first impulse is to call the police, but I nail that in the bud, fast. I'm not getting involved in this unless I have to, I've already decided that. The fact that I have proof is no reason to change my thinking.

I make a fast decision: no one in the world except me knows these pictures exist. And unless there's a good reason for me to come forth with them, no one is ever going to.

I save the pictures in my computer. Then I put the mounted transparencies of the birds into a file drawer, noting the date and subjects. I've become an efficient cataloger. This collection could be valuable someday.

The other transparencies, the crime evidence, are a potential land mine. I need to keep them separate from the bird shots. Locking the cabinet behind me, I stash them in an old pair of wingtips I haven't worn in years and bury them in the back of my closet.

Time to get motivating. I shower, shave, apply liberal amounts of antiperspirant to each underarm, foot powder in between my toes. Then I don a short-sleeved white dress shirt, the kind one associates with nerdy accountants and computer geeks, and take my good summer suit out of the closet, still in its plastic laundry wrap. I haven't worn it once this summer. I hope my mother appreciates the sacrifices I make for her.

There will be eighteen at table, including my mother, my brother, Sam, his wife, Emily, and me. My mother's idea of a small, intimate gathering. I'm acceptably late, twenty minutes, but most of the other guests have already arrived and are on the back veranda, drinking and chatting.

Conversation lulls for a moment as the others take notice of my entrance. My mother, looking cool and comfortable in a summer dress she's undoubtedly owned for fifty years (waste not, want not), excuses herself from her conversation, bustles over, and gives me a dry peck on the cheek.

"You're not too late," she says approvingly, giving my apparel a once-over, but wisely not commenting on it.

"What's the occasion?" I ask, looking around. "And why was I invited?"

"You're my son, why wouldn't I invite you to my party?" she asks indignantly.

"Because you often don't."

"Well, this time I did."

"Just because you wanted to." I'm looking around for the reason I'm here.

"I wanted you to meet our newest neighbor, who bought the old parcel at the edge of Swanson Creek last year, shortly before you . . . moved back," she says, having a hard time, as always, with my current status. "He's an interesting individual someone of your intellect might cotton to. I've been meaning to get you two together, but the opportunity never presented itself until now. He's a very busy man," she adds, almost conspiratorially.

My pulse rate begins spiking immediately: the parcel at the edge of Swanson Creek is the farthest parcel from our original property. It's the place I was spying on this morning. Maybe this recent addition to the neighborhood is one of the men I saw. Jesus, that would be a bitch. I'm intrigued by the possibility of coincidence. And scared, too. I'll try not to show it.

"If you say so," I tell my mother.

"I do. So be good." She drifts back to the old friends she was in conversation with when I arrived. My brother, looking spiffy as usual in one of his British-made custom suits, this one a beautifully cut charcoal gray silk shantung, ambles over and sizes me up.

"Nice suit," he says, grinning wide, fingering the material at the lapel. "You buy this at an outlet store in Moscow?"

"Dubuque, Iowa," I correct him. "And I paid retail." It's a tan and white wide-wale seersucker of a style that peaked around 1949. Harry Truman wore such a suit. He was a haberdasher before he went into politics, he knew from clothing. Brooks Brothers still sells them, which is where I bought this. They're comfortable, and they're supposed to be wrinkled. They go good with bow ties and two-tone shoes, neither of which I'm wearing, since I don't own either.

"A bargain at half the price," he says sarcastically, using one of our late father's pet epigrams.

"I have to keep up with you, Sam."

"You have a warped sense of humor, Fritz."

"Takes one to know one."

This initial sparring aside, I say hello to his wife, who's wearing a simple cocktail dress that I'm sure cost at least a thousand dollars, and cross over to the small temporary bar to greet Louis, the black bartender who's been working functions at my mother's going on sixty years now. He's as old as she is, maybe older. He is the only black person visible (Mattie's in the kitchen overseeing the caterers—there are too many guests here for her to manage, at her advanced age, by herself). My mother is liberal by her standards, but the generational separation of races is ingrained in her too deeply for her to have black friends on this kind of social level, unless they're of the Vernon Jordan caliber.

"How you doing, Louis?" I ask him as we shake hands. "I thought you were retired."

"I am, Mr. Tullis," he says warmly, starting to fix me a Jack Daniel's Manhattan, "but for old clients, like your mother . . ." He hands me my drink. "You're looking fine. Being home agrees with you."

"It's a ruse," I stage-whisper, grinning at him like a conspirator.

"Well, you're pulling it off well," he tells me, smiling back broadly. Being the youngest, I was always the jackanapes of the bunch. Loved and tolerated by all, with much head-shaking and forgiving of my youthful fuckups, some of which weren't so innocent.

Drink in hand, I join the gathering. Some I know, old friends of my mother's, who are happy to see me, we exchange innocuous pleasantries. They don't know the true facts of why I'm living here, instead of in Austin, Texas, where my job was. I'm easy about playing along with the fiction my mother's created, academic burnout and such. I do like to shock and upset people for sport, as Shakespeare says famously in another context, but these are old codgers. Some have weak hearts.

My mother links my arm with hers. "Come meet our new neighbor."

She's happy, in her element, with two of her three children in tow, a rare occurrence. My brother, Sam, and I don't keep each other's company, for reasons varied, complex, and ancient.

She leads me to a tall, ruddy-faced fellow with graying, rust-colored hair cut JFK-style who's in his early-to-middle sixties, I'm guessing, but in great shape, the kind of man who will always look a decade younger than his true age. He's dressed in a finely cut summer suit that hangs well on him. Compared to this guy and my brother I'm strictly tobacco road, which fits my current personality-approach to life.

Our new neighbor is talking to a couple of mom's old-lady friends. They're smiling, almost giddy, so he must be charming them. He looks like a charming sort of guy.

"James," she says, butting into their conversation, her prerogative as the hostess, "this is my other son, Fritz."

The man turns. He looks inquisitively at me for a moment, as if trying to read me, or place me. Not able to do either, since we've never met, he smiles pleasantly. "James Roach." He offers a hand.

"Fritz Tullis."

We shake. His grip is firm.

"James recently bought the farm at the edge of Swanson Creek," Mother informs me again, in case I'd forgotten.

"It's been almost a year now," he says with a smile.

"A year," I say, trying to figure out if this is one of the men I saw there this morning, either the pilot or the killer. I'm pretty sure he isn't the pilot. The alternative is not good, from my perspective. "Are you a permanent resident?" I ask politely.

He smiles again. If he's noticed my lack of sartorial cachet he's good at not showing it. That qualifies him as a gentleman in my book. "Not yet, unfortunately, although I hope to be able to live here more permanently someday."

"James is assistant secretary of state," my mother says proudly, as if he's an expensive urn she's brought out to show off.

"That's impressive," I reply, not that I give a shit. But it is impressive, this man's important.

A modest shoulder shrug. "One of several." His eyes are locked into mine, unblinking. Someone taught him a long time ago that would give him a psychological edge. He strikes me as a man who always wants to have an edge, psychological or otherwise.

"James was heavily involved in the Balkan peace process," my mother prattles.

I change the subject away from politics—I have more pressing questions on my mind. But I have to tread lightly. "What do you own, about a hundred acres?" I start out innocuously. My father sold the parcels in even amounts, although they got mixed up in later transfers.

"Eighty," he answers crisply. "Eighty-two, to be exact. Most of it's heavily wooded, as you'd know," he adds without my asking, letting me know he's not a strictly absentee owner.

"Do any farming?"

He shakes his head. "Not now. I might want to try to grow some grain. I'm thinking of bringing in a few horses for riding."

"Do you spend weekends on your farm?" I now query, getting closer to my target.

"As often as I can," he says, "although I usually don't get out of Washington until Saturday afternoon. Mine's not a nine-to-five job, as you can imagine."

"James has his own airplane," mother says admiringly, as if that makes him a better person somehow.

He's not a career government apparatchik, obviously—you can't afford a multimillion-dollar piece of prime waterfront property on a government salary, let alone an airplane. "A corporate jet, no doubt."

"Yes," he answers comfortably, implying "what else would I have?"

"What kind?" I ask, pushing harder than I want to but unable to hold back on my curiosity. "A Gulfstream?"

Roach shakes his head. "They're a bit expensive for me," he says, his tone insinuating that he could, in fact, afford such a plane if he so desired. "Mine's a Lear. And it's leased," he adds, as if to say, "I'm just a regular guy."

The plane I saw this morning wasn't a Learjet. I push my line of questioning anyway. "Did you fly in this morning?" I can feel the water forming under my arms. The antiperspirant I used wasn't strong enough to cover fear-sweat of this power.

Roach shakes his head. "I was tied up in my office until this afternoon. And I don't normally fly from Washington to the farm. By the time you get to the airport, get the plane ready, and fly out here, you've spent more time than it takes to drive. Besides, a flight of that duration costs too much. I'd only fly in if I was going somewhere else from here, but this weekend I'm not, I have to be back in Washington tomorrow afternoon." He smiles. "We're hosting an international conference on terrorism, which is one of my specialties. You've heard about it, I'm sure, it's been on the news."

I shake my head. "I haven't been following the news."

If he didn't arrive until this afternoon, and came by car, then he wasn't one of the men I saw this morning. I feel the tension flowing out of my body like air escaping a balloon. "It must be convenient, having your own airfield," I say. "Friends want to visit you, they fly right in. Although I guess for someone in your position, security's always a concern."

"I'm on every terrorist hot list in the world." Said flatly, but the gravity is manifest.

It occurs to me, suddenly, that he could be a target, like the man I saw murdered this morning. That raises a moral issue for me—should I tell him about what happened out there this morning?

The answer, simply, is no. I don't want to get mixed up in this, especially with someone this powerful. I don't want to be the target. I'm not involved, I'm not going to get involved. If he's that important, he's under tight security anyway.

"Speaking of friends flying in," he mentions, "that rarely happens. Again, security issues. And I don't have many friends with their own planes—it's a luxury for me." He frowns. "We have had uninvited aircraft using our strip."

I give him the most nonchalant "Oh?" I can muster. "Doesn't that bother you? Being intruded on?"

"It bothers the hell out of me. I'm sure you know what a haven this area is for smuggling, drugs especially."

I nod. "Don't you try to stop it?"

"We ever catch one, we sure will," he replies vigorously. "But it's only been a couple of times; I hope that's all it's going to be. It's either that or plow the strip under, which would be cutting off my nose to spite my face."

My mother, who's been a silent observer to our conversation, breaks in. "Fritz lives near you," she tells Roach. "On the north side of the river, down there." She doesn't mention what kind of house I live in. My situation makes her teeth grind.

Roach nods, like he's thinking about that. "Where, exactly?" he asks.

"It's not that close," I say, correcting my mother. "About twenty minutes, by boat."

"You've seen my airstrip, then," he says. "It's right on the water."

I feel like biting my tongue off—that was really stupid, letting him know I've been by his place from the water side.

"I may have, a couple of months ago," I lie. "I normally don't go down that far on the water. Mostly I hang around my house."

"You should come down sometime. I'll take you up in the Lear. It's a kick." Changing the subject, he asks, "Do you sail?"

I've sailed all my life—if you live on the water most likely you know your way around boats. But I don't want to get into talk about the water, particularly around his property. "I fish from my dinghy. That's about it for me and boats these days."

"Fritz is an excellent sailor," my mother butts in pridefully, happy to trumpet any accomplishment of mine, given the other side of the coin she's had to live with this past year. "He's been in big sailing races all over the world."

"That was a while ago," I protest mildly. "I haven't sailed competitively since college."

"I'm having a sailboat built for me," Roach says. "It's almost finished. Perhaps we could take it out together when it's delivered. I'm not a pro like you, but I enjoy it."

"I'm no pro," I demur modestly, "but that would be fun. It's been a while."

My mother breaks into the conversation to excuse us and steer me in another direction, toward two women who are standing on the edge of the veranda, watching the early evening sun as it bleeds slowly into the marsh at the edge of the deep back lawn, a particularly radiant spectacle tonight. "Be nice," she says in a no-nonsense tone of voice.

"I'm always nice."

"No, you're not. Work at it for me tonight."

How can I say I won't do that? She's my loving, aged mother, who puts up with all my shit.

The two women, I can tell as we approach them, are mother and daughter. I see the blood-likeness in the faces, the shapes of their bodies. The mother's in her mid-sixties. The daughter is about my age, I'm guessing a few years younger. Tall, slender women, pale of hair and complexion. They're both wearing summer dresses that show off their legs. They have nice legs, long and thin but with good definition, although the daughter's are better, since she's half her mother's age. The daughter is sensibly barelegged in the heat. The older woman is tolerating the discomfort of opaque white pantyhose, to hide the varicose veins. They've undoubtedly been competing since the kid reached puberty and bought her first trainer bra. From the looks of her, the size hasn't increased much in the ensuing twenty years.

Keeping her voice low, my mother says, "She's a . . ."

". . . lovely woman," I finish for her. Meaning the daughter, of course.

"She is," my mother says, almost hissing. "I'm serious, Fritz."

"Well, I'm not." I smile.

Both women are drinking tonics in tall, sweaty glasses. They turn to mother and me in unison as we approach.

"Agatha, Johanna," my mother says, "this is my son Fritz. Fritz, Agatha and Johanna Mortimer. I believe you've met Agatha, Fritz, she's from the historical society."

My mother is chairperson of the King James County Historical Society, a duty she takes seriously and conscientiously.

Agatha's the mother. "Of course," I say smoothly. "Nice to see you again." I don't remember ever having met the woman.

"Well, thank you." She's flirting with me, the way aging women fighting to hang on to their looks can't help doing.

I shake their hands. The mother's already sizing me up; the daughter also, but less obviously.

"Johanna's from Boston," mother informs me, saying

"Boston" as if living there automatically makes one a unique and special person. "She's a stockbroker."

"Managing director," the woman's mother corrects my mother. "Merrill Lynch. That's like a vice president, except higher," she informs me with a mother's brag.

"Mother . . ." Johanna's a sophisticated woman of the world. She doesn't need her mother acting like she's in fifth grade.

"You're a professor at the University of Texas?" the elder woman asks, pushing, knowing the answer, which my mother must have fed her. Poor mom, having to stand up for me under this woman's sky-high praising of her accomplished adult child. "What is your field?"

"American history," my mother answers for me. She is going to navigate these perilous waters before I can run us aground. "On sabbatical this year," she adds quickly, before other bothersome questions can be raised.

Sabbatical. How many times have I heard that word come out of my mother's mouth?

"Burnout?" The daughter regards me presciently.

"You could call it that," I say.

"I've come across a wonderful old book from the 1880s about the old county horse shows," my mother says, placing a hand on her counterpart's arm. "It's in the study. Come, let me show you." To me, she says, a glint in her eye, "We'll leave you two to acquaint yourselves with each other."

Off they go. Johanna and I stand next to each other. It's awkward, but not too badly. She leans against a post, smiling at me cagily. She's a pretty woman, high-cheekboned, a stockbroker—make that managing director—she must be intelligent, making plenty of money.

"Mothers," she says.

"Yeah."

She fingers my puckered seersucker, like my mother did. "I haven't seen a suit like this since Humphrey Bogart stole the Maltese Falcon."

"It was Sydney Greenstreet," I correct her, "and he wore white linen."

"Whatever. It takes a man of courage to wear a suit this distinctive," she says. It sounds like flattery, but I'm not sure.

"It's a retro thing," I say. "If we were in California I'd be wearing a zoot suit, pants pegged fourteen."

Juggling her drink, she takes a pack of Camel Filter Hundreds and a Bic lighter from a small beaded handbag. "Do you mind?"

"Light 'em if you've got 'em."

"I'm trying to quit, but I'm not doing too well on my own. I'm going to have to go to Nicoderm or something."

"What's life without a vice?"

"I agree. What's yours?"

"Almost all of them, except this one." I smile.

She hands me her lighter. I light her cigarette for her. She touches my hand softly with her fingertips as she takes the first drag, standing there next to me on the far end of the veranda, away from the others, wide-hipped, wide-shouldered, small-breasted, smoking and drinking, looking at me, sending a clear message, *I came here to meet you and I'm not disappointed.*

There is a hot, humid, decaying-flower sweetness in the air, and she's had enough to drink that she is without reserve. Her forwardness is an aphrodisiac of a schoolyard nature, and I'm looking at her and feeling the fuck-heat coming off her, and thinking, okay, if that's what you want.

"I'm sitting next to you at dinner," she says, knocking back the rest of her drink and crunching the ice cubes between her teeth. "I snuck a peek at the place settings."

"Mothers," I say. We both laugh.

As the honoree of the evening, James Roach is sitting at the head of the table, to my mother's right. I'm situated toward the other end, the lovely Johanna on one side, Dolly MacBride, another old-biddy friend of mom's whose family are tobacco billionaires, on the other. The caterer has provided a nice selection of California chardonnays and cabernets, but half the guests, the older ones, eschew the wine, sticking with hard liquor. There's also some lighting of cigarettes during the meal. They're old, they don't have to worry about dying of lung cancer, they're going to die soon anyway, it doesn't matter from what.

Roach is an entertaining guest. He regales the table with tales about current affairs and the players who are deciding the fate of the world, and the casual, even reckless manner in which high-level decisions are made. Some of the late-night sessions he describes at the State Department and the Pentagon sound like scenes right out of *Monty Python* meets *The X-Files.* It's incredible and lucky, he says, how many times we go to the brink without even realizing we're there. He's particularly critical of the Russians, none of whom, according to him, are ever sober, and are either crooks or incompetents, or both. He's equally scornful of the members of Congress that he and the other "professionals" at State have to deal with.

Dinner is vintage summer Chesapeake Bay: rockfish and crab cakes and fried chicken, fresh vegetables and salads, homemade biscuits dripping with butter. Cholesterol through the roof, but nobody's shy about digging in, including the old dowagers, who shovel it in by the forkful.

After dessert, coffee and Remy Martin are served back out on the veranda. The temperature's still in the 80s, but there's a cooling breeze coming off the water. My new lady-friend and I are tossing cognacs back, match for match. Her mother tacks in our direction.

"Johanna, darling, I have to make an early exit." Turning to me, she says, "Would it be too inconvenient for you to give Johanna a ride to my place? It isn't that far out of your way."

I look across to my mother, who's talking to the guest of honor. She feels my stare and turns; then she smiles, and turns away.

"No problem. If that's all right with you," I say to Johanna.

"I'd appreciate that," she says, deadpan.

"She'll be safe and sound with me," I promise Agatha.

"I know she will." The woman's practically purring.

Now that that's settled, we can relax. We drift over to the rest of the group, where Roach, holding court, has picked up the thread of the subject he was discoursing on at dinner.

"The Russians today are a much greater threat than they were when the Soviet Union was at the peak of its powers," he's telling his captive audience. "At least then there was stability in the government. Now it's total chaos. Everything in Russia is for sale, including military items—the military there is totally corrupt, we've caught them selling tanks, airplanes, you name it. The real power in Russia now is their version of the Mafia—they're running the country, and they have their tentacles spread out all over the world, even in this country—enclaves in New York, Miami, other big cities are controlled by hooligans who emigrated here from the former Soviet Union."

Personally, I find this regurgitated post–Cold War talk boring—but the old folks are listening with rapt attention.

"The most frightening thing," Roach continues, "are the huge quantities of weapons of mass destruction that are unaccounted for. One of these days we're going to wake up and find that the Iranians or Iraqis or some other rogue government has acquired a nuclear submarine from the Russians, complete with atomic warheads. For all we know, they may already have. I can't tell you the number of hours every week I spend trying to stay on top of this."

I'm sure the man is sincere, but I'm irritated with this. It's the same old Red Scare, in new clothing. But these old folks, for whom the fear of Communist domination hung over their lives like a thunderhead from the end of World War II to Reagan, are hanging on his words.

"The Russians can't even feed themselves, let alone worry about stirring up mischief in the rest of the world," I interrupt.

Roach stares at me coldly. "I agree about the poverty. But you're wrong about causing trouble. They're too proud to admit they're a second-tier power, as Britain has been for decades."

I don't want to argue anymore, but I can't help taking another dig. "So what're we supposed to do, go into Russia and take over their nuclear sites? We don't even know where they are. *They* don't even know where some of them are."

"My point exactly," he responds with a ferocious smile. "We don't know and they don't know. But somebody does. And we have to be prepared to make sure that whoever that might be never gets to activate them."

I can feel Johanna's heat as she stands beside me. It's turning her on, my engagement with Roach. She's just on that edge of drunk-high that she thinks I'm doing this to impress her. "And how do we do that?" I ask.

"By creating alliances with democratic forces within Russia and other nuclear powers who believe as we do. So that if a rogue element does decide to play with fire, we have the means to stop them. From within."

"What do you mean by means?"

"Sufficient organization and arms to combat them, if it comes to that."

The old folks don't understand where Roach is going with this, but I do. "We're arming a rebel faction inside Russia, is that what you're saying?" I ask. Jesus, this is a cocktail party out in the boonies. What kind of loose talk is this?

Roach laughs indulgently. "Of course not. Russia is a legitimate government. It's all theoretical. We have to be ready for any eventuality. Strategic planning and vision—that's what we do. If you don't anticipate the future and plan for it, you have another Hussein or bin Laden. It's better to take preemptive steps before there's a real conflict. If we've learned nothing else over the past decade, we've learned that—hopefully." He puts a friendly arm around my shoulder. "We don't interfere in the internal affairs of other governments. We don't cowboy out there like we used to in the old days. We're just a bunch of old boy scouts now. We want to be prepared."

The party's over. I kiss my mother good-bye. Outside, walking to my car with Johanna Mortimer, my brother stops me, pulls me aside. "What's going on with you?"

"Like how?" I don't enjoy getting into discussions of my life with Sam.

"What the fuck are you doing?"

"I'm giving this woman a ride home." I point over to Johanna. "Her mother had to leave early."

"I'm not talking about her, numbnuts. I mean with your life. Your career."

"My so-called career?"

"You've got to make amends." He's forceful, right in my face. "You can't throw a career away."

"Right now there's not much I can do."

"You've got to do something. It's killing mother."

That was low, although I know it's true. "She's tough," I say, feeling blue about our mother. "She's been through worse. She doesn't have to worry about me, I'm a big boy."

"Then start acting like one. Do what you have to do and get back on track. You're a Tullis. Don't disgrace our name. More than you already have."

He walks away. Emily stares at me as they get into their Mercedes and drive off. I know what their conversation on the way home will be about.

"Big brotheritis?" Johanna asks as I walk her to my mud-spattered Jeep.

She is smart, even half-looped. "Family business," I explain.

"Ongoing. You ready?" I open her door for her like a proper gentleman.

"I've been ready for hours."

I get in and start the engine. "How do I get to your mother's house?"

She laughs, then stops. "Are you shitting me? You're shitting me, right?"

"I didn't say immediately."

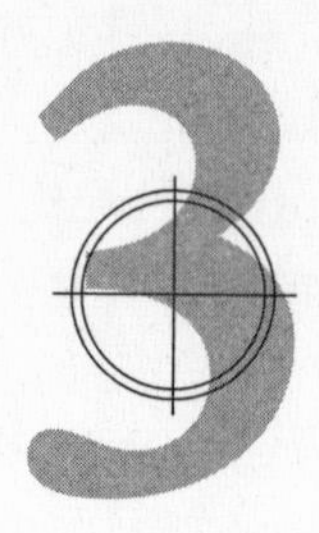

Under normal circumstances, my mother's meddling in my affairs of the heart would've been a bull's-eye. Johanna Mortimer is smart, pretty, financially in good shape. But I'm not living a normal-circumstances life these days.

Before we jumped into bed I gave her the nickel tour of the place. My prints of the birds blew her away. I didn't show her any of Ollie, of course. That's my secret, not to be shared, even with a lover.

Now her fingertips idly caress my flaccid penis. We're lying on top of the soggy sheets, passing a bottle of blue agave tequila back and forth.

"Do you mind if I smoke? That old nasty habit again."

"On the porch, please."

She props herself up on her elbows, looks around. "This place is kind of a tinderbox, isn't it?" she comments. "All this dry wood and exposed wiring."

"I guess."

"You're not concerned?"

I shrug. "As long as I'm not asleep in my bed, not really. It's not a permanent dwelling place. The only thing I give a shit about is my equipment and my pictures."

She heaves up from the bed, crawling across me to go fetch her cigarettes from her evening bag. Her small, firm breasts brush my chest. She's easy to be with, which was a surprise. Of course, we're on first-time behavior.

I roll a joint and join her outside, bringing the bottle. The dark humidity brings forth strong nighttime aromas, sweetness of honeysuckle and pungency of marsh water. A choir of bull-frogs is singing a loud call and response. We sit in battered Adirondack chairs that are set at 45 degree angles, facing each other. Her bare feet, long and slender, so milk-white they're almost translucent, are perched in my lap.

"This is a neat place," she says, flicking her cigarette ashes into a coffee cup ashtray as she looks out through the screen into the darkness. "And private. Who knows about this?"

"My mother, my brother and sister. A few friends, not many."

"You enjoy your solitude," she observes, missing the mark.

"It's where I am for now." *Enjoy* is the wrong word. *Endured* would be closer to the truth. A self-imposed exile while I sort my life out.

I pass her the joint. She takes a hit, passes it back. Some cactus juice to wash it down.

"So you're on sabbatical," she throws out, probing delicately. On the drive over, and then post-lovemaking, she told me about herself. Her age—thirty-five; where she went to school—Williams, Harvard MBA, which is why she's living in Boston, actually Cambridge, she owns her house; the sports she enjoys—skiing and tennis; the music she likes—classical and jazz, but she basically "digs" all kinds of music; that she's never been married, but has had two long live-in situations, the last one ending a year ago; and that she's great at what she does and makes a shitpile of money, but isn't career-consumed.

The personal résumé, in other words, of an accomplished woman who is now ready to fall in love, get married, and have kids. Oh, and she's also a gourmet cook, it's her passion, she loves to cook so much she's taken cooking school vacations in Provence and Tuscany.

"Kind of," I parry in response to her probing about my career status. "I don't know if I'm going back or not."

"You don't want to teach anymore?"

"It's not that. I love teaching, most of the time, anyway. It's the place—I don't know if it and me are the right match."

We aren't—that's already been decided. I'd like to change the subject, but I don't know to what. I don't want to get personal, even though we just made love and are now sitting nude next to each other in easy contentment.

This woman would be a catch. In another life.

"Have you ever been married?" she asks. She's getting personal, she knows she shouldn't, she can't help it. She just gave one of the most special parts of herself to me on what wasn't even our first date. There's commitment there, already. And she can sense my goodness.

It's true. I'm a good guy. Sometimes too good for my own good, I don't say no, don't hurt people's feelings when I should, so that later on, they're hurt much worse. It's a distaste for conflict, sweeping-the-dirt-under-the-rug, which is always never more than a short-term solution to a long-term problem. That's normal, I know, human beings are better at avoidance than at confrontation, but I've left too many bodies lying in the dust. Not that I haven't been hit and run over myself.

Johanna here doesn't know any of this. She knows she likes me, is liking me more by the minute, especially naked and sated like we are now.

"No. Never have been," I answer.

"Not the marrying kind." Spoken as a teasing joke, but she can't mask the seriousness. I like her even more because of that.

Which is not a good thing, for her. "No, I wouldn't say that. I'm not against it." *With the right woman* goes unspoken.

I don't know. This might be the best woman I'll ever meet

in my entire life, and it isn't going to happen. I'm not ready for emotional involvement, and that's all there is to it.

"It's late," I say. "I'd better be getting you home."

She sits bolt upright. "What?"

I play dumb. "To your mother's."

"I don't need to go home. I'm a grown woman. My mother isn't waiting up for me."

"Yeah, it's just . . ." Shit.

She stands, her body touching mine. No more trying for cool now. "Don't you want me to stay?"

Here comes the lie. Fuck, I hate this. But I'm going to do it. "I'd love it. But I have to go down south tomorrow morning before six, which is the opposite direction from your mother's place."

She wants to believe me. "Where are you going?"

"Sussex." The first town that pops into my head. Sussex is a sleepy burg at the far southern end of the Eastern Shore. There's a ferry that crosses over, one of the few still running. "An Audubon Society meeting," I improvise off the top of my head. "Regional."

"I like bird-watching," she says with grit. "I could go with you. If you don't mind my tagging along," she adds, not able to let go.

Don't, please, I'm thinking. I have too much respect for you for this.

"It's a board meeting, boring as hell." I pause, as if considering her supplication. "You're not dressed for it."

She looks down at her nude body. "I'm not dressed at all." Trying to lighten up a heavy situation.

"What you wore last night."

"I was kidding."

"I know."

"You're not trying to get rid of me." Her eyes are searching my face for clues.

"Of course not." Which is both the truth and a lie—I can't

have her here any longer, but I am attracted to her, in spite of myself.

She swallows the bitter pill. "Okay, then. As long as you're not bullshitting me."

"I don't bullshit." What's one more lie? I bullshit myself all the time. I'm doing it right now, even as she throws her ego out the window. I wish I had the guts to do that. And the character.

It's four o'clock in the morning now. I'm sitting alone on my back porch. The bottle is two-thirds empty. It was full when sweet Johanna and I started in on it earlier in the evening.

We said our good-byes on her mother's doorstep (all the lights were out inside the house, her mama's no fool), and I was smart enough to remember to ask her for her phone numbers, here and in Boston both. That took the edge off the tension I knew she was feeling.

It's not like she'd fallen irrationally in love with me off a one-night stand. She's a mature, grown woman, real grown-ups don't do that. She simply liked me, and wanted to get to know me better. More important, she didn't want to be rejected. That she'd fucked me our first time together, maybe the only time she'd done that her entire life, certainly since she was old enough to know better—she's an attractive, desirable woman, she doesn't need to be chasing tail—wasn't as meaningful as that she'd given of herself, spilled some emotional blood. I hadn't, and we both knew it.

Which is why I need to go celibate for a while, because the way it's working now isn't working. It isn't about sex, or sexual conquest, or good sex, or any of that. The fucking's inconsequential, compared to feeling. Which is how it should be, because sex, in and of itself, is transitory. It's love that's real, feeling something. I'm not ready for that, not after what I've been through. I used to think I knew what love was, but I'm not sure anymore. And until I am, I shouldn't be screwing decent women around.

Sex coupled with misunderstood love is the reason I'm living in a sharecropper's shack on my mother's property instead of toiling at my profession, which is teaching college students. Sex with the wrong women, at the wrong time. Particularly one.

Actually, that isn't true. That's me bullshitting myself again. Sex—having sex—is the manifestation of the problem, the tip of the iceberg. The real issue was, and still is, my inability to grow up and be a responsible man. All this skating around my tenure situation, watching my poor mother covering my sorry ass because I can't, is chickenshit. I'm a grown man, my mother's apron and the strings that tie them on her bony hips should have been rolled up and stuck in a drawer long ago.

I'm not on sabbatical. I was permanently let go. Fired.

I am the third and last child in my family. My parents, who were comfortable financially, going back generations, were well along in years when I was born; I was an accident, no one's ever made any bones about that—my mother was forty-six when I came along, my father fifty-two. My siblings, Sam, the Baltimore lawyer, and my sister, Dinah, a gynecologist who lives in New York, are seventeen and twenty years older than I am, respectively. Both departed from home ere I barely saw the light of day, they're more like uncle and aunt to me than brother and sister. We never knew each other well, and since my fiasco at Austin they've washed their hands of me. I don't blame them.

I grew up privileged and wild. My parents couldn't handle me, they were too old, I was an entire generation removed from my siblings, on which they'd based their understanding of kids. I plumb wore them to a frazzle, so they boarded me out, starting in the seventh grade. I moved from one minor league prep school to another before I landed at Andover for my last three years.

Besides having money and little parental control, I was smart, a jock, tall—six feet two, broad-shouldered—and better than okay-looking. Women were attracted to me before I even knew why, and once I did, around the tenth grade, I started making hay. I was golden, and I was just beginning.

I went to Yale, where I did well—I was getting my shit together by then, at least academically and socially. I rowed varsity crew, was a member of the debate society, played trumpet in the university orchestra and several impromptu jazz groups, and graduated with high honors, Phi Beta Kappa. A demonstrably bright boy.

From Yale I traveled cross-country to Stanford, where I racked up my doctorate in American History in three and a half years, which is flying. My doctoral thesis, *The Confederacy Within the Union* (inspired by incidents that took place in my own backyard—a lucky accident of place and time that informed my desire to choose the teaching of history as a profession), was picked up by a mainstream publisher and subsequently has done very well—many universities and high schools use it as a primary text.

While waiting for my thesis to be published, I instructed at Northwestern for a couple of semesters and followed that with a two-year stint at the University of Wisconsin as an assistant professor. Then Texas beckoned. I went in as an associate professor: good salary and benefits, fine choice of courses to teach, the whole nine yards. Three years later, I was granted tenure—they knew I was the real goods, a serious scholar who was also popular with students, the best combination a teacher at my level could have.

I was thirty-one years old, and I was set for life in the world of academia. I could stay forever at UT in Austin, the coolest city in Texas, a great school with a huge endowment, they pay fabulously and attract top-notch talent in their faculty—or, if something in the crème de la crème category came along, Harvard or back at Yale, I'd have that option, too. I could mature into being a beloved university professor, get married eventually, have kids, live a great life.

The settling-down part of my life-style fantasy was in the future—I wasn't ready for that yet, I had too many wild and crazy things I wanted to experience. I have always had a tendency—some would call it an obsession—to take risks, which took full flower at this time. In my circle of friends I got a reputation as a daredevil who sometimes exhibited more guts than brains—their conclusion, not mine, I always felt I had things under control. As I said, I was a wild child, and this reckless streak stayed with me into manhood. Teaching is a sedentary profession, and I had the need to test myself physically—I've always been a physical animal, I get antsy if I sit too long. I developed a compulsion to push the envelope further and further, taking risks for the sake of taking risks, for the heart-stopping joy of going to the precipice, trying to see how far out on a limb I could go without breaking it off. I became an avid solo rock-climber, traveling around the country to various mountain ranges whenever I had some time off to test my skills on some of the hardest faces in mountaineering. I also indulged in bungee-jumping from spectacular heights, free-falling thousands of feet at times, watching the ground get close and closer until, just before shattering my bones on the rocks below, I would be jerked back to safety. Hang-gliding, another wild ride, virtually became an obsession with me. Soaring high in the air, catching thermals and staying aloft for long periods of time, was one of the most exhilarating things I had ever tried (which may be the reason I've become so enamored of birds and all things related to birds—flying on your own, lord of the skies).

My friends, those who knew of these breathtaking adventures, would shake their heads at my latest escapade, calling me a crazy bastard, while secretly wishing they had the guts to try what I was doing. Most people, I'm convinced, live that way—vicariously, through others. I didn't want to be one of them, a member of the herd. I wanted to be the lead stallion, the first to see over the next horizon.

My life, in almost every way, was rosy—if I wanted to do something, anything, I did it. I had no one to answer to, no one to be accountable to. And I was lucky enough—I take no credit for this, it must have been purely genetic—that I had some kind of inner governor, a little voice deep inside my brain, that told me when I was, finally, going too far, that I had pushed as hard as I could without being so out of my control that I could fail. So fail I never did. I always survived to tell the tale and to try yet another dangerous venture.

This testing of my limits, which had a strong core of self-centeredness, extended to my relationships with women. If I was attracted to a woman and I could score, I did. I wasn't an indiscriminate pussy-hound, I didn't screw everything in sight. I didn't have to, I could pick and choose.

For the first few years in Austin, then, everything was peachy. The teaching went well from the start, and I was involved, for various periods of time, with some excellent women. I had set definite parameters for myself regarding who I'd allow myself to get involved with sexually. No undergraduates, no women on the faculty, and most important, married women were off-limits, regardless of whether or not they wanted to play.

Unfortunately—and inevitably, given my disposition—I started sliding. My initial falling off the wagon was with an undergraduate who was twenty-six, several years older than the usual undergrad. Thelma had been in the Navy and had worked before starting college. I think what attracted me to her initially was her name. There can't be any Thelmas in existence under fifty, except for this one. Thelma McGraw. She hailed from Lubbock, which is in West Texas and has nothing going for it according to her, except that Buddy Holly and the Crickets and some other famous singers of that bygone era came from there. And never went back, she added, nor would she. She was quite a Buddy Holly fan and knew the lyrics to all his recorded songs, which she would sing at various weird times, including while in the throes of hot sex. "That'll Be the Day" is actually rather appropriate for a transitory love affair, which ours certainly was. The point is, since she was twenty-six and experienced—she'd also been married for a short, forgettable time—I didn't feel I was violating my no-undergraduate oath, only technically, not in spirit, which is what really counts. She would have laughed at me if I'd told her of such an absurd credo, so I didn't.

That liaison lasted a few months and petered out naturally at the end of the semester with no hurt feelings on either side, which turned out to be a curse rather than a blessing, because pulling the affair off so comfortably and guilt-free emboldened me to expand my boundaries—not much, just a smidgen (I was conning myself, of course)—and once I did that, it was an easy downhill descent. It isn't the miles that do you in but the inches, because you don't notice them slipping away.

To begin with, I widened my self-imposed parameters, so more applicants could apply. Instead of no undergraduate women, I set an age limit of no one younger than twenty-three, which I eventually loosened to twenty-two, drinking age plus one, more than enough time to become an adult and be accountable for adult choices, including fucking professors if you want to. That expanded the field tremendously, because in most universities, especially public ones, students don't graduate in four years, it takes longer, generally five or six. So virtually every senior undergraduate woman was fair game.

That worked incredibly well; it was like hitting three cherries at a Vegas slot machine. My appointment book was filled to overflowing.

Those women had a lot going for them: beauty, wonderful tight bodies, uninhibited attitudes. But they were also lacking in life experience, and not being able to talk about things I found interesting—being more than a decade older (by now I was thirty-four), or being expected to enjoy and embrace college-age stuff, which was often immature and banal, even with the bright ones—became a turnoff. Also, there was the fear of exposure. None of them ever filed a complaint against me, which was a miracle, when I think back on it, considering how some of those relationships ended, but the nervous-making possibility was very present.

So I expanded my boundaries yet again, to include female colleagues. Single or divorced only, of course. That was okay legally, because those relationships were between responsible adults. That they were frowned upon by the administration stopped me not in the least. From childhood on I'd been given to understand that rules were for other people and didn't apply to me; or if they did, it was okay to flout them, because I was never punished, I never paid the price. And why obey stupid rules, wasn't that the point of all those revolutions of the 1960s, civil rights, sexual, political?

What was wrong, I knew, was hurting someone, or being hurt back. Inflicting pain on another person, women with whom I'd been intimate, not only sexually but emotionally, never felt good, even though it was never intentional. I'm not shallow. But there was pain in all these relationships, because unless you spend the rest of your life with someone, the relationship is going to end. None of my relationships lasted forever, or even remotely, so I had some bad endings. Terrible endings, crying and screaming and pleading. My pain wasn't as strong or deep, because I was always the one to end them, but it still felt bad, seeing the hurt I had caused.

Then the roof caved in.

Two years ago this coming September I was driving west out of Austin into the Hill Country, Lyndon Johnson's old stomping ground. It was a Sunday afternoon, the last weekend before the beginning of the fall term. I'd brought a camera with me, to shoot whatever pretty or interesting sight crossed my eye.

This is the most beautiful area of Texas. It extends west about a hundred miles, from Austin in the north to San Antonio in the south. The air is incredibly clean, the plant life, particularly in the spring, is gorgeous, it's the best of what this country used to be a hundred years ago. It's touristy as hell now—all the old quaint German towns are jammed with visitors from all over the world from spring until fall, but it's still a wonderful place to come to.

A sudden rain shower came up, as happens at that time of year. They bluster crazy for about half an hour, then they're gone. As I meandered along one of the backcounty roads I spied a car, a vintage Jaguar, that had lost traction on the wet pavement and skidded off the road and into a drainage ditch on the far side.

I pulled over and jumped out to take a look. The car had blown a tire. The sole occupant, sitting dazed in the driver's seat, was an attractive woman of means, judging by her clothes, makeup, general demeanor, and the car. She wasn't hurt, but she was shaken by the accident.

I helped her out of her car and into mine. As she settled into the passenger seat next to me, slipping her wet pumps off and shaking her neck-length hair dry, I couldn't help but notice that she was married: she was sporting a diamond on her left hand that had to be two or three carats at least, along with a smaller, matching wedding band. I judged her to be older than me by five or six years.

She introduced herself as Marnie Hamilton. She was on her way to Austin, where she lived. She'd been in San Angelo for a week, visiting with her sister. As had I, she'd detoured off the main road to savor the pleasures of the early fall countryside, only to almost flip her car in the rain when the tire blew. She was very happy to see me, she smiled gratefully—she'd forgotten to recharge the battery on her cell phone. And, she admitted with chagrin, she didn't have a spare tire—her old spare had gone bad and she hadn't gotten around to replacing it.

I contemplated what to do. I didn't want to turn around and head back to Austin; I'd planned on a few days off by myself, as the semester didn't begin until Wednesday. But I couldn't strand her, of course.

Before I could figure a way out of this dilemma she read my mind and told me I need merely take her to the nearest town that had a garage that could haul her car in and fix her tire or sell her a replacement. Worse came to worst, she could call Austin and have someone come out and pick her up.

That sounded like a plan. We waited in my car until the rain slacked, then she grabbed her suitcase from the trunk of her car for safekeeping, threw it in my backseat, locked up the Jag, and we headed off.

It became evident almost immediately that there was going to be a glitch in this scheme: there were no open garages in any of the little burgs we drove through. Sunday, day of rest. Finally, as evening was approaching, I came to my destination, a rustic bed-and-breakfast in the tiny town of Yamparika. I'd booked my room sight unseen—a friend had touted it to me as a cozy place that served a hell of a good dinner, with a not bad wine list. People drove a hundred miles to eat here, not a great distance in this part of Texas. I'd made a dinner reservation for myself when I reserved my room.

"You can call Austin from here," I said.

She followed me inside to the reception area, which was tucked in a corner of the Southwestern country-style living room. Behind the desk stood a stout, elderly woman. Her name tag identified her as Mildred Hertzburg.

"Mr. Tullis?" She smiled. As I looked at her in surprise, she continued, "you're the last guest to check in tonight. Am I right? You are Mr. Tullis?"

"Yes," I smiled back.

She rotated the registration book in my direction. Then she noticed Marnie, standing a few paces behind me.

"Oh," the woman said. "This is Mrs. Tullis?"

I didn't connect for a moment. "I'm not—"

"We thought you were a single," Mrs. Hertzburg said before I could finish. "No matter," she said efficiently, "your room has a queen-sized bed. So that'll be two for dinner rather than one," she added.

"Well, there's a—" I was going to say "mistake here," but she was too fast for me again.

"It's good you reserved in advance, because we're full up tonight. I've already turned two parties away. You'd have to drive clear to San Angelo to find a place."

I didn't know what to say. I signed her book, and she handed me two keys.

"Upstairs, third door on the right. It's one of our nicest rooms, a bed–sitting room combination. The tub has a Jacuzzi, in case you're inclined." She smiled past me to Marnie, who was staring at her damp shoes. "The dining room opens in twenty minutes, and we serve until nine-thirty. Do you have bags?"

"In the car. I can . . . we can get them."

Marnie followed me out to the car. "This is very embarrassing," she said as I opened the trunk and grabbed my small overnight bag. "I'll call home right away."

We went back inside and up the stairs. I slipped the key into the lock and opened the door.

The room was L-shaped, tastefully decorated in the same fashion as the common room upstairs. There was a large sitting area with a couch and two wing chairs flanking a fireplace, a small table off to the side where you could eat breakfast if you were so inclined, and a high, four-poster bed with a down cover. The large bathroom was dominated by the octagonal tub. French doors led to a balcony outside that overlooked the low, rolling, flower-covered hills.

"How lovely," Marnie murmured. She sat on the couch. "Can I ask you a favor? Before I make my call?"

"Sure."

"Could I get my suitcase out of your car? My shoes and stockings are wet. I'd like to change into dry."

"No problem," I told her. "I'll get it for you."

I went back downstairs. As I was heading out the door I bumped into Mrs. Hertzburg. "Your wife is lovely," she commended me.

I didn't tell her Marnie wasn't my wife. She'd find out soon enough, when Marnie's husband or whoever was picking her up arrived from Austin.

Marnie was by the telephone when I came back into the room. She looked morose. "There's no one home."

I stared at her.

"I left San Angelo a day early. I wasn't expected until tomorrow."

Now what? I thought. Then I made a decision that is going to haunt me for the rest of my life. "Not a problem," I told her. "You can sleep here, on the couch."

"Are you . . . sure?" Her right hand went to her wedding band reflexively.

"What're your alternatives?"

"I don't know."

"It doesn't look like you have any." I smiled reassuringly, trying to put her at ease. "We're adults, we can handle this. I'll be respectful of your space, don't worry. We can get your car taken care of in the morning."

"Thank you." She looked so grateful, both at my offer of sharing and the gallantry about her modesty, that for a moment I thought she was going to cry.

She didn't, though. She changed in the bathroom. She looked

nice—she was a conventionally sweet-looking, married woman, some years older than me, and judging by her car, her large diamond ring, and the cut of her clothes, hair, the full package, conservative in her life. Not a Fritz Tullis woman, who runs to wild and crazy.

Dinner was full-on gourmet, nothing Texas shit-kicker about it—there was not one fried fish on the menu. We lingered over the meal, enjoying a nice bottle of wine, sharing a piece of rich chocolate cake for dessert. When the bill came, she grabbed it before I could sign.

"Please. It's the least I can do to repay you for your generosity."

This was true; and since I knew she could afford it, I let her. It wasn't the money—the gesture made her feel better, that she wasn't completely freeloading.

Back in the bedroom, we each had a cognac from the minibar and watched a Goldie Hawn comedy on HBO. It was a romantic setting, except we weren't romantic, carefully so. We sat fully clothed on the couch, and kept a discreet distance between us.

Then it was time for bed. She used the bathroom first, emerging wearing a pair of plain-jane cotton pajamas. Her face, redolent of lilac soap, was clean of makeup. Unadorned, she looked her age. Youthfully scrubbed, but there was no denying the age lines around her eyes and mouth. She was into her middle age, and she would never get any younger.

I put together a sleeping outfit of running shorts and a T-shirt. When I emerged from the bathroom she'd already fixed up the sofa with an extra blanket from the closet and a spare pillow.

"You're all settled," I observed.

She nodded. "Good night, Fritz. And thank you again for being so kind."

"I'm glad I could help."

She got into her makeshift bed. I waited a moment to make sure she was secure, then I crawled into mine and turned off the lights.

The fragrance of lilac soap woke me up. I'd been dreaming; for a moment I was discombobulated. Then I wasn't.

Marnie was in bed with me. She wasn't wearing her pajamas. She wasn't wearing anything.

"Please forgive me," she whispered.

What was to forgive?

Who can explain it, who can tell you why? Corny, but in our case, true.

Neither of us slept that night. Even given the emotional awkwardness of this being our first time together, it was glorious. Unlike some of the young goddesses I'd known, her body was ordinary, but we fit together flawlessly.

After we made love the first time we rested, talked, had drinks from the minibar, then made love again. This was not two heat-seeking animalist forces, the way I was used to it. This was lovemaking, the real thing. I'd never been in this place before: it was exhilarating, overwhelming.

It was also scary as hell: she was married.

She filled in some of her blanks. Forty-three years old. Married for nine years, her only marriage. No children, her husband didn't want them, he had adult children from his previous marriage. He was older, almost sixty, he didn't want to start a family all over again. He had left his first wife for her. She had not wanted him to, but once he did, she felt obligated to marry him. Which did not mean she hadn't loved him. But breaking up his family, even if that was the perception in the community rather than the reality (he was going to leave his wife no matter what, he just needed a reason to do it sooner than later), had weighed heavily on her. He had become estranged from his children, a man and a woman in their early thirties (my age, I thought, as she recited this litany), after the divorce and remarriage. It bothered her, Marnie, more than it bothered him.

Her husband, Mark Hamilton, was a doctor. Rich, successful, narcissistic. They lived, palatially, in Austin. His circle was their circle, his interests their interests. She'd been a social worker before they got married—they'd met while serving on a United Way committee, of which he was the chairman, she a lowly volunteer. She had tried to resist him, but he was irresistible. In everything, not only the pursuit of his own, self-centered happiness.

She had a wonderful material life, but it was bereft of love, of passion. Until yesterday, when her car blew a tire in a rainstorm and I, by pure random (or divine, so she felt) chance, came along to help her out.

Is there such a thing as love at first encounter? I'd never believed so. I don't know if I did then, or do now. Marnie did, unquestionably; she wasn't being disingenuous, she was honestly smitten. She had fallen in love with me.

As had I with her, to be brutally honest with myself, looking back on it. *On some level.* I don't know if it was on a par with the love that she said she felt; to me, that kind of intensity, involving depth and complexity and extensive knowledge of the other person, takes time, it's not to be entered into quickly or lightly or frivolously, because you're talking, ultimately, about a lifetime commitment; but I fell for her like the proverbial ton of bricks.

I didn't realize the extent of my emotional involvement until we checked out late that morning. Earlier, she had arranged for a tow service to pick up her car and take it to a garage about fifteen miles away. The tire would be fixed by the time she came to fetch it.

"You can drop me off and continue on your way," she said as I was signing for the bill.

I started to say okay. Then we looked at each other, and knew that wasn't going to happen.

She called her husband at his office. He wasn't in, fortunately; she left a message with his secretary: the Jaguar had a mechanical problem, it would take a couple of days for the local garage to get the part from Austin and fix it, she was going to stay in the area until she could drive it home. She didn't know where she'd be staying, she'd call and let him know. No mention where she'd been last night; if her husband ever asked her, which was unlikely, she'd make up a lie. He would believe her; she had never been unfaithful before, he had no reason to distrust her. And he was so busy, he'd barely notice she was missing.

Marnie Hamilton had been unfaithful to her husband of nine years for the first and only time, so she confessed, and had now lied to him about her infidelity without a second thought, after having spent one night and part of a day—eighteen hours—with me. But our one-night stand was going to go way beyond that. She was willing to throw it all away—money, prestige, security. Sail into uncharted waters, with no guarantee of a safe harbor at the end of the journey.

It scared the shit out of me, once I realized the enormous repercussions of our getting involved. But we were in the maelstrom of first love, where everything's right and nothing can ever go wrong.

It's nerve-wracking, carrying on an affair. Nothing's in the open, everything you do is conducted in the dark. It's a dirty feeling, it cheapens the experience, which should be joyful and liberating. You've finally found someone to be in love with—now go hide.

Marnie didn't like sneaking around any more than I did—we talked about it, at my apartment, in the out-of-town hotel rooms where we went for clandestine weekend breaks, on the telephone. She wanted us to be able to show our love freely. But she was married, and as she explained to me, when I griped, adolescently, about our situation, she wasn't ready to make the final break yet. Not because she didn't love me—I was the only man she had ever loved, she knew that, now that she'd had a taste of the real thing—but she had to figure out how and when to tell her husband in a way that would cause him the least amount of pain. He was an important man, a man respected in his profession, a man of great pride. For his wife to leave him for another man, especially one who was hardly more than half his age, would be crushing and humiliating.

I understood the situation, but I didn't like it. Still, I was patient. Marnie wasn't going anywhere, I wasn't the one who had the secret rival, it was her poor shlump of a husband who was going to look up one day to see the safe falling on his head. And it wasn't as if I wanted to jump right into domestication with her. On the contrary—I had been carefree my entire life, being housebroken went against my grain. I wanted to be clean, that's all. But these things take time, as I was discovering.

And it was great being with her, even if I was often looking over my shoulder, figuratively and literally. She was loving, smart, humorous. She wasn't pretentious, either, despite her station in Texas society. She had been living in a golden cocoon for nine years, she wanted to break out and goof. We had a lot of fun together, even if we had to do it under the radar.

It went on like that for the entire first semester, until the week before the winter break. I was going home to spend Christmas with my mother. It would be the first time Marnie and I would be physically separated for more than a few days. We'd talked about her coming with me, but that would be too risky—she had to be home to prepare for Christmas, it was the most important holiday of the year for her husband, especially since he no longer shared it with his children. We had been very careful our entire time together. Not one person either of us knew had ever seen us together—we had taken great precautions.

"When you come back," she declared a few days before I was scheduled to leave, "I'll tell him. We can't go on like this anymore. I can't imagine ringing in the new year without you, Fritz. A new year, a new beginning."

I felt a tremendous sense of relief upon hearing that, because the deception had been weighing heavily on my shoulders; although I must admit the idea of us going public made my sphincter pucker. Once Marnie made the break, she and I would be partners—for life, or a goodly portion thereof. Middle-aged women don't leave affluent, albeit loveless, marriages without a safety net.

"Are you absolutely, totally positive?" she asked me for the umpteenth time. "This is enormous, for both of us. I don't want you to commit to something you'll regret later on. You'll still be young when I'm old," she reminded me without flinching.

"I won't regret it," I swore valiantly. I meant it. I had been touched, I felt, by the inexorable finger of fate. And you can't escape your fate.

Did I wish she was younger, closer to me in age? Of course; we both did. There was no guilt in feeling that, we wanted our future to be as perfect as possible, particularly since it was beginning with a fundamental imperfection. But love isn't a neat arrangement, all tied up in a pretty pink bow. You can only take it as it comes and rejoice that you've been given the chance.

It was the last day of fall classes before the beginning of reading period, final exams, and winter break. I was fifteen minutes from finishing my last session, a graduate seminar on Madison's contributions to the *Federalist Papers,* when a harried-looking secretary came striding into the room—no knock, just flung the door open and marched up to me. Barely glancing at my students, who were regarding her with undisguised hostility—you don't walk into a classroom, particularly a graduate seminar, the way she had—she said to me in a stage whisper, "Dean Marshall needs to see you."

"I'm teaching," I said brusquely, turning my back on her.

"He needs to see you right away."

I turned to her. "I'll come over to his office as soon as I'm finished here," I said icily, managing to restrain my temper. She should have known better than to barge in on me like this. Some of my colleagues would have cut her to ribbons for such an indiscretion.

She held her ground. "He said now."

"Get out."

She glared at me for a moment; then she turned on her heel and left.

"Goddamn administration," I heard from one of my students. A female voice. My students, particularly the women students, were very protective and supportive of me.

"Don't sweat it," I told them. "She didn't know any better."

That brought a laugh, based on elitism. Faculty and students on pedestals, secretaries, like janitors, in the muck. I don't like that caste system; if she hadn't been so rude, I wouldn't have taken the cheap shot.

We finished our work and I bade them good luck on their exams. Then I put on my outer coat, wound my scarf around my neck, and went outside.

Paul Marshall, who had requested my presence through the rude secretary, was the dean of the college; still is. My boss. We weren't close friends—he's old enough to be my father—but I was one of his favorite faculty members of the younger bunch. He'd recruited me from Wisconsin, so he had a proprietary interest in my future.

I assumed this would be a short, casual meeting, a pre-holiday drink with a few others. I had no concerns regarding my performance—my classes were ranked among the most popular and sought-after in the school; they were always overenrolled. There had been speculation on the faculty grapevine regarding the impending retirement of some of the older professors in my department; maybe they were thinking of moving me up to full professorship, and Paul was going to tip me off—an early Christmas present. Considering my age and relative inexperience that would have been a big step upward, but when they'd hired me, that was the plan. I was a rising star, and the university wanted to foreclose the possibility of my bolting to greener pastures.

I walked through the campus from my classroom to Dean Marshall's office. It was dark out, there was a chill in the air. The tower where Charles Whitman had gunned down all those people decades ago loomed up to my left, while to my right, a few blocks away up Congress, the State Capitol glistened in the early evening moonlight.

"Close the door behind you, Fritz."

Dean Marshall was leaning back casually in his chair, hands clasped behind his head, cordovan-shod feet propped up on his desk. He was tweedy as usual, the prototypical university don. His hair, cut Marine-short on his mottled balding head, gave him a monkish appearance. He was anything but monkish in real life, however; he had a martini-dry sense of humor and was very supportive of his people, especially the younger faculty. I enjoyed him more than any other authority figure at the school.

There was no one else in the office, just the two of us. "Going home for the holidays?" he inquired politely, a bland conversation opener. He motioned for me to make myself comfortable.

"Yes." I took off my pea coat and scarf and hung them on the coatrack in the corner, then sat down across from him. "My mother throws a hell of a Christmas."

"Being with family's always the best way to spend the holidays," he observed. He swung his feet down off the desk, leaned toward me. "We have a problem."

"What kind?" I assumed he was talking about something pedagogical.

He reached into his center desk drawer and took out a legal-sized manila envelope. Almost formally squaring the corners, he set the envelope in front of me. "Take a look at these."

Thinking back on the situation later, I don't know how I could have been so blind, so naive. Love can do that to you, I certainly know that now. Still clueless as to what was going on, I picked up the envelope and opened it. Inside were several photographs.

"Take them out," Dean Marshall instructed.

I pulled the pictures out of the envelope. And almost had a heart attack.

The entire affair was there, almost from the day Marnie and I returned to Austin. Pictures of us locked in hot, passionate embraces. Pictures of her entering and leaving my apartment. Pictures of her *in* my apartment, taken through the open window blinds. There was even a topless picture of Marnie sunbathing on my rooftop deck, with me applying suntan lotion to her breasts. The only details that weren't there were pictures of us actually fucking.

My hands were shaking so badly I could barely hold on to the photographs. I dropped the incendiary bundle onto his desk. "What sick fuck did this?" I could barely speak, my throat was so dry. I was scared, but I was enraged, too. "Who gave these to you?"

"A better question, Fritz, is why were you having an affair with this woman?"

"That's none of your business, Dean Marshall," I snapped at him. Now that the element of surprise was over, my anger was overtaking my fear.

"It's very much my business," he responded piercingly.

"Why? This woman is an adult and so am I. This is between us."

"And her husband."

"Is that who gave you these?"

Rather than answer, he picked up the incriminating photos and looked at a few, shaking his head sorrowfully. "You weren't very discreet, were you?"

"We tried to be. Damn it, Paul, this is an invasion of my privacy! This is lower than low, it's practically blackmail." I forced myself to reduce my pitch. "Okay. We had an affair. I'm certainly not going to deny it, the evidence is sitting on your desk. I'm sorry we did it this way, but affairs happen. All the time, everywhere."

He shook his head. "Not this way. Not with these people."

I had no clue of what he was talking about. "What does that mean?"

"You don't know what I'm talking about? Who your paramour is married to?"

"A doctor." What a stupid, archaic word, *paramour.* Like she's my concubine, an object.

"That's all?"

"A rich doctor."

Marshall cradled his head in his hands. "Oh, Fritz. You stupid, oblivious son of a bitch." He leaned forward and gave me this incredibly pitying look. "Mark Hamilton is a distinguished transplant surgeon. He's world-famous, he has pioneered some of the most important advances in medicine in the past thirty years. On top of that, he's a power in the Texas Republican party. And—I hope you're listening carefully, Fritz . . ."

I was listening. I didn't want to hear any of this, but I was listening. And squirming. "Okay," I gave him. "The man's a certified big shot."

"He has given millions of dollars to the university."

There it was. "What's he going to do, ask for a refund?"

My mentor shook his head. "No. He's not like that. And for one time," he grumbled in exasperation, "I wish you weren't such a smart-assed kid."

That stung. "I'm sorry," I said, trying to be properly humble, which, given the circumstances, was the posture I needed to be embracing, obviously. "I can see how serious and compromising this is to the university."

"You don't know the half of it." Marshall gathered up the photographs, holding them between his fingertips as if they were dog turds, and inserted them back in the envelope. "Mark Hamilton is the dean of our School of Medicine."

Tenure or no tenure, my dismissal was a slam dunk. The arrangement was signed, sealed, and delivered in seventy-two hours. I would stay on until after exams were completed—to leave before then would be a red flag that something ugly had happened. The university didn't want this tawdry information going out into the world. And my leaving before then would be an injustice to my students, who had been under my tutelage all semester.

The only question was how much the university was going to pay me to keep my mouth shut and not raise a stink. In the end, we settled on a year's salary, maintenance of my health plan, and confidentiality regarding the particulars of my leaving, so that in the future I could apply for positions at other schools and this wouldn't be on my record. For said record, I was taking an extended leave of absence to pursue "other interests." What those "other interests" were, no one ever told me. In due time, I'd officially tender my resignation.

By the time we managed to get in touch with each other late that night, Marnie was hysterical. I was alone in my apartment. The lights were out, the shades drawn—I wasn't going to give the peeper her husband had hired any fresh material. A fifth of Gentleman Jack, freshly bought after leaving Dean Marshall's office, sat within arm's distance. A generous portion had already been consumed.

The good doctor had already given her the news. Not only were there pictures, he'd also had her phone tapped. All of our intimate conversations that had emanated from her house were on tape. There was some very embarrassing material there, about the variety and intensity of our lovemaking, terrible comments she'd made about him, all kinds of rotten, incriminating shit.

"What are we going to do?" she asked, sobbing.

That question threw me—what could we do except slink out of town with our tails between our legs and start fresh somewhere else? Before I could answer, however, she told me she had to get off the phone—she was afraid Mark would hear her. We'd meet in the morning and discuss everything.

After she abruptly hung up on me I sat back and pondered what that meant—we'd discuss everything. What was there to discuss? And the fact that she'd called from her house really bothered me. Why was she there? Hadn't he kicked her out? And if, for some perverse reason, he'd allowed her to remain, why had she? Why wasn't she with me, sharing our sorrows with a bottle of Tennessee sour mash?

I got the answers when we met for coffee the following morning at an obscure working-class lunchroom way off the beaten track. Marnie was ultracautious. A woman who dressed with impeccable, rather conservative taste (we were the classic opposites-attract), she was clad in dark baggy sweats, sunglasses, a floppy hat that covered her face. She had ditched her car at a downtown hotel, walked through the lobby, exited via the back entrance, and grabbed a taxi. She was paranoid, absolutely convinced that her husband was still having her tailed.

To me it didn't matter anymore that her husband knew about us—the genie was out of the bottle. I didn't press that point, though, she was too emotionally blitzed. She looked awful—no makeup, hair unwashed, bags under her eyes. Her age was clearly showing that morning, a preview of attractions to come. I didn't care; her unadornedness made her even more beautiful to me. I couldn't help but notice that the big rock was still on her ring finger; for some reason I'd thought she would have taken it off, a symbolic gesture of rejection of the old and embrace of the new.

We hugged; then we sat in a back booth, side by side. The breakfast crowd had departed. We were the only ones there, except for the bored waitress and the kitchen staff. Marnie was fidgety, nervous as hell. I couldn't blame her; I was, too.

We had to talk, but neither of us wanted to go first. Finally, after the waitress brought us coffee, I plunged in. "Do you want to move in with me? Until we figure out where we're going?"

She looked at me, then into her coffee cup. "I . . . I don't think I can do that."

"Yeah, I guess that would be throwing oil on the fire. Do you have a friend you can stay with—" I stopped. Something in her body language told me there were problems going on within her, more than the catastrophes I already knew about.

"I can't move out right now," she said, her voice almost inaudible.

"But how can you stay? Isn't he going to kick you out?"

"No." She paused. Then she swiveled around so that she was facing me. "Where are *you* going to go, Fritz?"

That was a good question. I hadn't given the issue much thought. The immediate problems—losing my job, my career—had occupied whatever time I'd had to think when I hadn't been thinking about her and me.

"I don't know. I was planning the trip home. I guess I'll still do that." A bright idea came to me. "You can come with me. We'll be together, away from the pressure, we can work things out together."

"Work things out? What things?"

"Our future. What else?"

She looked away, out the window. We were in an industrial area; eighteen-wheelers rumbled down the road, making an awful racket. "What future?"

I wasn't getting it. "You and me. What other future is there?"

She turned back to me then, and before she spoke again, I knew what she was going to say.

"We don't have a future." The words were flat, devoid of emotion. Dead words from a numb brain. She put a hand on mine, the hand that wasn't wearing the ring. It was dry, almost scaly to the touch. "How would we live? You don't have a job."

"I'll get a job."

"Where? How?"

"I don't know," I said, starting to panic. This was spinning out of control, beyond the out-of-control that already enveloped us. "I haven't had time to think any of this through. Jesus, Marnie, this is a fucked situation. For both of us." I gripped her hand. "We'll figure it out, that's all. We have to, we don't have a choice."

She was shaking her head no.

"Look," I plunged on. "You were going to tell him anyway. The process got moved up a month, that's all."

She kept shaking her head.

"I'm sure I can catch on as a temporary instructor somewhere," I continued. "For the spring semester. There are lots of schools that would love to have me. I'm always getting feelers." I forced a smile.

"I can't leave here," she said.

"What?" I took a sip of my coffee. It tasted terrible, metallic and oily. "This is a free country, you can go anywhere you want."

"I've lived in Texas all my life." She wasn't looking at me; she couldn't. She was staring out the window, at the big rigs rolling down the road. They were going somewhere. She wasn't—she was stuck.

"I'm from here. All my family's here. My friends. My life. I can't just up and leave all that, for a man who doesn't even have a job anymore." She hesitated. "A man who'll leave me soon enough anyway, once he realizes how fast I'm aging."

Self-pity was the last thing we needed now. "We've been through that, honey." I pulled her chin around, forced her to turn and look at me. "That's not what it's about for me. You know that by now."

Her eyes started tearing, big silent drops running down her cheeks. "I can't leave, Fritz. Not like this."

That got me mad, and I had to express it. "What do you want, an amicable separation served up on a silver platter? Shit, Marnie, my whole fucking career's in the toilet, not just your marriage. We need each other, now more than ever."

She pulled some tissues from her purse and dabbed at her eyes. "I'm sorry. This has all turned out so badly."

I tried to comfort her as best I could. "That's how it is . . . now. But it'll get better. It can't get any worse. Sooner or later I'll get another job, a good one, we can settle in somewhere, start our life. In the meantime, we'll work it out. People do. You're a strong woman, you can handle this." I said that with as much conviction as I could, because I was beginning to doubt it.

She shook her head. "No. I'm not strong at all."

I leaned back against the cracked Naugahyde, exhausted. I'd had an awful sixteen hours, and things weren't getting any better. "What're you trying to tell me?"

She didn't pull her punch. "That it's not going to work."

I wasn't buying that—I couldn't. "It has to, Marnie. We don't have any other choices."

Her gaze went to the window again. "Mark wants to take me back."

That took my breath away, hearing that. "You can't go back. Not after . . ." I put my hands on her shoulders, pulled her around to face me. "You love me. You can't walk away from that. You can't . . . we can't not be together . . . you love me, I know that you love me. We love each other . . ."

I heard myself babbling semicoherently, thinking "shut the fuck up, fool," and not being able to. I ground to a halt. "We love each other. We can't not be together."

She shook her head, a tiny shake. "And we can't be together."

I felt myself melting away. I was going to be a puddle of crap on this dirty linoleum floor, and the busboy was going to mop me away.

Now it was she who took my hands in hers. "If I leave Mark for you, I'll have nothing. I signed a prenuptial agreement when we got married. He'll cut me off, I won't even have the clothes on my back. He's a brutal, vindictive man when he's crossed. He'll bury us. I know, I've seen him do it."

"So how can you think of staying with a man like that?" I was so fucked up I couldn't think crooked, let alone straight.

"Because he loves me. Or what passes for love for him. And he wants me to. He doesn't want the humiliation of my leaving him."

"Fuck that. He'll get over it. Or he won't, it's not our problem anymore."

"It's my problem, Fritz. There's no way around that."

Jesus, Mary, and Joseph. "So are you saying . . . what *are* you saying, Marnie?" Don't say it, I was praying.

She said it.

"It's over, Fritz. You and me."

By that time I didn't know what I was feeling, or even if I was feeling. "You can't live without me. That's why we did what we did. Because we had to. You can't live without love, Marnie. You lived your life without it, but now you've tasted that apple. We can't turn back now. I can't, and neither can you."

She tried to smile, but it wouldn't come. She looked like a clown with the tears streaking her face, her lower eyelids charcoal-black from lack of sleep.

"I couldn't, you're right. But now I'm going to have to. There's no other way for me. I know it makes me sound like a materialistic bitch, but I'm into a style of life too deeply to leave it."

Love conquers all, I thought as I looked at her. Except when it doesn't.

"If you had kept your job, if we could have stayed here—"

I cut her off. "Given the circumstances, that never was a possibility, which you had to know." My anger started rising again. "Why didn't you tell me you were married to the fucking dean of the medical school? A doctor, that's all you said. Shit, that's like saying your husband shoots hoops, but you don't mention that he's Michael Jordan. How could you ever have thought we could slip away into the night?"

"Because if I had told you, you would have left me. We would never have been involved like we were . . . are," she caught herself. She was already thinking of us in the past tense. "You never would have gotten involved with me, would you?"

"I don't know. Maybe I wouldn't have. It doesn't matter, I did."

"It was selfish," she admitted. "I couldn't bear not to have you, from that first night we were together, even before we made love. I thought . . . hoped . . . childishly, I know, that somehow it would work out."

"Like what? He'd die of a heart attack or something?"

She started crying again. I wasn't so sympathetic anymore. She'd burned me down for a temporary pleasure she knew couldn't be lasting. And she hadn't clued me in, she'd made me her unknowing accomplice. Now we were finished, according to her, as was my career and my entire life. Shattered pieces, dust under my feet.

"So you're going back to the mansions and the Jaguars and the diamonds and a sterile bed."

She stared blankly out the dirt-streaked window at the shitty morning.

"Until when?" I lost it then, I wasn't going to hold back anymore. "Until the next poor asshole comes along and shelters you from the storm?"

"Don't, Fritz. Please don't."

"Don't what? Make you feel bad? Shit, Marnie, you've ruined my entire fucking life! No job, no you, nada. What am I supposed to do, act gallantly? Stiff upper lip, like Shane or some other horseshit movie? This is my life, godfuckingdamn you! My life!"

That outburst emptied whatever air was left out of my balloon. I couldn't help it—I reached for her and hugged her. She went limp in my arms.

We stood inside the lunchroom foyer, waiting for the cab the waitress had called for her. A couple of truckers came in and sat down at the counter. One of them dropped some coins into the jukebox.

"I'll have a blue . . . Christmas . . . without you . . ." Elvis at his most mournful. Talk about shitty, prophetic coincidence.

Marnie started crying again. I pulled her to me and held her tight. What else could I do?

The bottle of tequila is empty. There's other stuff in the house, but that's it for tonight. Tomorrow, I think, I'll start cutting back. Booze has never been a big deal with me. I'd rather get stoned than high on liquor, it doesn't hurt my head so much the day after.

While Johanna was here I was able to blot out the murder. Now that I'm alone I can't, it's here with me, in the house. Not only in my head, but literally, on film.

I know I should do something. It's immoral not to. Tell Roach, or go to the cops. But if I do that, I'm right back where I vowed I wouldn't be: involved.

It already might be too late to tell Roach. If I was going to, I should have figured out how to do it this evening. Now, if he ever does find out, he'll think I'm an asshole and a flake. He'll be joining a sizable list.

I guess I'm going to have to go to the cops; but I sure as hell don't want to. I imagine the sequence of future events—it's scary. Getting involved means going public, which means I would be exposed. Being exposed means becoming a target. If the mysterious murderer could kill someone he obviously knew, in such a cold-blooded manner, he certainly could do it to me without thinking twice.

The tree fell in the woods and no one heard it, so it didn't make a sound. I'll rest on that chickenshit solipsism for a few days, until I figure out how to buck up my courage and do the right thing.

Buster Reilly, who I roomed with at Yale and is still one of my closest friends, is a partner at Parkinson, Miller, and Clements, one of D.C.'s gigantic law firms, the kind that has two or three former cabinet members on board so they can make gazillions a year hand-holding multinational conglomerates and lobbying for foreign governments. Although their practice is primarily corporate, they also have an excellent criminal law division. That's Buster's turf. Fred Thompson, the former actor and before that Watergate counselor, now a U.S. senator from Tennessee, told Larry King that if he ever needed a criminal lawyer, Buster would be at the top of his list. That's how highly esteemed my old buddy is.

The firm's offices are on four floors of a high-rise at the edge of Foggy Bottom, a few blocks west of the George Washington University campus. Buster can walk to the office from his Georgetown brownstone, which he does. He's a big, strong guy, very fit (he was on the Yale crew, too); he works out in the firm's private gym at lunchtime. He's been on me to shape up, as I've gone a bit flabby these past months, living out in the sticks by myself and drinking too much. I keep meaning to add a training regimen to my list of need-to-dos. So far, I haven't progressed past running a couple miles two or three days a week; it's too damn hot, and I don't have the facilities that are available to Buster. Come fall, when the weather slacks off, I'll pick up my exercise program—another item on my to-do list. It's getting to be a longer and longer list.

"So what's so important you drag yourself all the way up here in this god-awful weather instead of talking to me on the phone?" Buster asks.

We're sitting in his corner office, which has the nice view of the Lincoln and Jefferson memorials and the Potomac River. I'd told him yesterday, over the phone, that I might have a problem and wanted to discuss it in person. As usual, Buster's in the middle of a bunch of big cases, but he's making time to see me. He even asked his secretary to hold his calls, to show me he's taking me seriously. Buster knows about what happened to me down in Texas; we've drunk several cases of beer commiserating and discussing. He's optimistic about me—he's sure I'll bounce back. I appreciate having that kind of friend in my corner. There aren't many of them.

"Before I get into specifics," I say for starters, "let me ask a hypothetical question."

"Ask away."

"If I see a crime being committed, I'm obligated to go to the police, right?"

He gives me a sideways look. "This is hypothetical?"

"Hypothetical, right."

He leans back. "The answer to your hypothetical question is no."

"No?"

"No."

"Even if—"

"The question isn't hypothetical?"

"Let's say."

"The answer is still no."

I want to make sure I've got this right. "So a witness to a crime doesn't have to come forward."

"That's correct."

"What if . . ." I hesitate.

"What if what?"

"A witness to a crime has evidence that the crime was committed."

"Like what kind?"

"Oh, I don't know . . . a taped phone conversation, some documentary records . . ."

"Still no," he says.

"So there are no circumstances under which a witness to a crime has to go to the police."

"Not voluntarily," he counsels me.

"What's the difference?"

"No one has to come forward and give evidence that a crime was committed. It goes back to English common law, the right to privacy. In this country, it comes out of the Wild West tradition, where the only law was a gun. If a man had to come forward and give testimony that he'd seen a crime, he could become a crime victim himself. Understand?"

"Completely," I answer. That had been my concern—that in getting involved in the killing at Roach's farm I'd become a target. Now my friend the crack lawyer tells me it's legal for me to protect my ass.

"On the other hand," Buster continues, "if the authorities think you have evidence, and *ask* you about it, and you lie and say you don't, then you *are* in trouble, because you'd be committing perjury. It wouldn't be about not reporting this hypothetical crime, it would be in lying about it if you're asked directly."

I relax and sip from the excellent cup of coffee Buster's secretary gave me before she closed the door to his office behind us.

"You're not in any trouble, are you?" Buster's concerned about me, given my recent history.

"No," I assure him. "No trouble."

"This theoretical crime . . . to your knowledge, has anyone else come forward about it?"

I shake my head. "As far as I know, no one else saw it. Theoretically."

He looks at me quizzically. "The police don't know about it?"

"I don't see how."

"In that case, you definitely don't come forward."

"If something like this ever happens to me," I assure him, "I'll do just that."

"Make sure. Don't forget."

"I won't."

Buster regards me with a skeptical eye. "You're a crazy fucker, Fritz. You've always taken chances for the sake of . . . taking chances. In this case—this hypothetical case—don't," he warns me sternly. "I'm telling you this as your friend and your lawyer. I don't want to have to pull your ashes out of the fire because of the old 'Fritz couldn't help himself' syndrome."

I nod vigorously in agreement. "Not to worry. I've put away my childish things." I hold two fingers up in the Scout's honor salute.

Buster smiles. "So what else is happening in your life?" he asks, leaving the subject behind us. "Any job prospects?"

"I'm not looking currently. I'm not ready yet."

"Don't let it get cold," he advises me. "Out of sight, out of mind."

"I know. It'll be soon—don't worry."

"How's your love life? You getting enough?" Buster's a bachelor, like me. He's very popular with the ladies.

"As much as I can handle. I met a nice woman at a party my mother threw last week. She's from Boston, though, and she has serious intentions."

He smiles. "Hardly your type."

"No." Actually, I have been thinking about Johanna. But he's right. I'm too much of a fuckup for a serious contender like her.

"How is your mom?" Buster asks, changing the subject

again. Like all of my friends who know her, he's fond of my mother.

"Feisty as ever." I pause. "Hey," I say, as if the thought just now occurred to me. "She had this fellow at her party, her guest of honor, so to speak. James Roach. He's a wheel in the State Department. You know him at all?"

Buster's expression darkens. "Yes, I know him. He's close to some of the senior partners here, the big rainmakers. Why?"

"He bought a farm adjacent to ours, part of our original property. Recently, less than a year ago. He built a runway on it big enough to land jets, just bought a big expensive sailboat. Likes to brag on himself. He wants to take me out sailing."

"Make sure you're wearing a life jacket," Buster says dourly.

"What's that mean?"

"Short and sweet: the guy's a world-class prick."

I'm taken aback. I found Roach somewhat pompous, but he didn't arouse such visceral, angry passion in me. "He did seem a little nutty about terrorists under the bed," I say, "but he was pleasant, heavy on the charm. My mother was all ga-ga over him. All the old ladies were."

"Your mother would find something nice to say about Pol Pot." Buster shakes his head. "'Prick' is the wrong word. 'Motherfucker' might fit him better."

"A close personal friend, I take it."

"Yeah, like Hannibal Lecter. I'm not shitting you, Fritz, he may be charming and all that at a party, but he is not a nice man. He'd cut you off at the knees if you crossed him. I know people he's left for dead at the side of the road."

"I'm just a neighbor," I remind Buster. "Not a competitor."

"Fine. Then enjoy your sailing. Maybe he'll give you some good investment tips. The guy's made a shitload of money over the years."

"What's he do?"

"International trade. He was big in weapons brokering back in the 1970s. He dodged some legal bullets over that, but nothing ever stuck to him. He's from the old Joe Kennedy–Bill Casey school, which Clinton turned into an art form—if I do it, it's legal, don't read to me from the lawbooks."

"That's interesting."

"Meaning . . . ?"

"He used to sell arms, now his job is to keep the Russians from selling theirs."

"That's 'cause he doesn't make a profit from them selling theirs."

"How does someone with that kind of dossier get a high-up job in the State Department?" I ask. "Wouldn't that be considered a conflict of interest?"

Buster shakes his head dismissively. "He's a big contributor to this and previous administrations. And he knows the playing field, he's been running up and down it for decades. Besides, you need some pricks to do the stuff the diplomats cringe over. The James Bakers and Madeleine Albrights smile and make speeches, the James Roaches put the whip to the mule train." He leans back. "Bottom line, the wheels of governance and commerce need pricks who can get the job done. But I don't want any of them marrying my daughters, and I know how far to trust them, which is half as far as I can throw them." He checks his watch. "I'd take you to lunch, but I'm booked. Let's party soon. I'll call you."

A week has gone by since the "incident" at my neighbor's airstrip, as I prefer to think of what was a chilling murder. My meeting with Buster had set my mind at ease about not having to come forward with my evidence, but for the first couple of days afterward I checked the newspapers and watched the local news on TV anyway to see if there was any mention of it.

There was none, as I'd suspected would be the case. This had been some kind of gang-style execution. Over what, or by whom, I didn't know, didn't care. As far as I'm concerned, it's over.

I spent today as I've been spending most of my days, taking care of chores around my house, shooting pictures of birds, particularly Ollie, and fishing on the way home from the birds' refuge. I caught two nice-sized yellow perch, big enough for a substantial dinner for one. I'll make up a salad out of my garden, pan-fry the fish in butter with some diced onion and spices, crack a bottle of decent white wine, smoke a joint, and I'll be styling.

Check of my voice-mail—nothing urgent. Ditto my e-mail. A couple messages I save for later; one from my mother, another from Johanna, back in Boston. How much she enjoyed our evening together, trusts that I did, too, she'll be back down to see her mother and hopes we can get together. I'll send back a pleasant reply. Another night of fun and games with her wouldn't be hard to take.

Having disposed of what passes for business for me these days, I flick the TV on to the CNN Headline News. I have a satellite dish that brings me more television than is good for me. It's a lonely life out here, but it isn't primitive. I don't watch too much, mostly nature shows on the Discovery Channel, the news, and some of the bio stuff on A&E.

A few minutes into the top of the show, while I'm drinking my first glass of sauvignon blanc and cleaning my day's catch, a story comes up that catches my eye. Vassily Putov, the third-ranking member of the Russian delegation to this country, who has been missing for a week and has been the subject of a quiet but intense search by the Metropolitan police force and the FBI, has been found in a Dumpster in an alley in Baltimore. The man was murdered: two gunshots to the head. The body is badly decomposed—he's been dead a long time, probably for most of the week, according to the coroner's preliminary examination. They flash a picture of the victim on the screen, taken before he was murdered.

It's a big deal, with international overtones. Representatives from the State Department, along with those from the Russian embassy, are shown discussing the tragedy, speculating as to why it happened. It appears that he was the victim of a mugging—his wallet and other personal effects are missing. The body was found in a mean area, where gang and drive-by killings happen too often.

I know that part of Baltimore—it's a shithole, one of the worst in the city. If this man was hanging around there, he was asking for trouble. The more pertinent question is, I'm thinking as I'm watching, why would an important diplomat be around there at all?

For a moment I glimpse my neighbor James Roach in the background of one of the shots—he doesn't talk on camera, he's standing in a group, looking solemn. Then the picture of the dead man is flashed again.

I turn away from the television; then I turn back. Something about the man jogs my memory. But before I can get a better look at him the picture is gone, and they're on to another story.

I channel-surf; the Washington and Baltimore local news programs are on. The murder of the Russian counselor is getting big airplay. I look at the picture of the man again as it comes up on the screen. He looks familiar, but from where, I can't recall. The anchorwoman says there is an unsubstantiated rumor that the man frequented street prostitutes, particularly transvestites. If that's the case, he was in the wrong place at the wrong time with the wrong people—a most unsavory and embarrassing situation. But it would explain why he was found there.

If that's true, I don't know the victim—hookers and gay cross-dressers aren't my bag. Anyway, it doesn't matter now—he's dead. I turn the television off and finish cooking my dinner.

Before I know it, it's almost eleven o'clock. I've been listening to some jazz CDs, old standards like Miles and Sonny Rollins, and catching up on my Faulkner—*As I Lay Dying,* one of my favorites of his, I read it every five years or so. I've smoked half a joint and drunk most of the bottle of wine—I'm in a mellow place.

Bedtime. I'm going to get up early in the morning, do some bird-watching and photography, my usual routine. These birds, especially Ollie, have really gotten to me. They're my boon companions, most days my only ones.

I turn the tube on again to catch the late sports news. The Orioles are out of the race as usual, but I like to keep up with Cal Ripken, Jr. He's heading down the final stretch of his great career, this could be his last go-around. I make a mental note to get up to Camden Yards before the end of the season. My brother has season tickets, good ones of course, only the best for Sam. I'll hit him up for a game.

The murder of the Russian counselor is still a big story. No clues, but plenty of speculation. On camera, the CBS State Department correspondent says there's a theory being floated by the usual "reliable but unidentified sources in government" that this may have been the work of a right-wing dissident militia from within Russia who are unhappy with the current regime. I wonder, fleetingly, if my neighbor Roach is one of the unidentified sources. In a more cynical vein, I also wonder if this so-called theory is really about saving face. If the guy was known to be a hooker freak, with a particular yen for transvestite prostitutes, being killed by foreign agents is a hell of a lot more dignified than being killed by some flaming cross-dresser, his pimp, or some street kids who waylaid him.

The slain counselor, according to the TV reporter, was considered a moderate in Russian politics. As the announcer drones on, the dead man's picture comes up on the screen, a different one from the early evening broadcasts. I look at it. I swear I've seen this face—but where?

A sudden thought occurs to me; and as it does, my pulse begins to quicken. Keeping the image of the dead man in my mind's eye as best I can, I go into my closet and pull out the old shoes in which I've hidden the transparencies of last week's murder. Taking them out—my hands are shaking, I don't deny it—I examine them under a magnifying glass.

The faces of the two men—the murderer and the victim—are dark, due to the early morning backlighting. Even under magnification the killer is basically indistinguishable—the cap and sunglasses he's wearing cover most of his face. I could blow the slide up to get a closer look at him but that would blur the picture, and it wouldn't help me see him any better.

The other man, the victim, is a clearer image. Still dark, but he wasn't wearing anything on his head or face. I strain to see if he's who I now think he might be.

I can't tell. There are similarities in size, head shape, and so forth, but his face is too dark for me to venture a conclusive opinion one way or the other.

If the man in my pictures turns out to be the dead counselor, though, the shit is going to hit the fan like a Caribbean hurricane. A high-ranking foreign diplomat is killed in southern Maryland and a week later his body turns up in a Dumpster in a Baltimore slum, a hundred miles away? That's not hookers, and it's not a dissident Russian group, either. I don't know squat about global politics, but the man I saw getting killed, even from far away, wasn't a stranger to his assassin. He and his killer knew each other.

A diplomat being murdered on the property of a high-ranking State Department official is too important for me to bottle up. I should have realized that a week ago, when I found out who owned that property, and taken prompt action, even though Buster warned me not to. The police should have these pictures.

I'm going to look like a jerk, going to the authorities so late. When Roach finds out, he'll be outraged, and he'll have a right to be. A high-stakes murder took place on his estate. Run-of-the-mill criminals don't travel by private jet. These people were big-time players. Further complicating the matter, I witnessed the murder *before* I met Roach. I exchanged pleasantries with a man who was a guest in my mother's house and deliberately didn't tell him about it, because he struck me as an asshole and because I was worrying about my own safety and didn't want to get involved.

It's too late to do anything tonight. Tomorrow I'll do something. After I get back from my birds. By tomorrow afternoon for sure.

I put the incriminating transparencies back in their hiding place and get into bed. I left the light on in the kitchen, but I'm not getting out of bed to turn it off. Tonight, I'm leaving it on.

I get up early and go out and hang around with the birds and take pictures of them and check out Roach's property. Not a creature is stirring. I watch the farm for a couple of hours while attending to my birding duties, wondering if someone will come by, some form of human life, but nada—not a soul. Roach had mentioned that he had a foreman and staff people, but I see no one. If I didn't know better, I'd think the place was uninhabited.

Now I'm back in my house. It's mid-morning and I have a raging headache, little men are beating on anvils all over the inside of my skull. My pain is not from the wine I drank or the grass I smoked last night—by my current standards I was abusing moderately. And it isn't from the heat of the day, I wore a hat and was back by ten, before the temperature really started blasting into the stratosphere. This is a panic-attack headache I'm experiencing.

I sit down with my mid-morning red one and a cup of black coffee to think about what I'm going to do. If, despite Buster's admonition to stay clear of this, I go to the cops and tell them I witnessed a killing, that would be bad enough. But to have the actual proof in my hot hands—that'll be a Pandora's box. It'll be like owning the Zapruder film—I could be drawn into a maelstrom over which I'll have no control.

I wash down a couple of Tylenol with the red one, sip at my coffee. The pounding in my head is going down, but my stomach is growling, and my skin feels clammy.

I need to know if the man in my pictures is the dead counselor before I do anything else, including wasting any more of Buster's expensive time. (He doesn't charge me, but he could be seeing a paying client while he's with me.) I don't know why, exactly, I have this need. I didn't kill the man, I didn't know him, so what if his death tilts the balance of power in the old Soviet bloc or even the entire world? Is that going to make my life any better or worse? I don't think so.

As best as I can figure it out—and I hate psychoanalyzing myself more than anything—is that I feel so guilty over so many crappy things I've done over the past several years that I've suddenly developed the need, fueled by this awful event that I witnessed, to atone for my sins by doing good deeds, starting now. I'm like Rip Van Winkle waking up into a new world. One of my worst sins (except with Marnie, where I sinned in the other direction) has been lack of involvement in the world of people—the cynic keeping everyone at arm's length, like I did with that nice lady Johanna Mortimer.

Doing the right thing in this situation, the moral thing (as opposed to the *legal* thing), is to turn my evidence over to the authorities. If the man I saw being killed a few miles from here is the counselor, why was his body picked up and transported a hundred miles away, then dumped in a shithole slum and made to look like a mugging accident, with kinky and humiliating sexual overtones to make the victim look bad, as if he deserved to be killed?

Why would his killer go to all that trouble? Why did the murder occur on the property of an American assistant secretary of state? If the killer wanted to discredit James Roach, ruin him, the body would have been left on his property, not taken away. So that's not the reason. Maybe the killer knew this was Roach's property and specifically *didn't* want Roach implicated. Would that mean the killer knew Roach? And how could the killer and his pilot have known they could land on the airstrip, commit the crime, and get away without being seen? Did they know no one from the farm would be there? Did they know the farm staff's schedule? Or was there collusion between the killer and people who work for Roach? Between the killer and Roach himself? That would be fucking scary—the man lives a couple of miles from here, practically on my back doorstep. Was the killing premeditated, as I've been assuming, or could it have risen from an argument that got out of hand? What were the victim and the killer arguing about?

The possibilities are endless—*if* the man in my pictures is the Russian counselor. The million-dollar question. I don't know if he is—this could be all smoke, no fire. But I do know, for my own peace of mind, that I have to find out.

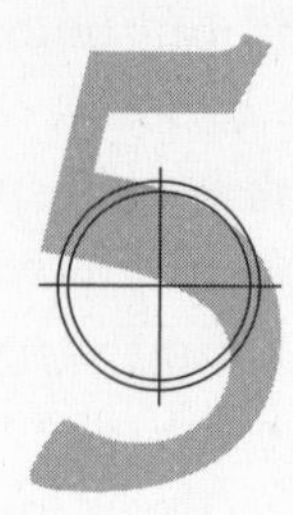

My pal at King James Community College, Pierce Wilcox, has good contacts in the photography business. I phone him up and tell him my problem: I have pictures of some people in which the features are unrecognizable. I want to try to digitally enhance the slides to see if I can make an identification. "It's a delicate situation," I tell him. "I don't want anyone knowing I have these pictures."

"You moonlighting as a detective now?" he asks with curiosity.

"Kind of," I answer evasively. "It could be embarrassing to the parties involved."

"What honey pot are you dipping into now that you shouldn't be?" he asks. I can feel his salacious old-man's smile across the wire.

"You know me too well, Pierce."

A couple hours later, he calls me back. "There's a lab in Washington that should be able to handle your problem. My guy there will do what he can to help you out."

"This is kind of sensitive." I'm nervous about anyone seeing these pictures and figuring out who they're of.

"Not to worry. My friend will bring you in after hours. No

one else will know you've been there, and he's the height of discretion—he's handled delicate situations many times."

"Okay," I answer reluctantly. I'm taking a chance, but I have to find out. "I'm trusting you on this, Pierce."

"I'm doing you a favor here, man," he says peevishly. "So's my friend."

"No offense meant," I assure him quickly. "I'm still paranoid these days, from what happened down in Texas."

It's a lame excuse, but Pierce buys it. He knows the story of my crash and burn in Austin.

"None taken," he says forgivingly.

I need to trust people. So far Buster's the only person I've confided in, and he's a lawyer, sworn to secrecy. I either need to widen the circle, or start sleeping with a gun on my bedside table. I don't like guns, never have.

"Thanks for the help, Pierce. I appreciate it."

I park my car in an enormous, dimly lit, almost empty parking lot located in an industrial section of Anacostia, in southeastern Washington, and walk toward a long, concrete-slab building with slit windows that are set high above street level. The building is flanked by others that are architecturally similar, monstrous block-square tombstones that were constructed to be anonymous. High-tech companies that perform exotic, ultramodern work for government and industry occupy these cheerless structures. Their drab exteriors mask the originality and artfulness of the activities that go on inside them.

The company that is housed in the particular building I'm going to is an ultra-high-tech photography lab. Some of the exotic jobs they perform include monitoring images from satellites all over the world, and inventing and perfecting state-of-the-art camera devices to deal with infrared imaging; anything that involves any type of cutting-edge photography can be handled here. They also have beautiful printing and reproduction facilities—they do work for the Smithsonian and important public art galleries around the world. And they also specialize in what I'm here for—they can enhance images so as to make the obscure or indefinable identifiable. A considerable portion of their work comes from federal agencies like the CIA, the FBI, and the Defense Department.

My host, who tells me his name is Jack (but deliberately doesn't offer up his last name), explains all this to me as he leads me through the building to the area where we're going to be working. He'd met me outside and walked me in, giving me someone else's ID card to wear to get past the guards, who knew him and didn't pay us any attention. So much for security, I'm thinking—no wonder the Chinese have our nuclear secrets.

Jack's a prototypical old-school nerd from back in the days when the geeks wore slide rules on their belts like holsters and cinched their pants up to their chests. Rayon shirt, of course, old-fashioned Converse All Stars in black, eyeglasses with chunkier frames than Clark Kent's. Classic, except that Jack is no older than twenty-five. I can't tell if his accent is northern British or Irish; it's thick, working-class, like the Beatles when they hit the scene back in the '60s.

It's ten-thirty at night. There are other people working in the building, but I don't see any of them. Jack doesn't want me to; and he doesn't want anyone to see me, either.

"Let's see what you've got," he says when we reach the area where we're going to work. It's a windowless rectangular room full of computers, imagers, scanners, digital cameras, similar to a science lab in a university, except there are no petri dishes or microscopes.

I hand over the transparencies I want to enhance—the *before* shots, not those of the actual killing. No one's going to see them.

"First off," he says briskly, "we'll feed 'em into the computer. Then we'll tweak 'em, see what we can pull up."

I perch on a stool and watch him do his thing. There are a

dozen monitors connected to his computer, like a video bank in a broadcasting booth. He scans the transparencies into his computer, brings them up side by side on the center screen. On this large screen they're less clear than my originals.

"We'll fix that," he says, alluding to the quality.

He fiddles with the color and contrast, changes the pixel dimension on the screen, plays with them a bit more, and voilà!, the photos displayed on his computer screen are as bright and clear, even more so, than my originals.

"Quality okay for you?" he asks me with a nonchalant air. The guy's a pro, and usually handles much more complicated problems than mine, I'm sure.

"Excellent."

"Dandy. Let's move on, then. I see your problem, of course. You can't make out any of the features, can you? What time were these taken?"

"An hour after sunrise."

"Shooting right into the bloody sun. I take it they weren't posing for you."

"You take it correctly."

"Who interests you the most?"

I point to the face of the man I think could be the Russian counselor.

Jack peers at it through his thick-lensed spectacles. "This'll be a bit of a challenge. The sun's directly behind his bloody head. The other one"—he points to the man who pulled the trigger shortly after these pictures were taken—"he'd certainly be a problem, since the shades and that hat hide most of his face anyway. Almost as if he was taking precautions not to be seen," he muses.

"Probably his style," I say, realizing that Jack's statement might be true. Almost certainly is true, as I think about it.

Jack points to the third man in the picture, the pilot. "What about him? He'd be the easiest, he's standing at more of an oblique angle."

"I'm not concerned about him, although if you can do it, I'll take it. This one"—I point at my objective—"is why I came."

"Any idea of where this man you're looking for lives?"

"Washington, I'm pretty sure. If not D.C. proper, Virginia or Montgomery County."

"Good, that'll narrow down the field, save some time." He squares his shoulders. "Let's give it our best shot."

He turns his attention to his computer, starts typing in a series of commands, and all the screens start going crazy. Images flash across them almost faster than the eye can take them in—faces, all different. They seem to be similar to the general outlines of the face in my photos.

"Who are these people?" I ask, trying to keep up. "What's going on?"

"This is everyone in the computer's database who bears a basic resemblance to the man in your pictures," Jack informs me.

"How . . . where did these come from?"

He smiles morbidly. "Big Brother's watching you. Didn't you know that?"

"That sounds like CIA stuff."

His smile turns into a laugh, right in my face. "Of course it is, for God sakes. CIA, FBI, plenty of agencies, here and abroad. This is the digital age, the computer age, or have you not noticed? Modern technology's opened the world up to infinite possibilities—and it's also taken away any vestige of privacy that you have, or think you have."

In front of us, the screens are still going crazy with images of faces—they're dissimilar in many respects, but the basic shape of the head, the hairline, the features, and so forth, is of one general variety.

"These matches are close enough to warrant looking at more deeply," he tells me. Then he asks, "Do you have a driver's license?"

"Yes." I start to dig for it in my wallet.

He waves me off. "I'm sure it's a beautiful portrait, like all driver's license pictures. That's not my point. You have a driver's license, you have credit cards, you have bank cards." He points to the screens. "You're in the system. Every man, woman, and child is in here, almost. Only people who don't use any of those things escape the dragnet. Give me your Social and your birthday."

I tell him my Social Security number and my birthday by month, day, year. He punches the numbers into his computer, starts a series of commands. Almost instantaneously, my Texas driver's license picture pops up on one of the screens.

"You live in Texas?"

"I did," I say, dismayed at what I'm seeing. "I haven't switched back to Maryland yet."

"Well, if I wanted to, I could find out a lot of things about you, from knowing no more than your birthday and Social Security number, which anyone can find out. It's how insurance companies and credit companies and banks keep track of you, Fritz Patrick Tullis." He's reading from the license data on the screen. "And government agencies that don't have your best interests at heart."

"This sucks." Goddamn, there really is no privacy left, if this is true, which it obviously is. What do they know about me, how detailed is their knowledge? Do they know I hang out with exotic birds? Are there satellites flying over my head recording my every move? Was I photographed photographing the murder? The prospect is chilling.

"Yeah," Jack says with a shrug, "but it's the way of the world. Too late to change things now. We're living in the information age, don't you know? And you and me and everyone is a piece of that information, a couple of bytes in the massive vortex. Don't fight it—you'll be pissing against the wind. If you want to escape, give up all your credit cards, driver's license, move into a wilderness area. Better yet, leave the country entirely, move into the deepest recesses of the Amazon, or some remote former

Soviet republic, where they still farm with oxen and stink their breath up with garlic to ward off the evil eye. Maybe you'll be safe in one of those places—for a while. Sooner or later, they'll track you down, if you leave any kind of paper trail."

"Thanks for the warning," I tell him sourly.

"You want to find this man, don't you?" Jack says bluntly as he points to the screens, bringing me back to earth. "If so, you have to take the good with the bad and hope that the big boys who have access to all this stuff don't abuse it." He shrugs. "There's so much of this stupid information floating around out there in cyberspace no one knows where most of it is, nor does anyone care, unless you're deemed dangerous by someone who can access this and use it. If it really worked, half the population would be in jail, not just the druggies and the dumb shits who can't get out of their own way."

He turns back to the computer. "Enough jawboning. I can't have you here any longer than's necessary."

He plays with the computer some more. More pictures come and go; then about a dozen and a half fill the various screens and remain, frozen in two dimensions. They're small, no more than an inch square. I look at each of them, straining to see if one of them is the Russian counselor. I can't tell.

"Okay." Jack smiles. "Now we're starting to make sense of this." He scrolls a forefinger in front of the images. "These men are the closest matches to your photo. If the man in your picture lives in the metropolitan D.C. area, he's one of them. Now . . ." He brings my scanned pictures up on the one screen he's left blank. "Let's start painting."

He starts playing with the man in the picture whose face is in backlit shadow. Quickly, a portion of the darkness goes and the face becomes lighter, so that some features begin to show. He twiddles the computer some more, and more features become apparent—not enough to make an identification, but clearer than it was when we started looking at it.

"We're getting there," he whispers intensely. "Come on, baby."

Slowly, bit by bit, a face begins to emerge. I'm staring at it intently; is it who I think it is? I can't tell—it still isn't clear enough.

"Fuckin' backlight," Jack mutters under his breath. "What kind of photographer are you who takes pictures of faces in this kind of crappy light?"

"They weren't posing for me," I remind him.

"I know," he says with aggravation. "If they were, we wouldn't be here, would we?"

He works at it some more. "I don't know," he says, beginning to sound pessimistic. "I don't know if we're going to have enough to—"

Suddenly, one of the screens that's filled with the miniature frames of the possible matches flashes a silent explosion—and there, full-screen, is one face.

Jack sits back, a big smile on his face. "Ah! The machine comes through." He pats the computer like it's a pet. "Good girl," he praises it. "Good doggie."

I'm staring at the face on the computer screen—and begin to shake. I hope Jack doesn't notice. I don't think he does—he's too happy with his success to pick up on my reaction.

"Well?" he asks me. "Is this who you're looking for?"

"I don't know who I'm looking for," I lie. "I needed to know—" I stop.

"What?" he asks impatiently.

"You don't need to know," I tell him abruptly.

"Well . . . okay." He sounds miffed.

"You don't want to know."

"Like that, huh?"

I don't answer. Instead, I tell him, "Can you print this up for me? Both images, side by side?"

"Sure."

He highlights the images, hits Print. The printer spews out the pictures. I stuff them into a manila envelope.

"You can shut it down now," I tell Jack. "And if there's any of this stored in memory, get rid of it."

He hits some keys. The screens go blank. "I already have."

I sit in my car in the empty parking lot, the pictures from the computer in one hand, the newspaper clipping in the other.

There's no doubt—the man I saw murdered on a remote farm in a small southern Maryland county is the same man who turned up a week later, still murdered, in a Baltimore slum, a hundred miles away.

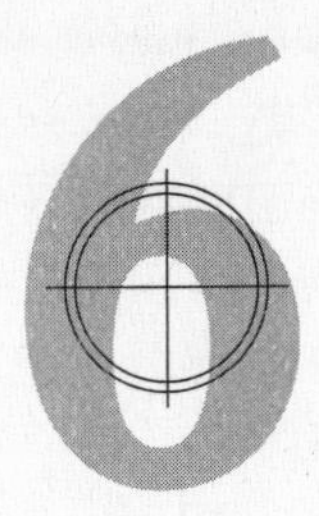

The invitation comes via e-mail: *"My new sailboat is being delivered this weekend. I'm taking her out on her maiden voyage Sunday, around nine in the morning. I'd be delighted if you would join me. Sincerely, James Roach."*

My instincts tell me to stay away from Roach. On the other hand, I love to sail, and I haven't been out on a big boat in years.

In the end, my appetite for adventure gets the better of my caution. I respond to Roach's e-mail, thanking him for the invite, that I'll be there. I'll have to be on guard that he doesn't find out I was lying like a rug when I told him that I don't venture down there, which of course I do, almost every day, when I go to see my birds. But I can handle that; if I can keep my mouth shut about a murder that happened on his property, I can finesse my way through a day's sailing.

Bright and early Sunday morning I'm driving to Roach's farm. It's a roundabout route, doubling back by my mother's place, up to the two-lane, drive a mile south, then turn onto Roach's private road. I could get there in half the time in my little putt-putt, but I don't want him to know I navigate those waters.

I pull up to his dock at the appointed hour and spot the new boat sitting in the water, pretty as a Winslow Homer painting. The name *Helena* is freshly stenciled on the side. If this is Roach's idea of "nothing special," I'd like to know what he considers "special." This is a beautiful vessel. I eyeball it to be at least seventy feet in length.

"Glad you could make it!" Roach, standing on the teak deck, a glass of champagne in his hand, booms out a welcome to me. He's dressed in old boat shoes, well-worn baggy shorts, a New York Yacht Club polo shirt frayed at the collar, his head covered by a long-billed cap, the kind you see Hemingway wearing in the old deep-sea fishing photos.

Standing next to him is a large, white-haired man his age, maybe a few years older. Unlike Roach, this man is showing his age. His florid complexion and big nose crisscrossed with broken veins remind me of Tip O'Neill, the late speaker of the house from Boston. He's wearing a short-sleeved shirt and khakis, and expensive hand-tooled cowboy boots. I knew people in Texas who wore boots like his. None of them had ever punched a cow—the closest encounter any of them had ever had with one was when they cut into a steak.

"Come aboard!" Roach calls out jovially as I approach.

I jump onto the deck.

"Fritz, I'd like you to meet an old friend of mine, Ed Flaherty. He's going to join us today."

Flaherty and I shake hands. His grip is solid—he could have been a football player forty years ago.

Flaherty smiles broadly. "Perfect weather for sailing, isn't it?"

He definitely isn't from Texas—his accent sounds pure Chicago.

"The gods are smiling today," I agree.

"Ed and I go back a long way," Roach says. "We fought the good fights shoulder to shoulder, in the trenches."

"And survived, although it beats the shit out of me how," Flaherty laughs.

Roach nudges his friend in the ribs. "You'll have to change

out of those fancy boots before we take off," he joshes the other. "I don't want my brand-new deck scuffed up."

"Got a brand-new pair of Sebagos," Flaherty says. "I'll put 'em on now."

A college-aged kid comes up from below. "All secure below," he announces, giving me a sideways glance.

"Joe Pitts," Roach says to the kid, "say hello to my guest and neighbor, Fritz Tullis." To me, explaining: "Joe's going to be taking care of the boat."

"Nice to meet you," I say.

The kid grins. "Same here."

He disappears back down the hatch, leaving the three of us on deck. There's an ice bucket at Roach's elbow. He hands me a glass, fills it with bubbly. Veuve Clicquot, Grande Dame. This guy goes first-class all the way.

"Cheers." He raises his glass.

"To your new boat," I reply. "*Helena.* Is there any personal significance to that?" I don't know if he's married—no women here today, and he bachelored it at my mother's.

He shakes his head no. "I named her after the woman whose face launched a thousand ships." He smiles. "A thousand and one, now."

"And whose abduction caused one of the bloodiest wars." I'm a history professor, I can't help putting in my professional two cents' worth.

He laughs. "I prefer the reference of tragic beauty to that of bloodshed."

We sip champagne. It's exceptional. "Let me show you around," Roach offers.

He proudly points out various features as we walk the length of the deck. Twin head stays with Reckmann hydraulic furlers, Lewmar electric winches all over the place, North sails, top-of-the-line Brooks and Gatehouse nav instruments, Furuno radar, a Zodiac Sport Boat hanging on the stern. This boat was built without compromise. Down below, three computers and every possible piece of nav equipment is here: a Furuno 1850 chart plotter with differential GPS, Robertson autopilot, satellite phone, single sideband high-seas radio. The engine's a Caterpillar diesel.

The galley is equally impressive. Granite countertops, an Alpes Inox vent and stove, Smeg oven, a microwave, a dishwasher, washing machine. This yacht has all the bells and whistles, bar none.

Joe Pitts is putting provisions away in the refrigerator. He grins as I gawk.

The master stateroom should be featured in *Architectural Digest.* A queen-sized bed, custom cabinets—all the wood on the boat is custom, teak, mahogany, cedar. The master bath has a tub with Jacuzzi jets, stainless steel fixtures, the full works.

Roach waits while I take all this opulence in, then silently opens a wooden door in a corner of the bathroom. I look inside. It's a sauna, big enough for six.

This is a level of sailing beyond any I've ever known. "A hell of a boat," I tell him. What else can you say?

I follow him back up on deck. Flaherty's changed out of his cowboy boots into brand-new boat shoes. Looking around, I calculate in my head. This yacht had to have cost three million dollars; maybe more. Add a jet airplane. A private airstrip. As my father used to say in his wry, understated way, a million here, a million there, pretty soon it adds up to real money.

Roach pours more champagne for the three of us. As he's about to drink he looks off abruptly, over my shoulder.

Another man is approaching us. He moves lightly; I didn't hear him coming, which unnerves me—I don't like people sneaking up on me. This guy's in his mid- to late forties, bristly blond flattop, muscles cut sleek. He's wearing a WWF T-shirt, tight bike shorts to mid-thigh, new boat shoes, is carrying a small day pack. Mirror shades from the old Paul Newman prison movie *Cool Hand Luke.* There's an ominous aura about him.

Roach introduces us. "Fritz Tullis, Ed Flaherty, say hello to Wade Wallace. Wade's the new head of my security detail," he informs me. "A recent addition," he adds, "a necessary but intrusive drawback of the job. The sensitivity of my recent activities has forced me to do this. It's not all wine and roses, being in a position of prominence."

Flaherty gives Wallace a good looking-over. I get the impression he's had plenty of involvement with men like Wallace. "Are you a sailor?" he asks the newcomer. Like me, he seems to have taken a gut-reaction antipathy to this man.

Wallace shakes his head: a firm no. "I'll tolerate it for the job, but it's not my thing. I prefer firm land under my feet."

"You'll learn to love it!" Roach barks happily, clapping the security man hard on the back. "You'll be a regular salt in no time. Right, Fritz?" He smiles at me like we've been best friends and sailing companions all our lives.

"Whatever you say, James," I answer in a spirit of good fellowship. The man's taking me on the nicest boat I've ever boarded. I can mind my manners.

"I'm Jim to my friends," he corrects me, winking at Flaherty. "James is for the press and the bureaucrats."

"Jim it is," I say sprightly.

Joe pops out from down below. "We're set, Mr. R."

The master-of-all-he-surveys looks out toward open water. "Let's not lose any more precious time." He starts the engine. "Cast off, Joe."

The kid unties us from the dock. Roach takes the helm, and we head out.

Once we've cleared the narrow channel and are out into the river we hoist the sails and cut the engine. Young Joe and I are the crew; Roach is at the helm, as befits the captain. Flaherty stands next to Roach while Wallace, looking green and queasy, has planted his ass on the deck, his back firmly lodged against the side of the cabin. He wasn't faking about being a landlubber; he's fighting hard to keep from throwing up.

After a short time the river flows into the Bay: we're in open water. We turn downwind and hoist the spinnaker. There's ample wind to fill our sails and get us up to seven brisk knots. Roach has charted a course that will initially take us south, in the vicinity of Tangier Island in the Virginia section of the Bay, back up northeast toward Pokomoke Sound on Maryland's Eastern Shore, from there circling back into the middle of the Bay, where we will skirt Bloodsworth Island, then head west for home. A full day's sail, a nice shakeout for Roach's new prize possession.

We're running with the wind on the first leg, so there's not much to do except sit back and enjoy the ride. Overhead, the sky is cobalt blue, unusual for this time of year, when it's generally bleached white. Large billowy cotton-candy cumulus clouds in the shapes of animals and plants drift through it—I see an elephant's head, a walrus, a running hound among the formations. The sun, a fat yellow-white shimmering jellyfish, lies listlessly high above us. The clouds obscure it on and off, tempering the fullness of the heat. There's a different feeling to the moisture in the air than the normal torpid humidity—it's wetter, cooler (90 degrees instead of the normal 100). Somewhere in the Caribbean a storm must be brewing, fixing to crawl up the coast with its drenching rain and howling winds. We don't get the full brunt of hurricane action very often, we're too inland. But the air feels good, tropic-like. The water below us is dark, green-black, small whitecaps lapping up against the hull. It'll feel good to swim later on, after lunch, when the heat of the day is at its peak.

I take my camera out of my day pack and snap off some pictures of the boat, some birds flying overhead, Roach at the helm, Flaherty standing near him.

Flaherty gestures at my camera. "Are you one of those photographers who take it with you wherever you go?"

"Pretty much. If I think I'll get good shots."

"Do your own developing?"

"Only black and white. Color's too complicated. It's a hobby, something to occupy my time."

I don't want anyone, Roach especially, thinking I take pictures of everything I see, not with those transparencies hiding in my wingtips. It was a mistake, I realize, bringing the camera at all.

Roach gestures to the wheel. "Want to drive her?"

"Sure," I answer eagerly.

I can feel the power as I take hold of the wheel—it's like I'm a jockey trying to rate a twelve-hundred-pound thoroughbred who wants to run as hard and fast as he can. I turn to Roach. "She tracks beautifully."

His smile is wide. "I know."

Three o'clock. We've been out on the water for six hours. I'm slathered up with suntan lotion, but after going bareback for a few hours before lunch, which included taking a quick dip, I put my shirt back on. The swimming wasn't enjoyable—the water's too hot, it was like swimming in a warm bathtub.

Lunch was simple, but good: crab cake sandwiches, cole slaw, potato salad. We washed the meal down with beer. In weather like this you have to stay hydrated—rivulets of salty water are running down my underarms and back.

Roach has done most of the skippering, as he should, since it's his boat, but Flaherty and I have taken turns, too. The only one of us who hasn't had a good time is Wallace. The man's been miserable. He tried to eat some food but wound up puking it up over the side, which embarrassed him and riled him up, particularly when Roach teased him about it. I doubt he'll come sailing again—he'll find someone else to take on this duty. I don't know if the guy's surly because he's feeling shitty or if it's his natural state; I suspect there are elements of both working. I wouldn't want him on the other side in a fight. For an hour now he's been below; this man doesn't want to see water, let alone be out on it.

We're cruising along in the shelter of Pokomoke Sound, leisurely tacking back and forth, heading toward the more open water of the Bay proper. We'll get back to Roach's dock by five-thirty, which will work out good for me—I told my mother I'd have Sunday dinner with her, and she doesn't like to eat late. I can be back to my shack, shower, and get to her place by six-thirty. She'll want to know what the sailing was like, of course, and she'll be pleased that I'm getting along with our neighbor—she disapproved of what she considered my bad manners toward a guest. She's a proper lady; she was raised to be gracious and nice to everyone you invite into your home, even if they're assholes. I was raised that way, too, by her, but the lessons didn't take, like many others she and my father tried to teach me.

"Take 'er for a while, will you, Fritz?" Roach calls to me from the wheel.

I realize I've been daydreaming. I snap to. "Sure." I scramble along the deck to the helm.

"Roll up the jib, bring her into the wind, and douse the main," he says. "I'll be right back," he says, and disappears into the cabin.

I turn to as he ordered—he's the captain. Joe helps me drop the mainsail. The in-boom furling works seamlessly. We slow down, almost stopping, the big yacht bobbing gracefully on the still water. A moment later Roach emerges with a shotgun cradled in one arm and a trap and some clay targets in the other. "Joe, give me a hand."

Joe takes the trap and the targets from him and starts setting up the apparatus on deck.

"What're you doing, Jim?" Flaherty asks, eyeballing the shotgun dubiously.

Roach ignores his friend. "Do you shoot trap?" he asks me.

I shake my head. "I don't hunt."

"These pigeons are clay, not real."

"I don't shoot, period." I'm uncomfortable with this—I don't like guns in general, certainly not on a moving boat.

"I thought everyone native to this area hunted," Roach replies.

"Not my thing."

He shrugs. "You don't mind if we do?"

I do mind, but I'm not going to press it. I don't want to make a big deal of this, it's his boat, I'm his guest, we've been getting along nicely.

"No." I force a smile. "Just point it away from me, okay?"

"Don't worry," he says easily. "We're shooting out into open water. I've been hunting and shooting for decades, I've never hit anyone yet."

That's reassuring; I guess.

"Count me out," Flaherty says.

"Fine, you're counted out," Roach replies. He's pretty curt, considering it's an old friend he's talking to. He's not a man who likes to be disputed, that's obvious.

"Ready, Mr. Roach," Joe says from his position at the back of the boat.

"Good, thank you." He holds the weapon up for my inspection. "You have to admit, it's a beautiful tool."

I look at it—it is a fine-looking piece, if it wasn't a gun I'd want to hold it, feel the smooth wood and metal in my hands.

"It's a Purdey. Custom-made, in England. Finest shotguns in the world. Takes two years to have them make one for you. I had to fly over twice to be custom-fitted."

Flaherty slides over to me. "Have any idea how much that cost?"

"Not a clue. Five grand?" I venture, naming what I think is an extravagant figure.

"Add another zero."

"Fifty thousand dollars. Are you serious?"

He laughs. "Some men overindulge themselves. Have to have the best of everything. Jim's one of them."

Roach loads his shotgun, snaps the barrel shut, sights down the barrel, and calls out to Joe: "Pull!"

Joe springs the trap and the first plate flies up into the sky. Roach tracks it, calmly taking his time, then fires. The target explodes, a puff of dust in the air.

"Nice shot, Mr. R.," the kid says admiringly.

"Thanks." Roach breaks the barrel, ejects the spent shell, reloads. "Pull!"

Another target flies skyward, another shot explodes close to my ear. Another clay plate bites the dust.

I feel I have to say something. "You're a good shot," I tell him.

"It's the weapon, not the shooter. Anyone can look good with this shotgun." As if to prove his point he turns to the kid and says, "Here, Joe. Give it a try."

Joe eagerly takes the gun from him.

"Nice and steady, Joe," Roach counsels.

"I know, I know," Joe says impatiently. "Pull!" he yells.

Roach lets fly the target. The kid swings the gun around and squeezes off a shot, staggering from the slight recoil coupled with the boat's gentle rocking.

There's no explosion.

"Shit," he mutters.

Roach reloads the shotgun. "Lead it like it's a receiver you're throwing to in football," he says patiently. "Then squeeze the trigger, don't pull it. You don't need to put hardly any pressure on it."

"Okay, okay." Joe's embarrassed at having missed. "I know how." He brings the gun to his shoulder, sights down the barrel. "Pull."

Another target flies skyward. Again, an awkward shot, another miss.

"Fuck." Now the kid's really pissed. "Let me try again."

"My mother can shoot better than that. And she's in a nursing home."

We turn. Wallace is standing at the entrance to the cabin, smirking.

"That's uncalled for," Roach admonishes him.

"Sorry," Wallace says. He's still smiling, though. He's a bully, plain and simple. Maybe that's a good qualification for his job, but it makes him a pain in the ass to be around.

Roach nods tightly. "You look better than you did earlier."

"I took that Dramamine you gave me. It helped." He walks toward Joe, holding on to the lines to steady himself. "Let me try one."

The kid looks at Roach.

"Go ahead," Roach challenges Wallace. "Let's see how you do."

"Yeah, hotshot," Joe says, really pissed. "Let's see you do better."

Wallace snatches the shotgun from Joe's grasp. "I'll do better, don't worry."

He breaks the barrel, ejects the spent shell. Roach hands him a fresh one. He loads the weapon, snaps it shut. "Pull!" he growls.

The target arcs skyward. Wallace tracks it patiently, waiting, waiting, then fires off the round. And misses.

Joe snickers. "You call that better?"

"I slipped," Wallace says defensively. "I can shoot up a gnat's ass at a hundred yards."

I don't like the feeling of this—an embarrassed bully with a gun in his hand. "Take it easy," I caution Wallace. "This is a pleasure cruise, not a contest."

"He made it the contest, not me," Wallace answers in a surly tone.

"It's not a contest," Roach says sharply. "Here, give it to me. We're done shooting for today."

"Hey, I'm sorry, okay?" Wallace steps back. He tries a smile on Joe. "No hard feelings, okay?"

"Okay," Joe answers uncomfortably. He's a kid, he doesn't know how to assert himself in this situation.

"It's not okay. Let's put this gear away," Roach says. He signals to Joe to pick up the trap and the remaining targets.

"One more," Wallace demands stubbornly. "I don't want to go out on a miss."

Roach stares at him. I'll bet he's seething inside—he's a man who isn't used to his employees contradicting him. Especially assholes who cross the line.

"Just one," Wallace pushes. "One more won't hurt anything."

Roach breathes strong out his patrician nose. "Okay," he acquiesces. He's not going to make a scene, lower himself to this man's level. "One more. But that's it."

Wallace loads the shotgun, takes a few steps back, steadies himself. He might be feeling better, but I can see that standing firm on a boat, even one that's bobbing slowly in the water, is foreign and uncomfortable to him. It's reckless for anyone to shoot off a boat, but seeing someone who isn't comfortable on the water try it makes me doubly nervous.

"Ready?" Roach stares at Wallace. Joe has stepped back away from the action, toward me.

Wallace nods. "Pull."

Roach springs the trap. The clay target takes flight, curving out over the water in a high, spinning arc. I watch as it reaches the height of its arc and starts to fall. Better pull the trigger soon or you'll lose it, I'm thinking.

It happens so fast there's no time to react. Two waves, one on top of the other, hit the boat, causing us to pitch sideways. Normally, I wouldn't have noticed it, boats are always in movement, but there's a man with a gun in his hand and he isn't comfortable standing on the deck of a moving boat. Wallace is losing his balance, not a lot, but enough to throw him off.

He's not going to shoot, I realize I'm thinking. He can't shoot now. And I'm diving for Joe and we go down in a heap as the shotgun explodes, the trajectory of the shell going directly over our prone bodies.

"Got it!" Wallace crows triumphantly, just as Roach is screaming at him, *"What have you done?"*

Wallace, startled, realizes exactly what he's done. *"Oh, shit!"* he shrieks. "Did anyone . . . ?"

My heart's pounding three hundred beats a minute. Joe's on his hands and knees, shaking uncontrollably. His lunch is all over the deck, all over him. Flaherty kneels down next to him, a supportive hand on the kid's shoulder.

Roach tears the shotgun from the security man's grasp. "You stupid idiot!" he screams at Wallace, who falls to the deck, slipping in a puddle of Joe's puke. "You almost killed them!" He looks at Joe and me. "Are you all right?"

My voice comes out in a hoarse whisper. "I'm okay," I manage to tell him. I'm okay, rather than dead, by a tenth of a second, or less.

"Me, too," Joe says in a gasp. He looks up at me from his hands and knees. "You saved my life." He's about to go into shock. "Jesus, you saved me, my life, you saved . . ." He breaks down crying.

Wallace looks distraught, anguished. "I didn't mean—"

Roach is incensed—I can see the veins pulsing in his neck. "Shut up! Just shut up!" he rages. "Go below and don't come up until we're back at the dock. I'll deal with you when we're ashore."

"Mr. Roach," Wallace grovels, "I'm sorry, I didn't—"

"Now!"

Wallace staggers to his feet. He shuffles belowdecks.

"You saved two lives," Roach says to me, his own voice shaking. He puts a hand on my shoulder. "I'm sorry. Can you forgive me?"

"Sure," I say. My mouth is dry. "Sure." I'm too numb and shook up to say or do anything else.

We engage the engine, and slowly make for home.

Motoring up the small river that bisects our property from Roach's, I look skyward as I see a flurry of birds flying overhead. Roach looks up also.

"Lots of birds around here," he comments. He's trying to make nice toward me; for good reason. "Some pretty exotic types, I'll bet."

"I wouldn't know," I say carefully.

He looks at me, puzzled. "I thought you were an avid bird-watcher."

I'm caught off guard. "What?"

"You're supposed to be an expert on local birding."

"I'm no expert on birds," I protest, not too strenuously, I hope. "I hardly know anything about birds at all. Where did you hear that?" I ask nervously.

"From your mother's friend, Agatha Mortimer. Her daughter told her you're the local expert on birds around here."

I close my eyes and sigh. This is why lying is stupid—you get caught, and wind up looking like an ass. And feeling like one. "I'm . . . not."

Roach looks at me for a moment; then he smiles. "You were blowing her off, weren't you?"

"Excuse me?" I say stiffly. I don't want to have a conversation about my personal life, particularly when it's about an incident in which I behaved badly.

"Come on, Fritz," he says man-to-man. "I've been there, every man has. You needed to extract yourself from a delicate situation, you didn't want to hurt the lady's feelings, so you told her an untruth. You can't have a clinging woman hanging around your neck like an albatross, can you?"

That stings. "Johanna Mortimer's not an albatross," I say in her defense.

"No," he agrees, "she's pretty decent. But you know what I mean."

"Yeah," I say lamely, "I know what you mean."

I look up. The sandhills and Ollie have been luffing in the low thermals. Now they drift down out of sight, heading for home. Roach, his back to them, didn't see them, fortunately. I doubt that he'd know what they were, but I don't want anyone spotting them under any circumstances.

"I can't see you as a bird-watcher," he goes on. "You're too much a man of action to take up an activity that sedentary, aren't you?"

"Yes," I say. "Bird-watching's not for me."

Roach looks up the river. "We're almost home." He sighs. "It's been a long day, hasn't it?"

"Not one I'm going to forget soon," I tell him.

"Nor I."

Joe and I tie up the boat to Roach's dock. The kid's still shaken; he threw up twice more as we crossed the Bay.

Roach turns on Wallace as soon as we're on dry land. "Get off my property," he says tersely. "You're fired. I should never have hired you."

Wallace stares at him, stunned. "It was an accident!" he protests vigorously. "Besides, you're the one who brought the shotgun on the boat."

Roach's face is purple in anger at Wallace's insubordination. "I'm not the one who shot at two people point-blank. And who the hell are you to talk to me in this fashion?" he declares. "You're a hired gun. You work at my pleasure and you leave at my pleasure. Now take off, before I really lose my temper."

Wallace looks at him, starts to say something in return, decides not to. He glances at Joe and me. "It was an accident. I slipped."

Roach puts up a warning hand. "Don't make a bad situation worse. Do us all a favor and leave peacefully. I'm going to forget this happened, and I suggest you do the same."

Wallace stares at him rigidly. Then he turns on his heel,

marches down to the end of the dock, gets into his Toyota 4Runner, and peels out, leaving a cloud of dust.

"I hope you won't hold this against me," Roach says to me as he watches his security chief disappear down the road. He seems to be genuinely shaken up by the near-fatalities. We all are.

"It wasn't your fault," I answer listlessly. I want to get home and have a stiff drink. I'm not going to tell my mother about this part of the day—she's a spry old lady, but I don't know if her heart could take this news.

As Roach talks to Joe about the yacht's maintenance, Flaherty sidles over. He looks at me almost as if he's looking at a ghost; which I nearly was. "Wallace is an oaf, but he was right—Jim was a fool to have brought that shotgun out," he says quietly, so Roach, his friend and host, won't hear him. "Jim's ego can't tolerate criticism of any kind—one of his imperfections. We were lucky you were with us today." He takes my hand in both of his, like a priest with a supplicant. "Very, very lucky."

I can barely move, I'm so limp. I walk down the dock, get in my Jeep, and slowly drive home, where I have two stiff belts of Maker's Mark bourbon before I have the energy to jump in the shower, put on fresh clothes, and head over to my mother's house for dinner.

That was too damn scary. I've never come that close to dying before, and I don't want to again—not for several decades, until I've lived into my ripe old age, like my mother. The only consoling thought I have is that if troubles do come in threes, as I had thought about when I heard Marnie's voice on my phone machine, then this near-death experience was number three. I'm safe—I hope.

It's been a week since the shooting incident on Roach's yacht, more than two since the murder on his airstrip. I've had nightmares about the boat shooting, and I've thought about the murder more than I've wanted to. The two scariest experiences of my life. A few times I've thought about digging into that murder, but then I remember Buster's fierce admonition to keep my dumb-ass amateur nose out of it and I push the thought under the pile, along with the rest of my dirty emotional laundry.

It's early morning. I return from a session of shooting pictures of the birds to find a wild woman sitting on my front porch, on the old metal rocker swing I salvaged from a junkyard. Wild-looking, anyway. Her hair is a thick tangle of coal-black coils that frame a heart-shaped, strawberries-and-cream face. Blossomy tits strain against her *Save the Whales* T-shirt. She's wearing shorts to mid-thigh, her tanned legs are stupendously long, her inseam must be thirty-six inches.

She sits up as I approach from behind the house, where I've tied up my skiff. Her gray Dodge Stratus is parked in the yard next to my Jeep; a rental car, I see the Dollar sticker on the bumper.

This woman is one of the most exotic-looking females I've ever seen in my life. And she's sitting on my front porch. Emerald eyes staring at me like she's a bird of prey and I'm the rabbit she's about to have for breakfast.

Maybe she's a dream. I was drinking last night, and smoked some righteous grass, too; what else is new? I thought I was okay; I've been out hanging with Ollie and the other birds since dawn, now at nine o'clock I'm back, ready to screw around for the rest of the day. Eat a high-cholesterol breakfast, maybe write some in my journal, which I've been keeping haphazardly since I returned home, play with my computer, nothing heavy. My usual routine. But maybe it's all been a hallucination, and I'm dreaming this.

"Are you Fritz?"

I'm not dreaming. "Who're you?"

"I asked first."

"You're sitting on my porch."

"So?"

"So you're on my property, so I want to know who you are."

"This property belongs to Mary Tullis." Pause. "Fritz. You are Fritz?"

"What?" Where is she coming from? How does she know this? Who the hell is this apparition?

"Mary Tullis is your mother. She owns this"—she makes a dismissive hand motion—"dump, right?"

"Don't change the subject, okay? My property, my mother's, it doesn't matter, it's my family's. So tell me again—I missed it the first time—your name is . . . ?"

"Maureen O'Hara." Said with a perfectly straight face.

I've never met this woman and already she's playing head-games with me. "*Maureen O'Hara?* What is this, some kind of joke? Why not Scarlett O'Hara?"

She locks me in place with those eyes. "My mother was a movie fan." Defiantly: "My name is definitely not a joke, although I was teased about it plenty as a kid. Anyway, what kind of name is Fritz, if you want to talk about names? Nobody in the world is called Fritz, except in Germany." She smiles. "Or in the comic books."

"It's a family name," I say stiffly. When I was a kid they used to rag me about my name, too. "Anyway—back to my question. What're you doing here? Who told you you could come here? This is private property."

"Your mother."

"My mother?"

"Your mother said I could come here. She said you'd help me."

The sun's beating down on my head. It must be giving me heatstroke. My mother said I could help her? I know damn well my mother doesn't know this woman from Courtney Love. I walk closer to the house, into the shade. "How do you know my mother?"

"I don't. We talked on the phone. She told me how to get here, that you'd help me."

This is getting more and more convoluted. "How did you get my mother's phone number?"

"From Johanna Mortimer."

Oh, fuck.

"Johanna's a friend of mine, from Boston. She said . . . never mind what she said about you. Do you remember her?"

"Yes, of course." Between this and getting caught in my lie by Roach, I'll remember Johanna Mortimer to my dying day.

"Johanna told me you're an avid bird-watcher." She pauses. "And a very nice man. A helpful man."

"Johanna said that?"

"She did." Then she laughs. "With a straight face, even."

I hate being hoisted on my own petard. I'm feeling tired, suddenly, from what I ingested last night and getting up early. I walk up onto the porch and sit down next to her on the rocker, keeping plenty of distance between us.

"So, Maureen O'Whatever. What are you here for, anyway?"

"I want to look at birds."

I almost choke. "Look at birds?"

"Yes," she says. "That's what I do—look at birds. I'm an ornithologist. I teach ornithology. You know—bird-watching. What you do for a hobby."

Christ Almighty. You tell one little white lie, like throwing one harmless snowball, and look at the avalanche of shit it causes.

She digs into her purse, takes out a card, hands it to me. The card has the Harvard University crest on it. It lists her name, with a Ph.D. behind it, just like me, her address—so and so, Cambridge, a phone number, and her position—associate professor, Department of Biology.

If I didn't have crappy luck I wouldn't have any luck at all. This woman is a Harvard professor in *ornithology!* for crying out loud. A freaking bird-watcher, the one class of subspecies I've been working like crazy to avoid.

If this woman sees my bird, it's all over. Bye-bye Ollie. Bye-bye peace and quiet.

"I'm not a bird-watcher," I tell this creature whose own plumage is itself as extravagant as that of a bird from the Amazon.

She looks at me as if she's misheard me. "I don't understand. Johanna told me you're such an avid birder that you . . . never mind about you and her, that's your business and none of my own. But she did tell me, very clearly, that you are a birder."

I look her straight in the eye, as straight and unwavering as I can look given the shock my system has just suffered.

"I was lying."

She stares at me.

"I'm not a bird-watcher. I'm not a nature lover in general, except to catch a few fish that I eat."

"Then . . ." She still isn't getting it.

"Sometimes things happen fast between people and one of them can't handle the speed," I explain. "So they have to get off the train. Telling her I was a bird-watcher—that's how I got off the train."

She nods slowly. "Now I get it."

"Look," I say, feeling like an ass, "I could've done it differently, I know that. It was late, I had a lot on my mind, I was feeling the pressure of—" Why am I telling this to a complete stranger? Even if she is drop-dead gorgeous and a brain to boot.

She finishes for me. "Entanglement. The possibility."

"Yeah."

She reaches over and takes my hand. It feels like a thousand volts rushing through my body. "You've been hurt not so long ago. You don't want to take the chance of that happening again, not yet anyway."

Who the hell is this woman and how does she come up with this stuff? "I thought you were an ornithologist, not a psychologist," I answer stiffly.

"I've been through that mill pretty recently myself," she says. "I know how it feels. How you can't be honest about anything, even if it's meaningless or unimportant. Or worse, you can't be honest about what is important."

"I guess."

I stand up, move away from her a few feet, so as to not lose my edge. I'm at the best place I can be, given the circumstances. I don't need to reopen freshly healed scars. I need peace, quiet, serenity. No surprises, no rocking the boat.

"Hmm," she says from her throat, pulling her legs up to her chest. "This messes me up but good."

"Sorry about that, but it's not my fault."

She turns, staring at me accusatorily. "But it is your fault. If you hadn't lied to a friend of mine I wouldn't have called your mother and asked if I could come down here and go bird-watching with you. I wouldn't have given up a trip to the Andes. So yes, it is your fault."

"You should've checked up on the situation more. Called me, for openers."

"I did," she says. "You never called back. That's when I called your mother, who couldn't have been more gracious."

Now I remember. There was a message on my machine last week. A woman's voice I didn't know, asking me to call back about bird-watching on the Chesapeake Bay, particularly around here.

I didn't return the call, of course. I erased it from my machine and hoped never to hear that voice again.

Now I have.

"I'm sorry. But I can't help you. Wish I could."

She nods. I can tell she's thinking about what to do. "Well," she says, after some time, "I'll have to do it on my own."

"Do what?" I ask apprehensively.

"Go birding. It would be preferable to go out the first time with someone who's familiar with the area, but I can do without that. I do it all the time, all over the world."

"Go bird-watching? Around here? On this property?"

"Of course. I'm here. I'm not going to waste this trip."

Fuck. This can't be. "You can't do that," I tell her.

She looks up at me; then she stands up. Her eyes are almost level with mine. She might be over six feet tall.

"And why not?"

"Because . . ." Shit, I might as well tell the truth, a partial truth anyway. Lies haven't done me much good. "Because I couldn't handle you being around me. I need solitude now. No people, not in any kind of close contact like what you're talking about."

"Okay, fine," she answers breezily. "I'll go by myself, or with another birder from around here, there's lots of them, this is one of the prime birding areas in the country, the lower Chesapeake Bay." She favors me with another brilliant smile. "I'm not pressuring you, believe me, but you ought to try it, one time. It's really fun. It might help you lighten up . . . Fritz."

"Thanks, but no, not now. Having you on my property,

even if I'm not with you, I can't have that. I'd feel your aura. It would put me off balance."

She stares at me. "Your mother gave me permission," she reminds me.

"I don't care," I answer curtly. "I'll have her unpermission you. I live here. And I don't want you around. Or any other bird-watcher."

Her eyes widen. "You're more fragile than you look," she says bluntly.

That stings, even though I set myself up for it. "I'm fine with the way things are," I tell her. "It's none of your business or anyone else's, including my mother."

She hesitates a moment; then she nods. "I guess if I lost my university position I'd be fragile, too."

I stare at her. What the hell?

"Professors on sabbatical don't screw around taking pictures and drinking beer all day," she says, looking me square in the eye. "They do work elsewhere that's related to their field. You're not at Texas anymore, are you?"

This rips it. "Not that it's any of your business, but no, I've left. My decision," I add hastily. I have to preserve my status, even if it's unwarranted.

"I'm sorry," she says quickly. "I've gone too far."

"No shit."

"I've embarrassed you," she says. "I apologize." She looks around. "I don't want to intrude where I'm not wanted. I know about respecting space, I feel the same way about my own. So . . ." She puts out her hand. "There's other places I can go birding besides your property. Maybe we'll run into each other."

I take her hand. "Maybe we will." And maybe we won't.

She starts toward her car.

"Hey . . ." I call after her.

She turns to me.

"I wish I could help you. But I can't, not now. I hope you understand."

She nods. "Like I said, I've been there myself, not too long ago."

" 'Bye, then."

" 'Bye. And listen—I'm not going to tell anyone about your job situation. In case you're worried."

"I'm not," I tell her. "You can tell anybody whatever you want, I'm not hiding anything from anyone."

She raises an eyebrow, contemplates me for a moment, then leaves.

In less than an hour, the telephone rings.

"Fritz," my mother reprimands me over the line, "how could you be so rude? I didn't raise you to have bad manners, son."

The exotic and pushy Maureen O'Hara hadn't wasted any time. "I wasn't rude, mother."

"You told this sweet young woman to bug off," my mother insists. "That is being rude."

"I never used the words 'bug off.' "

She isn't budging. "It amounts to the same thing, whatever you said."

I get a grip on myself, as she's been admonishing me to do for a year. "I know you have my best interests at heart, mother, as well as those of every single human being in the world. When you die and go to heaven there's going to be a special place for you, right near Mother Teresa."

"Fritz! Stop that foolishness. I am no saint, nor am I close to dying, I hope."

"You're definitely not, mom. Close to dying. But you are a good woman, and God will reward you. And in your infinite compassion, I want you to do one little thing for me, Fritz, your son, the sinner, the prodigal son who did not deserve to eat of the fatted calf."

"Stop this theatrical talk, Fritz," she complains, "you're

giving me a headache. What is wrong with helping this woman? She has a Ph.D., she must be intelligent. And if she's a friend of that lovely Johanna Mortimer's she must be a worthwhile person."

I hold the phone away from my ear for a moment and stare out the window at the water and the bald cypresses that grow in the middle of it, my own private jungle. I can't stand up against these women, not the old ones like my mother, the middle-aged ones like Marnie, or the younger ones, like Johanna Mortimer and now Maureen O'Hara, who's as beautiful as her famous namesake was in her prime.

"Mother, listen to me. Just listen, and don't talk for thirty seconds."

I pause, waiting for her to interrupt in protest. But she doesn't, she's wisely giving me my space. That's the thing about mothers, they know how to handle their children.

"It's not that I don't want to help this woman, or anyone. It's that I want to be left alone. I, me by myself, am all I can handle. Besides, we don't let strangers gallivant around here. You and dad set that policy years ago. I'm merely enforcing it."

There is a moment's silence. Then my mother says, "May I speak now?"

"Sure, mom."

"That is such a crock! You sound like some pathetic little weakling and I know you are not. Taking this woman out on the property for a few days will not harm you in any way, or intrude on our rights of privacy. So knock off the sorry-little-me role you've cast yourself in, and start acting like a man." She pauses. "The man you are."

Does she know which buttons to push, or what? "You're right, mother. I've been feeling sorry for myself lately. But I can't help this woman now. I'm working on a project and I don't want to be distracted."

"You are?" she says suspiciously. "What kind of project could you be working on in the swamp down there?"

"Job research."

I can feel the mood change over the wire. "You're looking for a job?"

"A new semester's starting up soon. I need to see what's out there. I have friends who are checking things out for me as well."

Nothing I just told her is a lie. It's only a lie when you put the sentences together.

"It's about time," she says. "All right, then. I won't impose on your time on this woman's behalf. When she calls back, I'll explain that you're too busy to help her and she'll have to do her bird-watching elsewhere."

That's one load off my mind. "Thanks, mother. I appreciate it."

"Your career comes first," she says stoutly.

"Yes," I agree. "Careers are important." Mine was, when I had one.

"Well," she says, signing off, "come to dinner in a few days and let me know what you've come up with. I'm getting weary of lying about you."

Me, too. "Don't worry, mother," I finesse her, once again. "You won't have to do that much longer."

My sump pump isn't working so I spend most of the afternoon screwing around with it. The work takes longer than it normally would because my unexpected visitor keeps intruding on my thoughts. What the hell was that all about? A stunner who's a Harvard professor, with a movie star's name to boot?

The whole thing, particularly the timing, gives me a queasy feeling. What if I was wrong about the three troubles? Maybe Marnie's out-of-the-blue phone message wasn't one of them? What if this is the third trouble?

I take her card out of my pocket and pick up the phone.

"What city and state, please?"

"Cambridge, Massachusetts."

"What listing?"

"Harvard University. Department of Biology."

"One moment, please." There's a short pause. "Here's your number."

I dial it up. One ring. Two. Three. Four. I'm about to hang up—school's out of session, the offices would be closed.

"Biology Department."

A positive break for a change. "Dr. Maureen O'Hara's office, please."

"I'll connect you through," the receptionist says crisply.

My wait is short. "Hello?" A woman's voice, dry, with a pronounced Boston accent.

"Is this the office of Maureen O'Hara?"

"This is Dr. O'Hara's office," the woman answers stiffly.

"May I speak with Dr. O'Hara?"

"Dr. O'Hara is out of the office," she responds curtly.

"When do you expect her back?"

"When the fall semester starts. Dr. O'Hara is doing fieldwork this summer." A cautious pause, then: "She checks in with me, so if you'd care to leave your name and state your business, I can pass on a message."

"That's okay," I answer, feeling my paranoia level going back down to a manageable level. "It can wait until she's back. Thanks for your time."

I hang up. This isn't my third trouble, after all. That's a relief.

It's coming on cocktail time. I take a shower, put on clean clothes, and drive down the road to Peewee's to get some whiskey and barbeque.

Peewee's Rib Shack, a low-slung cinder block building festooned with neon beer signs, is set back from the road amongst a stand of pines and cypresses. It's popular among the locals for the best-cooked meats in the county, done low and slow over hardwood. It also serves up a fine crab feast, both hard-shell and soft.

Like most Peewees, the proprietor of this joint is a monster of a man: six-eight, four hundred pounds, hands the size of Smithfield hams, a bullet-shaped ebony head bigger than a basketball, shaved bald. He's a genial fellow, but no one messes with him. Peewee is the chef as well as being the owner, and when he isn't cooking he will tend bar, doling out libations in large quantities along with unsolicited advice, much of it scatological and sexual. Peewee's is one of those happy joints where when you ask for a drink, a gin and tonic for instance, it comes in a quart Mason jar filled to the brim, with more gin in the mix than tonic. In the summer the place goes through a half-dozen kegs of beer every day. There is no wine list.

The gravel parking lot is almost full when I drive up. I squeeze my car into an empty space, park, and go inside. The place is jammed up, noisy with talking and laughing and the clanking of knives and forks scraping plates, glasses and mugs banging on the battered wood tables. The dim lighting is filtered through a gray-blue cigarette haze. Heavy rhythm & blues is blasting out of the jukebox: "Little Red Rooster" by Big Mama Thornton, a classic from the 1950s. I work my way through the crowd, saying hello and exchanging handshakes with a few regulars I know, and take the last available seat at the bar, where I order a shot of Crown Royal and a draft Michelob from the bartender, who's new and doesn't know me. She gives me a quick look-over before getting my drinks. I'm one of only a few white people in here (the others are tough-looking white women with equally tough-looking black men).

I take a sip of whiskey and look around. Except for an old, barely working air conditioner and changes in clothing, hairstyles, and such externals, this place doesn't look much different now than it would have thirty-eight years ago, when I was born. It is a black establishment, where black people go and few white people do. In those days it was because if you were black you had to, you had no choice. Now it's because they choose to.

I come here because it's close and I like the food, the overall ambience. Enough customers know me, and have known me since I was young, that my presence doesn't bother anyone.

If I'm going to be drinking, which I am, I need to put some food in my stomach—I haven't eaten since breakfast. I ask the barmaid for a menu, planning to eat at the bar here. As I'm contemplating short ribs versus baby backs, I feel a hand settle on my shoulder.

"Now I know this place has gone to hell," a voice says.

I turn with a smile—I know who the voice belongs to. "Hey, Fred," I say. "You coming or going?"

"I'm in the middle," Fred Baxter tells me. "You by your lonesome?"

"Me, myself, and I."

"You gonna eat, or just drink yourself into the usual stupor?"

I hold up the menu.

"Well, then, come on over and join us."

I grab my drinks and follow him through the room to a small corner table, where another man is seated. The man is about Fred's age, which means he's about my age. Fred introduces me: "Marcus, this here is Fritz Tullis, a friend of mine from around here. We go back a long time. And this ugly sonofabitch," he says to me, giving the man a whack on the shoulder, "is my cousin, Marcus DeWilde. He's in the same business I was in."

Which means he's a cop. Fred was a county deputy sheriff, number three in the chain of command. He quit the department a couple years ago to become a private investigator. He makes more money now, and he's his own boss.

"From Baltimore," Fred adds.

The cop cousin from Baltimore reaches across the table and shakes my hand. "What do you do?" he asks.

"I'm coasting on my laurels at the moment," I reply.

"He's a lazy bum." Fred laughs, clapping a hand on my back. "Seriously, he's a schoolteacher." He winks at me. "Excuse me. A professor. Serious educator here."

"At a college?" DeWilde asks.

I nod.

"Which one?" He's a cop, it's his nature to ask questions.

"Well . . ." This is awkward, which is why I avoid the topic whenever possible. "I was at the University of Texas. I'm on a leave of absence at present."

"Whatcha teach?"

"History."

"I liked history in school. One of my favorite subjects."

"Me, too." I change the subject. "What department are you in?"

He sits up a little straighter. "Homicide. I'm a detective. Lieutenant."

Homicide detectives are the cream of the crop, and lieutenant is a high rank—this man's a serious player.

"Marcus is into some serious shit at present," Fred says, bragging on his cousin.

"Like what?" I ask.

"Later," Fred says. "I don't want to get into that crap on an empty stomach. Depress your appetite."

We get down to the business at hand: eating and drinking, something Fred's good at, my equal or better. His cousin's no slouch in the drinking department, either, I see, as we quickly go through one pitcher of draft beer and get a good start on a second before we order dinner. Bourbon shooters on the side. I'm feeling no pain, and I can see my companions aren't, either.

The food arrives, covering the table with slabs of barbecued meat: baby back ribs, short ribs, brisket. Side dishes of fries, pickled beets and cucumbers, corn on the cob, fresh sliced tomatoes. We tuck our napkins into the tops of our shirts and commence to eating it up, washing the meal down with pitchers of beer.

We feast until there's nothing left on the table, not a crumb. Then we push back, burping and farting, three contented, sated male animals.

The waitress plunks down three mugs of hot coffee. We lace it with brandy, and the cop talk begins. The two cousins immediately engage in a contest to see who can outgross the other, with me as the captive audience. Grisly stuff, the more stomach-turning the better. Not that I object; I like a good war story, I accept mayhem as part of our intrinsic nature. Although having been on the receiving end firsthand had been much harder to deal with than I could have imagined.

"We dredge the body out of the channel," Fred says, alluding to his days as a sheriff, "it's all swollen up, it's been down there a couple weeks, all white and crinkly-like even though it is a black man, like a dead whale or something, and Prescott, my partner? He says, 'Stick a fork in this one, it's done,' and he pulls out his Swiss Army knife and jabs it into this sucker's stomach, which is as big as a twenty-month-pregnant elephant, and the body explodes! All that damned trapped gas. Pieces all over the place. And man, it stunk like you cannot believe. Everybody about threw up on the spot, the stench was so rank. Like you about to go down on some woman and you realize she ain't had a bath in a week, middle of summer? This was worse."

"I don't eat pussy," Marcus says staunchly. "I don't put my mouth on anything I stick my dick in. But here's one. You might've heard about it. Jeffrey Dahmer wannabe?" He looks over at me.

I shake my head.

"Guy gets married, wife disappears. Says she run off on him. Gets a divorce, marries again. Same story. Does it a third time. Then we get this complaint from the trash collectors, they're emptying his trash cans and out falls body parts. Burnt parts, like they were cooked. Coroner determines the man been eating them. Like we were eating these ribs here."

I'm glad I've got a buzz on, otherwise I'd be sick.

"That tops mine," Fred says, admitting defeat. He winks at me, checking out how I'm taking this. "See why I wanted to wait until after we ate?"

"Thanks for sparing me," I answer. "What are you working on now?" I ask Marcus. "That isn't cannibalism."

"He's on a big case now," Fred says. "Could be international."

Marcus picks up his cue. "You follow the news?"

I nod. "Casually."

"You read about the Russian diplomat who was murdered in Baltimore? Some hooker's john might could've done the deed? Or maybe it was a straight-up stickup, or he was buying drugs?"

I perk up. "I saw something on television. You're working on that?"

"I'm running the investigation."

This gets me in the gut a lot more than the war stories they were telling. "Have you arrested anyone?"

He shakes his head. "We've dragged in every hooker, pimp, drug dealer, every lowlife there is around there. None of them knows a damn thing. If they were lying, I'd know it." He pauses and looks around, as if someone might be eavesdropping on us. "I shouldn't be talking about this." He looks at his cousin.

"Fritz is good people," Fred vouches for me. "He knows how to keep secrets to himself."

Marcus grunts. "That man was not murdered where he was found."

So they know. What else do they know? My leg starts doing a St. Vitus' dance under the table; I put my hand on my thigh to steady it.

"I didn't know that," Fred says, surprised.

"Not many do, only me and my team and the assistant DA who's running the case." He stares at us, me especially. "You're not saying shit about what I'm telling you here, right?"

"Not me," I vow. If the three of us weren't half in the bag he wouldn't be telling these important secrets to a stranger, even if the stranger is a friend of his cousin's. I hope he won't be angry at himself and me tomorrow, when the sunup brings a headache and sobriety. An angry cop is a dangerous cop.

"How do you know he wasn't killed where he was found?" Fred asks.

"Condition of the body, other forensic stuff. You know how it works."

Fred nods.

"Why would they do that?" I ask. "Whoever did it. Kill somebody and dump the body somewhere else?"

"So it isn't found where it . . . he . . . was killed," Fred explains. "Clouds the trail to the murderer."

"Partly," Marcus concurs. "But in this case the bigger reason, we think, is about motive. We know this wasn't a hooker thing, or a petty drug buy, or a street robbery. This man had no history of any of those activities, we would've found out by now if he'd had." He pauses. "There's a piece of physical evidence that makes it almost certain it wasn't that kind of killing."

"What's that?" I ask.

"I'm not at liberty to tell," he says. His tone tells me not to push any further.

"What kind of killing was it, then?" I press. "The reason." Stay cool, man, I admonish myself. Don't do or say anything that can get you involved.

"Something more significant is my guess—political, international." He pauses. "I shouldn't be telling you this. Not even you," he says to Fred.

"Blood's thicker than water, cuz."

"Not with all the booze we've been drinking," Marcus replies.

"Come on, man. We're cool. You know that."

Marcus relaxes, pours some more brandy into his coffee. "You get paranoid, you know what I mean?"

"Amen," Fred says.

I know what he means, too. Right now I'm more paranoid about this than either of them, but they don't know that, thankfully.

"So what could the motive be?" I'm pushing, I shouldn't be, but I can't help it. I want to know how close they are to tying it in to where it really happened, which is not far from where we are presently sitting.

Marcus eyeballs the room again: instinctive reaction. "Hell, I've told you too much already, I might as well tell you this, too. We think the counselor was involved in criminal activity, but not some petty shit thing like a dime bag or a blow job. Something big."

"Drugs?" Fred voices the logical suspicion.

"Could be. Or arms on a large scale. Or . . . worse."

I can't hold my tongue. "What could be worse than guns or drugs?"

Marcus turns to me. His dark brown eyes are flat, emotionless. "Secrets. Or—" He shuts up as the waitress approaches.

"How're you boys doing here?" she asks. "You want another taste?"

"Not for me," Marcus tells her. "I've got to be rolling."

"You driving back to Baltimore tonight?" Fred asks his cousin. "That's three hours, man. Why don't you bunk with me?"

"I've got an eight o'clock court date. I'll drive partway and take a motel." Marcus throws some bills down. "That ought to cover me."

"You gonna be all right? Driving?"

"Yeah, I think so."

"Well, be careful you don't get a DUI," Fred laughs. "These cops around here are motherfuckers on drunk driving, especially the county sheriffs."

"They're motherfuckers, period."

We say our good-byes, then it's Fred and me and the brandy makes three. We order fresh coffee and spike it.

"That's heavy," Fred says, alluding to his cousin's disclosure of his investigation of the killing. "We country folk don't get that kind of heavy stuff."

If only you knew, I think.

We drink a while longer, talking about light stuff, sports, music, weather, families, women. Then it's time for me to go. We pay our check and walk outside. It's still hot and humid. I'm immediately sweating through my shirt.

Fred gets into his Ford Crown Victoria and fires it up, the exhaust rumbling low. He takes off, throwing gravel off the back tires. I walk to my own car and sit in it for a moment before turning the ignition over. Listening to Fred's cousin Marcus ruminate on the Russian counselor's murder and his frustration at trying to solve it, along with the bizarre aspects of how and why things might have occurred, has rekindled my apprehension about the killing, and my inquisitiveness about the people, like James Roach, who might be connected to it.

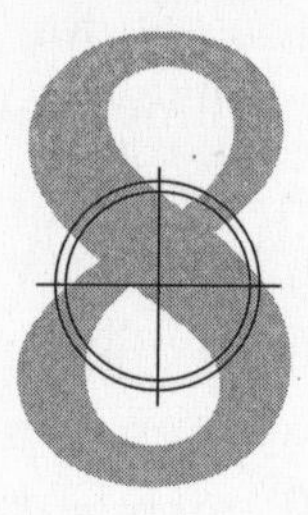

I wake up early, sweating more than usual. Drinking does that; and worry. It's black outside. The moon is down, there's a heavy cloud cover over the stars, not a shimmer or sliver of light penetrates the darkness.

I think about the events of the past month, how I've reacted to them. The conclusion I've drawn, particularly after the disturbing information Fred and Marcus gave me last night, is that despite Buster's insisting that I keep away from this, I can't; pretending nothing happened and that I won't get involved is no longer an option. I'm already involved. The question now is: how am I going to end up in all of it? And how do I protect myself?

I'm not going to be able to fall back asleep. I haul myself out of bed and make a pot of coffee. I'm going to have to face the day sooner or later, I might as well begin the process.

A low fog blankets the water. I don't have much energy for being out here this morning, my presence doesn't affect the birds except that I feed them, and if I don't they can take care of themselves, they don't need me. The need is mine for them, and from the time all this shit's gone down—the murder and the events regarding it that have followed—some of the pure joy of watching this marvel of nature has lost its allure. But sitting around my house with nothing to do but worry isn't good either.

I need to get a life. Exile, either involuntary or self-imposed—mine is both—has its spiritual and emotional growth points, but I'm not Thoreau or Robinson Crusoe. I need to live in the world. I have to get active about resuscitating myself in academia or, failing that, find another line of work.

I tie my boat up, grab my paraphernalia, and wade ashore. Thousands of birds, aware of my presence, flock to the center of the island where I drop loads of feed. I stand back and watch them peck and eat. Ollie and the sandhills have their own area, a marshy spot where the other birds, except for some egrets and other long-legs, don't flock.

The early light, diffused by the fog, is particularly good today for picture taking. There's a quality to it that's almost Impressionistic, reminiscent of Monet's paintings. I focus on a group of birds, featuring Ollie. Today, I decide as I peer through the lens, I'll concentrate on feathers.

"Holy Mother of God." A woman's voice—low, awestruck.

I spin around so hard I almost fall over my own feet. Maureen O'Hara, the Harvard bird-lady, has snuck up on me, catching me unawares. She's frozen in place, staring at Ollie through binoculars, her mouth open in an astounded O.

Her focus shifts to me as she sees me glaring at her. She comes a few steps closer, drawn to Ollie as if to a magnet.

"What are you doing here?" I'm flummoxed by this unexpected and very unwelcome intrusion. I slide my body so that I'm between her and the bird.

She ignores my question. Instead, she inches closer, staring at him intently. "Do you know what that is?" she asks, as much to herself as to me.

"Birds," I snap. My camera hangs from my neck. "How did

you get here?" I bluster. "You were told—*ordered*—not to come on this property." I'm pissed off; also chagrined for having been busted. "Get the fuck out of here. Now!" I point an accusatory finger at her.

She drops her binoculars down. They hang from her neck. "I followed you," she answers my question.

"How?" I maneuver to try to keep my body between her and the cranes. She moves in step with me, keeping them in sight.

"In a canoe," she says matter-of-factly. "Upstream from your place. It's a good thing I was able to keep track of you or I'd have gotten lost, these creeks go off every which way, it's worse than the Minotaur's labyrinth." She smiles at me disingenuously. "You didn't think I was going to take no for an answer, did you?"

"Yes, I did," I say, mustering as much menace in my voice as I can. "You are trespassing, lady. Now haul ass out of here."

She stares at me directly; no smile. "Or what?"

I stare back at her, trying to be intimidating, although she doesn't look like she's easily intimidated. "Or I'll call the sheriff and have you hauled out of here and cited."

She actually laughs, right in my face. "Oh, yeah?"

"Yes."

She takes a cell phone out of her satchel, holds it out to me. "Be my guest." Another smile—this one downright vicious. "And while you're talking to him, make sure you inform him that you're violating the Federal Wildlife Endangered Species Act, so he's prepared to arrest you and throw you in jail."

I play dumb. "What are you talking about?"

She points to Ollie in the center of the flock of sandhills. "Do you know what that bird is?"

I glance back at them. "Sandhill cranes. They're not common around here, but they aren't endangered. I know that much about birds."

"Not them," she says, pointing directly at Ollie. "Him."

I turn and look again. "Oh, you mean the white one," I fake. "The wood stork. Yeah, I know the difference."

"That bird is not a wood stork," she says, her voice laden with disgust.

"Sure it is." I'm tap-dancing around this like I'm Fred Astaire. "I looked it up."

"You didn't look hard enough," she tells me. "Or else you're lying."

The best defense is a good offense. In this case, the only one. "Lying? Who the hell do you think you are?"

"It doesn't matter," she says dismissively. "You're breaking the law." She holds the phone out to me. "Go ahead. Call."

I back away a few steps. "You're the so-called expert. If it isn't a sandhill or a wood stork, what is it?"

"You know full well what it is. If you didn't, you wouldn't have objected so strongly to my coming out here."

I've been nailed, but I still play dumb. Actually, mute. She answers for me, as I knew she would. "That bird is a whooping crane. Wood storks have dark heads and dark underwings. A blind man can tell the difference." She looks at me in disgust. "But you knew that . . . didn't you?"

I hold my hands up in supplication. "Okay. You've got me. Now what?"

"Now . . ." She hesitates.

"Go ahead." I'm finished; maybe it's for the better—the responsibility of being the guardian to an endangered species has been weighing on me. I already have enough problems without carrying that burden, too. "Call whatever agency you have to call. U.S. Fish and Wildlife Service, whoever." I turn my back on her, begin preparing to leave.

"Where are you going?" She seems taken aback at my abrupt capitulation.

"I don't want to be here when they take him away." I pick up my bag. "But I don't ever want to see you on this property again, you hear me? If I'm violating the law, it's out of ignorance. You're doing it deliberately."

I grab the rest of my stuff, start down the footpath toward my boat. "I mean it," I call back over my shoulder. "If I see you anywhere near here again, I'll shoot first and ask questions afterward."

"You'd shoot me?" she asks, truly shocked.

"It's an expression. I don't own a gun. You know what I mean." I start walking away again.

"Hey, wait a minute! Stop!"

Slowly, I turn back to her.

"Listen . . ." She runs toward me. "Can we talk about this for a minute?"

"What's to talk? I only come here for Ollie. Otherwise, I'm not interested."

She smiles. "Ollie? That's what you call it?" She turns and looks at him, feeding in the marshes. "He does kind of look like an Ollie, doesn't he?"

"See you later." I'm done with her. "I mean, I won't see you later. *That* is one thing I am serious about."

"Okay, wait, wait."

"What now?"

She looks back at Ollie again. "Who knows about this bird, besides you?"

"No one."

"You sure?"

"Positive. Otherwise, there'd be a jillion of you out here."

She puts her hand on my arm. Gooseflesh rises, involuntarily. "I'll make you a deal."

"A deal?" I look at her distrustfully. "What kind?"

"I won't bust you. I won't tell anyone." She pauses. "If you let me come with you and observe him for the time I'm here."

"How long is that going to be?"

"Only a few weeks. I have to be back at Harvard right after Labor Day."

"Just you. No one else." I take a step back, stare at her—everyone has their angle, I've figured hers out. "You want some mileage out of this, don't you? The big article in *Scientific American* or *Nature.*"

She nods. "Exclusivity," she admits candidly. "Observing this bird under these unique conditions could be a huge feather in my cap. The world of academia can be pretty cutthroat, you need every advantage you can get."

Her pronouncement brings back a flood of unpleasant memories. "Tell me about it."

"So . . . ?" She stares at me.

"Okay," I say wearily, giving in—what choice do I have? The truth is that I'm not ready, emotionally, to let go of my prize. He's the only thing going in my life that makes me feel special.

"All right," I tell her. "You can come down here with me. But only with me," I state emphatically. "Not by yourself, ever again."

"That's no problem," she agrees promptly. "I'd get lost trying to come here by myself."

"And there's one more condition to this shotgun marriage."

"What's that?" she asks with a trace of a smile.

"No picture taking by you," I tell her firmly. "I'm the only one who shoots film of Ollie."

"Wait a second," she protests, "I can't agree to that. I need—"

I put up my hand: a traffic cop's signal to stop, on a dime. "That's nonnegotiable."

She looks dismayed. "Why can't I take pictures?" she argues. Then she gives me a shrewd look. "You want your own exclusivity, don't you? To be able to use these pictures for your personal gain someday."

I hadn't thought of that angle—I'm naively deficient in the mercenary department. But it's true—photographs of a lost whooping crane in the wild could be a financial windfall for me. And more important, maybe a way back into the teaching world, through a side door.

"You're right," I tell her. "But that's not my main objection to you taking pictures of him. You can study him all you want. You are the expert, after all. But he's my bird. He lives on my land, which makes him mine while he's here. I'm not going to abuse that, or harm him for my selfish desires if I can help it, but that's how it is."

"That is selfish," she says in sharp agreement.

I shrug. "You wanted a deal, here it is. Take it or leave it." I smile at her. "I suspect you're going to take it."

She nods reluctantly. "I don't have a choice, either. Okay—I'll agree to your conditions—although I don't like them," she hastens to add.

"Life's imperfect." I throw her a bone. "I'll let you use some of my pictures, after he's gone."

"Thank you," she says crisply. "That's very generous."

I choose to ignore the sarcasm. We're a team now, teammates have to get along.

We stay until mid-morning. I shoot film, Maureen watches the birds, takes notes. When it's becoming uncomfortably hot, I stow my stuff again.

"Time to go."

She looks up in surprise, caught in the moment. "Can't we—?"

"I'm leaving. You come and go with me. You agreed."

She starts to argue, catches herself. "Okay."

As we start walking down to the water I see, in the distance, a small jet airplane flying low, coming in for a landing. I put a hand on Maureen's arm. "Where did you tie up your canoe?"

"Next to your boat. Why?"

If her canoe is next to my boat, it won't be seen. "I don't want anyone seeing boats from the air. It could lead to—"

She gets it immediately. "Right."

We walk a little farther, until we have a clear line of sight across the water to Roach's property and airstrip. I put my hand on her arm again, hunker down on my heels.

"Crouch down."

"What—"

I pull her down to my level, reach into my bag for my camera, quickly screw the ultralong lens onto the body.

"What is it?" she asks.

"I don't want us to be seen."

She stares across the water through the high reeds. "No one can see us from over there."

"Doesn't hurt to be careful."

"What's with the camera?"

"I want to see what's going on. Just hang tight a minute, this won't take long."

"What . . . ?"

"I'll explain later."

The small jet touches down and taxis along the runway. It's a Lear. Roach's—it has to be.

"What is . . . ?" she starts up again.

I'm trying to focus on the plane as it slows down and stops. Then I have it, sharp and clear.

"Please be quiet," I order her quietly. "I'll explain in a minute."

"Who are they?" She can't stop talking. "What are you looking for?"

I ignore her, zeroing in on the plane.

The door opens, swings down. A figure stands in the doorway, peering out. Sure enough, it's Roach. He walks down the steps. Two more men follow him off the plane. The three talk for a moment. Then Wallace, the security asshole who almost killed me, comes out and jogs down the steps.

"What—?" she begins to whisper yet again.

"Quiet, damn it," I hiss. I'm shaken by this, more by seeing

Wallace than anything else. I force my hands to be steady, so I can shoot pictures without blurring them.

"Do you know them? Is there something wrong?" she asks apprehensively.

"There's nothing wrong," I lie, not wanting her to freak out and do something dangerous like make noise, which will travel over the water in echoing sound ripples and cause them to look over in our direction. I do not want James Roach to discover that I'm here.

I wait to see if anyone else gets out, but no one does. I spy on the four of them through the long lens as they cross the tarmac, get into a Range Rover that's parked at the edge of the field, and drive away.

As I watch them leave I'm wondering: what in hell is Wallace doing here? Roach fired him. I heard him.

We wait, motionless. After I'm sure they're out of sight, I stand up and stretch my cramped muscles. Maureen stands beside me.

"What was that all about?" she asks, her voice vibrating with nervous energy. "Who are those men?"

"One's the owner of the property. The first one off. James Roach. He's a big deal in the government and a friend of the family's. I wanted to make sure it was him and not someone else."

"Like who?"

"Like anyone else. He doesn't like other people using his airstrip. He's had some problems with that." I shouldn't be telling her this, but I have to explain my behavior in a way she'll buy without arousing any suspicion.

"I don't think you should let anyone else in on what we're doing," she advises me sagely.

"So no one will horn in on your discovery?" I ask pointedly, wanting to deflect her interest.

"That's exactly right," she answers unapologetically. "I want to keep it all to myself."

We wait until I'm sure the coast is clear, then we go down to the water's edge, untie our boats, and head up the channel. I keep her in front of me, maintaining a watchful eye on the far shore. But there's no one there to see us.

Back at my house, Maureen maneuvers her canoe to my dock.

"Want to come in for coffee?" I ask. If I'm going to have to accommodate her I might as well be hospitable—within strict boundaries, of course.

She ponders the invitation for a moment before answering, "Yes, thanks."

She follows me inside. The coffee's still hot in the carafe. I hand her a cup.

"Milk's in the fridge."

"Black's fine." She blows on it, sips tentatively. I take out the ingredients for my red one.

"What's that?" she asks.

"Devil's brew. Want to try one?"

She makes a face as she watches me crack a raw egg into the mixture. "No, thanks. That's nasty-looking."

I mix it all up, drink it down in two swallows. It helps; it always does.

"Is this your everyday breakfast?"

"Only when I've been imbibing the night before. So yes, most of the time."

She looks around. "It's quaint, I'll give you that."

"Suits me okay." I don't need this interloper bad-mouthing my house.

"Reminds me of camp," she comments. "I assume you have a good smoke detector," she adds, looking at the wires that run along the walls from my outside solar panels. "You wouldn't want to fall asleep smoking in bed."

"I don't smoke inside and I don't let anyone else, either, so I don't worry about it."

I pour myself a cup of coffee. She follows me out onto the back porch. We sit in the Adirondack chairs. She unlaces her expensive-looking boots and pulls them off, dropping them onto the wooden floor. Then she takes a notebook from her pack, starts scribbling in it.

"What're you writing?" I ask with curiosity.

She looks up. "Notes from this morning. Technical stuff. Nothing you'd be interested in."

"Where are you staying?" I continue, making idle conversation.

She closes her book, puts it back in her pack, blows on her coffee to cool it so it won't scald her lips. "Lighthouse Motel, in Jamestown."

"That's thirty miles away. You're going to come out here at six every morning? You'll have to get up damn early, 'cause you can't go to watch the birds without me. If I've already left, you're out of luck."

"I can manage it." She stretches her legs out like a cat, then crosses one over the other. "I'm not staying here with you, if that's what you're insinuating."

"What're you talking about?"

"Johanna told me about your evening together." She runs a finger along the rim of her cup. "Everything about that night."

My face is hot. How mortifying. "So?"

"So she likes you. You hurt her feelings, but she likes you anyway. She said you're going through a rough patch and have to be forgiven for acting boorishly."

"I didn't mean to," I say sheepishly.

"I'm sure you didn't," she replies charitably. "My point is, Fritz, she's my friend. I'm not going to have sex with a man my friend's slept with and wants to see again. I wouldn't sleep with you anyway, I'm too discriminating. Besides, you're not my type, but even if you were, I wouldn't. It would mess up our working relationship."

"I see."

"I wanted to make sure we understand each other."

I don't like playing games like this, particularly when I'm losing them. "I don't have eyes for sleeping with you, Maureen. Don't worry about that."

"I'm not your type, either?"

She's fucking with my head, which normally I could handle, except I'm scared now, having seen Roach and Wallace together. "I'm on the shelf," I add defensively.

She starts to reply, but manages to hold her tongue.

"You're taking a huge risk, going out there with me and keeping your mouth shut about it," I say, changing the subject to one less personal.

"How so?" she asks, blowing on her coffee again.

"I've done some studying up. Whooping cranes are the most endangered birds in this hemisphere, outside of California condors. Every one of them is vital—I'm amazed this one wasn't reported missing."

"So am I," she agrees. "They must have missed him in the count they do every year."

"The point I'm making is, if you're caught it could be the end of your career. Harboring a whooping crane, as you forcefully pointed out to me, is illegal. I'm an amateur, I can plead ignorance. But you can't."

She nods gravely. "I know. I've been thinking about that all morning." She stares into her cup.

"Ambition supersedes ethics?"

She gives me a baleful look. "I'm not perfect. Yes," she admits, "I want this, and I'm willing to take the chance I won't get caught, or he won't get hurt." She pauses. "I hope our situation—our arrangement—doesn't blow up in my face. It's a chance I'm willing to take."

On that note, we finish our coffee. I walk her to her rented canoe. She'll be on my doorstep at the stroke of six tomorrow morning. Driving her rental car from now on.

"We have a secret," I remind her.

"I'm good at keeping secrets."

I push her off from my dock, watching her paddle away. She does it well—she's much at home in this world.

Back inside my shack, I flop down at my kitchen table. My uncomplicated, semimonastic life has gotten complicated all of a sudden. Way too complicated. The murder, the near-fatal shooting on Roach's yacht, now this woman. I've got to simplify, but I don't know how.

Roach has become a specter hovering over me. The six degrees of separation between him and the other elements in this drama are too coincidental to be ignored: the murder took place on his property, he's with the State Department, so most likely would have known the slain counselor, plus the weirdness regarding Wallace, who is a stick of dynamite ready to go off—not the kind of security chief a man in Roach's position should have.

I have to check up on Roach. Passive research, nothing that will put me at risk. It won't be hard to find information about him, he's been a public figure for decades. I'll try to find out what I can about Wallace, too.

I don't know where this snooping around will lead; but too many coincidences are piling up for me to ignore this and hope it will all blow away in the first strong wind. After that conversation I had with Fred and Marcus, I know that's not going to happen. And if the shit does hit the fan, I don't want it splattering me. For my peace of mind, as well as my own protection, I have to know more about what's going on.

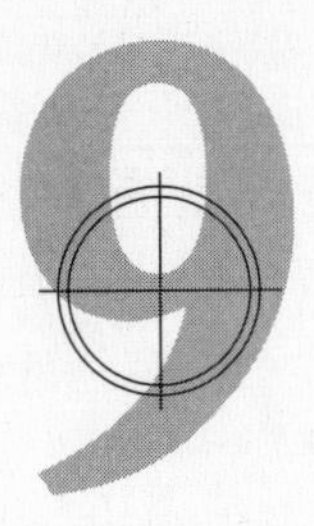

My alarm wakes me, which is unusual. I'm almost always awake before it goes off. Anxiety—not wanting to face the day. Unfortunately, it arrives despite my perturbations regarding it.

I was dreaming. It's vague now, bits and pieces of airplanes, dark corridors, women's body parts, frightening rather than sexy or romantic, the devouring cunt, the turning of the lips away from the kiss, a cold, almost frozen breast. And guns being fired, cars driving away, being left behind, alone, cut off from all hope. An abandonment dream at its most basic.

It's still dark out—I had mistakenly set the alarm for five instead of six. I'm thankful for the jolt into reality, though, I wasn't enjoying that dream.

Okay, I'm up, so I might as well get up. Wash my face, balls, pits. My body feels fuzzy, like I slept in a bed infested with caterpillars. When I come back after my early morning bird-run I'll have a proper shower and a good scrubbing with a loofah.

I step out onto the back porch and send a leisurely stream over the railing into the murky water below. The first piss of the day always feels good. Out with the old to make room for the new. Idly, I stroke my member as I release my fluid. It doesn't respond—it knows this is merely pissing, not a precursor of sex. It's been a while since the little guy got to stand up and salute; my night with Johanna was the last time.

I feel them. Eyes. Something is watching me.

I shake off the last drops and take a furtive look around. This area is teeming with nocturnal wildlife: raccoon, possum, muskrat, bobcat. Creatures that have more claim to this territory than I do, they've been here a lot longer.

I don't see any shining eyes. Back inside, I paw through my clean-clothes pile for a pair of shorts and T-shirt that aren't too wrinkled. Then I hear a noise and know I am being watched, for real.

Still naked, selected shorts in hand, I peer out the front window. There, perched on the old porch swing, is Maureen O'Hara, staring at me. The moon, almost full, is still up, radiating enough light for me to see her. She, of course, sees me plainly, I've already turned on the inside lights. She's reclining on the sagging swing, her feet propped up on the bench, her back against one side, a leisurely pose, as if she owns the place. She's wearing beach flops, rather than the boots she had on yesterday. She sees me staring back, and smiles.

I drop the shorts to below my waist, a protective fig leaf. Smiling more broadly, she cocks her head as if to say, "I've seen everything already, what's the point in hiding it?"

Turning my back on her—I've never been particularly modest, but this is too much—I shimmy into my shorts. Then I cross the room and fling open the front door.

"What the hell're you doing here?"

"You invited me," she answers sweetly and logically.

"Our appointment was for six o'clock. It's barely past five."

"I didn't want to be late. I was afraid you'd take off without me."

"Six means six, not five," I say brusquely.

My attempt at anger doesn't faze her. "I'll remember that in the future." She stands up, reaches down, retrieves a couple of paper sacks, holds them aloft. "I come in peace."

"What have you got in there?" I inquire suspiciously.

"Coffee. And Amish strudel."

The Amish are a strong presence in St. Mary's County to the north of us. There are a few small pockets down here as well. They make great pastry. I can smell it through the bag. The coffee, too. Far superior to the supermarket brand I'm used to.

"May I come in?"

I nod—the damage has already been done. Holding the door open, I stand aside as she enters and plops her goodies on the kitchen table.

"Do you have cups and plates?"

I point to the cupboard above the sink. She takes two cups and a plate down, sets them on the table, dives into the refrigerator for the milk.

"You're not going to have one of those weird drinks, are you?"

"No. I didn't drink enough last night to need one."

"Good." She opens the large cardboard container of coffee and pours into the cups. It smells great, what coffee should smell like. "I couldn't stomach that this morning. Milk?"

I nod dully. She's revving at the red line, while my engine's barely started.

I sit across from her. She takes the pastries out of the other bag and arranges them on the plate.

"I hope you like my selection."

"It's fine." I reach for an apple strudel, bite into it. Like honey straight from the comb. Too decadent for this early in the morning, but what the hell, I'm not on a schedule.

"Thank you," I mutter through a mouthful of pastry.

"The least I can do. For imposing on your privacy."

"Let's not get into that," I caution her.

"Sorry."

We munch and drink in silence for a few moments. Then I

get up, pull on my T-shirt and running shoes. “Excuse me a minute.”

“Sure.”

I open the door to my cabinet, shielding her from the combination with my body. I grab the equipment I’ll need for our morning sojourn, lock the door.

“Ready to go?” I glance at her feet. “You’re not wearing those, are you?” I ask, alluding to the flops. “It’s thorny out where we’re going.”

“I left my boots in the car. It’ll take a second.” She sips her coffee, lifts a foot for me to observe. “Do you like the polish? It’s a new shade for me, I put it on last night.”

“It’s bright,” I say. Fire engine red.

She wiggles her toes. “Sometimes I’m embarrassed by my feet.”

“Why?”

“They’re humongous. Like a man’s.”

“You’re a tall woman. You’d look silly with small feet. Out of proportion.”

She straightens one leg out, appraising her foot. “I’ll bet they’re almost as big as yours.”

“What size are they?” This is a silly conversation.

She almost blushes. “Twelve.”

“That is pretty big. One might even say humongous,” I say with a straight face.

She laughs. “Touché. In men’s it would be eleven,” she informs me.

“I’m thirteen. So you’ve got a ways to go to match me.”

She shakes her head. “I’m not growing anymore. I hope.”

We finish the coffee and strudel. She goes out to her car, comes back in, boots in hand.

“Nice boots,” I comment. They have a logo on the side I’ve never seen before. “Where’d you get ’em?”

“Switzerland. I led an Audubon Society tour across the Alps last summer.” She laughs. “We went native. Lederhosen, the whole schmear. I looked like a refugee from *The Sound of Music,* but everyone else did, too, so it didn't matter." She puts on socks, pulls a boot on. "They are great boots, very well constructed. Custom-made, it's hard to find made-to-order in my size. I'll keep them forever."

She laces her boots tight and ties them. Then we go outside, load up my skiff, and take off for the birds.

You shouldn't feed them."

I'm doling out grain from my sack. "I know, but I do."

"They'll become dependent on you."

"They do fine on their own the days I don't come."

"It's not good," she persists. "If they become too friendly with people they'll lose their natural instincts to stay clear of us. That's a sure recipe for trouble. Some of us carry guns."

I toss the last handful of grain. "It's not for much longer." I stand back, watching the birds swoop down to the food, feeling her watching me watching them. Ollie stands out, royalty among commoners.

"He's become a pet to you," she observes. "But he's a wild creature, he doesn't belong to you," she says gently. "He belongs to his own."

I have no rebuttal to that.

"But he's fine here for a while longer," she says, trying to cushion my disappointment.

"What'll you do when the time comes?" I ask her. I'm assuming she'll want to take charge of him when he has to be taken away.

"There are different possibilities," she says. I'm sure she's been thinking about this from the first time she spotted him—it's her job. "One option would be to take him up to the Patuxent Reserve in Prince Georges County, where they're raising cranes. Another possibility is that he could be taken to Florida, where there's a permanent colony of nonmigrating whooping cranes. The best thing for him, and the species, would be if he could be united with an existing migratory flock, perhaps one of the new ones from Operation Migration. They're doing great work with young cranes."

"Can that be done, given how he's been living?" I'm skeptical about that—I've read enough about the migratory pattern of whooping cranes to know that integrating a new one into an existing flock is almost unknown in nature.

"It'll be difficult enough separating him from these others. But maybe it can be done. I'll have to bone up on the subject, whooping cranes aren't my field of expertise. The sandhills will definitely have to be taught how to migrate. But don't worry," she goes on, reading my thoughts. "Whatever happens to your crane, it'll turn out all right."

"If you say so. You're the expert."

"Trust me. It will."

I don't tell her I don't trust her yet, but I'm going to try. Because I have to.

We spend a few hours in the marsh. I take some pictures, rote behavior. My head isn't in it this morning. I watch Maureen as much as I watch the birds. She has a battered *Petersons Field Guide* in her pocket, which she takes out a couple of times to reference some of the hundreds of varieties of birds that have made this area their home.

I can't not be attracted to her—I'm a man who likes women, it's part of my essential nature. I know she's off-limits, most notably because of her friendship with Johanna, but libido disagrees.

How I feel, however, doesn't matter. She's in the driver's seat and she's made it clear there's going to be no romance between us. Which is good for me, her resolve removes temptation and the likelihood of my doing something stupid; but still, I can't help but feel pangs of arousal. To paraphrase Woody Allen, the cock knows what it knows.

I take some more pictures of the birds. While Maureen is preoccupied with studying them I shoot off a couple of her, too. She'd be a great subject for a photo session, with these exotic birds in the background.

When I feel the heat rising on my face and neck I look up at the sky. The sun has climbed to the nine o'clock position. "Let's call it a morning."

I gather up my gear. She follows me down to the boat. "Do you ever come out in the evening, after dark?"

"Not often. Can't shoot without light. Birds roost once it gets dark," I add. She's the expert, she knows that better than I do.

"I meant in the hour before sundown. It must be beautiful light for pictures then," she says, hitting me on my soft spot.

What the hell—I've got nothing else to do. A few more hours in her company won't be painful. "Okay. Come by around seven. Bring insect repellent," I caution her. "The mosquitoes can be a bitch."

She beams. "That'll be great. Thanks."

We push off and head upriver toward my place. I glance over in the direction of Roach's farm. Nothing's shaking.

Maureen follows my look. "I have a feeling you aren't telling me about things that are going on over there."

"Like what?"

"How should I know? You seem preoccupied with it."

"It's a throwback instinct. That property used to be part of our holdings. I still feel proprietary toward it."

"Like Rosebud," she says understandingly.

"Sort of. Although Rosebud was destroyed in a fire, as I recall from the movie. Vanished, up in smoke."

"I meant emotionally."

"I know. Anyway, that's the past. I can't go there anymore." Although that's precisely what I've been doing.

"None of us should. Until we get old and that's all we have."

She turns her back on me and stares straight ahead as I

guide us back to my place through the maze of low-hanging cypress trees.

Mid-afternoon, I throw out a line and pull in some rockfish. My crab traps yield four nice-sized hard-shells, enough for a couple of dinners. I gut and clean the fish and stow them in the refrigerator.

On the stroke of seven Maureen's rental Dodge pulls up next to my dusty Jeep and she jumps out, raring to go. We get into my boat and head down-channel.

The late afternoon light is marvelous today. The sun is already beginning to bathe the horizon, particularly where the sky meets the water, in a golden glow that's spackled with tendrils of orange, pink, vermilion, purple. The birds, thousands of them, are packed into this small space, all vying for position. Maureen is giddy with delight, jumping around to get a look at one group, then another.

Her focus, of course, is on the cranes, Ollie preeminent. He stands head and shoulders apart from the throng, looking at the world through his yellow, unblinking eye. He knows he's special. It radiates from him. He is a regal being, a lost king in a foreign kingdom.

Maureen watches the birds. Her pleasure in them is almost childlike, rather than professional. I remember feeling that way in my classrooms when a spark caught with the students and we were all on one adventure together, discovering new truths in old passages.

Time slips by. Before we know it, darkness is almost upon us.

"Time to go." I point to the sky, where the sun filtering through the trees is no more than a sliver now on the horizon. "We're out of light." I look to the birds, who are settling in for the night. "They're done for today," I point out, "and so are we."

"Ten more minutes," she begs.

"Okay. But don't say I didn't warn you." I sit down on a grassy knoll, employing my bag for a backstop. The mosquitoes and other insects are out in force now; I spray insect repellent in the air, on my damp T-shirt. It won't help much—we'll be eaten alive if we don't skedaddle pronto.

She starts slapping at her arms, forehead. "Ouch!" More slaps. "Okay," she yells at the unseen provocateurs. "I get the message. Let's get out of here before they eat us up alive."

I resist saying "I told you so," since I just did. Gallantly, I grab her gear and we walk down to my boat.

Across the water, lights come on. Two long lines—Roach's runway. From a near distance, I hear the sound of an airplane approaching.

"Company," I tell her, immediately stopping. "And we're not invited. Stay still until they land."

She stands next to me as Roach's Lear comes in, lands, taxis to a stop.

"This feels creepy," she says. I can hear the apprehension in her voice. She slaps at an unseen tormentor.

"Not a problem," I assure her. "We're not trespassing." I've got to stay calm; if I show panic I'll freak her out. "No one knows we're here."

But I'm apprehensive, too. Roach had told me he only came here on the weekends. What's he doing here in the middle of the week? I wonder. This is the second time this has happened. Something's going on, and it isn't an ordinary visit—I feel that in my gut. Instinctively, I reach into my bag and take out a camera, the one with the long lens, and load a cassette of 800 ASA black and white film. You can shoot in near pitch-blackness with this film and still get an image. And I can process it in my darkroom.

Roach emerges from his plane, followed by Wallace. No one else follows.

"Why—?"

I put up a hand to silence her.

"Be quiet." No time for politeness. "Don't move."

She stands stone-still next to me. I can smell the sweat on her. Not all of it is from the heat and humidity. Then I hear the sound of another plane, approaching on a different flight pattern.

"More company," I observe in a whisper. "It's a regular hoe-down over there."

We watch as the second plane lands, taxis near Roach's. This, too, is a corporate jet. Not a Lear like Roach's, but about the same size. It looks smaller than the airplane the counselor and his killer came in on, but in the diminishing light I can't be sure.

The door swings open. Men start coming out. Three are dressed in dark suits. A fourth man hustles out after them. A machine gun is slung over his shoulder, a serious piece of business.

"What in the—"

I put a hand over her mouth, to silence her. "They're not looking for us," I say. "But they wouldn't like it if they found out we were looking at them. Just chill." I wait a moment until I know she's going to be quiet, then I move my hand from her mouth. There's a trace of lipstick on my palm. I wipe it on my shorts.

A fifth man emerges from the airplane. He's dressed pilot-fashion, similar to the pilot who flew the plane that had transported the slain counselor. He buttons his craft up and joins the others.

Roach greets the other newcomers, then turns his attention to one in particular. The two talk for a moment. The conversation seems easy, but animated. I take pictures of them. Maybe I'll get an exposure, maybe not. It's worth the try.

After a few moments, Roach points toward a couple of Range Rovers that are parked off the runway. They all walk toward them, get in, and drive off—toward Roach's house, I assume.

Maureen and I watch until the lights of their vehicles can

no longer be seen. A moment later the runway lights also go out and we're standing in darkness, but for the moonlight overhead.

"This is weird," she says, once she's sure they're gone. "What's happening that you aren't telling me?"

"I don't know," I tell her honestly. It's nice not to have to lie for a change.

"Why are you taking pictures of them?"

"In case."

"In case what?"

"In case I don't know why. Can't hurt, can it?"

"I'll bet if they knew you were taking pictures of them it could," she says.

"Let's not tell them then."

I dump our bags in the boat, help her climb aboard, follow her in. Pushing off, I start rowing into the channel. I won't start the engine until we're well out of range, both visual and auditory.

"Were we in danger?" she asks. She's scared, she can't hide it.

"I don't think so. Although we were spying on a high government official. I don't know who those men with him are, but they don't want to be seen, that's for sure."

"So we were."

"No, because they didn't know we were there. If Roach doesn't want people spying on him, he knows how to avoid it, I'm sure."

"But he doesn't know," she persists. "He must think he's safe, doing that."

"Well, I'm sure we're the only ones who know. And we're not talking, so it's all right."

I don't believe that, and I don't think she believes that, but she doesn't argue the point further.

After I'm sure we're deep enough up-channel that we won't be heard, I start the little engine. In the moonlight I can see her smiling at me. "It's kind of exciting," she says. "Like being in a James Bond movie."

"I don't want to be James Bond," I tell her. "Too many people get killed in his movies."

She puts a hand on my knee. "You're fine as you are." Her hand is warm. I look down at it. She catches herself, removes it. But she doesn't stop smiling.

Care for a drink?"

"I could use one, thanks."

"Anything special?"

"Whatever you're having."

We're back in my house. Maureen excuses herself to wash off the insect repellent. She emerges from the bathroom a few minutes later, having wet down her hair and combed it back in a twist. Her face is scrubbed clean of makeup; she looks like a schoolgirl, not a professor—the prettiest coed on campus.

I assemble my mai tai fixings and make us a couple of stiff ones. We click glasses. "Skoal," I toast.

"And to you." She knocks down a hearty swallow. "Whoa!" She wipes foam off her lips with the back of her hand. "Strong."

"I'll back off the next one."

"I'll drink to that. Although I can't handle another one of these. I've got a thirty-mile drive to look forward to."

"Your choice. Although it's no fun if you stop after one."

"Says you." She takes a more temperate sip. "I can't drink at your level, Fritz. A man who drinks beer mixed with raw eggs for breakfast is out of my league."

Funny, I'm thinking, I feel exactly the opposite about who's out of whose league. "I could fix you something to eat, to absorb it."

She considers that. "If it isn't any trouble . . ."

"I haven't had dinner, and cooking for two's the same difference as one."

"Thanks. I'm ravenous, actually."

Putting the hard stuff aside, I open a bottle of white wine. Maureen watches while I dice potatoes and onions and stir-fry them in my wok with a slice of chopped-up bacon for flavor, then pan-fry my catch of the day. The crabs and rockfish steam in a couple of minutes. Some lettuce from my little garden for a salad, and we're set. We take our plates and glasses out to the screened-in back porch, eat off the battered telephone line spool I use as an outdoor table. All the elements are in place for a late candlelight romantic dinner, except there's no romance, and lighting candles would be pushing it.

"Hey, this is pretty damn good," Maureen praises me as she tastes a bite of fish. "Why didn't you tell me you could cook?"

"You didn't ask." I'm pleased I've done something that impresses her. Sometimes a vicarious experience is enough, if that's all that's available. "Most of the great chefs are men. Not that I'm in any category like that," I add modestly.

"I've never known any of them. Not up close and personal. You're plenty good enough for me tonight." She whams a hammer down on a crab shell, splitting it apart, picks pieces of crabmeat out with her fingers and devours it. "You're uncomfortable taking compliments, aren't you?"

"I'm okay with them," I say a bit stiffly. I need to be careful that I don't cross the line with her and make a fool of myself. It would be easy to do.

"Well, you're a good cook and a nice guy. Nicer than I was expecting."

I don't reply to that—I know when to quit while I'm ahead.

One bottle of wine doesn't last long in the evening heat and humidity. "Another?" I toss the empty into the oil drum which serves as my trash barrel.

She doesn't flinch. "Why not?"

I carry the dirty dishes into the kitchen and dump them in the sink, crack open a decent zinfandel. We sit on the porch, feet propped up on the railing. I'm barefoot, she's kicked her fancy boots off. It's all very comfortable and easy. I'm waiting for the other shoe to drop; after a long silence, it does.

"Aren't you the least bit curious about what's going on with your neighbor?"

She's trying to sound like it's a casual thought that just popped into her head, but I know that isn't the case. I'd be curious, too, if I were her and didn't know the full story. She's already seen more than she should.

"Sure, but it's none of my business. I learned a long time ago to mind my own business." I wish.

"Isn't he like a secretary of state or something?"

"Not like, is. Assistant. What I think is going on," I tell her, spitballing a story, "is he has meetings with people who don't want to be seen in an official capacity in Washington. He's got the perfect location—close, but out of the way."

"I don't know," she says dubiously. "It feels awfully hush-hush."

"Meetings like that would be."

She thinks about that. "Why were you taking pictures of them?"

"Force of habit. I see it, I shoot it."

"But couldn't it get you into trouble, if the wrong people found out?"

"It's a free country. Anyway, who's going to tell on me? You? No one else knows except you."

"Why would I do that? I wouldn't be able to observe the birds anymore," she counters logically.

"Then there's no problem, is there? And why do you care what I do? You're getting what you want."

"I'm curious, that's all."

"What Mr. Roach does is his business and not mine, and it's going to stay that way."

She backs off. "Okay. Listen, I'm here for the birds. Whatever else you do isn't any of my affair." She smiles, touches my arm with her hand. "You're not going to hog that wine, are you?"

I refill her glass. "You going to be all right, driving back to your motel?"

"You know the saying about how do you hold your liquor?" She laughs, a hiccupy kind of laugh. She's getting high, which amuses me. If the circumstances were different . . .

"Yes, I've heard that saying."

She laughs again. We're on the same loopy wavelength. "I shouldn't jabber like this," she says. "You'll get the wrong impression." She's definitely high, and enjoying it.

"What impression should I get?" I shouldn't be pushing this, but I can't help it. She's too damned sexy for me not to. She'll stop me when she wants—she's feeling frisky, but she's still in control.

"The right one."

"I think I've got that."

She looks up at me. Is there genuine feeling there, or am I kidding myself?

"I hope you do."

All too soon, our evening comes to an end. I don't know where to go from here, we don't have much to talk about, we don't know each other beyond the superficial details. I'm about to say "I guess you'd better be hitting the road" when she preempts me.

"Can I sleep here tonight?" She stretches luxuriously, a big cat after a satisfying meal.

"I don't . . ."

"On your couch. It looks comfy."

It is—I've fallen asleep on it countless times. "I don't think that's a good idea."

She gives me a peculiar look. "Why not?"

"Because you're sexy as hell and I've had too much to drink. We both have. I might do something stupid, like hit on you in the middle of the night, which would fuck things up."

I look at her, for her reaction. She's still staring at me, but there's no clue.

"And I don't want that. I mean, I do, you're a beautiful woman, desirable as hell. But I can't get involved with anyone now, and I wouldn't want to have casual sex with you." I'm getting nervous, just thinking about the possibilities. "We're going to be together almost every day for the next few weeks. It wouldn't work. Even if you wanted to. Which you don't."

"Yeah." She pulls herself together. "We don't want to put ourselves in the path of temptation." She gives me a sisterly peck on the cheek. "You're a nice guy. I've already said that, haven't I?"

I don't say "nice guys finish last," but I feel it. "Yes," I say instead. "I'm a nice guy."

I drive her to her motel—she doesn't know the roads that well, and she's jagged around the edges. Parking in front of her unit, I walk her to her door.

"I'll pick you up tomorrow. Not too early. We both can use a good night's sleep."

She leans over and gives me a kiss. A mere brush of the lips, but it's a real kiss. "Thanks for everything." She goes inside, closing the door behind her.

I drift back to my car and take my time driving home. Her taste lingers on my mouth, but not as long as I want it to.

I fetch Maureen the following morning and take her to Maizie's Lunchroom (formerly the Tobacco Broker's Bar & Grill) for an old-fashioned country breakfast. A local landmark, built at the turn of the century, it features dark wood walls, beat-up leather banquettes, a pressed-tin ceiling. Faded prints of Scottish country scenes adorn the walls. The restaurant's popularity peaked in the heyday of King Tobacco, when the high rollers—the growers and auctioneers and out-of-town buyers for the tobacco companies—bellied up three-deep to the bar at the end of the day, abused their livers with Old Grandad and Jim Beam, and gorged themselves on two-pound porterhouses. Tobacco's not as much of a cash crop in this country anymore, but the restaurant keeps chugging along. Maizie, whose real name is Frank Wheatley, a teetotaling retired fireman, bought it twenty years ago and turned it into a luncheonette. The place quit serving liquor soon after, and now closes at two, after lunch.

By mutual consent we're not going to do our usual birdwatching today. We both feel the need to steer clear of Roach's property for a few days, let our emotions settle down.

After a leisurely, gut-stretching chowdown—eggs fried in

butter, spicy sausage, grits, biscuits with homemade jelly, strong chicory-flavored coffee—I give her the deluxe tour of the area, such as it is. There are a few pre–Revolutionary War homes in Jamestown that are open to the public, but nothing much else of historic interest. Still, this is an engaging region, if you appreciate the throwback life, because it is rural and slow. There are two car dealerships, a Ford and a GM, a John Deere store, various small shops that sell items you can find anywhere. Mostly it's a farming community, lots of dairy cattle, chickens, hogs, vegetables. Except for the basic life-style improvements—electricity, indoor plumbing, cars, TVs, etc.—much of it is still as it was a hundred, two hundred years ago. Certainly in attitude. Hardly anyone lives here who isn't from here—there's nothing for an outsider to do, except buy a local business; and since it's insular, it can be boring and closed off to a newcomer.

After that we jump into my car and tour the countryside. I point out some of the Amish farms and we stop at one to examine their crafts, in this case wooden cabinets, beautifully made in the old-fashioned way, without nails. Maureen thinks about buying one for her place back in Boston, but it won't fit into my Jeep.

It feels domestic, cruising around with her, looking at this stuff. A good feeling, comfortable. It reminds me of similar forays I made with Marnie, out in the Texas countryside.

By early afternoon we call it a day for sightseeing and head on down the road toward my place. It takes the better part of an hour on the narrow back roads. I put an old Grateful Dead CD on and we groove with it as we cruise along. The first time I laid eyes on her I thought she could be a Deadhead, or at least a connoisseur.

I wasn't wrong. She even knows the lyrics.

"Want a cold beer?" I ask as we park and get out of my car. Her rental Dodge is where she left it, in front of my house.

"Sure," she answers willingly. "Only one, though, Fritz. I can't be having you driving sixty miles round-trip again."

I pop a couple of cold ones and we sit around the kitchen table, drinking our brews from the bottle. "I'm going to be gone for a couple of days. Shit to take care of in Washington," I tell her. "So we're on hiatus until the day after the day after tomorrow."

"That's fine," she replies cheerfully enough. "I've been wanting to hook up with some local Audubon Society members, check out other sites. Don't worry." She smiles as I look at her anxiously. "Ollie is our secret, no one else's."

"I wasn't worried," I fib. A fib is a small, acceptable lie.

"I want you to know you can trust me."

"I trust you okay. I don't trust myself all the time."

I walk her outside to her car.

"Have fun in the big city. Stay out of trouble," she says in a teasing tone of voice. Then she leans forward and gives me a light kiss on the lips, like the one from last night.

I could get used to those kisses.

I ride the elevator up to Buster's floor and present myself to the receptionist, who's trying to handle five phone lines simultaneously. Barely glancing at me, she informs me that Buster's in conference with a client and is running about twenty minutes behind schedule. She'd get me something to drink, but there's no one to relieve her. She goes back to her phone juggling.

There's a magazine rack on the wall behind her station, near the hallway that leads to the inner sanctum where Buster and the other stars have their offices. I walk over and peruse the selection. Heavy on the financials and techs. I find a copy of *The New Yorker* I haven't seen and start leafing through, checking out the cartoons. As I'm about to sit down and amuse myself, I hear a familiar voice. I look up, my face obscured by the Art Spiegelman cover.

James Roach has come out of a conference room and is standing in the hallway about forty feet from me. He's in urgent conversation with an older man whose face seems vaguely familiar.

I back off so they can't spot me if they look up. That's the last thing I want, James Roach seeing me here. I glance around the reception area. It's a circular space, nowhere to hide, except in the men's room. But if I go in there and Roach has to drain the snake, I'll be trapped.

Another voice joins Roach's and the man he's with. One that I know, much better than I know Roach's. Slowly, I turn back to the hallway.

Buster has joined the two men. He greets Roach. They talk; I don't know about what, I can't hear specifics.

This is unnerving. The reason I'm here is because I've decided to tell Buster what I know about the murder that took place on Roach's property. I figured that was the safest way to go, given Buster's virulent antipathy toward the man, the way he'd put Roach down so hard that day I picked his brain about going to the police. Now I don't know what to do.

I have to get out of here—I can't let them see me. I look over at the receptionist. She's too busy to be aware that I'm still here.

Carefully, I back up to the bank of elevators and press the down button, holding the magazine in front of me for cover. I can hear the three of them talking; they seem to be coming closer.

Behind me, the bell rings, an elevator door silently slides open. I duck inside, push the button for the ground floor, stab at the door close emblem. As the three enter the reception area the door slides shut with a pneumatic whoosh, and I'm safe.

I watch from across the street as Roach emerges from Buster's office building and gets into a limo parked curbside in front of the building. As his car pulls away into traffic, I dial Buster's office number on my cell phone.

"This is Fritz Tullis," I tell his secretary when she picks up the line. "I'm late, the traffic was worse than I anticipated. Would you apologize to Buster for me, and tell him I'll be there in about ten minutes?"

She assures me that my tardiness isn't a problem, Buster has been running behind schedule himself.

Ten minutes later, Buster greets me in the lobby and ushers me to his office. The harried receptionist gives me a quick "weren't you just here?" look, but doesn't comment, thank God.

"You wouldn't believe who was here earlier this afternoon," Buster says as he shuts the door behind us.

"Who?" I ask, the picture of innocence.

"James fucking Roach, that's who." He gives me a Cheshire cat grin, like we're in on a secret no one else knows; which we are, except he's on the outside, too. "Too bad you missed him, ace."

"I'll pass," I say dryly. "What was he doing here?"

"Business with Rex Clements. Something shady, I'm sure," he says with a wink. "Rex is the last founding partner still active in the firm. He's pushing eighty now, but he's still a force to be reckoned with. The old man was Roach's mentor, years ago."

Clements. That's the man I saw with Roach, now I remember. He was a player in the Nixon-Ford era, too, as I vaguely recall. "Did you see Roach?"

"For a minute." Buster gives me a shit-eating grin. "I told him to go fuck himself. I really despise the guy."

"You used those exact words?"

"What're you, nuts? Of course not, I'm not suicidal. But he knows I think he's a shit, that's no secret."

"How do your partners feel about that? Isn't Roach important to them?"

Buster crosses to his minibar. "You want a brew?"

"Make it a scotch." I want something with a kick, to help digest this.

He pours a couple tumblers of Laphroaig, hands me one. We toast.

"Roach is very important," Buster says in answer to my question. "He and Clements and some of the old guard, they ran the world. Still do. But that doesn't mean I have to like what he stands for, and my partners know that. This office covers the political spectrum, we speak our minds. If we couldn't, we wouldn't be able to do the job." He sips from his drink. "This is the majors, man. We play hardball here. James Roach doesn't care how I feel about him, as long as I don't fuck him up. Which I wouldn't—unless I had to."

That may be sooner than you know, I'm thinking as I stare at him.

"So," Buster says, "what's on your mind? Hey, before I forget. We're on for tonight, dinner and whatever, right? You're staying over?"

"Sure."

"Good. We're going to have a good time." He leans back. "So . . ."

The moment of truth. Either I trust Buster, or I don't. That I saw him and Roach together doesn't mean they're in cahoots over anything. He's explained their relationship. I have to tamp down my paranoia or it's going to overwhelm me.

"Do you remember what we were talking about, back aways?"

"That hypothetical crime you witnessed?" He pauses. "Which wasn't hypothetical, was it?"

"No," I answer. "It wasn't."

He leans forward. "Has anything changed?"

Slowly: "Yes and no."

"Yes and no how?"

"No one else knows about it, but . . ."

He's getting antsy. "You saw a crime being committed. For real."

"Yes."

"What kind?" he asks, sounding like he's afraid to know what it was.

"Murder."

He stares at me. "That's . . . big." He gets up and pours himself two more fingers of scotch. "Where did you see it?"

"Near where I live."

"Like a few days before we talked about it?"

"A week. A little more."

"Do you know who it was? The victim?"

"I didn't." I pause. "Now I do."

"Someone you knew?"

"No."

He thinks about that answer a minute. "Then how do you know now?"

"I saw his picture in the paper. And on TV."

"Somebody famous?" Buster leans toward me.

"No. But he was important."

Buster shakes his head impatiently. "Let's quit beating around the fucking bush, Fritz. Who did you see get murdered?"

I brace myself with another swallow of scotch. "The Russian senior counselor to the United States. He was based in their embassy."

Buster sits up like he's been zapped with a cattle prod. "You're shitting me," he says. "I mean, that's impossible. That guy was found in an alley in Baltimore. He was cruising for gay hookers."

"He was found there, but he wasn't killed there." I take a deep breath. How far can I trust him, having seen what I just saw? Partly, I decide. "Take my word for it; or don't, I've got the proof."

"You *what?*" Buster flies out of his chair. "What the fuck kind of proof could you have?"

I take two pictures out of the envelope where I've stashed them—my original of the three men on the tarmac, and the ID that came off the computer. I hand them to Buster.

"This man," I say, pointing to the picture I took, the one in which the faces can't be seen because of the lighting, "is this man." I point to the computer image. "And both"—I take out the newspaper clipping I'd cut out of the *Post*—"are this man. The counselor."

Buster looks from one picture to the second to the third. "Are you sure?"

"Yes," I say heavily. "I'm sure."

He looks at the computer image again. "This is a diplomatic driver's license photo. Where did you get it?"

"I can't tell you."

"What do you mean, you can't tell me? How did you get access to this?"

"From a friend. And I can't tell you his name or what he does. I promised him I wouldn't."

Buster shakes his head. "That's bullshit. I'm your lawyer, for Godsakes. Everything between us is confidential. I need to know, man."

"Why?"

He looks like he wants to throw me out his window. "To protect you, you asshole. You could be in trouble over this, Fritz." He brandishes the driver's license facsimile. "You're not supposed to have access to these records."

I hadn't thought of that. I knew I could be in jeopardy from the killer, but not in trouble from merely having the picture. "I didn't even think about that." I'm in over my head, and I'm beginning to realize how deeply.

"Shit on a fucking stick." Buster starts pacing the floor, running his fingers through his unruly hair. "Who knows this picture exists?" he asks, holding up the one I took.

"No one. Except me and the guy who helped me out. And you, now."

"That's one too many. I'm going to have to talk to this guy who helped you out."

I shake my head. "You can't. Don't worry, he erased everything from his computer. Anyway, he doesn't know who this is. He thinks it's part of a divorce proceeding."

"Absolutely no one else knows? Don't bullshit me, Fritz," he says gravely.

"No one. Who else would I tell?"

Buster thinks for a minute. "Where did this murder happen?"

I take a beat. "On James Roach's farm."

Buster sways. "For Christsakes! You saw this diplomat get assassinated on property that's owned by an assistant secretary of state?"

I nod.

Buster slumps into his chair. "Do you know if Roach was there when this happened?" He looks panicked—I've never seen him lose his cool like this before.

I shake my head firmly. "No, he wasn't. He doesn't know anything about this—I mean, that it happened at his place."

Buster regards me suspiciously. "How do you know Roach wasn't there? Are you holding anything back from me? I'm a lawyer, remember? You don't keep secrets from your lawyer."

"I'm telling you everything," I aver, fighting not to sound defensive. *Except that I have other pictures, transparencies to back them up, and a pushy Baltimore cop is chasing after this as well.*

"So okay, you and I are straight, but you haven't answered my question—how do you know for sure Roach wasn't there?"

"I asked him."

"You *what?*" Now he's out of his chair again. He looks like he wants to strangle me.

"Not directly. Give me some credit." I realize how idiotic and naive I sound. "I met him the same day the murder happened, that evening. At my mother's, a social occasion, pure coincidence. We got to talking about his job and I brought the conversation around to his schedule, and he mentioned that he'd been at a meeting in D.C. that morning and hadn't gotten to his farm until late afternoon."

Buster stares at me. "And while you and he were talking about his schedule, and he convinced you of his honesty—through what, his body language?—did he also sell you a nice piece of property?" he asks sarcastically. "The Brooklyn Bridge, for example?"

"Come on, Buster," I answer peevishly, feeling stupid. "It

sounds dumb out of context, but it was just conversation. He wasn't trying to sandbag me with some alibi or anything."

"Of course not," Buster says caustically. "You're positive about the time frame? Where he was—said he was."

"Yes."

"Tell me what happened," he orders me. "Where, when, the usual suspects stuff."

I tell him what went down, except that instead of birding I say I was out fishing, a plane landed, I looked through my camera lens to see what was going on, and I saw the murder occur, the body taken away.

Buster stares at me when I'm finished. "That's it?" he asks. "The whole kit and kaboodle?"

"That's it."

He starts pacing the floor like a fretful husband whose wife has been too long in labor. "Roach is in a dangerous position. He could be fucked if this ever gets out." His brain is working overtime. "Or he could have knowledge of it and for whatever reason isn't letting on, which would really be a bitch." He makes a note. "I'll try to figure out a way to find out what happened. I'll have to test the waters gingerly—I don't want to set anybody's neck hairs on edge, particularly Roach's." He gives me a bracing stare. "The important thing is to keep your name out of everything."

I feel greatly relieved, hearing him say that. "Thanks in advance for doing whatever you can on the q.t. Because I sure don't want to get involved."

"You don't know how much you don't want to get involved." He holds the incriminating photographs up to me. "Are there any more of these?"

"No, they're the only ones," I lie.

"Okay," he says. "Here's the drill. This never happened—the pictures, you taking them, you seeing anything. You with me?"

"All the way."

He crosses to the far corner, where there's a small machine that looks like a copier. He lifts the lid of the machine, drops the photos in, closes the lid, pushes a button. I hear a high-pitched grinding sound.

"A shredder?" I ask. I don't know why I'm surprised that there's a paper shredder in his office—he must have use for it dozens of times a week, for occasions such as this.

He nods. "Now they never existed, for sure." He walks back to me. "Fritz, listen to me. Carefully. Do not talk to Roach about this. Not even indirectly. You listening to me?"

"I hear you, Buster. Loud and clear."

"I'm serious. You're out of your league when it comes to stuff like this."

"I know that, believe me."

He shakes his head. "I know you know it, Fritz, but I don't think you *know* it, if you know what I mean."

Too many "knows." "I understand what's going on, Buster."

Buster gives me a worried look. "You wish. *I* wish. You are one reckless, impetuous SOB. You always have been, from our first week at Yale, when you jumped out your dorm window on a bet. Do you remember that crazy stunt?"

I grin. "Of course I remember. I made twenty bucks."

"And damn near broke your neck." He groans. "You jump into things without thinking about the consequences. I know you, Fritz, I've known you half our lives. You know what I'm afraid of?"

"What?" I ask. I don't like being chastised by someone my own age—I get it enough from my elders, particularly my older brother.

"That you're going to chase after this."

"I'm not," I protest.

"I hope not," he says fervently. "I sincerely hope not." He puts a brotherly arm around my shoulder. "I love you, man. I don't want to see any more misery coming your way. You've already had your full ration of shit."

"Thanks." We're the same age, but I feel like he's the grown-up, and I'm still the kid. He's wearing a tie, and I'm not.

"Okay." He grins, a big smile that says maybe all's not right with the world, but the important stuff is. "We're out of here." He tosses down the dregs of his drink. "You're in good hands with me, Fritz. Beats the crap out of Allstate."

I smile wanly. He really wants me to trust him—as much for him as for me. Maybe more.

Buster's is a blonde, mine's a redhead. Otherwise, two peas in a pod. Tiffany and Whitney. I assume those aren't their real names. The women, both in their mid-twenties, are pleasant enough, bubbly, sweet, savvy. Built like *Playboy* centerfolds, of course. Buster's idea of the cure-for-whatever-ails-you.

We get to know each other over a bottle of champagne—Krug, only the best for Buster—and a few lines of quality blow. Whitney, my date, asks the obligatory questions: am I a lawyer like Buster, are we partners? She's met a couple of his partners. They're cool guys, the younger ones all drive Porsches. I tell her I'm a university professor, and drive a Jeep. She thinks that's neat; "you must be a real brain" (although I have to explain what "sabbatical" means). And where do I live now? She scrunches up her nose at my address. The boondocks as far as she's concerned; she comes from a two-stoplight hicksville in Ohio and doesn't ever want to go back to the small-town life, she's a big-city girl through and through. Until she gets married and has kids, then that would be okay, if it's a hip little town like Aspen or Santa Fe (neither of which she's actually been to). She likes outdoor activities (she's recently taken up golf, her instructor says she's a natural), music, dancing, moonlight walks along the C&O Canal. She recites these things like she's composing an adult ad, although a woman with her looks is never going to have to scrounge for a date.

So now we know each other as well as we need to, as well as we're ever going to. We've been in each other's company for fifteen minutes.

The ladies are in high heels but they're game for walking, since we aren't going far, and Buster wants to. We stroll a couple of blocks to 1789, a Zagat top ten restaurant that Buster uses as his local since it's close to his house and they treat him like the crown prince, and have another bottle of champagne at the bar before we go upstairs to the dining room for dinner. They're out of Krug, we have to settle for Dom Pérignon.

By now, Whitney has become quite amiable toward me. Several glasses of champagne on top of some righteous blow can bring out the friendliness in just about anyone. Besides, that's why she's here—to make me happy. As we work our way through dinner she's very touchy-feely, fingertips on thigh, foot brushing against ankle, finger-feeding me from her plate. I'm enjoying the attention. Her nails brush my crotch under the table; I react predictably. Buster's lady is doing the same with him, but not as much—this isn't their first date.

We pig out like madmen, eating and drinking with gluttonous abandon. By the time dinner's over we've knocked back two bottles of '95 Haut-Brion (three hundred dollars a bottle and worth every penny; I can blithely say that since Buster's buying) on top of the champagne, plus a half-bottle of Château-d'Yquem that absolutely blows my head off. This is a thousand-dollar dinner, easy. I know the bill is going on Buster's expense account but the hedonistic excess staggers me, particularly since the two women don't know great wines like these from a decent twenty-dollar bottle of cabernet from the supermarket. That's not a put-down of them; twenty bucks is my speed, too. I come from money but I never learned how to spend it like this. Maybe the difference is Buster's earned his, mine fell into my lap.

Finally, almost mercifully, we're finished. Buster barely looks at the check as he signs it on his house account.

"Thanks," I say. "That was awesome, and that's an understatement."

"Perk of the job." He smiles, satisfied with himself. "When

Philip Morris gets their monthly bill they won't even notice, this is a pimple on their ass. By the way, you were Roger Thomas tonight."

"Who's Roger Thomas?"

"Chairman of Philip Morris. Another of Rex Clements's classy buddies."

"Your partner knows all the right people."

"We're the sweepers that clean the elephant shit off the street after the circus parade's passed by. Someone has to do it."

The ladies are in no shape for walking, especially in their four-inch fuck-me stilettos, so we cab back to Buster's place. Whitney sits on my lap for the short ride. We make out like bandits. Ditto Buster and Tiffany. Whitney's breath is musky. She tastes like sex.

As soon as we're inside Buster's house it's stripped-down hot and heavy, no polite chitchat. I'm loaded and I'm horny. I lead Whitney to my guest room, shoes, jackets, shirt, pants, skirt coming off as we go, a trail of discarded clothes. She was okay to talk to and lovely to look at, but this is why we're together tonight. That I have no feelings for her beyond pure lust doesn't matter. I'm living in the moment.

The foreplay goes on and on, I'm riding a whirlwind. She's a gumby, she really has me going.

Then it's over. And we're left with each other.

Standing in the vestibule in a guest bathrobe, I say good night to the two women. It's well after midnight. Both of them are dressed, pretty much put back together as they were when they arrived. Buster took care of them; I saw two envelopes discreetly passed, quickly tucked away in their small evening bags. He's in bed now, sound asleep.

We hear the sound of the cab honking its horn outside. "Thanks for a nice evening," I say to Whitney.

"Me, too."

"I'll be in the taxi," Tiffany says. "Don't take long."

"Just be a minute."

Tiffany staggers down the front steps to the cab. Whitney fishes in her purse, pulls out a card, hands it to me. I look at it—her name and telephone number, nothing more. The number looks like it's an answering service. She takes a pen from the purse, scribbles another number under the printed one.

"Maybe we could go out sometime," she says uncoquettishly. "A regular date, like a movie, the next time you're in Washington." She points to the handwritten number. "That one's my personal number."

"Well . . ."

"I'm not a regular at this, only with a straight-up person like Buster. Then, if I like the guy . . . when I saw you, I liked you."

It's late, I'm half-stoned, wiped out from the sex we had. And tired, it's been a long day. "A movie. That could be fun."

"I hope you call." She opens the door. "But if you don't, I still had a good time."

She's gone before I can say, "Me, too."

It's five o'clock. I slept fitfully for a few hours, but I'm up now. I don't want to go back to sleep—I don't want to be here at all. It was a nice act of friendship for Buster to fix me up with a sexy lady, wine and dine us like royalty, and foot the bill to boot, but that's not what I want. I want resolution; I need it. What I don't want is having to stare at Buster across a morning cup of coffee and face more questions about the killing at James Roach's farm.

I fumble into my rancid clothes, splash cold water on my face, scribble Buster a thank-you note. It's still dark when I close his front door behind me and drive off in search of an open diner.

I sit in my assigned carrel in the Library of Congress main reading room, waiting for the magazine articles and journals I've requested. Earlier, over coffee and scrambled eggs in a coffee shop near Dupont Circle whose other night-owl patrons were cops and assorted graveyard shifters, I'd checked my answering machine. There were a few messages of no consequence and one from my mother, requesting my presence at dinner tonight. And that I bring my new friend, Maureen, so that my mother can meet her and Maureen can pass muster. She didn't use the words "pass muster," but that was tacitly implied.

That'll be fun, watching my mother size up Maureen. Sparks may fly.

The runner, an old geezer who looks like Bartleby the Scrivener, wheels his cart up to my cubicle, hands me my box, and shuffles on. I dump the contents onto the desk and start sifting through them.

What I have in front of me is everything I could find in the library's files on the subject of James Roach, going back over three decades, to the hot center of the Vietnam War. I arrange the literature in chronological order, oldest to most recent—political science magazines and journals like *Foreign Affairs* that deal with the CIA, the military-industrial complex, and matters of state and the interlockings of economics and government. I pick up the first piece, a *New York Times* Sunday magazine article from May 1967, and begin reading.

Three hours later, I'm finished. I push back from my cramped position, stretch the kinks out of my back, and reflect on what I've learned.

James Roach is a complex, disturbing, fascinating character who's led an exciting, turbulent life. Married four times, once to a member of the Dutch royal family. An Army Special Forces officer in the early 1960s, with a stint in Vietnam, he left the service and signed up with the CIA, based in Southeast Asia—Thailand, Laos, Cambodia, South Vietnam—where he was involved in various furtive activities. Roach was, among his many shadowy enterprises, a go-between for foreign weapons merchants and U.S. agencies that wanted to arm various rebel factions but were barred from doing so by U.S. law. He made a fortune dealing guns, and also ran afoul of the law.

In 1979 he was charged with violating laws governing illegal transfers and sales of weapons to foreign governments, but after two years of pretrial investigation and depositions the case was dropped on the eve of going to trial for "national security reasons." The case was never resurrected, despite the protestations of the U.S. attorney handling it (a Democratic holdover from the Carter administration). The files were permanently sealed.

That, as far as I could find, was Roach's only official brush with the law. Other allegations about him, mainly regarding other arms dealings, have surfaced over the years, but nothing's ever stuck to him.

The contacts he'd made over his years working for the government helped him build a thriving international trading firm. He still brokered arms, but legitimately now. In the 1990s he began investing heavily in tech stocks, emerging as an early, savvy Internet entrepreneur, alongside his other businesses. The latest *Forbes* estimate of his personal wealth is over two hundred fifty million dollars.

Also starting around 1990, he began buying his way back into the political mainstream. He contributes substantial sums of money to both political parties, and has friends in high places in both camps. In 1998, the Democrats rewarded him with an assistant secretary of commerce position dealing with the World Trade Organization, and after the 2000 elections he was given his present post. He still owns his trading companies, but his holdings are in blind trusts.

James Roach is a textbook if depressing example of the revolving door that spins between the public and the private sector, where the lines are so blurred as to be nonexistent. He is, clearly, a man who's accustomed to having power and isn't reluctant to use it.

There's lots of intriguing information, but nothing damning—

except the decades-old situation involving the failed arms prosecution. I jot down some notes on a sheet of legal paper, and leave the cool confines of the library.

It's a long shot—the case has been closed for over twenty years—but it's the only lead I can pursue on my own, so I might as well give it a try.

The federal prosecutor who tried to put Roach away is long retired; I don't even know if he's still alive. His last listed address was on Woodley Place in Northwest D.C., but when I find that number in the reverse directory and dial it, it isn't him, the party on the line had had this phone number for ten years.

Late afternoon. I'm back home now. I sit at my PowerBook, running the man's name, Maxwell Simmons, through various databases, starting with the regional telephone directories for the metropolitan Washington area. Simmons is a common name, but not with a Maxwell in front of it. There shouldn't be many of them around. Hopefully, if he's alive, he didn't move to some faraway burg in the Smoky Mountains in North Carolina or some other such remote outpost where people like him retire to because it's cheap.

No luck in D.C., no luck in any of the Maryland counties in proximity to Washington, going as far north as Baltimore, east to Annapolis, south to St. Mary's; nor can his name be found in the nearby Virginia counties—Arlington, Fairfax, Loudon, or Prince William.

He could be anywhere; or nowhere. I should check the obituaries—the *Washington Post* would have run an obit on him if he died. Or his number could be unlisted, certainly a possibility.

I'm about to get out of the telephone search and start looking through federal records when the name Maxwell Simmons pops up on my screen. It's in Essex County in Virginia, which is due west from where I am now, on the other side of the Potomac.

The specific location is Taneyburg, a graceful Revolutionary War–era village much like Jamestown, located not far from some of the great battlefields of the Civil War—Chancellorsville, the Wilderness, Fredericksburg, Spotsylvania. When I was a kid my dad and I toured the Civil War battlefields of Virginia, Maryland, and Pennsylvania. That trip was one of the principal reasons I became a teacher of American history. Those two weeks I spent with my father were my most memorable vacation.

I dial the number. It rings several times—five, six, seven. I'm ready to hang up when a voice comes over the line. An old man's voice—frail, tentative. "Hello?"

"Is this Maxwell Simmons?"

There's a pause, then: "Yes."

"The former federal prosecutor?"

"Who is this?"

I've flushed my quarry—no point in beating around the bush. "Someone who's looking into James Roach's past."

A longer hesitation than the first. "What about it?"

"The case you were prosecuting over twenty years ago, that got thrown out. I'm trying to get information about that."

"Are you a reporter?" he asks apprehensively. "One of these Woodward-Bernstein types?"

"No, sir," I assure him. "I have no connection with the press."

"Detective? Police?"

"No. I'm a private citizen. I'm not connected to anything. Or anybody." I get a quick idea. "I'm a history professor. I'm researching for a paper I'm doing on arms dealing over the past quarter-century. Your name came up in conjunction with Roach."

"A paper," he says flatly. "You want to write a paper about Roach?"

"I might," I tell him, "if I can come up with an angle."

The old man sees through my ruse. "What's the sonofabitch done now?" he rasps.

I smile—I like hearing him describe Roach like that. He might be willing to spill some beans. "I don't know. Nothing. I'm . . ." I don't want to say I'm a neighbor, in case this blows up in my face. "Can I come talk to you? In person?"

There's another pause. Then: "Where're you calling from?"

I can picture him fearfully looking out his window, to see if I'm camped outside his house. "Maryland," I tell him. "I could come see you tomorrow, if that's convenient," I continue, pressing him.

The line is silent for some time, but he hasn't hung up. "Mr. Simmons?" I prompt.

"I don't think that's a good idea," he answers with an attempt at finality. "All that's buried in the past. And I prefer to keep any dealings I had with James Roach buried."

I can't take "no" for an answer, not after the trouble I've gone through to track this man down, and everything that's led up to this. "Look," I say, half groveling, half persuading, "just let me come visit with you. If you don't want to tell me anything, I won't force the issue. But let me come see you. There's truth that needs to come out."

There's another long silence.

"Don't you want to set the record straight, even after all this time?" I push. "So the rest of the world can know what you knew, back then."

I've touched a distant chord—I can feel it over the line. "Okay," he consents. "Got a pencil on you? I'll give you directions."

Maureen's dressed to kill. "Am I presentable enough for your mother?" she teases me as I gape, taking my arm as we walk from her motel room to my car. "Have you been behaving yourself, Fritzie?"

The image of Whitney, in all her bodacious, naked glory, flashes in my mind, along with the image of me, equally naked, entwined with her. We were there less than twenty-four hours ago, a blink of the eye.

My emotions are roiled. I don't owe Maureen any allegiance, emotional or sexual—she's the one who set this agenda between us. But I feel guilty anyway, as if I cheated on her.

"I only have eyes for you." Which is the truth, as we stand here. And beyond this moment, if I'm being honest with myself.

"Good."

I look at her again. Her smile says nothing more than . . . what? I can't figure her. The Mona Lisa could take lessons in inscrutability from this woman.

Dinner is to be an intimate group: Maureen and me, my mother, and the Franklins, an elderly couple who have been friends of mom's since before I was born, here tonight as a beard, so mother's machinations regarding Maureen won't look so obvious. The Franklins are among the last of mother's friends who are still alive. That's an ongoing burden on her psyche, her friends dying on her. She must think about how much more time she has, and how she'll spend it.

Seeing me married and settled down is her number one priority. Grandkids would be a bonus. I wish I could make her that gift. It would be nice to give her back one thing to make up for all she's given me.

My mother comes out of the house and strides to us as we get out of my car. "Mother, this is Maureen O'Hara, don't ask. Maureen, this is my mother, Mary Bradshaw Tullis, the doyenne of King James County."

"Stop showing off your vocabulary, Fritz," my mother scolds me, her eyes twinkling. She gives Maureen the once-over, extends a parchment-thin hand. "It's a pleasure to meet you at last. You don't look the least bit like an ogre."

"Mother . . ."

Maureen laughs. "I'm harmless. Trust me."

"She's tall," my mother informs me, as if I didn't notice. "Almost as tall as you. You have a regal bearing, my dear," she compliments Maureen.

"Thank you, Mrs. Tullis. That's lovely for you to say."

She's trying to seduce mom. But my mother can't be easily seduced, she's seen way too much in her long life.

We walk through the house to the veranda, where the bar's been set up. Mother seems to want to like Maureen. The woman is a Harvard professor, after all—good credentials. "Come let me introduce you to my friends," she says, interlocking Maureen's arm in hers.

She escorts Maureen over to the Franklins, who already have their drinks. Even in her low sandals Maureen towers over my mother, but they make a striking couple. Two formidable women. I'm overmatched tonight, I know that already.

Dinner is delicious, as usual. We serve ourselves from the sideboard where Mattie has laid out the dishes—it's her night off, she went into town with a friend after she cooked the meal. My mother has strategically placed Maureen next to her, on one side; I'm opposite them, sandwiched between Mr. and Mrs. Franklin.

The meal proceeds convivially. My mother and Maureen are in animated conversation throughout, most of it in tones too low for me to hear. I know that they're talking about me; both keep stealing glances in my direction and then turning back to each other, giggling behind their hands like schoolgirls.

"Let us have a short break before dessert," my mother suggests when we've finished. "Will you help me clear, dear?" she asks Maureen.

"Of course, Mary."

It's already "dear" and "Mary." It isn't a man's world, despite the old aphorism; women only say that to humor us.

"We'll join you in a moment," my mother tells the Franklins and me, shooing us outside.

The Franklins decline; it's late for them, they need to be on their way. We say our good-byes and I escort them outside to their old Cadillac. Mrs. Franklin clings to me as we walk to the driveway; her night vision is shot, she's like an old dog, only comfortable in her own surroundings.

"I don't know how your mother does it," she says, sadly envious of mom's robust health. "She'll outlive us all."

"Who knows," I say diplomatically. It's true, though; she will. Which she dreads more than anything. No one wants to be the last of a dying breed.

I watch the old couple successfully negotiate their way out of mom's driveway and onto the road, then I walk back to the veranda, nursing the last of my wine from dinner. As I slouch against the porch railing my mother comes out and joins me.

"I like her," she says without preamble. She lights up a Kent, using my father's old World War II Navy Zippo, a cherished keepsake. I don't chastise her about her smoking—at her age it doesn't matter.

"Good. She was worried about that. Well, maybe not worried. Concerned."

"She's strong. She can tame you. You need taming."

"I'm a pussycat, mother."

"You're an alleycat is more accurate." She takes my wineglass from me, sips. "Try not to mess this one up."

"Mess what up?"

"You know what I'm talking about. You botched it with that lovely Mortimer girl. Don't do that with this one."

Man, oh man. She wants to marry me off, she doesn't care who it is, as long as it's to a presentable woman of childbearing age. "It's not like that, mom. We're friends."

Her laugh is derisive.

"We are." I'm on the defensive again with her. Parents can guilt-trip their children without breaking a sweat. "She and Johanna Mortimer are friends, that's how we met. You know that. This is a platonic relationship. It's better that way, believe me."

She shakes her head in disagreement. "I'm an old woman, Fritz, but I still have my eyesight. Maureen likes you." She pauses. "And you like her. Admit it."

I'm busted. "I do like her, okay? But it's not going to happen."

She smiles. "We'll see." She stubs out her cigarette. "I'll go help Maureen bring out the ice cream. You stay here."

"Yes, ma'am."

She goes back into the house. She's going to be disappointed when Maureen returns to Boston in a few weeks and nothing's happened between us. Ah God, mother, what a disappointment I am to you.

The three of us sit outside, spooning up our chocolate sundaes. I feel like a specimen under a microscope that's being scrutinized by two competing but collegial scientists; my mother with a critical eye toward promoting further engagement between Maureen and me, Maureen enjoying watching me squirm at knowing that I'm being watched. Her pleasure in my discomfort is not malicious, but she's above the fray, so to speak, while I'm mired down in the pit.

The sound of tires crunching oyster-shell gravel breaks me out of my musing. "That must be our neighbor," my mother announces.

"James Roach?" I ask, surprised and dismayed.

Maureen gets a look of anxiety on her face, hearing me say Roach's name. I make an imperceptible head shake—leave it alone.

"Yes," my mother answers, oblivious to our distress. "He's asked about how you're doing, so I invited him over for dessert. He's such a nice neighbor, don't you think?"

No, mother. I don't think he's a nice neighbor. I think he's a hot-air balloon with a scary agenda. But I keep my mouth shut.

"Hello?" Roach appears in the doorway to the veranda. "Am I too late?"

My mother rises to greet him. "Of course not," she says brightly. "There's plenty of ice cream for everyone. Did you have your supper? I can fix you a plate."

"I've eaten, thank you." He steps onto the veranda.

I slouch to my feet and reluctantly stick out my hand. He shakes it vigorously. Then he turns to Maureen. "Have we met?" he asks, looking at her closely. The tone of his voice implies that they have.

Maureen, who stood when I did, shakes her head quickly. "I'm sure we haven't. I'm not from around here."

"This is Maureen O'Hara," my mother says, introducing her without missing a beat about her name. "From Boston. She's down here on a research project. This gentleman," she tells Maureen, "is our part-time neighbor, James Roach, the assistant secretary of state."

Maureen doesn't offer her hand to be shaken. "I've never met a secretary of state before," she says with a straight face.

I manage to hold my laughter. She is one tough cookie, this woman. One of the many reasons she turns me on.

"Assistant," Roach corrects her with transparent false modesty. "So—Boston." The word rolls around on his tongue like he's sampling a first-growth Bordeaux. "We had another delightful young woman from Boston here recently." He turns at me. "You remember Miss Mortimer, don't you, Fritz?"

Asshole. "Sure."

"Johanna's a friend of mine," Maureen informs him. "That's why I'm down here. She recommended it. For my work."

"What sort of work is that, Miss O'Hara?" He catches himself. "Excuse me. Is it 'Miss'?"

"Yes. Or Ms., either one. But you can call me Maureen, Mr. Roach," she says, sparring with him.

"James," he responds. "If you don't mind."

"I don't mind, James." She glances over at me.

"And your project?" Roach politely asks again.

"I'm a biologist. I'm studying the local plant life."

"And animals," my mother chimes in. "Maureen's—"

Maureen cuts her off adroitly. "May I get your dessert for you, Mr. Roach . . . James?"

My mother's a wise old owl—she gets it. "Allow me." She walks back into the house to get Roach his ice cream.

"Animals?" Roach asks. He wants to know what everyone who comes into his sphere does, even if obliquely.

Maureen sits down next to me. "All kinds of stuff," she says dismissively.

"Birds as well?" he asks.

"Birds?"

I watch this verbal tennis rally with intense interest. She isn't going to let him sucker-punch her.

He looks over at me with a crooked smile. I know his use of the word *bird* is a double entendre, and he knows it, too, but he doesn't know that she knows. "Fritz is an avid bird-watcher."

"Really?" She looks at me, turns back to Roach. "We have done some bird-watching," she acknowledges. "It's hard not to, there's such an abundance of wildlife all around here."

"Here we are!"

My mother comes out with Roach's dish of ice cream. The bowl is huge, a serving bowl rather than a dessert size. She hands him the bowl and a spoon. "It's homemade, my cook made it."

I turn away to hide the smile on my face. Mattie's never made ice cream in her life—this is Häagen-Dazs, straight from the carton.

Roach looks askance at the huge portion. "I don't know if I can eat all of this."

"Fiddlesticks," my mother says with a wave of her hand. She can get away with using archaic expressions, it's part of her old-lady charm. "Any real man can eat tubfuls of ice cream. My boys could never get enough of Mattie's ice cream when they were little. Dig in, James," she commands him.

Dutifully, he spoons up a bite, tries it, smiles gamely. "This is delicious."

Mother beams. "Mattie will be delighted to hear that."

Roach turns to me. "Have you been out sailing, since our last time?"

"I haven't had the opportunity," I mutter. I don't want to have a conversation about his boat, because I don't want my mother to know about my near-fatal accident.

"Don't let your ice cream melt, James," my mother trills, oblivious to any tension between us.

Maureen, however, immediately picks up on my uneasiness. She glances over quizzically, as if to ask "what's he talking about?"

I don't acknowledge her unspoken entreaty, but I'm pissed off by Roach's bringing up such an ugly incident. The man is altogether too arrogant and confrontational for my taste; it's almost as if he's baiting me. Buster was right—this man is not to be trusted. I need to keep him and this topic at arm's length.

"I haven't been out on the water much recently," I tell him. "I've been busy doing other things," I say evasively.

"I trust that's not a permanent situation," Roach counters. "You know my boat is yours to use."

I give him a noncommittal shrug. This man really makes me queasy—not only because of my having spied on him, but more important, because of what I've seen. I'm going to have to figure out how to tell my mother, without alarming her, that I don't want her to have him here again, certainly not when I'm around.

Why he's around at all is bothersome to me, and not only because of my own situation with him. What's he doing hanging around with an octogenarian and her wayward son? This guy rubs elbows with presidents and kings—we should be off his radar screen.

"This is such a beautiful spot you have here, Mary," he says to my mother. "What are your plans for it? I don't mean now, of course. I'm talking down the road. It must be difficult to manage an estate of this size." He glances over at me. "Of course, it'll go to your children someday. Then it'll be their responsibility."

My mother shakes her head. "It's theirs, of course, when I go, but they don't want the responsibility, do you, Fritz?" she says, staring at me intently. "Living here, this life in general, is not for my children."

There she goes, guilt-tripping me again. But that's how it is—this is not my life, nor my siblings'. We made that decision decades ago. We just want her to be here for us so we can cherry-pick, use it when we want. But she's right—we won't keep on with it. Tullis ownership of this farm will be finished when she is.

"A shame," Roach comments. "It's such a desirable piece of property." As if the thought just came to his head, he says offhandedly, "If the occasion were ever to arise that you wanted to sell it, I would hope you'd speak to me first. Since I have the adjoining property now."

Of course! That's the reason he's sniffing up our asses. It's so obvious—he wants this property. Put it together with his, he has several miles of contiguous waterfront tied up, virtually impenetrable from the outside.

"It's not for sale," I jump in firmly, almost harshly.

The vehemence of my response seems to take him aback. "I was merely dipping my oar in, so to speak," he says with alacrity. "Please don't take any offense." He smiles at my mother—the cat that wants to eat the canary so bad he's almost salivating. Let him drool all down his shirt. I'd put down stakes here myself before I'd ever let James Roach own this property.

Maureen doesn't know the subtext of what's going on between Roach and me. She's been with me when we've spied on Roach, but she doesn't know about the shooting incident on the boat. Still, she's keenly aware of my uptightness, I can feel her vibe. She reaches over and strokes my hand, a gesture for which I'm grateful.

"Would anyone like a glass of port?" my mother asks, unknowingly but welcomingly breaking the tension.

It's late. I have to take Maureen back to her motel, then drive home. "'Bye, mother. I'll call you in a few days."

She gives me a dry kiss on the cheek. "Stay out of trouble."

"I'll do my best."

She gives Maureen a kiss, too. "Don't be a stranger, Maureen. You're always welcome here—with or without *him.*" She gives me the eye.

"Thank you. I'll be back soon," Maureen promises.

Roach is leaving, too, since we are. "Thanks for having me over, Mary," he says.

"That's what neighbors are for, James."

She goes inside and closes the door behind her. The three of us start down the front steps. A recently polished black Lincoln sedan with dark-tinted windows is parked in the driveway next to my road-dirt-speckled Jeep.

"Good night," Roach says to us, offering his hand. "Don't forget about my offer," he reminds me yet again.

I shake his hand reluctantly. "Good night," I say perfunctorily. "I won't forget."

"Good night," Maureen throws in.

I take her arm to lead her to my car. As we draw near the Lincoln the driver's-side door opens and out steps Wallace, blocking our path.

I recoil. *"What the fuck . . ."* I cry out involuntarily.

Maureen, brought up short by my vehement reaction, looks at Wallace, who holds himself military-erect, staring at me.

"I sure as hell didn't expect to see him again," I say to Roach, trying to will myself to stay calm. Inside, the butterflies are swarming in my stomach.

For a moment, no one says a word. I glare at Roach, whose expression indicates that he's aware he's committed a faux pas.

Wallace, who isn't encumbered with a conscience, breaks the silence. "What happened out there was an accident."

Maureen stares at Wallace quizzically. She doesn't know he was with Roach when we were spying on them; she was too far away, she couldn't see them through the long lens, as I did. So she doesn't know why there's so much tension between him and me, but she can feel it. It hangs over all of us, thicker than the humidity. She squeezes my hand in silent support.

"I thought I mentioned it," Roach finally says, lamely.

"Mentioned what?" I ask heatedly. I'm so angry I'm almost incoherent. I'm shaking; I want to punch someone in the face. Roach first, then Wallace. "What did you think you mentioned? That this asshole was still around? Is that what you forgot to mention?"

"Hey, look—" Wallace starts.

"Hey look, nothing! What the fuck is he doing here?" I yell at Roach. "I don't want him on my property!"

"Okay, okay, okay." Roach has his hands in front of him in the posture of a supplicant. "Calm down for a minute, will you? Will you let me explain?"

"What's to explain? He's fired, then he isn't? I can see that, I don't need an explanation for that." What I really want is an explanation for what they've been doing out on Roach's property with all the mysterious flying in and out, but I don't think this is the best time to bring up that subject.

"What's going on?" Maureen asks. She's scared—she's never seen this kind of violent reaction from me.

I point at Wallace. "This asshole almost killed me, that's all." I glare at him. "You gonna draw on me again?"

Wallace is fighting to control his emotions—I can see the muscles quivering in his face. "I never drew on you."

"Bullshit semantics. You pointed a gun at me and fired."

"It was an accident."

"That would've soothed my mother when she was putting me in the ground," I say, moving toward him. "Get your ass off my property, and I mean *now!*"

Wallace holds his ground. "I am not a killer, and no spoiled shit like you is going to call me one." He points to Roach. "And don't tell me what to do. I go with him, wherever he goes," he says, goading me. "He gives me my orders, no one else. And if you don't like that, junior, you can fucking well stuff it."

That rips it. I jump him, smashing him hard across the face. "You sonofabitch!" I yell.

Caught flat-footed at my unexpected physical assault on him, Wallace loses his footing and staggers back, his hand to his face. There's blood on his mouth, where I split his lip.

"What the hell?" He looks at the blood on his fingers, not believing that I'd hit him, and worse, that I'd beaten him to the punch. "That was the wrong thing to do, ace," he says with a bully's smile. He brings his fist up to pay me back, and then some.

"Fritz!" Maureen is grabbing at me. At the same time,

Roach jumps in between us, denying Wallace the chance to strike back at me.

"Shut up," he yells at Wallace, pushing the man away. "You never know when to leave it alone, do you?" He turns to me. "This has gotten way out of hand. I'm sorry. I didn't expect anything ugly like this to happen."

"You should have, after what happened before," I tell him unforgivingly. "That's who he is, you heard the words come out of his mouth. He's an asshole, pure and simple."

Wallace, his hand at his mouth, glares at me. Maureen, caught up in something I badly wanted to keep from her, is wide-eyed in shock and dismay.

Roach nods. "You're right. I should have. Please."

I allow him to take my arm and lead me a few steps away, so he can talk to me without being overheard.

"I *was* going to fire him," he says softly. "He certainly deserved it."

He's distressed—this situation reflects badly on him. This is a man with a huge ego, who's very concerned with how he's perceived. And right now, he looks stupid; and worse, incompetent. "But for reasons which I can't get into with you right now," he continues, "that course of action was not possible." He looks back at Wallace, who is rigid with anger. "But it's obvious that your take on him was right: I should have gotten rid of him, and now I will. So please—let this go. You don't want to lower yourself to his level," he adds, appealing to what he thinks (or hopes) are my better angels.

He's overestimating my capacity for forgiveness, but I don't want this ugly scene to go on any longer, especially not with Maureen watching. Thank God, at least, that my mother wasn't out here to witness this. She's upstairs in her bathroom getting ready for bed, she wouldn't have heard the ruckus.

"Okay," I say woodenly. "I'll let it go this time. But if I ever see that piece of shit again, anywhere on my property, we'll have a real problem."

"It will all be handled, don't worry," Roach says again. He's trying as hard as he can to placate me.

"Good," I say, finishing it. "Now if you'll excuse me . . ."

I walk back to Maureen, who has been watching all this in disbelief. I take her arm, escort her to my car. As we drive away I can see Wallace through my rearview mirror. He's staring at me with unconcealed hatred.

Maureen and I sit on the cheesy fake-leather couch in her motel room. On the way, we stopped at a bottle store and bought a pint of tequila. I needed something potent to cleanse the bitterness of the encounter with Roach and Wallace out of my mouth, and to steady my nerves. Maureen joins me—the incident shook her up, too, even though I haven't told her the reason why.

"What in the world is going on, Fritz?" she asks. "What was that about with Roach and that other man? He was creepy." She spasms involuntarily, a frightened shiver. "What were you talking about?"

I tell her about the sailing excursion, and Wallace almost shotgunning the kid and me. She shudders. "Roach should've fired him on the spot," she says forcefully. "There's no excuse for keeping a loose cannon like that around. The man used terrible judgment, shooting a gun off on a sailboat. He's supposed to be a professional, isn't he? A professional wouldn't do that."

"It was Roach's idea to bring the gun on board in the first place."

She shakes her head dismissively. "Doesn't matter. Roach isn't the pro, Wallace is, the way you describe him. I don't think Mr. Roach is telling you the truth about their relationship, Fritz."

I knew that as soon as I saw Wallace get off the airplane with Roach, but I didn't want to admit it to myself. Now she's forcing me to. "I don't know," I temporize. "Maybe." If she really knew the full story, she'd freak out.

She knocks back her shooter of tequila, picks up the bottle, pours herself another. I'd join her but I have to drive home. And I know if I stay, she's going to bombard me with questions I don't want to answer.

"I'm bushed," I tell her, heaving to my feet. "I have to get going."

"Fritz." She takes my hand. "Do you want to stay here tonight?"

Ah, Jesus. At last. "I can't."

"Why?"

"Because . . . I can't."

She turns away. "I thought . . ."

"You thought right, you're not mistaken about that. But the timing's wrong."

"Because of Johanna? I don't care that you slept with her. That stuff happens. And it seems to be finished." She hesitates. "I'm jealous, actually."

It's hard to disengage from her after hearing that, but I do. "You're going back to your real life in a few weeks. I can't get emotionally involved with anyone right now, knowing there's no future to it."

"So if you *didn't* care for me, we'd sleep together?" she asks.

"Yes." Which I did last night, with Whitney. Now I wish I hadn't.

"That's stupid, Fritz."

"It's what it is."

She closes her eyes, opens them. "You're right, I know that. But I wanted to anyway, and worry about the consequences later. There'll be consequences to wishing we had, too."

"We've become good friends, Maureen. Let's stay with that for now."

She walks outside with me. "You could take a room here."

"And stay in it all night? I don't think so."

She nods, accepting it. "I'll see you tomorrow?"

"Tomorrow night. I'm busy during the day. Family business."

"Be careful driving home, Fritz. Just . . . be careful."

"I will."

As I drive away I look in my rearview mirror. She's standing where I left her, watching me go.

I drive across the Potomac River to Virginia and head west through the low countryside toward Taneyburg. It rained earlier, a long thundershower, so it's cooler and less humid today than it has been for weeks, a welcome relief. The drive is pleasant, taking me through low lush countryside—much of it overgrown woods of pine, oak, ash, hickory. About every ten miles the verdant landscape is interrupted by a small town, comprised of a few blocks of commercial and residential streets, a couple traffic lights, cemeteries on the outskirts. Civil War monuments and plaques, of ancient skirmishes and impoverished bivouacs, adorn the sides of the road. That terrible war raged all around here, back and forth, for almost the full four bloody years it was fought. Even in a moving car you can feel the history.

I'm not in a hurry; my appointment with Simmons isn't until lunchtime. I got an early start, so I'd have time to meander. At one of the small towns I stop at a Mobil to gas up and have a cup of coffee. Across the street there's a statue of a man on a rearing-up horse, dressed in Confederate garb. I cross over and read the inscription. Colonel Thaddeus Whitherspoon, 11th Tennessee Cavalry. Killed in battle following the retreat from the Wilderness, 1864. Statue erected in 1913 by the Daughters of the Confederacy. I sight the man and horse, frozen forever in time, through my camera lens, and take a couple of pictures.

Taneyburg is old and quaint, but it isn't touristy, it's far enough off the main interstates and other big highways that it has avoided rampant commercialization. A typical Southern village, dominated by a town square with the mandatory Confederate statue in the center, bordered on its four sides by wood-frame two-story buildings—a movie theater, a Walgreen's, The Gap, Banana Republic, and some older, local establishments. A couple of restaurants. Nothing remarkable, but comfortable, homey. A good place to raise a family, which some residents do. Expatriates from the city, they commute to Washington or Richmond, an hour in each direction.

Simmons's house is easy to find, a modest two-story wood colonial on a shady street a few blocks from the town center. It could use a paint job around the trim, but looks solid otherwise. There are flowers in the front yard, the grass is neatly trimmed, the stone walkway is clean, uncracked. Mr. Simmons is proud of his house.

"One minute." I hear rustling around inside when I ring the doorbell. "Cassie, stay." The heavy wood door opens. We peer at each other through the screen door. He's leaning on a cane.

"Mr. Tullis?"

"Yes, Mr. Simmons."

He opens the screen door, one hand holding on to the collar of an ancient golden retriever. "Come in. She's harmless, but she wants to run outside, chase squirrels. She's blind, so I can't let her. She's my last remaining companion."

I follow him into his house. The furnishings are a hodgepodge, a few good pieces interspersed with heavy department store–style stuff from the '40s and '50s. The wallpaper is faded, some curled edges around the floorboards and ceiling trim. Newspapers and magazines clutter the tables and chairs.

"Excuse the mess. I'm not a good housekeeper, and the cleaning lady doesn't dare discard anything." His gaze wanders the room. "If my wife was still alive she'd throw three quarters of this out. She was a tidy woman, I vexed her with my pack-rat ways."

He leads me through a sunroom that overlooks a spacious backyard. Through the windows I see a vegetable garden against the back fence; corn and pole beans are growing high, alongside running melon vines, squash, tomatoes.

"Gardening's my hobby," he says with pride. "Gets me outdoors, and I don't have to get in my car to do it. I gave up golf when my eyesight started going, so now I work in dirt."

"You're going to have a passel of beans," I observe, a sincere flattery. "Corn, too."

He smiles at the compliment, but doesn't reply. We sink into cushiony wing chairs. A sweaty pitcher of iced tea is set on the glass-covered side table between us.

"Thirsty?" He pours a glass for me, one for himself. I take a sip; it's heavily sweetened.

"You want to know about James Roach."

"Whatever you know about him that you can tell me."

"Are you in litigation with him? I won't allow my name to be dragged into a court mess. I don't want to go through any more aggravation."

"Nothing like that," I assure him. "You won't be involved in anything, I can promise you. No one knows I'm here, or that I've contacted you. No one's going to."

He nods, assured enough to go on. "What I know about James Roach." He leans back in his upholstered chair, gazes at the ceiling. There are some water stains in the corners.

"James Roach is a murderer."

"A murderer?" I sit up on the edge of my chair.

"Figuratively. I don't know for a fact that he's actually ever killed anyone. But the weapons he's profited from sure as hell have. He got away with murder, is how I would describe it." He looks off for a moment, recollecting. "He committed crimes and got away with them. Scot-free."

"You were prosecuting him."

"*We* were prosecuting him. The government. It was my case. But it wasn't any kind of personal vendetta, like some of these special prosecutors have embarked on. The government—the Justice Department—brought him to trial. I ran it."

Retired prosecutor Simmons might not have had a vendetta against Roach when he was trying to prosecute him, but he took losing personally, that's obvious, listening to him—twenty years after the fact he still loathes the man.

"Roach was selling arms to Libya, a country that was off-limits for us to trade with. Which meant to dictatorships and anti-government insurgents all over the world. Iran, China, the contras, the Hezbollah, IRA, whoever. Massive sales, billions of dollars."

This information dovetails with what Fred's cousin had speculated on. Roach's farm is a natural for clandestine activity—isolated, with access to shipping anything anywhere, via the Bay, plus the airstrip, which was built long enough to accommodate jets.

I take out a notepad and pen. "Do you mind?"

"Go ahead. It's in the public record. But only the summations. Not the rest of it. The dirty parts."

"Sealed files?"

He nods. "National security, so-called." He coughs derisively. "National security, my behind. There were no breaches of national security, except the laws he was breaking." He grits his teeth, remembering. I'm sure he has relived this over and over for the past twenty-odd years.

"Those were very sensitive times." He's going back in the past now, I can see the faraway look in his eyes. "Terrible times for this country. This was happening during and right after the Iran hostage crisis, our government was tied up in knots, especially after the failed raid in the desert."

"How could Roach get away with doing that on the huge scale you're describing?"

"The usual way that they all did, through dummy corporations set up in third-party countries. Layers and layers of cover, almost impossible to penetrate." His fist is clenched, remembering. "But we did it, this time. We broke through."

"And you felt you had him dead to rights?"

"We *had* him dead to rights, no ifs, ands, or buts."

"Then why didn't you go ahead with it?"

"Because the Reagan administration didn't want to."

I scribble quickly, to keep up. "Did you go to trial?"

He shakes his head. "We were a month away from formally indicting him. One short month. And Roach was scared to death, let me tell you. His lawyers were trying to cut any kind of deal they could, anything that would keep him from going to trial."

"What reason was given for shutting down the process?"

Simmons scratches his old blind dog's head. "Everyone was weary by this time, from the hostage situation, the aftermath of Watergate, all the garbage. The new administration didn't want to drag the old administration's manure along, they were looking to a more pragmatic future. Pragmatic meaning accommodating skunks, of course. You have to remember, by this time almost everyone in Washington hated Carter, even in his own party. He'd crash-landed them into the ground." He drinks some of his iced tea. "They knew that down the line other things like this might crop up and they didn't want to deplete their ammunition on what they said was an iffy case. It wasn't iffy—it was solid." He puts his glass down. "But they shut my operation down."

"National security."

He nods. "A big rug. Lots of dirt gets swept under it." He fixes his gaze on me. "And there was money involved. Big money."

"Are you saying Roach bought his way out of the indictment?"

"He could've, but I doubt it was that blatant. Campaign contributions, insider information about deals he was making; it amounts to the same thing. You see it all the time—someone leaves his position in the government, a short time later he has a cushy job with a company he was regulating. The pot of gold on the other side of the revolving door."

I look out the window at the tomato plants ripening in the sun. This is much more complicated than I ever imagined. What the hell am I doing pursuing this, sitting here in this old man's living room, dredging up the ancient past?

Because I'm too stubborn and stupid and reckless not to. "Do you have any material about this I could look at?" I ask.

He's thrown by the question. "I told you, it was classified."

"I thought maybe you held on to some things, for your own records."

"In case I write my memoirs someday? The frustrations of a spoke in the wheel?" he says self-deprecatingly.

"You were a federal prosecutor. That's an important position."

"It secured me a decent pension, that's all it was. We're all fodder, son. We oil the machine, and then we let it eat us."

"So you don't have anything."

He shakes his head. "They cleaned out my files. The FBI, the CIA. This was before the computer era, remember, when you couldn't copy the world onto a floppy disk. They took everything that was in my office."

I close my notebook. "I guess that's it, then."

"I wish I had it to give to you. I'm sorry."

"Don't be," I tell him. "I shouldn't be looking into any of this. I should leave James Roach alone, and let him leave me alone."

He looks at me, startled. "Do you know James Roach?"

"I've met him," I admit abashedly. "He's a neighbor of my mother's. I went sailing with him once."

"So this is personal."

"He didn't screw me over, if that's what you mean. We get along all right. He's an important, interesting guy. I'd like to know more about him."

Simmons puts his glass down, looks down at his old dog, lying at his feet. "I knew you had some kind of agenda. You lied to me over the phone, son. Not nice to do to an old man, although I knew there was something up your sleeve."

"You've caught me," I admit. "Although technically, I didn't lie to you. You asked me if I was a reporter or a cop. I'm neither."

"Private eye?"

"None of the above."

He looks at his dog, curled around his feet. "Are you trying to bring Roach down?"

"I'm not trying to—"

He interrupts me. "I shouldn't have asked that. I don't want to know." He looks at me again. "I wish someone would, though. That case ruined my career. I never got a good one after that, I wasn't a team player. I had to take early retirement. More important, though, was the shameful miscarriage of justice. Things like that should never be allowed to happen."

The interview is over. Simmons walks me to the front door. I opened some old wounds in him today, which I regret. His final days, like my mother's, should be without stress.

We stand in his doorway. "I wish someone would go after that bastard," Simmons says wistfully, blinking against the afternoon sun. "To think that he's with the State Department today—talk about inviting the fox into the henhouse!"

"Doesn't help you keep faith with the process, does it?"

"The ends justify the means," he says with sad anger. "They always have, and they always will."

I call Maureen's motel on my way home. She isn't in. I leave a message that I'll be back at my place before nine.

She's waiting for me when I drive up. "Did everything go okay?" she asks as soon as I get out of my car.

"Could've been better." I don't elaborate, she doesn't push.

We sit in the battered wooden deck chairs on my back porch and watch the last rays die into the water. Cold bottles of long-necked Budweisers help ward off the heat. She sheds her fancy boots and socks, props her long bare red-toenailed feet in my lap. Just like Johanna did. I feel guilty about that for a moment, but it passes. Johanna was a transitory encounter that was over before anything got started, as almost all encounters between men and women are. This is much deeper. I haven't felt like this since Marnie. It's a scary feeling. Wonderful, too.

I drink from my bottle. Past her, in my line of vision, I see phosphorescence on the water from the early moonlight. It feels dreamy, but there's nothing dreamlike about what's going on in my life—it's all too real.

"I'm going to tell you about some of what's been going on," I say, once we're comfortable. "I can't keep you in the dark any longer. It isn't fair to you, and I need to confide in someone." I pause. "I want to confide in you."

She runs a bare foot along my leg. "I'm glad." She pauses, drinks from her own bottle. "You're safe with telling me anything, Fritz," she tells me seriously. "I want you to know that, up front."

I look at her and think, how much should I tell you? That I saw a man murdered on Roach's property? That the victim was an important diplomat? That his body was found a week later a hundred miles from here, deliberately planted there to draw any possible suspicion away from Roach? That I have pictures of the killing?

The answer, for now, is none of the above. She wouldn't be able to handle any of that. She'd want me to run to the cops as fast as I could, and if I didn't, she would. For my protection, of course; but protecting me isn't her job. I can take care of myself. And if it turns out I can't, I'll live with the consequences. Under these circumstances, though, it is my place to protect her; she's the one in the dark. She has no connection to this, except through me.

"I think my new neighbor is dirty," I begin.

"Dirty as in criminal?" she asks.

"Yes."

She takes my bold declaration with more equanimity than I would have expected. "After what I've seen, I can believe that. What do you actually know?"

I have to be careful the way I craft this. The truth, and nothing but the truth. But not the whole truth.

"Why did he buy his place out here?" I ask rhetorically, momentarily skirting her question. "This isn't where people with money are buying. They're buying on Solomons Island, or St. Michaels, or other places closer in to Washington and Baltimore. We're still nowhere out here. We're too far gone for weekenders."

"Maybe he likes the privacy, the same as you," she responds reasonably.

"Then why is he flying people in and out of here like the Delta shuttle, if he wants privacy? We don't know who those people were that we saw, but he could have met with them somewhere else, couldn't he? Unless he didn't want anyone to know they were meeting."

She nods, slowly. "That makes sense. What do you really know about Roach, besides his job description?"

I give her my first concrete fact. "He almost went to jail once, for illegal arms dealings."

That shakes her up. "Where did you find that out?"

"I've been doing research. Most of it's in the public records. You have to go back a couple of decades, but it's there."

"What happened? Was he convicted, or—"

"No." I shake my head impatiently—now that I've started telling her this my anger toward Roach is in my throat again, a poisonous bile I have to exorcise. "The case never went to trial, so technically he's never done anything wrong. The official line—ha, ha, big fucking joke—was that a public trial would compromise national security issues, so the government was forced to drop it. The same bullshit they always use. But the lawyers in the Justice Department who were prosecuting the case, who once in a blue moon actually gave a shit more for the truth than politics as usual, were sure he would be found guilty. They also felt that using national security was a chickenshit excuse for covering up other crimes by other big players." I sag. "They fought like sons of bitches to keep the case going, but they were overruled. The files were sealed and the whole episode was buried."

She looks at me warily. "How do you know all this if the case was sealed?"

"I . . ." Be careful here. I can't bring Simmons into this. "I met a newspaper reporter who covered the story," I lie. "He filled in the blanks. The stuff that isn't in the public record."

"When did you meet him?"

"A while ago."

"Before we met?"

"Around then," I answer elusively. I'm beating myself up inside for having opened this can of worms.

She ponders what I've told her. "Do you think Roach is still selling weapons illegally?" she conjectures, savoring the possibility of scandal. "Fritz, I know you have bad feelings for him, but think about it. He's an assistant secretary of state. If what you're saying is true, this would be a scandal that could bring down an entire administration. Why would someone in his position be that reckless? It sounds crazy."

"Like Willie Sutton put it so well, for the money. We're talking hundreds of millions of dollars potentially, Maureen. Billions. People have done crazier things for that kind of money. And who better than a man in Roach's position to pull something like this off? He's the ultimate insider."

She shakes her head doggedly. "Roach doesn't strike me as being reckless. Just the opposite, I think of him as being supercool and guarded. I've only met him the one time," she admits, "but I'm a good judge of character on first impression."

"He's trained himself to look sincere, even while he's picking your pocket. Do you remember Spiro Agnew?" I ask. "Nixon's first vice president?"

"Vaguely. I was nine years old when Nixon resigned."

"I wasn't much older, but we all followed it around here, because Agnew had been governor of Maryland. He was well thought of, even my father voted for him for governor, and he never voted Republican. Well, it turned out Agnew was taking bribes in the White House. He'd been a bagman for years, from when he was a two-bit local pol in the state here, all the way up to being a heartbeat away from the presidency. If he'd been smoother about it he would've become president when Nixon resigned, instead of Ford. So believe me, Roach could be dealing under the table. Anyone in his position could."

She shudders. "God. That's so scary to think."

"Yes, it is."

"What else do you know about Roach?"

"Nothing else concrete—yet. But I'm going to try to find out if there's more."

She slams her beer bottle down on the floor. "Oh, Fritz!" She gets up. "Have you gone totally brain-dead? If James Roach is involved in any criminal activities he's not going to let anyone get in his way, certainly not someone like you. You don't need to be a college professor to figure that out."

"I'm not a college professor anymore," I remind her. "And he doesn't know," I say, trying to reassure her. "I've been careful to cover my tracks."

She grabs a handful of my hair, jerks my head around. "How long do you plan to pursue this cockamamie scheme?"

"For as long as it takes to find out."

"Find out *what?*" she almost screams.

That's a good question. "I don't know. Whatever it is."

She lets go of me. "Oh, Fritz, Fritz, Fritz. What in the world is wrong with you? Do you think Roach won't ever find out you're sniffing his trail?"

"I don't—"

"Of course he will! He's a professional, Fritz, it's what he's done all his life. You're a college professor. A sweet man I've started to fall for, who's an amateur. Please, Fritz. Whatever you're doing, don't do it anymore."

She's started to fall for me. She said it.

"Fritz. I'm scared for you. Please—if there are things going on that could hurt you, please tell me. I want to . . ."

I wait. "Want to what?"

She takes a deep breath. "To be in this with you."

I shake my head. "That's not where we are." I look away from her, out across the water, now blank, in darkness.

"It's not where we've *been,* that's right." She takes my face, pulls it to meet hers. Oh, those emerald eyes. "But it's where we are now. Admit it to yourself, Fritz. I have. And it's been hard, because I know there are so many impediments between us. But I can't help what I feel."

My guts are tied up in knots. "I'm falling for you, too, Maureen." I moan. "Shit, who am I kidding? You blew me away the first time I saw you sitting on my porch. But this could turn out to be a dangerous situation. I can't involve you in anything where you could get hurt."

Her eyes light up. "Have you been lying to me, Fritz? How much danger could you get into? How much are you already in?"

I backstroke rapidly. "I'm not in any danger. But you never know what can happen. I'm not planning on getting into any dangerous situations, believe me."

I sound like an ass. I am an ass. This incredible woman, this object of my desire since the first time I saw her, is throwing herself, literally throwing herself, at me, and I'm fucking it up. "Shit happens sometimes, that's all I'm saying."

"I know that. I've been there." She won't stop pushing. Maybe she can't—what a terrific and frightening thought. "But if shit does happen, I want to be there to wipe it off your face." She kisses me. "I'm growing accustomed to this face."

It 's nothing like making love with Whitney, which was pure libido with no emotion, and it isn't like making love with Johanna, which was emotion coupled with clandestine teenage-style recklessness, we were doing it under our parents' noses, so to speak, nor is it like making love with Dakota Chalmers, two adult friends fulfilling each other's carnal needs on a practical level. It's closer to the way it was with Marnie, except Maureen isn't married, so we have the potential of having a future together, which Marnie and I never could. (If I'd realized that back then my life would be completely different. But you can't change your past, and at this moment, I don't want to.) Of course this is brand-new and may come to nothing, but the possibilities are whatever we allow them to be.

And man, does that scare the hell out of me.

Maureen's sleeping. I can't. Taking care not to wake her, I get out of bed, pad silently into the other room, unlock my cabinet, and take out the pictures I shot of Roach, Wallace, and the others, on Roach's runway. There's a link in these shots to something else—what is it? Is it the other men? Who are they, and what is their tie-in to Roach? Are they diplomats? Gunrunners? Legit or not? Whoever and whatever they are, they don't want anyone to know that they're getting together with Roach; and vice versa, maybe more so: Roach must have compelling reasons for not being seen with these men openly. Otherwise, they wouldn't be meeting clandestinely. Whatever this is, it has a bad aroma to it.

What else? The other pilot besides Wallace, the one who flew these men in? Have I ever seen this man before?

Leaving the incriminating pictures in the cabinet, I tiptoe into my bedroom. I don't want to wake Maureen. I know she wants me to trust her with everything and I wish I could, but I can't get her involved in this. Her reason for being here is to study birds, not to stick her neck out because of my dumb tenacity, with the possibility of having it whacked off.

She's sound asleep. Adorable little bubbles are forming at the edge of her mouth as she breathes in and out. Stealthily, I open the door to my closet and find the shoes I'd stashed the original transparencies in, the ones I took of the actual murder.

I peek at her again. Not an inch of movement; she's a sound sleeper. I creep back to the other room and look at the transparencies alongside the pictures of the second encounter, the one with Roach and Wallace and the mysterious visitors. Picking up a magnifying glass, I carefully study the face of the pilot who flew the second plane in.

He doesn't look familiar.

I turn back to the original transparencies, concentrating not on the victim or his killer, but on the third man—the pilot.

And there it is. This is a textbook case of not seeing the forest for the trees.

The airplane pilot I'm looking at in the set of transparencies is the same one I'm looking at in the prints. But he isn't the pilot who flew in Roach's guests. He's the pilot who flew Roach in.

Wade Wallace is the third man in my originals—the pilot who was there when the Russian counselor was shot to death, who then got into the plane with the killer and the victim and flew both of them away.

I don't even try to go back to sleep. I sit outside on the porch, waiting for the sun to come up. It takes a long time, too long.

"Hey."

I look inside, to my bedroom. Maureen's up, reclining on her side, looking at me through the mesh.

"What're you doing up so early?"

"Couldn't sleep."

"I can understand." She pats the empty space in the bed. I go in and lie down next to her. She smiles, kisses me. I nuzzle her breasts, stroke her stomach, kiss her neck. She tastes salty.

We make love slowly, tenderly; it builds on the special feeling from last night that both of us want to hold on to. We don't talk about the new place we've gone to; it's too raw, too scary—the implications for the future.

She's going to Boston for a few days—work. She'd put it off if she could, but people are depending on her. "I'll try to call tonight," she assures me. "What are you going to do with yourself? Stay out of trouble, I hope."

"I'll do my best," I vow, stoutly.

"Nothing stupid." She has a worried look on her face, as if she doesn't trust me to keep my word. "You promised."

"A promise is a promise."

"See that you keep it," she orders me sternly. "And stay away from Roach and Wallace."

I give her a parting kiss. "I will have nothing to do with either of them."

"This is going to sound like lovesick teenager crap, but you're the first man I've ever fallen in love with, I mean really deep down, Fritz."

"Maureen . . ." Jesus, how do you respond to that? I thought I'd gone off the deep end with Marnie, but that was nothing compared to the emotions I'm feeling at this moment.

"I don't want to lose you, Fritz. Promise me I won't."

"You won't lose me. I promise."

It's Fritz Tullis. I'd like to speak to Buster. Is he in yet?"

"He's not available at present, Mr. Tullis," comes back the crisp reply. Buster's secretary, Enid, is at least twenty years older than he, and she tends to mother-hen him. One of her ploys in that regard is to call everyone over twenty-one, except office staff, by his or her last name—it holds them at arm's length, so they can't wheedle favors from her, such as talking to her boss when he doesn't want to be disturbed, and provides cover for him when he's late coming to work, or is otherwise indisposed. "Shall I tell him you called?"

I can picture her pen poised over Buster's message list. "Yeah, please. As soon as possible, if you can," I say, trying to keep the anxiety from my voice. I glance at the clock over the stove. Almost ten—I'd thought he'd be in by now, his phone machine picked up when I called him at home, over an hour ago. "How long before he'll be in?" I ask as politely and casually as I can.

He and I need to talk, pronto. It's one thing to keep your mouth shut about a so-called hypothetical murder when it's an abstraction to you. But now that I know that James Roach's security chief, a loose cannon, as Maureen said, if there ever was one, was directly involved in that diplomat's murder, it's time for the bullshit to stop. Somebody in authority has to be told. I want Buster to hand-hold me through the process, because I know it's going to be gnarly, given that I've been sitting on important evidence for weeks.

"The day after tomorrow," she tells me.

"What?" I blurt out.

"Mr. O'Reilly is on a corporate retreat in Santa Fe, New Mexico," she explains. "He won't be back in the office until the day after tomorrow," she repeats. "He's asked that I hold all messages until he returns, unless it's an emergency. This isn't an emergency, is it?"

She thinks of me as Buster's main party-animal friend, not someone who might have serious business. Better I keep it that way.

"No," I answer. "Just let him know that I called, and need to talk to him. In person," I add. I hang up.

This is a bitch. I need to talk to Buster, and I don't want to do it over the phone—I'm paranoid about phones being tapped, especially cell phones, which would be how he would call me from wherever he's holing up. I'm going to have to keep my head down until then, out of the line of fire.

Since Buster's unavailable, I boot up my computer and begin delving into Wade Wallace's record. It doesn't take me long to find out that his background is what I'd feared it would be. He's a licensed commercial pilot with a jet airplane rating, for over twenty years he was a covert operative in the CIA, from before the Iran hostage crisis until less than two years ago, when he resigned and started his private security firm, specializing in clients in the government who need additional private security. People like James Roach.

I'm certain about one thing now: James Roach did not meet Wade Wallace recently, as he'd told me that day I first met Wallace, on the yacht. They've had to have known each other before then, their world is too interconnected.

Turning off my computer, I make a decision, one I'd never have thought I'd make. I hope my father will forgive me, from the grave.

Late in the afternoon, shortly before the end of the business day, I drive to Jamestown and enter a gun shop that's owned by Billy Higgins, an acquaintance of mine from my dissolute youth. I check it out before I go inside, to make sure no one's there, except him.

Billy's sitting on a stool behind his display cases, feet up on the counter, engrossed in a stroke magazine. He's fat as a sow now, his Harley lowrider has extra-strong shocks and struts. His temper is as hair-trigger as the action on some of the guns he sells.

"Hey, back there!" I call out. "You running a bid'ness or spanking your monkey?"

He whirls, about to jump the counter and engage me in mortal combat, when he stops in his tracks as he recognizes me.

"Jesus H. Christ!" he exclaims as he recognizes me. "What the hell're you doing in here, man?"

"You got any guns for sale?" I eye the weapons behind the locked glass counters and the racks that line the walls. George Washington could have outfitted the Continental Army out of this store.

"The hard-core gun-hater is gonna buy one?" Billy says incredulously. "Armageddon must surely be upon us."

"That's about right. I have finally seen the light, Billy."

"What brought you to this sorry state of affairs?"

"There are bad people who are out to get me," I say darkly. "Who only respect the business end of a .45."

"Spoken like Liberty Valance," he crows. "But you don't want a .45, son. That's old-school. A nine millimeter'll do you just fine." He opens his arms to the merchandise below him. "You got a price range?"

"How much is a good one?"

"I can outfit you like a white man for six to eight hundred dollars, or a nigger for two hundred. Your choice."

I wince inwardly at the crude racism, which is still common around here, but I don't show it, like I normally would. When in Rome . . . I'm here for a reason, not a crusade.

"What color do I look like to you, Billy?"

"The right color," he chortles, smiling broadly. I can imagine him tonight at Dargin's, the local white-trash watering hole, regaling everyone with the tale of how Fritz Tullis, the resolute gun-hater, finally changed his tune and saw the light. "Let me show you some selections," he says, unlocking the top case. "All premium quality, guaranteed to blow away any man, woman, or child who pisses you off."

He takes out three automatics, lays them on the counter in front of me.

"What's the difference, besides price?"

"Whatever feels good in your hand."

I pick up each gun in turn. A chill wind blows through me as I heft them. This is a true turning point for me. I've always been down on guns. They kill people, that's their purpose. Which is why I'm going to buy one today.

"I think I like the feel of this one," I say, handing one over.

"Sig Sauer. Priciest, but an excellent choice. More movie stars carry this weapon than any other, did you know that?"

"I didn't, as a matter of fact, but I'll take your word for it. Can I take it with me?"

He shakes his head. "There's a seven-day waiting period while your application's being processed." He pauses. "You need it right away?"

"I hope not. But you never know."

He thinks a minute. "You don't have a record, do you? No murders, arsons, rapes, any of that tawdry shit?"

"None they can trace back to me."

He walks to the front of the store, locks it, turns the sign on the door from OPEN to CLOSED, comes back to me. "I'm gonna let you take it now," he says quietly, as if we're being eavesdropped on, "then I'll adjust the purchase order date once you clear officially."

I wonder how many times he's done this before. I'm sure I'm not the first customer he's made this exception for, and I'm also sure he isn't the only licensed dealer who does this.

"Thanks, Billy. 'Preciate it."

He puts the gun into a spiffy leather case. "Case is on me, since you're my ol' pard. You need ammo?"

I buy two boxes of shells—full-metal jackets for target practice, hollow-points for the real deal. Billy tells me they'll stop a bull moose. That's what I want, maximum stopping power.

"Kill a commie for mommy," he advises me as I count out the money. I'm paying cash—less paperwork to get me into trouble with.

"Ain't no commies left, Billy," I tell him. "Cold War's over."

"Two billion Chinese beg to differ. Anyway, the real threat's within. Always has been, always will be," he says, spoken like a true believer.

"Pray for Charlton Heston," I tell him as I'm walking out the door.

"I pray for all sinners," he replies. "But you've gotta back up your prayers from the end of a gun barrel sometimes."

"The meek shall inherit the earth, Billy."

"Not while I'm still on it."

I sit in my house and load my new purchase with full-metal jackets. Then I stuff cotton in my ears, walk outside, set some empty beer bottles on a level piece of ground, pace off thirty steps, and start firing away.

I don't hit any bottles, but I bring up large clouds of dust, some close to the targets. Reloading, I cut the distance in half and try again. This time I hit two out of the six. Good enough for what I need—I'm not going to be using this thing unless I can see the whites of their eyes.

Back in the house, hefting the lethal weapon in my hand, I think about what I've done today, and the anger I feel at myself, that I've been sublimating, finally rises to the surface, a bilious gorge in my mouth.

What the hell am I doing owning a gun? How have I come to this state? I hate guns and everything they stand for. I've turned my core values on their head. For what?

I had a hole in my life, and something came along that filled it—the pursuit of justice. So I thought, and still do, on a righteously indignant level. Murder shouldn't be allowed to go unpunished. But I'm not the one who should be administering the punishment. If I take that responsibility myself, how much better am I than those I'm judging? And if I am afraid of retaliation, why am I not backing off?

Maureen calls after ten. She's in Cambridge, if I need to talk to her I have her cell phone number.

"I miss you," I tell her.

"Me, too." She pauses. "Darling."

That washes through me like an electric current, hearing her use that word. We're serious. We're partway to being a couple. Maybe more than partway.

"When're you coming home?" I ask her. Not "going" home, as to Boston, where she is, but "coming," as to my little abode.

"Day after tomorrow, I hope. I have some loose ends to tie up here. As soon as I can," she promises.

Loose ends? I tense. I'd assumed the friend she was seeing was a woman. But maybe it's a man. An old beau; or a current one, more likely? Will she be in bed with him after we hang up, or will she tell him it's over, she's met the man she's going to be spending the rest of her life with. Or neither, it really is a woman friend she's with.

Don't ask, don't tell. I'll find out, soon enough. If this is only a dream, I don't want to wake up yet.

But she did call me "darling," and she did say she was coming back.

"What have you been doing today?" she asks. "You haven't done anything reckless, have you?"

I bought a gun. That qualifies as reckless in my book. But I don't tell her that, it would scare the hell out of her.

"You need to be careful, Fritz," she cautions me yet again. "Being away makes me realize how defenseless you are out there."

I've thought the same thing. That's why I bought the gun.

"I'll be okay," I say, trying to reassure her—and myself. "I'll be watchful."

"I feel like coming back right now. I could be there tonight."

Wouldn't that be lovely? But it would be selfish, too.

"There's no reason to. I'll be all right."

"If you promise me to be careful. I really do have unfinished business here, some administrative problems that're too boring to talk about."

So it isn't a man. I feel a weight lifting off my shoulders.

"I'll be careful. I promise."

"No more Wallace, or Roach, or anything about this? Can you let it go, Fritz? Can you?"

Maureen's caution about my vulnerability gets my paranoia up and running. I decide to set up a warning system on my dirt road, which is the only passageway in here (except via the creek in back, which is virtually unnavigable if you haven't done it countless times). I can't imagine Wallace trying to ambush me that way, he's so uncomfortable on the water.

I call my mother, make some feeble small talk, ensure that she isn't planning on surprising me later tonight with a spontaneous, unexpected visit. She's done that a couple of times, although never after dark; like most older people she doesn't see that well at night, she doesn't like to drive or venture out past her home boundaries.

After she scolds me for not paying enough attention to her and gets my promise that I'll come to dinner soon and bring my delightful new girlfriend, I go outside to my perimeter and crudely booby-trap my entrance. My road, like many in this area, is covered with crushed oyster shells. I sprinkle some M-80s and other firecrackers that I brought with me from Texas (in case I wanted to celebrate a future Fourth of July the old-fashioned way) on top of the shells. If anything comes down the lane, driving or even walking, the pressure from their tire or boot will set off the explosives. It will also scare the shit out of whoever's trying to violate my space. I know this for a fact, because I've done it before, as a prank. If it happens now it'll be for real.

The question, of course, is what will I do if someone comes calling? I don't have an answer. I have a gun and bullets, but I can't see myself using them on a nighttime invader. Still, I make sure my new weapon of destruction is loaded and ready by my bedside.

No one pays me a visit, but I don't sleep a lick anyway. At first light I drag myself out of bed, where I've been lying rigidly, and clear my road of the firecrackers. Then I go back inside and give some serious thought to how I'm going to resolve this mess I've gotten myself into.

Being alone with my birds is the most therapeutic activity I do. I can admire their beauty, their uniqueness, their total birdness. Unlike humans, who have to think to be human, they merely have to be. So that's where I go. I sit on the ground and watch them from a careful distance, marveling about how easy life would be if I could only let that happen. I don't keep track of time, I go by feel—when it gets too hot in the sun to be comfortable I go back to my house, catching a glimpse of Roach's property from the river. Nothing's happening there, at least nothing I can see.

Back inside my shack, I have a red one for medicinal purposes, followed by a strong cup of coffee. My thinking lamp is lit about Wallace. He's the immediate imperative for me now, until I can get with Buster—his role in all this, and his true relationship to Roach. As I'm trying to figure out how to start that exploration, the telephone rings.

"Fritz Tullis?" A woman's voice. Deep, commanding. Not a voice I know.

"Who's calling?" I ask distrustfully. I'm distrustful of everything now, particularly voices I don't know.

"Are you Mr. Tullis?" The caller sounds impatient, aggravated.

"Yes, this is Fritz Tullis." I'm testy, I don't need attitude from a stranger over the phone, I have enough crap I'm already dealing with. "Who are you?"

She answers in a tone that is not friendly. "This is Lieutenant Mabel Ricketts, Prince Georges County police department."

I freeze. What the hell do the Prince Georges police want with me?

"Mr. Tullis?"

"Yes, I'm here. What can I do for you, Lieutenant?"

"We'd like to talk to you, Mr. Tullis."

"What about?" I ask suspiciously.

"We'll discuss that when you get here," she says firmly.

"Where is *here?*"

"Our main station, in Palmer Park. Are you familiar with the area?"

"More or less. But I want to know what you want to talk to me about, and why I have to come up there."

I can hear her annoyed sigh hum over the wire. "Look, Mr. Tullis. We have a situation here. You may be able to help us. Now you can come up here voluntarily or I can get a warrant and have a sheriff come down to where you are and pick you up. I've already got the warrant made up, and the judge is across the street waiting to sign it, so it's no skin off my nose. Your decision."

Jesus, I think, what the hell is going on? "That's not much of a choice," I complain.

"It's the only one you have," she replies immovably.

"Okay." This is fucked. "I'll come up there. Let me check my calendar."

"We'd like to interview you as soon as possible, Mr. Tullis. In other words, now."

Ricketts's directions in hand, I head up Highway 5. My mood is foul, and it isn't improved when I run into a roadblock in

Charles County that's caused by an eighteen-wheeler which has jackknifed across all the northbound lanes on the highway, stopping traffic dead in its tracks. I sit in my car with hundreds of other frustrated drivers, muttering to myself.

The truck is finally cleared to the side of the highway and the traffic inches by. Then it's pedal to the metal, changing from Highway 5 to U.S. 301, then again to Highway 202, the main drag into Palmer Park, one eye on the road while the other checks the rearview mirror for cops—there's a notorious speed trap around the Upper Marlboro area. But I make it without seeing a single cop. It must be my lucky day.

I'm almost an hour late. I'd thought about calling Ricketts from the road and explaining the delay, but then I decided, to hell with it. I'm the one being inconvenienced, for reasons she won't divulge. I'm coming here under duress. Let them cool their heels. What're they going to do, throw me in jail for not having a tardy slip from my mother?

The station is a fairly new light-brick building, one story, with several flags—county, state, U.S.—flying in front. I park and go inside, clear through the security gate, and announce myself to the duty sergeant at the front desk. A moment later a stocky, middle-aged black woman in civilian attire, an ID badge clipped to her waist, comes out to meet me.

"Mr. Tullis?" She squints at me. A cop's look, suspicious of everything and everybody. I should start to cultivate such a look. She doesn't ask why I'm late, it's trivial to her, I guess. I'm here, that's what counts.

I nod. I'm going to play this cool.

"Mabel Ricketts." She offers her hand. I shake it. It's calloused, and her grip is firm. She must chop trees down for recreation. "Come with me, please."

She leads me through a set of double doors, into the station proper. I follow her down a hallway, entering a door that reads CRIMINAL INVESTIGATIONS. The room is a regulation detective shop, the kind you see on every cop show on television—a bullpen area with desks facing each other, and small cubicles on the sides of the room for the brass. Ricketts qualifies as brass—she has her own eight-by-eight office, separated from the chaff by an opaque glass wall that extends halfway up to the acoustic tile ceiling.

Ricketts sits at her desk, motions to me to have the chair opposite her. She takes a notebook from a desk drawer and asks me for ID. I show her my driver's license. She jots down the information.

"Do you know this man?" She reaches across the desk and hands me a picture. It's a facsimile of a driver's license. I look at it, grimace, hand it back.

"Yes."

"For the record—do you know his name?"

"His name is Wade Wallace," I say stiffly.

"Was," she corrects me.

"Was?" This doesn't sound good.

She nods. "Mr. Wallace is deceased. He was killed," she specifies. Her tone of voice is even—all in a day's work.

Not to me, though. I sit back in my chair. "When? Where?"

"Sometime late last night or this morning. In his house," she adds, answering the second part of my question. "His watch was missing, ditto his wallet. Some other personal items. We don't know everything yet, what was taken."

"It was a robbery?" My gut reaction is that I find that hard to believe.

"Until we have evidence to the contrary, that's how we're labeling it."

I'm in shock. "You wouldn't think that could happen to someone like Wallace," I say. "Given his training and background."

"No," she agrees. "You wouldn't." She obviously knows Wallace's history. Shifting gears she asks, "Do you know where Wallace lived, Mr. Tullis?"

"No." I shake my head. "I know where he worked, but I don't know if he lived there."

"For James Roach," she says, keeping a tight watch on me. "Who he worked for. The assistant secretary of state."

I nod. "Yes."

She picks up a file, opens it, glances at the top sheet. "Wallace lived in Bowie, in this county, which is why the case is in our jurisdiction." She puts the file aside. "Tell me what you know about the deceased."

Is she trying to set me up? I don't know. I'll tell her the truth—that's all I can do. "He handled security for James Roach."

"And you know James Roach?"

"Yes, we're neighbors."

She makes a note in her notebook.

"Do you know what he used to do, before his present job?" she continues with her questioning. "The dead man, not Roach."

"I think he was in the military, in some capacity. He may have worked for the CIA, but I'm not sure about that. He was a creepy guy, that I can attest to." Screw the convention of not speaking ill of the dead—I'm not going to sugarcoat Wallace, just because he's been killed. He was a prick. I'm sure he pissed a lot of people off.

She grunts, a verbal shrug, briefly refers to the material in the file again. "Do you own a firearm, Mr. Tullis?"

Her question catches me off guard. "No," I answer reflexively; immediately, I know that was the wrong answer. "No, I don't."

Technically, my answer is true—I don't officially own my new Sig Sauer automatic, the paperwork hasn't cleared yet, Billy Higgins would have notified me. Still, it was the wrong answer. I hope I don't get tripped up on it. Looking across the desk at this woman, I'm afraid I might.

Too late, now. I'm going to have to brazen it out.

She stares at me for a moment, then sits back. "When was the last time you saw Mr. Wallace?" she asks.

"A few days ago. Why?"

She doesn't answer my question—she has her own agenda, and we're going to follow it.

"There was bad blood between you and Wallace, wasn't there." It's a rhetorical question.

"Yes," I say honestly. "He almost killed me, once."

"That was an accident, wasn't it?" she asks. Obviously, she's talked to others already regarding the incident on Roach's yacht.

"I guess. But if he hadn't missed me by inches, it wouldn't have mattered whether it was accidental or not, would it?"

"Did you hate him enough to want to kill him back?" she asks, ignoring my question. "Accidental or otherwise?"

"I don't hate anyone enough to want to kill them," I reply strongly. I don't like the direction this conversation is taking. "That's not me."

Another glance at the documents in front of her. "This last time you saw the deceased. That was on your mother's property, is that correct?"

"Our family's property, that's correct."

"And at that time . . ." She pauses momentarily, then gives me a strong, direct look. "At that time, did you assault Mr. Wallace and threaten him with further bodily harm?"

Oh, shit.

"According to eyewitnesses"—she glances at her notes—"you hit Mr. Wallace hard enough to draw blood, and you also told him that if you ever saw him again, there was going to be a problem. One could infer that to mean an escalation of physical violence against him," she says severely.

Fuck me. James Roach put those words in her mouth, he's the only eyewitness who was there, except Maureen, of course, who would never tell her anything like that, and would have called me if this cop, or anyone, had spoken to her. That bastard Roach.

"That was bluster, and everyone there knew it," I try to explain. "Going for him was a spontaneous thing, he goaded me into it. If there had been any more physical violence, it would have been the reverse. Him toward me."

"But you did strike him, as well as make that threat, didn't you?" She wants facts, not my self-serving opinion.

"Yes. I admit I hit him in anger and that I said those words." My body is flushing, I can feel it. "You're not thinking I had anything to do with his killing, are you?" I ask slowly.

She regards me coolly. "Where were you this morning?"

"At home."

"And last night?"

"The same."

I know what the next question will be before she asks it. "Was anyone with you? Can anyone verify you were where you say you were?"

I shake my head. "I was alone."

"Did you speak with anyone on the phone?"

I think for a moment. "What time frame?" I ask.

"Let's say from midnight until eleven this morning." She's sitting up ramrod-straight now. She must have been in the service before she took up law enforcement—she carries herself like a Marine.

"I didn't talk to anyone during those hours, or see anyone. I live by myself in a remote area, by choice. Not being with people or having to deal with them, unless it's on my terms, is how I like it."

She taps on the file. "That's not much help in this situation," she tells me frankly.

"I understand. But that's the way it is."

I didn't kill Wallace. If they think I did, let them try to prove it. But I'm still scared—I've never been in this position before, not remotely. I thought I was coming home to peace and quiet, to recuperate from my Texas meltdown. Instead, I've witnessed a murder, and have known someone who was also murdered. And I'm right in the middle of all of it.

I can't let this hang in the air. "Am I a suspect?"

"Should you be?"

"No."

"Then why'd you ask?"

"Because of the questions you've been asking me."

"Okay. To answer your question—not at the moment," she says flatly.

Not at the moment?

"So let me get this straight, one more time," she bores in. "You don't own a firearm. No rifle, shotgun, handgun, not a .22 for shooting targets, nothing."

"That is correct," I say stiffly. I'm in the shit now, I have to keep paddling as hard and as fast as I can and hope I reach land before I sink in it.

"Good," she says. "I needed to get that out of the way, for the record. If we check up on you there won't be any gun registered to you, that's your truthful statement?"

"Yes. I mean, no. There's no gun registered to me. But I'm thinking of getting one," I add. I need cover, in case she checks up on me later.

"Do you think you need one?" she asks.

"I hope not. It's my business, if I decide to buy one."

"Yes," she says. "It certainly is."

Abruptly, her body language changes. She's more relaxed. "You're not a suspect at present, Mr. Tullis. If you were, I would have Mirandized you already."

"That's good news," I say sarcastically. "Then what did you haul me up here for?" I ask.

"We're talking to everyone who knew or saw Wade Wallace recently, and might have had a grudge against him," she explains. "There are no witnesses to his murder, so we have to start somewhere. It's easier and more efficient for me if I don't have to run all over hither and yon interviewing people."

"That's going to be a long list," I tell her. "Have you talked to James Roach yet?" I ask, knowing the answer.

Ricketts stiffens. "That's being handled through other channels. For your information, Mr. Roach has an alibi. Ironclad. So we know it wasn't him. Not that he would have any reason to kill his own security chief," she adds.

Her reaction tells me she's out of the loop as far as Roach is concerned. Roach is a power, he'll be handled with kid gloves, and he'll never be treated as I'm being now—if he was questioned, and it sounds like he was, it was where he determined it should be, and when. And any tough questions thrown his way will be about his speculations regarding motive, and whether or not he, Roach, is also in danger. The way I thought, when all this first started with the Russian diplomat's murder.

Given all that, Ricketts still wouldn't like being cut out—a woman, black, who's worked her way up through the ranks. It's an unfair world. I'm sure she knows that better than I do.

I wonder about the kid. Joe. Wallace almost killed him, too. Maybe there was bad blood between them that I don't know about. I hope not—he's a good kid, and Wallace was a stone-cold prick.

She stands up. "You're free to go, Mr. Tullis. If you're going anywhere, though, let us know where and when."

I get up also. "Tell me the truth, Lieutenant Ricketts. Am I under suspicion?"

She looks at me squarely. "Not at the moment. But I can't rule anything out in the future."

The gun is out and loaded, with hollow points. If I fire it tonight—an unimaginable thought a week ago—it won't be at an empty can or bottle. It sits on the kitchen table, within easy reach, next to the bottle of Wild Turkey. I've only had a few belts. I can't be dull tonight.

Eleven o'clock. I turn the news on. The shooting is the fifth item, after a school board story and some other junk. Even the jackknifed truck gets bigger airplay. The cops are getting away with downplaying this for the moment, but I imagine that as soon as Wallace's background comes out, as well as his association with Roach, shit will fly.

Detective Ricketts is interviewed briefly on camera. A neighbor found the body. She speaks calmly, dispassionately. The neighbor's name is being withheld for privacy reasons. The deceased's wallet, watch, and jewelry are missing, as well as some electronic equipment—personal computer, etc.—which indicates the shooting happened in the course of a burglary. The police think the victim came home while the burglary was in progress and was shot by the perpetrator.

The station cuts to a commercial, which will be followed by the weather. I turn the set off.

I need to talk to someone about this. The logical person is my lawyer. I pick up the phone and dial Buster's home number. He won't be back from his retreat yet, but I'll leave a message that I need to see him, that it's urgent. He'll figure out what I mean, there's nothing else urgent between us.

To my surprise, he picks up on the second ring. "Hello?" He sounds distracted. Maybe he's jet-lagged. I wonder if he saw the story on the news.

I'm about to "Hello" him back—then I hesitate.

"Hello?" he says again, this time with agitation in his voice.

I hang up.

Calling Buster, then and now, was a careless move—I was reacting instead of thinking things through. Buster is connected to Roach through that founding partner of his, Clements, Roach's close friend. Clements was Roach's mentor—I remember that was how Buster described their relationship. That makes their bond very personal, a surrogate father-and-son kind of thing. Forget that Buster thinks Roach is a shithead—business is like blood, it's thicker than water.

He'll do what he can to protect my ass, but he's going to cover his own first.

Damn it! I should have thought of that before I called his office the other day. I need to be super-careful about how I handle this.

This is too heavy a load to carry by myself, though. I have to talk to someone I'm comfortable confiding in. There is one other person besides Buster I think I can talk to—at this juncture, I've run out of options. I look up his phone number in the telephone book and dial it.

"Whoever you are, it's damn late to be calling," a gruff voice answers on the second ring.

"It's Fritz Tullis, Fred."

There's a pause while he orients himself. "Fritz? What's up, man? You know what time it is?"

I glance at my kitchen clock—eleven-twenty. Not so late, unless you're a farmer. "I thought you were a night owl. Don't you watch Leno?"

"Not unless the battery's dead on my remote. I'm a news, weather, and sports guy. Sometimes the Discovery Channel." He knows I'm not calling to talk about his viewing preferences. "So what's the deal, Fritz?"

"You see the news tonight? The story about the man who was killed in Bowie during a robbery of his house?"

"Yes, I saw that."

"The Prince Georges police brought me in for questioning this afternoon about it."

A harsh exhalation of breath. "Say *what?*"

"I was questioned by the police. A few hours ago."

"That's what I thought you said. Shit, man. What for? Was he a friend of yours?"

"Hardly a friend, but I knew him."

There's a pause. "What was their reason?"

"They think maybe I know who did it, or that I could have," I explain. After a moment, I add, "I think I'm a suspect."

"Oh, come on!"

"Not officially—they told me I'm not—but I think I am, in their minds. He and I have bad blood between us and they found out about it. So they invited me to discuss it with them. It wasn't a fun hour."

"No shit," he commiserates. "This is heavy, Fritz." He goes into cop mode. "Where's this really coming from? I mean, what do you think? If you do have ideas about it."

"Yeah, I do. Do you remember the last time I saw you? At dinner with your cousin, the cop from Baltimore?"

"Yeah?"

"You remember what we talked about?"

"His case? The murdered Russian diplomat?"

"Yes."

"What about it?"

"It might tie into this. I'm almost positive it does."

There's a silence, then a sharp intake of breath. "You for real?"

"Too damn real."

"Shit, man."

"I hear you. Listen, can we get together tomorrow?"

Without hesitation, he answers, "We can get together right now, if you want to."

I can't handle anything more tonight. "Tomorrow will do. Can you come down here, to my place?"

"That's on your mama's property?"

"Yeah."

"What time?"

"As early as you can make it."

"I can make it at seven. Earlier, if you want."

"No, seven's fine."

I give him directions. "Don't talk to anyone about this yet, okay? Especially your cousin."

"Okay," he promises. "See you tomorrow."

I'm about to hang up, when he speaks again. "You safe down there?"

I glance at my new Sig Sauer. It's lethal just to look at it. "Safe as I can be."

"Okay, then. You be careful."

The line clicks off. I reach over and pour two small fingers of whiskey into my glass for courage, run my hand along the side of the automatic. It isn't comforting. I shouldn't have bought the damn thing. I shouldn't have met with Simmons. I shouldn't have taken the pictures of Roach and Wallace. I shouldn't have taken the pictures of the murder. I shouldn't have been down there at all. I should have driven by the Jaguar when it was stuck in the ditch, back in Texas.

But if I hadn't done those things, at least the Jaguar-in-the-ditch part, I wouldn't have met Maureen.

The ringing of the phone almost makes me jump out of my chair. Who would be calling at this hour? "Hello?" I say cautiously.

"What'd you call me for?" Buster asks abruptly.

"I didn't call you," I respond defensively.

"Don't bullshit me, Fritz. I have caller ID. Modern technology, fella. Can't hide anymore."

Think, boy. Fast. "Fuck, that's right. I did dial your number, by mistake. When I heard it was you, I realized and hung up. Hope I didn't wake you."

"You're lying."

"What do you mean?" I don't like the bullying tone in his voice.

"You're holding something back from me, Fritz. What is it? You left a message with my secretary that you needed to talk to me as soon as I got back from Santa Fe. Well, I'm back, so talk."

I will not talk about the new developments over the phone. It will have to wait until I see him. "I'm not holding anything from you. You're my lawyer, and my friend."

He doesn't bite. "You see the news?"

I can't play dumb, not on this. "You mean Roach's security

guy? Yeah, I saw it. I'm not shedding any tears, if that's what you're asking."

"Had you seen him lately?"

"Wallace?"

"No, asshole, Louis Farrakhan. Yes, Wallace. I heard you threatened him a few days ago. Took a piece out of the bastard's hide. That took balls." He chuckles.

"Where'd you hear that?" I groan.

"Roach told my partner, who told me."

Damn! That Roach is spreading that stuff, especially to someone who he knows would pass it on to Buster, my friend, gives me a powerful pain in my gut. And it heightens my suspicions about how much I can trust Buster, when push comes to shove. Like off the side of a mountain.

"I didn't threaten him," I say heatedly. "I told Roach to keep him out of my sight, nothing more. And I barely touched the prick, it was a reflex action to him getting in my face. Which Roach knows, he cooled the situation down, and admitted it was all Wallace's doing. Hell, you know me, Buster," I assert, trying to defuse this time bomb. "I'm a lover, not a fighter."

He isn't buying any joking around tonight. "You're out of your league, Fritz, fucking around with this shit. For some reason, you're trying to get something on Roach. I don't know what, or why. But whatever it is, don't do it. I've already warned you about meddling in this man's business, it's not a game. Witness this evening. 'Cause I'm going to let you in on a secret, ol' buddy. Wallace wasn't a robbery victim. He was hit."

I play dumb. "Hit?"

"Offed. Concrete-overcoated. Rubbed out."

"You mean murdered?"

"That's the word I was looking for. Yes, Fritz, my fucked-up friend. Wallace was murdered."

"How do you know? The police said it was a robbery."

"Because," Buster replies knowingly, "men like Wallace don't get killed in robberies. If Wallace had walked in on somebody in his house, the robber would be the dead one, not Wallace. Somebody wanted to kill him. Whoever did this was no break-in artist. That's how I know."

"Well, you'd know about stuff like that better than me," I say. "You deal with the criminal element. I'm only a defrocked history professor."

"That's what I'm trying to tell you, shit-for-brains. You're stuffed full of book learning, but you don't have much street smarts. And you need them to fuck with the Roachs. So one more time, Fritz, the last time: don't. You hear me?"

I don't like this. Buster isn't calling me at midnight with half a bag on from all the free booze he drank on the plane because he's concerned for my well-being. He has some other agenda. I wish to hell I knew what it is. It can't be good, not with his connections.

"Yes, Buster." I tell him what he wants to hear. "I hear you."

"So you're going to steer clear of Roach from now on."

"That's what I just said, isn't it?"

"For real this time?" He's pressing me, hard.

"For real," I say firmly.

"So . . ." He calms down. "You want to come in and see me, that was the message. In person, not on the phone or through e-mail. How urgent is it this time? It has to be about Roach, right?"

"I've learned some new things you should know, since you're advising me," I say cautiously.

"Umm. Can it wait for a couple of days? I'm swamped right now, I'm playing catch-up."

"Sure. You tell me when." I'm okay with delaying our next meeting—it'll give me time to figure out how to deal with him.

"Two or three days. I'll call you tomorrow, when I've gotten to the office and can look at my calendar."

"Fine," I tell him.

"Ixnay on fucking with Roach," he advises me, one more time. "Until we talk, at least."

"I hear you," I tell him, annoyed at being talked down to, like he's doing. "Loud and clear."

Enough with the telephone calls. I turn off my phone. If some catastrophe happens that I should know about, too bad. I want some peace and quiet.

Quiet I'll get. The loudest sounds are the hum of my refrigerator, the chirping of the grasshoppers, and the calls from the bullfrogs.

Peace I can forget about tonight. I lie in bed, eyes wide open, the gun on the table next to me. It's almost dawn before I fall into a fitful slumber of no more than an hour. By the time my alarm goes off at six, I'm more tired than I was before I went to sleep.

I've showered, dressed, and have drunk two cups of industrial-strength coffee by the time Fred arrives. We sit at my kitchen table. I pour him a cup. He stirs in three teaspoons of sugar, along with a generous dollop of milk.

"Sounds like you're riding a tiger," Fred comments, sipping his brew. "How'd this happen, Fritz?" he asks, genuinely puzzled. "You're an intellectual. You're supposed to have your head in the clouds, not your ass in the gutter."

"Because of where I'm living, that's how." I wave a hand toward the water outside my windows. "Right place at the wrong time."

Fred looks out the window, then nods knowingly. "To a smuggler this would be valuable property. Access and privacy."

I nod.

"How does this place tie into the murder my cousin Marcus is investigating?" He leans toward me, across the table. "You ain't involved in drug-running, or anything stupid like that, are you?"

"No. I'm not involved in anything illegal. Stupid, maybe, but not criminal."

"Then where's this coming from?"

I freshen my coffee, top his off. "Let's go back to the conversation we had that night at dinner. Your cousin is working on a murder case. The body was found in some dump in Baltimore, his city. Except he doesn't think that's where the murder took place. You remember that?"

"Uh huh."

"He's right. It wasn't."

"How do you know that?"

I trust Fred, but I have to be careful. "We're off the record, right?"

"Until you say otherwise. Or tell me you've committed a crime, in which case I'd be honor-bound to report it."

"I haven't committed any crimes, so let's keep going like we're doing." Now that I've started I don't want to get bogged down and lose my courage. "Does the name James Roach ring a bell?"

He thinks a moment. "Name sounds familiar. Didn't he buy property down here a while back?"

"Almost a hundred acres. On which he's built a big house, a dock for his big boat, a runway for his own private airplane. He's a rich man, he likes his toys."

"Sounds like it," Fred says. "But what does that have to do with Marcus's case?"

"The murder happened on that property."

Fred leans back, arms clasped behind his head, staring up at the ceiling. "How do you know?"

"I can't tell you, not yet. You're going to have to trust me."

His look to me is very skeptical. Casting his eye around my abode, the decor of which is ramshackle bachelor at its best—and these days it isn't at its best—he says, "Do you still smoke weed?"

"Come on, man, what does that have to do with anything?"

"Easy there, big fella. I'm not a cop anymore, I'm not out to bust you. I'm just wondering if you've been hallucinating these days. I mean, that's a pretty wild statement you just made."

"Maybe it is. But I didn't imagine it, Fred. I know it for a fact."

"Did you see it? Did someone you know see it? What?"

I shake my head. "I'll tell you everything—when I can. I'm not ready yet. Can I keep going?"

He sits back, waiting to be convinced, expecting not to be. "Go ahead."

"The man who was killed last night?"

"Uh huh?"

"He worked for Roach. He was his security chief. Before that, he was in the CIA." I pause. "Roach, in case you didn't know it, is an assistant secretary of state."

All of a sudden Fred's not so skeptical. "Damn!"

I take a deep breath. "I believe that James Roach is involved in both those murders."

Fred whistles, a sharp intake of breath. "You know how big a stink it would be if he was?"

"Of course I do. Which is why, before I go any further down this path I'm already too far down, there are things I have to know."

"Like what?" Fred asks suspiciously.

He *should* be leery of me, I'm a loose cannon, I'm accusing someone of multiple murder. A man of power and position. And if I'm right, a supremely dangerous man. "You're not a cop anymore. You can walk a looser line than the authorities. I'm not going to ask you to do anything illegal," I assure him. "I'm asking you to help me, before I cut loose with this officially."

He sits back, taking this in. We're casual friends, but he doesn't really know me. I could be a crackpot, a conspiracy freak. "What do you want from me?" he asks warily.

"I need to find connections to Roach. I can't do it by myself, I don't have your resources."

He thinks about the gravity of what I'm telling him. "We should go to the cops with this."

"No! Not yet."

The vehemence of my response surprises him. "Why not? Two men have been killed, Fritz. My cousin's already working on one of the cases. Let me go to him with this."

I shake my head obstinately. "I'm not ready."

"What does that mean?"

"Where's the proof? My word that I know about a murder? Or two? We can't move prematurely on this. Roach is an insider. You know how that works. Look how the Kennedy family's covered their shit for generations. This breaks too soon, Roach will cover his ass ten ways to Sunday. This isn't for the police yet," I tell him insistently.

"Maybe so," he grudgingly admits.

I reach my hand across the table. "You'll help me? Just you and me?"

He hesitates for a moment, then shakes my hand. "I'm in. But listen up, Fritz. If this gets real, we go to the cops straight away. We go to Marcus."

"Of course."

"I hear you say that, but I want to make sure you know what you're in for."

"I do. Believe me, I do. My session with the cops sobered me up real good."

This is as far as we can go now. I'm not ready to show him the pictures of the murder. But I will, if we get any conclusive proof that implicates Roach. "There's one thing I'd like to find out as soon as possible."

"What's that?" He's nervous; I don't blame him.

"Your cousin said there was a piece of physical evidence that led him to conclude that the diplomat's murder wasn't a random street shooting. Ask him if that evidence has to do with the caliber of gun used in the killing."

"Okay."

"And if that is the case," I continue, "see if he can find out from the Prince Georges County police if the bullets that killed the diplomat came from the same kind of gun that killed Wallace, Roach's security man."

"I'll try. Marcus can get a ballistics report from them, see if the bullets match up, his case and this one last night. But I've got to take it careful how I ask him. I'll figure something out," he assures me pridefully. He's excited about getting involved—beats the shit out of chasing down deadbeat dads. He puts a supportive hand on my shoulder. "Men like Roach have no conscience, Fritz. If you want to nail his ass to the wall, you'd better be airtight with your evidence. And if we do find out he's dirty—know it for real?—it becomes the police's business. Marcus's business. We square on that?"

"Yes," I tell him. "We're square."

I need to get my head out of this morass. I grab my camera gear, jump into my boat, and go down to my island. The birds rustle about when I arrive, a massive cloud of feathers, beaks, talons. Do they recognize me, I wonder, do they know me as anything beyond a form with a feedbag? I don't know, I'm not versed in bird behavior. That will be something I can explore with Maureen—learning more about these magical, wonderful creatures.

Ollie won't be part of that, though. Before Maureen leaves to go back to Boston he'll be transported to some new place, for his own good. That he won't decide whether it's for his own good, but human beings will, is beside the point.

Standing apart from the others, he stares at me with his gimlet eye from a safe distance, more for me than for him. Even though I've kept my distance, I believe that he knows me. If, as Jung postulates, there is such a thing as the collective unconscious, why should that not extend to all the creatures of God's kingdom, the beasts in the field, the fish in the streams, and the birds in the sky, like Ollie? Why should it only be humans that are afforded this wonderful, ongoing participation in the universe? Don't the Hindus believe that we return in another life as someone else? So why not as animals, or birds, rather than limiting the field to humans, such a young and imperfect species.

I don't stay long. It isn't the same anymore. A secret's no longer a secret when others know about it. And there's something else, more ominous. I have a strong premonition that, like Ollie, I'm being closely observed through someone's binoculars or telescopic lens, a specimen under magnification, to be studied, analyzed, dissected. And when my watcher decides the time is right, or necessary, to be captured and taken away. Or worse.

15

The two scary-looking men are waiting for me when I tie up at my dock. They're dressed identically: muscle T-shirts, designer jeans, running shoes, intimidating mirrored sunglasses. Clones of Wallace, still warm in his grave. They're polite, but firm. "Mr. Roach wants to see you."

"That didn't take long," I mutter to myself, under my breath. I push my way past them toward my shack, my gear slung over my shoulder. I'm putting on a brave show. Not how I feel. "I'll give him a call, figure out a time," I say over my shoulder, as if what they've told me is no big deal. The same bluff I tried to run unsuccessfully on the P.G. County lady cop.

They don't buy my act any more than she did. "He'll see you now." Not he'd *like* to see you now. A simple declarative phrase: He *will.*

They drive me to Roach's estate in one of his Range Rovers. I sit in the back, alone. My escorts are in front. The windows are heavily tinted. We can see out, no one can see in.

Security at chez Roach has been beefed up since my last visit. Two armed guards man a gated entrance. The gate swings open and the guards wave us through. I feel like I'm being driven through Checkpoint Charlie into the Soviet sector of Berlin, before the fall of the Wall.

We take the cutoff that leads toward Roach's house. After a couple hundred yards we enter into a clearing, and I get my first look at it—I've seen the airfield and the dock, but not the residence itself. Staring out the car windows, I catch a glimpse of water several hundred yards away, down a sloping lawn. The runway is located on the other side of the property, over a quarter-mile away. I can see only a sliver of it, not enough to tell if there are any planes there.

The car pulls up in front and stops. One of my escorts opens my door. I get out and look around.

The house is contemporary in design. Glass all around, supported by raw foundations of concrete overlaid with quarried stone and slabs of cedar siding, juxtaposed in a long, L-shaped one-story building. The front door opens. Roach steps out. "Thank you for coming on short notice," he greets me, without a trace of irony in his voice. The way he's acting it's as if Wallace never existed, let alone that he was just killed, almost certainly murdered.

We go inside. Roach shuts the door behind us. My escorts stay outside. This is going to be between him and me. No middlemen. No witnesses.

I look around. Several paintings hang on the walls. I spot a Diebenkorn, a Miró, a couple of Hockneys. Originals, not knockoffs. The man has taste. And a fortune to express it.

"The art wasn't as pricey as you'd think," he says as he observes me staring admiringly at his collection. We're passing through an atrium-like room. The roof, at least thirty feet over our heads, is a skylight of leaded-glass panes, while the floors we're walking on are marble. To put an exclamation point on the opulence there's an irregular granite pond in the center of the space in which several large koi, some over four feet long, are swimming back and forth. There could be fifty thousand dollars' worth of fish in that pool—koi are ridiculously expensive. One entire wall—glass, curtainless—faces out toward the water. I feel like I'm in a museum rather than a private home.

"I'm a lucky collector, fortunately," Roach informs me. "When I was young I had an older friend who was an art dealer. He took me under his wing, put me on to the artists who were going to appreciate. I have a Diebenkorn that I got for under five thousand dollars, for example. Same with my Julian Schnabels and David Salles. Hockney I had to pay considerably more, of course." He laughs. "My first wife and I were eating peanut butter and jelly sandwiches so I could buy art. Fortunately, I kept most of the good paintings when we divorced. I brought a few of them out here when I built this house, but most remain in my home in Washington. If I can ever manage to live here more permanently, I'll bring more of my art. As you may have noticed, the house was built with showing art in mind."

He leads me into a small room, his study. It's furnished traditionally—a room for work, not show. Papers and books are sprawled across a slab-stone desk. The floor, an exotic wood with an intricate pattern, is covered with a beautiful Persian rug. He indicates a leather chair in front of his desk. "Make yourself comfortable," he says ironically.

You're an asshole and a bully, I think as I warily settle into the chair. Roach sits across from me, steeples his fingers, sights me across them. "I think you bear some responsibility for Wade Wallace's killing," he says bluntly.

Okay—the shoe has dropped, with a thud. He wants to get into it? I'll oblige him, I have no choice. I'm nervous about what he might do—I'd be crazy not to be—but I'm not scared shitless. And I know that the more I back down, the worse it will be.

"You told the cops in Prince Georges County that I threatened Wallace, didn't you?" I reply aggressively. "Assaulted him physically," I snort. "It feels to me like you're trying to set me up."

"I also told them that, in my opinion, you're incapable of

killing. You're not the killer type." The way he says it, it isn't a ringing compliment. "When I said you had something to do with it, I didn't mean directly." He spreads his hands on the desk. I notice that his fingernails are manicured. "Let's cut the crap and try to have an honest conversation. Can we?"

An honest conversation with James Roach. I love it.

"Wallace's killing—murder—wasn't a result of a robbery," he says.

"How do you know that?" I parry. I want to see what I can pry out of him. "Just because Wallace was a security expert doesn't mean he couldn't be robbed, the same as anyone else, does it? If he was working for you full-time he wouldn't have been at his house much. An experienced burglar would have known that, wouldn't he?" I take a beat. "Unless you were there."

He jerks—I've zinged him, and he felt it. Almost immediately, though, he regains his composure. "That's too nonsensical a fantasy for me to even comment on. Wade was a professional. A common thief, even an experienced one, couldn't have gotten the jump on him."

That's how Buster had put it, which reinforces my concerns about him. Is he feeding information about me to Roach? What did he actually say to Roach, or to Roach's friend, Clements? Did he tell them I'd shown him a picture of the diplomat's killing? Does Roach know the murder happened on his farm? If he's dirty, as I think he is, he must.

Shit. My situation is getting worse by the day, it seems. Maybe I'm being watched around the clock, not just when I'm near Roach's property. That would rip it completely. I feel like I'm a yo-yo on the end of a string. Up, down, up, down, around the world, walking the dog. I'm the dog.

"What I do is very delicate," Roach says. "Much of it is classified. Even what isn't is extremely sensitive." He leans forward. "You're fucking things up, Fritz. You may not understand that, but you are."

"You mean I'm not playing the game by your rules?"

My continuing belligerence startles him—he's not used to being contradicted or challenged. But he maintains his outward calm.

"It's like this: there are actions I have to undertake that can be misinterpreted and used the wrong way. When that happens, catastrophic consequences can occur. Witness Wallace's death."

Or the counselor on your runway. How much blood do you have on your hands? "Are you telling me that Wallace's getting killed had something to do with your position in the government? That lets me off the hook as a suspect, doesn't it?" I smile—I've trumped you, you bastard.

His face clouds. He gets up, walks around the desk, hovers over me. "That's the least of your worries," he says darkly. "You're messing around where you shouldn't be, Fritz. That's what you really need to be worried about. Do you understand?"

I go rigid. That's a direct threat.

I cannot let this man intimidate me. Or more important, let him know that he is. Of course he can scare me, he can scare the bejesus out of me, he's doing it right now. But I have to put up a strong front. "No," I tell him. "I don't understand."

"You've been spying on me."

I grip the arms on the chair. "I don't know what you're talking about."

He points out the window. "From out there, on the water. You have a clear view of my compound. You're the only person I know who does," he adds ominously.

I wince.

"You didn't think anyone's seen you? You think you can outfox me, or outwit me?" He pats me on the knee, like a kindly country doctor patting a kid before he gives him a booster shot. Then he walks to the window and looks out. "I've worked hard for what I have. I'm not going to let some dilettante fuck things up. My work, my reputation."

He isn't looking at me when he's saying that. He's looking outside, at the fulfillment of some dream. He turns to face me. "Stay away from my property," he says harshly.

"That's fine with me," I answer. "But don't tell me what I can or can't do on mine. I was here long before you, pal." My feeling of proprietorship kicks in hard. "We owned this place, in case you've forgotten."

"And now you don't," he throws in my face. "I repeat—you stay away from me. My work, the people I employ, *everything.*" He stabs me in the chest with his forefinger for emphasis. I flinch at the unexpected physical encounter. "I'm advising you as a friend of your mother's, Fritz. Don't push this any further. I went to Wallace's funeral yesterday. I don't want to have to go to any others."

The two thugs drive me back to my house, and leave. I go inside. I'm shaken. One of my worst fears has been confirmed—Roach has been spying on me. For how long? Going back to when the counselor was killed? I doubt that. Roach wasn't around, no one knew about me—but anything's possible now.

They're pros, I'm not.

So much for my promising Buster I wouldn't fuck with Roach anymore, at least until he and I had talked. Roach is fucking with me, the situation is out of my control.

I can't be here now, knowing they're out there. I need a break from this.

My mother usually likes advance warning before allowing anyone, including her children, into her sphere, but she's happy to see me anyway. I find her in the spare bedroom she's converted into an office, sitting in front of her computer, typing away. An old photo album is open on an adjoining desk, piled on top of other albums. I sneak a look at the pictures on the open page.

The pictures are from 1940, over sixty years ago, when she

was a young bride, before the war. They are of her and my father, on their honeymoon. They sailed to the Caribbean and South America—Havana, where they got drunk on champagne and gambled all night, San Juan, Caracas, Rio de Janeiro, Buenos Aires. And smaller cities, and small islands with fine white sandy beaches.

This is one of the Havana pages. Mom and dad on the steps of the casino, dressed to kill, highballs in hand. They were a striking couple, the tall dark man in a pencil mustache, looking like Howard Hughes but more handsome, and the petite blond woman who could give Myrna Loy a few tips on style. Mom in a bathing suit, standing ankle-deep in the warm ocean water. Dad on a diving board, a lit pipe in his mouth, comically posing as if he's going to dive into the pool with the pipe still in his mouth, à la Bing Crosby. Some other pictures, of them and a second couple, another doctor and his wife from Fort Worth, who are honeymooning, too. My parents corresponded with them for a few years, until the war started. Then they were too busy. Both that doctor and my father went off to war, my father in the Navy, the other in the Army. My father returned from the Pacific, where he was a ship's doctor. The Fort Worth doctor died in France. My mother tried to rekindle her correspondence with the widow, but her letters came back stamped *Return to sender. Address unknown.*

Other albums have pictures of the family. My brother, sister, and me as kids, then teenagers. My brother and Emily on their wedding day. They were married here, on the front lawn. My sister and her husband were, too. The receptions were held in the house. Hundreds of guests attended both weddings.

There are no wedding pictures of me. If my mother can paste a wedding picture of me and a bride into one of these books, she'll die a happy woman. Although she would like to live long enough to see the grandkids, too.

It could happen, with Maureen. It's premature to think about that, but it could. Hopefully, before my mother passes away.

"What're you doing, mom?" I look over her shoulder to the

screen. She's writing something. I don't want to pry, but I'm curious. It doesn't look like a letter.

She stops typing and looks up at me over her shoulder.

"My memoirs. A history of the family as seen through my eyes."

I almost gasp. "Boy, mom. That would be something."

She is the repository of our history. When she dies, there will be a huge gap. There are records, of course, in our files as well as in the county historical society's, but there are many blanks that need to be filled in.

A great tenderness wells up inside of me as I look at my mother. She's been there for me my entire life, giving me much more than I've given her. My father's been dead a long time, but she's soldiered on. She's not going to be with us much longer, though; the thought of that, the physical act of her recording her history, is both wonderful and finite in the extreme.

"Can I see some of it?"

"Not yet. But you will, soon. You can edit for me."

"Nothing would give me more pleasure, mother."

I lean down and kiss her lightly on the cheek.

"Come to dinner tonight. Bring Maureen. I'm growing fond of that girl."

"Can't, mom. I have an appointment, and Maureen's out of town. As soon as she gets back, okay?"

"Yes. Call and let me know."

I give her another kiss and leave her to her labor of love.

Fred's office is a second-story walkup over a Chinese takeout restaurant in one of Jamestown's ratty strip malls. I arrive shortly after eight. I'd called ahead and ordered shrimp with lobster sauce, chicken chow mein, egg rolls. Fred's giving me his time and expertise, gratis; the least I can do is buy dinner. We sit at his desk across from each other, eating off paper plates and drinking Kirin beer from the bottle.

"I'll be hungry in an hour," Fred burps as he dumps his soggy plate into the trash container in the corner. He tilts his bottle back to get the last drop.

"I won't." I finish off my beer and loft the empty toward the trash can. Nothing but net.

The meal out of the way, he takes some reports out of a folder. "What's on the agenda?"

"Can you track an airplane through a tail ID number?" I ask him. "Who owns it, what dates it was flown, who flew it."

"Sure. There's a special program for that stuff. It's called Choicepoint. Tracks planes, boats, cars, you name it."

"Which you have access to?"

"Good detectives do, if they're up-to-date." He's letting me know he's not some backwoods hick.

I read off three airplane ID numbers: the one the counselor and his killer came and went in, and the two I saw land when Roach met with his visitors. I'm guessing the last two are legitimate, the first one maybe not.

"Can you narrow it down to an area?"

"Washington, northern Virginia, Maryland for openers."

"Okay. And dates?"

"Start back three months, to last week."

"That helps."

His computer is running—he logs on to the program. "This'll take a few minutes." He points to a stack of magazines on a corner table. "Check 'em out."

I thumb through his stash and select a recent *Car and Driver.* There's a good article on Porsches. A Carrera would be a nice toy to own.

A few minutes later Fred looks up from his screen. "Got one."

I put the magazine down. "What kind?"

"A Lear 35. Registered to your man Roach. Does that compute?"

"Yes."

"Any specific dates you interested in?"

"Later. Keep working on the other IDs."

He goes back to work. I go back to reading about Porsches.

"Got another one."

This is more important. It's either the one that landed with Roach, or the one the counselor was on. "Go."

"It's a King Air, owned by Landmark Charter, based at National. That's another small jet, like the Lear." He notices something. "This is interesting."

"What?" I get up and walk over to his desk, so I can read the screen over his shoulder.

"On one occasion this plane and Roach's were logged out the same day."

"When?"

"A week ago." He gives me the date.

A week ago is when I saw that plane alongside Roach's on Roach's runway. "Does it say who signed out for that plane?"

He scrolls down. "Name of Lance Edwards. Pilot for hire, looks like."

"Okay. Go back to Roach's Lear. Who was the pilot of record that day?"

He futzes with the program again, then looks up. "Wade Wallace."

"Who leased that plane?" I ask. "Not Roach's, the other one."

He looks at the screen. "Doesn't say. I can find that out, but we'll have to check flight logs. Not a big deal."

"Keep going." I want to know about the third plane, the one Wallace flew that the counselor was on.

I wait impatiently while Fred gets the third ID number.

"Here we are," he says after a few minutes. "It's a Gulfstream, GS4. That's a bigger plane. That's what the heavy players like Tiger Woods use." He peers at the screen. "Owner is Rampart Industries. Registered in the Bahamas. Currently hangared at Wilson Aviation. Private field in Virginia."

"Go back five or six weeks. See who's on the log."

He scans down a list of names. Then he smiles.

"Wade Wallace," I say, before he can.

He looks at me in surprise. "How'd you know that?"

"Intuition," I lie. "It fits."

"What now?"

"I'd like to know who Rampart Industries is, for openers. The players. I want to know who's been visiting Roach."

"That's going to take time," Fred tells me. "I'll get on it tomorrow, see what's there."

I put my hand on his shoulder. "I really appreciate this, Fred."

"Hey, that's cool. It's a kick, man."

We've worked enough for one night. A last beer, then I leave. As I'm going home I think about how neat it would be taking this drive in a Porsche Carrera.

My house is as I left it: lights on, television blaring away. I was sure Roach wouldn't ambush me tonight, not in my own house, not so close in time to our meeting and Wallace's murder. But I wanted to give the impression that I was awake and alert, hence the lights and noise.

I sleep fitfully, feeling the presence of the gun perched ominously on my bedside table. Waking before dawn, I clear the road. I almost go down to see the birds, a "fuck-you" gesture toward Roach, but for once I decide to act like I have a brain, and stay away. I have to remember to keep the big picture in mind, let the small stuff go.

When I hear a car approaching I tense; I actually go for my automatic. But then I see it's Maureen, back from Boston, and my pulse returns to near-normal. I hide the gun under my mattress, go outside to greet her.

We're on each other like two animals in heat, locked into a passionate embrace as soon as we touch each other. I would pick her up and carry her inside, but she's too tall and gangly, I might slip and fall on my ass, and how romantic would that be?

We make love, we tell each other how much we missed each

other. I wait until we're up and dressed to break the bad news.

"We're not going birding today."

"Why not?"

I could give her some bullshit about my schedule, the tides, all sorts of lies. I don't want to do that, so I tell her the truth, a sanitized version. "Roach knows we've been out there."

She pauses, turns to me. "So?"

"So he doesn't want us anyplace where we can spy on him."

That riles her. "He can't tell you where to go on your own property, Fritz," she says indignantly. "And if he isn't doing anything wrong, why should he care?"

"You know the answer to that as well as I do."

"Meaning?"

"That he is. Doing something wrong. At least something he doesn't want anyone knowing about."

"How do you know? Did he call you?"

"Worse. He had me come over so he could deliver the news in person."

"He asked you to come over?"

"He sent some men here to provide me with transport."

She looks aghast. "He sent goons over here?"

I nod.

"That's awful! What's he trying to do, acting like that? I thought he was trying to make things nice between the two of you. Although being spied on would upset anyone," she concedes. "I mean I can understand why he'd be upset about that, especially since there's all that weird stuff going on with the planes flying in and out and whatever. But how could he think you're a threat to him? You haven't done anything stupid that would make him suspicious of you, have you?" she asks sharply. "You promised me you wouldn't."

As she says that, I realize she doesn't know Wallace has been killed. It was a local story, it wouldn't have been in the news in Boston.

"There's another reason for him acting like he did," I say.

"Which is?"

"His bodyguard, security guy, whatever. The guy I hit?"

She nods.

"He was killed the other day."

Her hand goes to her mouth. "You're kidding!"

"I wish."

"Where? Was he with Roach? Oh my God!"

I shake my head. "He was in his own house, alone. The police are speculating it was a robbery. Stuff of his was missing."

"That's incredible. I mean, he was an asshole, but still . . ."

I nod. "Roach is upset about that, of course. He somehow has it in his mind that I had something to do with it. By my spying on him."

Now she's really flustered. "Why would he think that? It's preposterous."

"I know that and you know that, but he's a sinister man, he thinks everyone has sinister motives for everything they do, like he does. And should, the more I see what's going on."

"I'm scared for you, Fritz." Her voice is shaking.

I don't want her carrying any of this load. I've made this my fight—she hasn't. "James Roach isn't going to hurt me. I'm a gnat on his ass."

"After what you've told me? Hardly."

She's right—but I don't want to face that.

"Does this mean we can't go out there anymore?" she asks fretfully. "At all? I'm going back to Cambridge soon, I can't not see those birds. It's important to me."

"I haven't thought that far ahead."

"We'll let things cool down for a few days, then we'll go out again," she declares. "Roach can't stop you from going on your own property."

He can stop me from doing any number of things. But I don't say that.

I can't have her hanging around here today, in case Fred calls or comes by with some information I have to act on. "I've got stuff to do today anyway—more family business. So why don't we plan on getting together later on?" I feel bad about lying to her yet again, but there's no alternative.

She sighs. "Okay. I can find things to do. There are some other birding areas I haven't seen."

"My mother requests the pleasure of our company for dinner. Tonight okay?"

She gives me a smile. "She's the sweetest."

"She likes you, too."

"So you'll pick me up at the motel? Or should I meet you there?"

"I'll pick you up. A lady should always have an escort."

I phone my mother to let her know I'll be there for dinner and am bringing Maureen. She's delighted to hear it, she'll make it a special occasion.

I'm antsy, hanging here, but I feel I have to in case Fred calls, not wanting to miss him if he does.

I spend the rest of the morning anxiously waiting. Finally, too antsy to sit still, I pull on a pair of gym shorts and my Sauconys and head out the door, running along the overhung riverbank toward the southeastern end of our property. As I run I think about Maureen, what kind of life I'd have with her. It wouldn't be conventionally domestic—she's got a career, more important than I ever might, the way things are going. Which would be fine with me, I don't want a conventional life—I think. I've never let myself go to that place, so I don't really know. But if I never give it a try, I'll never know.

After thirty minutes of hard running I'm covered with sweat. I lick salt from the corners of my mouth. I've gone as far as I can go in this direction. From here, it's all water and foliage. If I was in my boat I'd be less than ten minutes from the birds, less than fifteen from Roach's property.

I can't go back there. But I have to go back there. I have no choice. Partly for Maureen, but mostly for me.

No message from Fred when I get back. But there is one from Billy Higgins, my gun dealer buddy. My gun application has been approved. I can come pick up my license whenever I want, but he has to talk to me. Like as soon as I get this message.

"Hey, Billy, it's Fritz Tullis," I announce myself when he answers the phone. "Got your call."

"You coming by to pick up your paperwork?" he asks. He sounds guarded. "You don't want to be waiting on it, since you're already in possession of the merchandise."

"How's about if I come get it today?" I can swing by his store on my way to fetch Maureen, it's not far out of the way. "What's going on?"

"I'll fill you in then."

He hangs up. I cradle the receiver. Whatever his news is, my gut tells me, it won't be good.

Billy's expression is sour when I walk in the door, like I laid a turd on his doorstep.

"Some nigger lady cop from P.G. County was in here, asking questions about you," he informs me as he hands me my gun license. He scrounges around his countertop, finds a card, squints at it. "Mabel Ricketts. Know who she is?"

My gut didn't lie. "Yes, I've had the privilege of meeting her. What did she want?"

"Did I sell you a gun? Not did," he corrects himself, "when."

"How did she know about that?"

"It's on the computer, lamebrain," he says harshly.

I scowl. She caught me in the lie, as I'd feared she would. "What'd you tell her?"

"That you came in and bought one, what else?"

"What about your giving it to me before I passed muster?" I ask, brandishing my new license.

"Well, I didn't tell her that, for Christsakes," he says, his voice rising half an octave. "My mama didn't raise no fools. I'd lose my permit to sell if I did that."

That's a relief. "So as far as she knows, I didn't have it then."

"That is exactly correct. Technically. But . . ." He leans over the counter toward me. "She is one suspicious lady, that cop. I don't think she believed me. What I did for you, it ain't uncommon. Hear what I'm saying?"

"But there's no record that I had that gun," I persist.

"No. You're in the clear—on the books." He shows a mouthful of missing teeth when he grins. "What dirt is she trying to dig up on you, Fritz?" he questions me eagerly. "You been a naughty boy?"

He doesn't need to know about the troubles in my life—his big yap would have me hanging from the gallows before sundown if I told him one iota of what's been going on. "It's bullshit," I throw away. "Some sorry asshole claims I gypped him on an old deal, he's out to make me look bad, he's grasping at straws. Nothing to raise a sweat about."

Billy grunts. "Well, it sure didn't sound like nothing, the hard-ass way she was coming on," he replies. "If I was you, man, I'd watch my back." He flicks a tobacco-stained finger at my license. "Good thing you did buy that gun, pard." He bangs me on the shoulder with his palm. "Don't you go chickenin' out on me when the time comes to use it."

"I hope I never have to," I say honestly.

He shakes his head like I'm a lamb being delivered to the shearing pen. "That's why you bought it, old son. 'Cause if you ain't man enough to use it, for sure you're gonna lose it."

Maureen's ready and waiting when I arrive at her motel. She's wearing a dress I haven't seen before. "I bought it in Boston. Do you like it?" She twirls for me. It's short, above her knees. She's wearing heels; we're almost the same height.

"Looks good on you. Of course, a paper sack would look good on you." I'm determined to put my conversation with Billy about that female cop out of my mind—I'll deal with my worries about that later, along with all the others.

"You're too kind," she banters.

I run my fingers along the inside of her bare thigh. She twitches.

"How about a quickie?"

"We'll be late. You don't want to be late for dinner at your mother's."

"She can wait." I take her hand.

She holds me off. "Later, big boy. We have all night, Fritz. We have all—" She stops.

Of our lives?

A surprise awaits us when we walk into mom's house. Not a pleasant one.

"I see you finally got rid of that stupid suit," Sam says to me, rising up out of his deck chair, Manhattan in hand. He looks over at Maureen, who's giving our mother a hug. "The new *femme du jour?*"

"A colleague," I say, stiffly. I wasn't expecting Sam and his windbag acridity.

"Colleague?" he scoffs. "With those legs? I'd be working nights and weekends if I had a colleague who looked like her."

So much for a congenial evening without sibling rivalry subtexts. "I'm sure Emily would be charmed to hear that," I fire back. I look over at his spouse, who stands stiffly near Maureen and my mother, looking ill at ease. I don't recall her ever giving my mother a hug, or of her receiving one from the materfamilias.

Maureen walks over, links her arm in mine. "Is this the

famous lawyer I've heard so much about?" she says, smiling at Sam. "Fritz is your biggest fan."

"I doubt that," Sam replies sourly, trying not to ogle her.

I know what she's doing—she's trying to make things nice between us, and hopefully, get on Sam's good side. What she doesn't know is that where I'm concerned, Sam doesn't have a good side.

Emily joins us, standing shoulder to shoulder with her husband. Her look to Maureen is pure venom—she's outclassed tonight, and it rankles. "I'm Emily Tullis," she says, extending a languid hand. "We're so pleased you could join us. Fritz always brings such *interesting* dates to our gatherings."

"Maureen O'Hara," Maureen responds, flashing Emily a million-watt smile.

Husband and wife give her identical "who are you kidding?" looks.

Maureen smiles. "There's no relation," she says, having endured such looks countless times before, I'm sure. "The name is just a coincidence."

Sam and Emily regard her dourly. This is going to be a long evening. Hopefully, without too much emotional bloodshed.

Maureen sees where this is going. "Would you get me a drink, Fritz? One of those gin rickeys you Marylanders are so famous for? Will you excuse us?" she says to Sam and Emily, even as she's pulling me away, toward the table where the drinks are set up.

"Sorry about that," I say to her, when we're out of hearing range. "If I'd known they were going to be here I'd have taken a rain check."

Maureen nods in understanding. "I'm sorry I'm making your life more difficult than it already is."

"It has nothing to do with you. You're caught in tonight's line of fire, that's all. It could be anyone I bring around. Sam and I have been at odds since I was born," I explain. "He could never abide not being the sole male heir."

"I'll try to be as accommodating as possible for the rest of the evening. For your mother's sake, if nothing else."

"Thanks." We're on our own tonight, no bartender. "Do you really want a gin rickey?"

"I don't even know what a gin rickey is," she laughs. She has a good laugh—full, rich, melodious. "I said that to get us away from them."

"How about a vodka tonic? That I can handle."

"Perfect." She bites my earlobe. "Have I told you lately that I'm crazy about you?"

"Not lately, no." It's hard to make drinks when you're distracted.

"I'm saying it now so if I get drunk later you won't think it's the booze talking."

"I'll remember."

"I'm joking," she says. "About getting drunk. Or even high. Not the way things are going. Besides, I wouldn't want your mother to think poorly of me."

"My mother's already enraptured by you, so don't worry." I hand her a sweaty glass. "Let's not think about that tonight. Let's just have fun."

She raises her glass. "To fun."

The food is excellent, as usual. My mother and Maureen spend the entire time talking and laughing with each other, to the chagrin of Emily, who feels—rightfully so—left out. If Maureen and I were to become permanent (I'm only musing, not projecting) Emily would disappear off the radar screen, as far as mother is concerned. Emily knows that, and her dismay is reflected on her face.

I'm sure my mother had the best of intentions, inviting Sam and Emily to dine with Maureen and me. She wanted them to meet her, so that if her wish came true we would collectively take the first steps toward being one big, happy family—the

Brady Bunch, Maryland division. That, however, is never going to happen. The lack of love between Sam and me is biblical, and any woman I wind up with is not going to be simpatico with Emily.

Fuck Sam and his dyspeptic wife. Let them hibernate in Baltimore, where they belong.

After dessert I go out onto the back veranda while my mother shows Maureen her collection of porcelain figurines. The hot, muggy air wraps around me like a wet cocoon. Despite the crap I'm going through with Roach, I'm feeling terrific. The reason is simple—Maureen's back. I hadn't realized how much I missed her, how emotionally involved I am with her, until today.

My reverie is broken by my brother, who ambles out with a bottle of cognac in one hand and a cigar in the other. He didn't know I was out here—he was expecting the porch to himself, where he could smoke his stogie and drink his brandy alone, away from Emily and the tension between them and the rest of us. Seeing me, he grunts, holds the bottle aloft. "Want some?"

The offer is ungracious, but we're trapped together out here, so he feels compelled to act civilized. I'm not going to turn down a good glass of cognac, however, regardless of intent.

"Sure."

"Grab a glass," he says gruffly. He's leaning against the railing. His face is flushed, his posture is a pronounced 45 degree lean. During dinner he was drinking wine as fast as he could replenish his glass. In short, he's snockered.

I get a snifter from the side table. He pours, spilling some onto my hand.

"I hope you're not driving home tonight," I say.

"Emily's driving," he replies thickly. "She's the designated driver."

I warm the glass in my hands. "I never see you this well lubricated, Sam. Had a bad day?"

He shakes his head, fumbles with his lighter. Billows of

gray-white smoke envelop his head as he draws on his cigar. "No worse than usual." He downs a healthy swallow of cognac. "That's quite a looker you brought to dinner." He winks at me lewdly. "This is your big brother, Fritz. You don't have to give me that 'colleague' crap. Where'd you pick her up, North Charles Street, by the statue?"

The statue he's referring to is the Washington Monument, not the famous one in Washington, D.C., the small one in Baltimore. It's a well-known spot for johns to rendezvous with hookers. The body of the slain diplomat was found not far from there.

If Sam wasn't my brother and we weren't at our mother's house I'd punch his lights out. "Don't be an offensive asshole, Sam. She happens to be a professor—at Harvard, no less. So shut up about what you don't know, okay?"

"A professor? Her?" He barks a nasty laugh. "If she's a professor of anything but mattress-testing, I'm Mel Gibson."

"Just shut up, Sam, okay?" I start to walk away. What a jerk my brother can be sometimes.

Sam speaks to my back. "I've been hearing some displeasing things about you, Fritz."

I turn around. "Like what?" I challenge him. He's all mouth tonight, it's pissing me off more than usual.

"Things about you and James Roach."

My antennae go up. "What about me and Roach?"

"That you're fucking around in his affairs, and that he's unhappy about it."

"Where'd you hear that?" This is bad news.

"Doesn't matter." He almost stumbles, braces himself against the railing. "Is it true?"

I'm fuming. "I want to know who told you, goddamn it!"

"Who do you think?"

"Roach?"

He looks at me like I'm the dumbest shit in the world. "Figure it out, moron."

Damn! Roach is calling my family now? I stiffen. "What I do, and who I do it with, is none of your business, Sam."

He straightens up. "This is my business."

"No, it is not."

He pokes me in the chest with a sweaty forefinger, the same kind of poke Roach gave me. I grab the finger, hold it tight. One twist of my wrist and I could break it.

"Hands off, Sam. I mean it."

I wait a moment to let the message settle, then let go. I don't want to break my brother's finger, not in my mother's house.

"Stay away from Roach," he orders me.

I explode. "Don't fucking tell me what to do! I'll do anything I want, you hear? I don't need to hear any of your shit."

I look toward the house. No one's heard us, fortunately. I start to turn away. This time he grabs me by the shirtsleeve. I yank loose.

"You're drunk," I bark at him.

"And you're suicidal."

"Enough with this shit. My life is none of your goddamned business."

He shakes his head. "It *is* my business, Fritz. Anything you do, anything stupid, which is everything, impacts on this family. Which makes it my business."

"Fuck off." I'm steaming. I start to walk away from him, before I lose it and deck him.

He won't let go. He gets in my face, right into it, an inch away. I almost gag from the booze and cigar on his breath. "Men like Roach are dangerous, you naive fool. They don't tolerate smart-asses like you in their lives, they eliminate them. I don't know what your beef is with him, but *leave him alone!*"

How many times have I heard this now? I'm sick of hearing it, I'm sick of the whole mess.

"Go home, Sam. Have your wife pour you into your car and go home. Sleep it off. You're making an ass of yourself."

He's a bulldog. "I'm telling you this for your own good."

"My own good? Since when have you been interested in my welfare? I can take care of myself. Now for the last time—leave me alone."

He backs off a step. "If you don't care about me, think about our mother."

Oh, that rankles, dragging her into this. "What about her?" I hear a nasty edge in my voice. I don't like sounding like this, but he's pushed me to it.

"She's getting older."

"Yes, I'm aware of that."

"Her heart isn't as strong as it was. She had a small seizure last year, before you came back here. You didn't know that, did you?"

I'm taken aback. "No one told me."

"You weren't around. You were too busy dipping your wick in the wrong honeypot," he says savagely. "We didn't want to disturb you."

"You're a prick, Sam."

"And you're a . . ." He doesn't say what he thinks I am. He doesn't have to—I already know. A wastrel, a fuckup. A lost cause.

He pulls himself together. "She controls her condition with medication. But it was a warning. She can't be stressed out, Fritz."

"I'm not stressing her out," I argue. It's feeble.

"You will if anything happens to you."

I want to say that nothing will happen to me, but I can't, because it wouldn't be true, and we both know it.

"If anything bad befell you, Fritz, it would kill her. Think about that, the next time you dive into the water before you know how deep it is."

Maureen and I detour by her motel so she can change out of her party clothes. She strips off her dress, washes the makeup from her face, puts on shorts and a blouse, packs a small overnight bag, throws her binoculars into her daypack, reaches for her hiking boots.

"It isn't smart for us to go down there tomorrow," I say with reluctance.

She turns, caught off guard. "We agreed we'd take a day or two off, then start going down again. This fieldwork is important to me, Fritz. This could be a big boost to my career," she says. She's being straight about her ambitions.

"It's not a good idea."

She stares at me as if trying to see into my brain. "I can't read your mind—the more I know you the more I realize that—but I do know there are things going on you aren't telling me. And it's bothering the shit out of me." She comes closer. "I've told you everything about me, whatever you've asked. But when I ask you point-blank about anything that's upsetting you, you clam up. You dance all around the subject, but you never home in." She bites her lip. "Am I pushing too fast? Or . . ." She closes her eyes, takes a deep breath, then opens them and looks at me. "Or have I been misreading all the signs? Am I in a different place with us than you are? Because if I am, tell me now, please. I'm this close"—she holds her thumb and index finger an eighth of an inch apart—"to falling for you completely. But I can salvage myself, if you tell me, right now, that it's not going to work between us. It would hurt like hell, but I'd survive. It's happened before. But you have to tell me." She pauses. "Or I have to go."

She's thrown down the gauntlet. The moment I've been dreading.

It's not the depth of the commitment. I think I can handle that; I'm willing to try, that's the best anyone can do. It's what I'm hiding, what I have to tell her to be completely straight and honest with her, that has my stomach tied up in a knot.

It's now or never. I can't conceive of the prospect of "never."

"I know more about Roach than I've been letting on."

"I assumed as much," she says. "Like what?"

I take her hand. "Let's sit down."

We sit side by side on the faded chenille bedspread. "The police brought me in for questioning about Wallace's murder."

Her face registers shock. "When?"

"The day it happened. That afternoon."

"Why?" she cries.

"They think I might have been involved," I say bleakly. Replaying my interview with Ricketts in my mind, there's no other explanation. I may not be a suspect, officially, but I'm very dubious in their eyes.

She shakes her head in disbelief. "That's crazy. Why would they think that?"

"Because Roach told the police about the dustup between Wallace and me, that night at my mother's house. That I'd hit him, threatened him. I'm sure Roach overblew what really happened, but it did happen, I couldn't deny it."

"That's ridiculous," she says hotly. Then she gives me a look that's both confused and angry. "The police had you in for questioning the same day Wallace was killed?"

I nod slowly—I can see where this is going. "That afternoon."

"So you'd already been to see the police when you told me he'd been killed."

"Yes," I confess.

"Fritz." She takes my face in her hand. "Why didn't you tell me then?" Her hand is trembling as it touches my cheek.

"I didn't want you to worry. It was over by then, there would have been nothing you could do."

"I could have been there with you. That's something." She looks at me, searching my eyes. "Isn't it?"

"Of course it is."

"That's what I've been talking about," she says. Her voice is shaky. "Trust. Communication."

"I know," I answer forlornly. I feel like such a self-centered ass. A complete dolt, a fool. "Which is why I'm telling you this now."

"Is there more?"

"A lot."

She sits back. "I want to know everything. *Everything.* Leave nothing out. Okay?"

I nod okay.

"A man was murdered near here," I commence, "not long ago."

"Where?"

"On Roach's farm. His runway."

That brings her up straight. "When did it happen?"

"Over a month ago. Before you came."

She whistles through her teeth. "I haven't heard anything about any murder. Why aren't people talking about it?"

"Because no one saw it happen."

"Then how do you . . ." She catches herself. "*You* saw it?"

I nod.

"When you were down there, watching the birds?"

I nod again.

She's stunned. "Did you go to the police?"

"No."

"They don't know about it?"

"No."

"I'm missing something. What happened when the body was found? The police had to be called in then, didn't they?"

"The body wasn't found there," I explain. "The killer took it away."

"And no one else saw it, except you?" she whispers.

I nod. "Do you remember when we saw Roach and those other people land their airplanes on Roach's property?"

"Of course. How could I not remember?"

"Wallace was one of those other people."

"Oh," she says, shook up now even more than she already was.

"That wasn't the first time I saw Wallace fly in there." I lean back, brace myself against the wall. "Wallace flew the victim to Roach's farm. He was the pilot."

"Who was he? The victim."

"The Russian senior counselor to the United States. The third-ranking member of their embassy."

"So Roach *was* involved," she says breathlessly.

I shake my head. "Roach wasn't there. He was in Washington."

I realize that Maureen doesn't know the counselor was found dead in a Baltimore slum a week later. There's no reason for her to—if she didn't see the story on the news over the next few days or read about it in a newspaper, she would have no idea. Most people wouldn't, it doesn't affect them—even if they had seen or read something, the information would have passed through, like yesterday's breakfast. Flushed from the system, gone.

She takes my hand. "No wonder you've been so uptight about this. You saw Wallace kill this man?"

I shake my head. "Wallace didn't kill him. There was a third man. He was the killer."

"Do you know who he is?"

I shake my head. "I don't know."

She stares at me, trying to understand. "I don't get it. There were three men there. Wallace, this counselor, and someone else. Who wasn't Roach."

I nod.

"Well, if you knew one was Wallace . . ."

"I didn't know it, then. I hadn't met Wallace yet."

That throws her. "Then how *did* you know?"

"I found out later."

She's off the track. "Later like when?"

"After I met him. I knew I'd seen him somewhere before. I figured it out."

She nods. "Okay. So if you knew one of these guys was

Wallace, then or later, and you knew the second one was this counselor . . . how did you know who *he* was?"

"I saw his picture on television, about a week later."

"Okay." I can see she's trying to image this, to figure it out. "So if you could figure out who Wallace was, and you could figure out the counselor, why couldn't you figure out who the third man was?"

I explain that it was early in the morning, that the direction in which the sun was situated placed the third man's face in shadow, unrecognizable.

"So you have no idea who he was, this third man?" she asks, wanting to make sure she's understanding me fully.

"Not a clue."

"Okay. So this third man—Mr. X—kills this counselor on Roach's runway."

Another nod.

"Umm." She thinks some more. "And the body was taken away, so no one could connect it to Roach."

"That's right," I affirm. "No one would ever know. Except Wallace and the killer."

"And you," she reminds me.

"And me. But they don't know that," I say. I'm not going to tell her that my pal Buster knows, and that Roach might also. "Aren't you sorry, now that you know this? You're in this a lot deeper than you should be. Than anyone should be."

"Including you, Fritz."

"I can't help it. I was there, I saw it."

"Shouldn't you have gone to the police?"

"My lawyer told me not to. You don't have to, legally."

She nods in agreement. "That was smart on his part. You go to the cops, whoever this killer is would find out about it, and you could be next."

"That's it. Stay uninvolved."

She taps her fingernails on the bedspread, a nervous gesture. "You aren't responsible for this. You didn't kill anyone. You don't have to put your life on—" A fresh thought occurs to her. "You saw this dead counselor's picture a week after you saw him killed?"

"About a week."

"So he did turn up somewhere. I mean, his body did."

"In Baltimore."

"Baltimore? That's what, a hundred miles from here?"

"More."

"Why Baltimore?"

"It was set up to look like a killing during a robbery, or while he was with a hooker."

"To throw the police off the trail," she reasons. "This killer's pretty smart." She pauses. "Do you still think it's smart not to go to the police? The more I hear, the worse this gets."

"I've got to try to find out who the killer was," I tell her. "I'm in too deep to stop now. But as soon as I find out—if I do—I am going to go to the police."

Her brow furrows. "Assuming you do find out who it is, how are you going to do that? It would just be your word. Is that enough?"

"Normally, it wouldn't be," I concur. "But the circumstances weren't normal." I get up from the bed and look out the window. Late-night vehicles rumble on the highway in the distance; not many, mostly trucks. I've driven this road late at night. There have been times, two, three o'clock, when I've been the only driver on the road. That's when you know you're very much alone.

"I took pictures of it."

She freezes in place, then she starts rocking, then she gets up and comes over to me. "You have pictures of this murder?" she asks, as if she can't believe what she just heard.

I nod. "I was shooting the birds, my usual routine. I saw the plane touch down, I swung the camera around, and I snapped some pictures. It was instinctive. I was just being nosy, really. But I got pictures of the killing."

She slumps against me. "Oh, Fritz," she moans. "If those pictures ever got out . . ."

"They aren't going to," I say quickly. "They're in a safe place."

"Like where?" She buries her face in her hands, then stares at me. "I'm going to slap you silly if you tell me they're in your house."

I don't answer. It's safer for her if she doesn't know, precisely.

"Fritz!" she rails at me. "Who are you kidding, besides yourself? Roach has already sent men to your house. It isn't a question of *if* he's going to come back, it's *when*. Hijacking you to his place—that was a shot across your bow. If he was suspicious of you before, he's still going to be suspicious. More, the longer this goes on." She grabs my arm. "Do you know what the smartest thing would be for you to do? The only sane thing?"

I want her to tell me, but I can't ask, because I would be admitting the truth of what she's saying.

She doesn't need my permission. "Get rid of the pictures, don't tell another soul what you've told me tonight, and then *forget about this!* Forget everything! You never saw it, it didn't happen, and you and I can start a life together." She puts her arms around me, leans her head against my chest. "Don't you want that, Fritz? To start a life with me, or at least give it a decent try?"

"Yes." The word almost chokes in my throat, but not for lack of feeling.

"Then give us a chance. Getting killed does not give us a chance." She's beginning to cry—not bawling, but tears are forming in the corners of her eyes.

"I'm not dead."

She looks at me, wiping at her eyes with the back of her hand. "You will be if you keep messing with James Roach. I don't know where you've hidden those pictures, Fritz, and honestly, I don't want to. But until you can assure me, honest to God, that they aren't in your house, I'm not spending one moment there. It's too scary." She grabs my face with both hands. "For you, more than me."

It's one in the morning. I'm sweating like a junkie, rivulets of stink are coming out of my armpits, my crotch. I can't sleep—I can barely breathe, the tension is so unbearable. So what if I have a gun two feet away, locked and loaded? I'm going to use it if Roach's storm troopers come after me? They'd shove it up my ass and pull the trigger.

Maureen's right. I can't keep the transparencies here.

Gathering up the evidence of the murder—the transparencies and the enhancements Jack the specialist made for me in Anacostia—I throw them into my camera bag with my cameras, my laptop, and my new gun. Then I leave the house and drive toward town, until I find a cheap truckers' motel that's still open and has an available room. I pay cash and check in under a phony name. As an extra precaution I park my car in back, where it can't be seen from the street.

The night goes slowly. I don't sleep, I don't even try to. I watch movies until dawn, curtains closed, door locked, chain on, my body so stiff with tension it aches, the loaded gun perched on the end table next to the bed.

At first light I drive to the nearest all-night minimart, get the largest takeout container of coffee they have, and go into Jamestown, where I sit in my car drinking the oily brew. Finally, at the stroke of nine, I walk into the First Bank of Jamestown (the only bank in Jamestown) the moment they unlock the doors, where I rent a safe deposit box and lock the film away.

That helps lift the burden. Now the pictures aren't in my house anymore, sending out evil rays via cosmic radar. I head for home, feeling greatly relieved.

The past few days have been hot and muggy, but bearable. This morning we're back to a normal Maryland summer—blistering heat layered on tropical jungle humidity. On days like this I fondly think about my supreme high school fantasy: cruising to Ocean City in a top-down red Cadillac convertible with two beautiful sixteen-year-old blondes jammed in the front seat with me and a cold case of beer in the back to quench our thirst.

It never happened. I never owned a Caddy, convertible or otherwise, and there were never two girls at the same time, unless there was another boy along as well. It's a nice fantasy, though.

I pass by my mother's house on the way to mine. I'm still nervous as hell, but I don't feel as bad as I did last night. Nighttime always brings out the sweats and heart palpitations. In the light of day, the shadowy creatures can be seen for what they are—frightening, but not fatal.

I hear the fire before I see it. It's loud, like gunfire or artillery shells, pops and explosions and a low rumble. Machines grinding, voices yelling words I can't distinguish. I round the final bend in the road.

The flames look like they're shooting out of the tops of the trees. In front of me is a wall of fire, crowned by massive cumulus clouds of black smoke that are billowing up to the sky. There are fire trucks parked haphazardly in my yard, men with hoses. Policemen as well.

The cop at the barricade doesn't know who I am. He tries to stop me, but I power by his outstretched hand, almost hitting him, braking to a stop at the edge of the fire-fighting equipment. Jumping out of my car, I run toward what remains of my shack. Most of it is already gone—no more roof, hardly any walls, charred timbers fallen on the floor.

"What happened?" I'm screaming. I try to run past the line of firemen into the house, but a burly cop stops me, grabbing my arms and pinning me back. Ralph Lomax, one of the firemen, a decent fellow I've known for years, rushes over. His face, like the others, is black with soot. He's shaking his head.

"It's a goner, Fritz. Nothing we could do about it, tinderbox like this. Getting water to it was a bitch, we tried to suction out of the creek, but no go. All we had is what we brought with us on the trucks."

My overwhelming thought is of my pictures of the birds, especially Ollie. Did any of them survive?

I stand there helplessly and watch as my house burns to the ground.

After what seems an interminable amount of time, the embers have cooled enough for me to go into what is now nothing more than a shell. The chief, Pat Summers, a man of poor humor who is a decade older than me, comes over and lays a weighty hand on my shoulder. "Sorry about this, Fritz."

I'm numb. "How did it happen?"

"Fault in the wiring or gas explosion, had to be." He pauses, gives me a dubious look. "You rebuilt this yourself, didn't you?" Without waiting for my answer he adds, "Didn't pull any permits, did you?"

I turn to him, angry as hell. "What's that supposed to mean?"

"C'mere." He leads me past the still burning embers to some exposed wiring, fingers the frayed edges. "This wasn't grounded properly. I'd bet next month's paycheck we'll find shoddy wiring like this everywhere." He glances at me as I survey the ruins. "That's generally the case with homemade places. That's why the county requires you pull a permit, so the pros can inspect it for you and tell you where there's going to be trouble."

My house has burnt down to the ground and this dickhead's lecturing me about chickenshit regulations. "I'll remember that the next time I build a house from scratch," I fume at him.

He gives me an "I could give a shit less" look and walks away. By this time, a news truck from one of the local television stations has shown up, along with some print reporters. Firemen and cops are walking around, poking at hot shards, treading cautiously on the floorboards, fearing that the weakened wood, what's left of it, will collapse out from under them.

All my equipment is burnt and twisted, nothing redeemable. The pictures and transparencies are scattered all over the floor. Most are scorched beyond recognition.

At least I still have my cameras. Thank God I had the instinct to take them and my PowerBook with me. I can take more pictures of Ollie—if I can summon the energy to go out there again, after this.

"Hey!" A young cop has wandered into the shell that was my bedroom. His voice is sheer panic. *"Hey! Over here!"*

The detective in charge, standing in the middle of what was my living room, turns to the voice. "What?" he calls back.

The young cop's voice cracks. In a broken falsetto: *"I think there's a body in here!"*

Everyone rushes into the bedroom; I lag behind. That could have been me. I look over, catch Pat Summers's eye. His face is set in a hard mask. We're coming from opposite directions, but we're thinking the same thing—maybe it wasn't an accident, after all. Maybe whoever this was torched the place and then got caught in his own fatal machination.

I'll feel a lot better if that's the case; although I'll be a lot more scared, too, because that would mean action has superseded threats. Which has to come from one source—my neighbor across the water. That's chilling to contemplate, but if it's so, at least it's out in the open now.

In the bedroom, men are pulling at a pile of support beams. The body is buried under them.

A foot is revealed. Wearing a woman's shoe.

I push past the assembled bodies, tearing at the beams, my hands are splintering, they're bleeding, I don't feel it, my heart is pounding, I'm trying to wrench the heavy beams away, the burnt wood is soft, it comes apart in my hands, my bloody hands. Others are shoulder to shoulder with me. We push the beams aside, one after another, the body beginning to be revealed, then the back of the head. The gray hair, the string of pearls.

"Oh, my fucking Christ!" This is Pat, crossing himself.

The remaining beams are cleared off the body. I kneel down, rocking mindlessly while I cradle the lifeless form of my mother in my arms.

The ambulance arrives. The coroner is a young Asian woman I've never seen. I watch as she and Pat Summers have a brief conversation. He shows her a section of the frayed wiring. She turns it over in her hands, scribbles some notes, approaches me.

"The cause of death was smoke inhalation, most likely," she tells me crisply, stripping off her latex gloves. "Since the fire was electrical in origin it would have started in the walls and gone undetected until the whole thing suddenly exploded. Probably a beam fell on her." She pauses. "If it makes you feel any better, she was almost certainly unconscious the entire time. She wouldn't have been in any pain."

That doesn't make me feel better.

"We won't know for sure until we do the autopsy." She nods

perfunctorily. "I'm sorry." She didn't know my mother from Adam.

The paramedics cover my mother's body, lift her into the ambulance, drive away. I sit on the ground, grasping a thick notebook in my hands. My mother's memoirs. It was under her body. She brought it down here to show it to me. The cover is burnt and the edges are charred, but some of the pages survived.

Another car comes tearing down the road and skids to a stop on the other side of the phalanx of police cars and fire trucks. Hearing the squeal of brakes, I look up. Maureen, eyes wide, hair wild, jumps out. She sees me, screams, rushes over to me. "I thought it was you!" she sobs. "I heard it on the radio. Thank God, you're safe. I was so scared."

"It wasn't me," I state the obvious in a dull monotone. "I didn't get here till it was almost over."

She's almost collapsing, she's so overcome with the emotion of what she'd feared had happened. "Who was it? Do they know?"

"It was my mother."

Everyone is gone now except Maureen and me. I sit hunched over on an edge of the burnt foundation, my head in my hands. Maureen is stroking my back, holding me. "We should leave," she says gently. "There's nothing you can do here now."

I shake my head.

"Where are you going to stay tonight?" she asks. Without waiting for my answer, she offers, "Why don't you stay at the motel with me?"

"I'll stay here."

"There is no here," she points out.

"At my mother's house, I mean."

She looks at me in alarm. "I don't think you should."

"Ghosts?"

She nods. "You're guilt-ridden. Staying there would only reinforce that."

"I should be guilt-ridden. I'm guilty."

"Of what?"

"This." I sweep my arm at the ruins. "I threw this place together with spit and shoelaces, and here's the result. You warned me that something like this could happen, the first time you were over. Remember? You were right. And you weren't the only one. Anyone could see what a piece of crap this was."

"It was an accident, Fritz," she says patiently. "Don't beat yourself up about it." She stands, pulls me to my feet. "Come on. Hanging around here isn't doing you any good."

I slowly get up.

"Come on back to my place. Stay with me."

I shake my head. "Not now."

She takes me by the hand like I'm a lost child and leads me toward our cars. "Well," she says, "at least one thing is resolved."

"What?"

"The pictures you took of the murder. They don't exist anymore." She points back toward the house, where everything's been consumed by the fire. "Without them, you don't have any proof of that murder. You're free of it, Fritz."

I shake my head. "No. I'm not free."

"But you have no evidence anymore."

I lean against the side of my car. It's hot from the heat from the sun and the heat from the fire. What I want more than anything right now is a beer. Lots of beers.

"I still have them," I tell her.

"You still have what?"

"The pictures of the murder."

She stares at me like I've lost my mind. "Fritz, I know this is a horrible, horrible time, but you have to try to think rationally. You can't live in a dreamworld, not now. We searched the remains together. There's nothing left here."

"They weren't in the house."

"They weren't?"

I shake my head. "I was so freaked with all that's been going on that I couldn't stay here, so I took off. And I took those pictures with me."

"You have them with you?" she asks in disbelief. "Where are they?"

"I can't tell you."

"Why not, for Godsakes?"

I feel my car against my back. My computer's inside. The scans of the transparencies are in the computer. But I don't want her to know that. "For your own protection."

She starts yelling at me, the way you yell at someone who speaks a foreign language, in the mistaken idea that if you raise your voice you'll get through to them. "*My* protection? *You're* the one that needs protection. You're going 'round the bend." She has real terror in her eyes, looking at me. "I'm scared, Fritz. I don't know what's going on inside your head, but I know you aren't thinking straight, how could you be with what's happened? You have to confide in me, darling, you can't hold all this in. You're going to explode. Fritz!"

I lean down and pick up a stone, toss it at my burnt-out shack. It hits a piece of hanging wood. The wood splinters, falling to the ground. Splinters—the shape my life is in now.

"Let's leave it alone," I say torpidly. "I need to go somewhere quiet, have a drink. Right now I'm too upset to think or do anything else."

We go back to my mother's house and have a drink. Screwdrivers, since it's still early in the day and they're easy to mix. Then another. I want to get drunk, blitzed, I want to blot out everything that's happened. But I don't, not even a buzz. My mind is clear as glass.

Maureen is drinking, too, but not at my pace. She's doing it to keep me company, to make sure I don't go off the deep end. I can see the fear and worry in her eyes.

After imbibing a sufficient amount of artificial courage I call my brother and sister, give them the awful news. Dinah, although shocked and heartsick, is relatively philosophical, considering the suddenness and randomness of it. Our mother had a full, rich life, and now it's over. Accidents happen. She'll see me at the funeral.

Sam, on the other hand, does not take the news well. He's devastated, and, of course, harshly accusatory. Our mother's death was all my fault, as far as he's concerned. If I hadn't fucked up in Texas I wouldn't have come home, rebuilt the shack, etc., etc., leading to our mother coming down there to see me. I've been nothing but bad news for the entire family ever since I came back; ever since he can remember.

He'll take care of the funeral arrangements. I offer to do it—I'm here, he's in Baltimore—but he brushes me off. He's a responsible adult, he'll make sure things are done properly. Show up for the funeral, that's all I ask of you, he tells me, alternately crying and yelling at me.

"Getting drunk isn't going to solve any problems," Maureen says after I've hung up on Sam and poured myself a straight shot of vodka. She isn't going to handle me with kid gloves.

"I want to forget problems, not solve them." I replenish my glass.

She gives me a stern look, but resists the urge to stop me. "What are you going to do now, Fritz?"

"Get through the funeral. After that . . ."

The weight of everything that's happened crashes down on me. I'm limp, I feel like all my bones have turned to jelly. "I can't talk about this anymore now. Let's just be with each other, okay?"

She nods. "Okay." She pauses. "That could have been you, instead of her."

I feel like I should take on the trappings of an early Christian martyr, exiled to the desert with a hair shirt as my only garment. "You're absolutely right. If it was supposed to be anyone, it was supposed to be me." I pace the room in nervous agitation. "Whoever did it came here looking for incriminating pictures, like you called it. Before dawn, I'm sure—bastards like that are vampires, they always work under cover of darkness. And here comes my mother, an old lady who got up early, like old people do, making her way down here to show me what she'd been doing on her memoirs. She knew showing up here early was okay 'cause I get up early, too, and she didn't like to be outside once the sun was up and it got too hot. She walked in on them, right into the middle of it, a lamb to slaughter." I'm in agony, visualizing this. "Scumbags like whoever did this don't leave witnesses. Then he set the fire to make it look like an accident. It all fits."

"You don't know that for sure," she says, trying to assuage my pain.

I shake my head angrily. "You don't believe the almighty James Roach masterminded this?"

She starts to answer, hesitates. "I don't know. I guess he could have. Anyway, it's over now."

I shake my head fiercely. "It isn't over. No way."

She grabs me by the hair of my head, pulls my face around. "How much killing does there have to be before you leave this alone? That diplomat and Wallace, that's one thing, but your mother . . ."

"I'm not supposed to do something about my mother getting killed?" I rail in anguish.

"No," she says firmly. "That's not up to you anymore. That's for the police to take care of."

"Fuck the police," I fire back angrily. "They think this was an accident. Case closed, next." My pulse is racing. "We're being watched, we know that. Whoever did this had to be spying on my place last night, saw me leave, knew it was empty. I don't know how long whoever did this was here, ransacking the place. Maybe hours. Roach knows I've been going by his property. That was the whole point of dragooning me over to his house, for Godsakes. To inform me he's on to me, and to keep my nose out of his business. That night we were out there and saw those planes, he probably had his spies taking pictures of us taking pictures of them."

Maureen shudders. "I'm beginning to understand how birds must feel when I intrude on their lives with my cameras and binoculars."

"Which is why," I explain to her, "if you don't know where the pictures are, you're not in danger. Or at least, in less danger." I reach out for her. "This is my fight. I know you want to be there for me, you *are* there for me, but I can't endanger you, any more than I already have."

She shrugs me off. "Fritz! Listen to your own words! If everyone knows we're together, then whoever is doing this would assume I know everything." She pauses to take a breath, so she can get down to the bottom line. "So—what *are* you going to do now, Fritz? About James Roach, the murder, Wallace. All that."

"Do you mean am I going to let it alone?"

"Yes."

I shake my head. "I can't."

Her body tenses. "What about me?"

"What about you what?"

"About how I feel, what do you think? The connection between us."

"I've already told you everything. Everything except where the pictures are, and I've explained why I can't do that."

"There's more," she says with iron conviction. "There's more you haven't told me."

"Like what?"

"How should I know? But I know there's more."

I feel like Sisyphus, pushing the rock up the mountain over and over. "We've already gone over this."

"Even if it means getting yourself killed?"

"That's already been decided," I remind her again. "Now it's a question of whether I take my medicine passively, or try to stop it from happening." I take her hands in mine. "I know in my heart James Roach brought about my mother's death, and I have to assume he masterminded the killing of the counselor, and Wallace as well. Someone has to shut him down, Maureen, don't you get that? And I'm the only one who can, because I'm the only one who knows what he's done."

"St. George rides in on his white horse and slays the dragon." She shakes her head forcefully, frustrated and angry with me, almost beyond words. "Do you really think you can stop him? Come on, Fritz, get real. Stop fooling yourself you're someone you're not. You haven't done a very good job so far," she blurts out hotly.

I turn away. That's way too painful.

For her, too. "I'm sorry. I shouldn't have said that."

"It's true."

"But I shouldn't have said it." She reaches out for me, her eyes full of pain. "I only did it because it hurts me so much. I love you, Fritz. I'm terrified I'm going to lose you if you pursue this insane chase. I don't want to lose you."

"And I don't want to lose you," I say, my heart pounding. "More than anything, especially now. But I can't stop. My mother was murdered! Fuck the cops, what they think. You know that's true. I have to nail him. I could never live with myself if I didn't."

"You may not live, period, if you do."

"Let's table this for now, please?" I beseech her. "I have to put my mother in the ground. Let me get through that, then we'll talk about the future."

"Everything about it?"

"Yes," I promise her. "Everything."

It's late. I walk Maureen to her car. She searches my face. "Are you going to be all right here by yourself?"

"I'll be okay."

I'm exhausted. I feel like I could sleep for twenty-four hours straight.

She leans over, kisses me. "You sure you won't spend the night with me?"

I shake my head. "I need to be here tonight."

She gets into her car. "Be careful."

I go back inside. The house is physically no different from the way it was a day ago, but it feels alien. A tomb, already a relic from a past that will never again be revived. Mother was the last link.

Each room bears witness to her, to my father, to generations of the family. Some of the furniture is over a hundred years old. There's cabinetwork from shortly after the end of the Civil War, refinished and repainted many times over the years, but the original design is as it was when Grant was president. God, what stories there are to be told.

Mary Tullis's journal is in my car. I haven't had the spirit to open it until now. I leaf through it, checking the condition of the pages. It had been underneath her body, protected from the flames.

A substantial life is told in those pages. Going back to before we entered the First World War, horse-and-buggy days in this area. People back then had to be strong to survive—only the strongest did. My mother was strong. She might have lived to be a hundred, the small seizure she'd had recently notwithstanding.

To die at her age is not unusual—it's normal. But to die the way she did, that's not common. It's wrong. She did nothing to provoke it, that's the worst part. The only thing she did wrong, in this case, was to be my mother.

I can't let this go. Maureen won't be able to understand that—she has no ties to this past, she only cares about the future. Her and me, healthy and safe.

My agenda, unfortunately, is different. It's not of my choosing anymore—it has been thrust on me, a second skin I cannot shed.

I don't know how much time passes—I've gone blank in my head. When the telephone rings it takes me a moment to realize it's ringing here, in real time, not in some dreamlike place.

"Hello?"

The voice is tentative, as if not wanting to intrude on my anguish. "Fritz? It's Fred Baxter. I figured you might be at your mama's place."

"Hey, Fred," I say wearily.

"I didn't wake you, did I?"

"Not hardly. I won't be sleeping tonight anyways."

"I'm sorry, man. I can't tell you how sorry I am."

"Thanks. And thanks for calling. I appreciate it."

I realize, talking to him at this late hour, that I don't have many friends around here anymore. Like my siblings and me, those who could flew the coop as soon as they were able. The ones who stayed, like Fred, had fewer options.

"Listen, Fritz, I don't want to intrude . . ." He pauses.

"You're not intruding. It's good to talk to someone."

"I found out some stuff. If you're still on the case," he adds. "I understand if you aren't anymore."

"More than ever," I tell him firmly. "That fire was no accident. Whoever set it murdered my mother. And I am going to nail the motherfucker who did it to the wall, if it's the last thing I do."

I hear his sharp intake of breath upon hearing my accusation. "When do you want to get together, then?" he asks.

"How's about now?" I say, before I can think twice about it.

"You sure?"

"I'm not sleeping, and it sounds like you're not ready to go to bed, either. I don't want to inconvenience you, but if you want to, I can do it."

Fred takes his coffee with milk and sugar. I lace mine with bourbon—Maker's Mark, my mother's house brand. Fred has brought a bunch of paperwork, which he lays out on the kitchen table. It's almost midnight, not that time matters.

"Rampart Industries. Very convoluted ball of wax," Fred begins, tracing his finger along the cover sheet, then flipping to the next page. "It doesn't seem to be a stand-alone company. It appears to be part of a larger multinational consortium group that's registered offshore, the Cayman Islands, Indonesia, Switzerland. And Russia."

He takes a sip of coffee, reaches across the table for the bourbon bottle.

"You mind?"

"Help yourself."

He tips an eyeball-measured ounce into his coffee cup, takes a drink. "Understand, Fritz, this is way out of my league. I'm into bail-jumpers, messy divorces, basic skip-tracing, you dig? Who pulled the knife on who. International finance ain't my strong suit."

"Mine, either. Just tell me what you've found out."

"There's a vein of gold in here you're gonna want to mine." He wets his finger, leafs through several pages until he comes to one he's marked with a Post-it. He points to a name halfway down the page.

I read over his finger. *James Roach.*

"James Roach." I say the name out loud. I don't need coffee now, or any kind of stimulants. "What does this company, or companies, do?" I ask. "What do they manufacture, sell, trade, whatever?" I'm pretty sure I know the answer.

Fred confirms my suspicion. "They're importers, mainly munitions. And planes, ships, big-scale stuff. They have deals with countries like Libya, Iraq, North Korea. Which is illegal for an American company to do, but not a Swiss company, or a Russian company, or whatever."

This dovetails into what Simmons had told me about Roach. If James Roach, who was almost indicted for exactly these offenses, is still involved in selling arms to countries we aren't allowed to trade with, he's a classic double-dipper. He's also a traitor, if that's true.

"This is dynamite." I'm excited. "He could be in shit up to his eyebrows."

"Maybe," Fred cautions me. "And maybe not."

"How so not?"

"These conglomerates"—he turns the pages, half an inch thick's worth—"are interrelated, but they're also separate entities, at least on paper. He isn't officially connected to this company now, or any organization that deals with the State Department, Defense Department, any American agency. Everything he owns is in blind trusts. He can't touch them, can't influence them."

"If he's involved in these companies, he's making decisions," I say scornfully. "You know that, Fred."

"Not officially, he isn't. And there's nothing in here"—he riffles the pages again—"that proves this company's doing anything illegal."

"But it could be."

"Yes, it could be," he admits.

"You think we can find out?"

"I don't know," he says pessimistically.

"It's basically legwork, though, isn't it?" I press. "Researching records, finding out whether there have ever been criminal charges brought against them, civil suits, government restraint of trade, stuff like that?"

"Some of it," he agrees.

"I'll give you a place to start looking." I tell him about the charges that were brought against Roach, then abruptly dropped in the early '80s, by former prosecutor Simmons. "Check up on whether Rampart Industries surfaces there," I instruct him. "And if any of these other companies that are connected to it are tied in."

"I'll try," Fred says gamely. He stuffs the documents into the accordian file he brought them in, hands the bundle to me. "I haven't done more than skimmed the surface. But you should read everything, you might find stuff in here I can't put together."

Our work finished for the night, we have a drink, a real one, without a coffee excuse.

Fred leaves. I go back inside. It's lonely in this big house, but for some unexplainable reason, I feel safe tonight. No one is going to come after me here. There's a sacredness to this place that can't be breached, not by Roach, or any of his hired killers. I'll keep my gun handy, though.

I retreat into my old bedroom, which still has Andover and Yale pennants on the walls. My father hung them—my parents truly were proud of me. It's time I showed them they had a reason.

I didn't think I'd be able to sleep but I get a few hours, waking before dawn. Catharsis sleep, aided by last night's bourbon. My head is clear, though—despite drinking whiskey, I have no need for a red one.

The lead story on the local television news before the *Today* show is about the fire and my mother's death. I watch like a ghoul. I'm sure there are prominent stories in the Washington, Baltimore, and Annapolis papers as well. My mother was well known and, more important, well loved.

I plug in my PowerBook and check my e-mail. There are dozens of messages of condolence. Buster, of course, sent one. He's blown away by this, is there for me any way he can be, just let him know. He'll see me at the funeral.

We still haven't had our meeting, I realize, but that's on the back burner for now.

Among the others is one from Johanna Mortimer, like everyone else expressing her shock and dismay; her mother had called and given her the awful news. She hopes I'm bearing up under this dreadful tragedy. She's flying down from Boston tomorrow morning, and will accompany her mother to the funeral. She adds that I need not reply, she appreciates how busy I must be, and how grief-stricken.

I compose a general reply and send it out to everyone, thanking them for their support and informing them of the time and place of the service—day after tomorrow, eleven in the morning, First Methodist Church.

The phone rings. My brother. He and Emily will be down later today, to finalize the arrangements—funeral service, burial in the family plot, caterer for the wake afterward. We'll talk about the future, if there's anything we need to discuss, when he gets here. They won't be staying in the house, too many memories he can't deal with. They've taken a motel room in Jamestown.

My sister, too, calls. She'll fly down the morning of the funeral, but she'll have to return home immediately after. Later, when her schedule permits, she'll come down and go through mother's things, help close up the house.

What strikes me, talking to the two of them about this unspeakable family tragedy, is how unemotional we are toward each other. The three of us haven't spent any time as a unit for years. Even when I used to visit New York I would get together with my sister for an hour or two, no more. Neither she nor my brother ever visited me in Austin, Madison, anywhere I lived. After this is over, we'll probably never be together again. We will go our separate ways, live our detached lives, as we've been doing. Our mother was the connective tissue. Now there's no glue.

Mattie, ever dutiful, makes breakfast for me. Her face is swollen—I'm sure she was up all night, crying. We talk about her future. She's been thinking about it, and she's decided she would like to leave as soon as it's convenient—she can't bear the thought of living here without my mother. She has an old friend in Salisbury, on the other side of the Bay, a woman her age, who has extended her a welcome for as long as she wants to stay.

"Whatever you need," I soothe her. "This house is more

yours than mine, or Sam's, or Dinah's. You put your life into it—we were just passing through."

Maureen shows up around ten. We hug each other, as much from need as from love. "Are you all right?" Her eyes search my face for clues.

"I'm getting by. Don't have a choice, do I?"

"I missed you last night."

"I needed to be here." I'm not going to tell her that Fred came over later, or what he and I talked about. She's here to help me get through my mourning, not play detective, which she wants me to drop.

"What can I do to help?" she asks.

"Nothing. Sam's arranging all the details. He'll be down later today."

Her face tightens. "I shouldn't be here when he comes."

"Why not?"

"Because he doesn't like me. I don't want to be a discordant note on what's already going to be such a sad couple of days. He has the right to be in his house without having to be polite to someone he doesn't like."

"He likes you fine," I say defensively, both of us knowing the opposite is true. "Sam'll be okay. Don't worry about him."

"Friction in your family is the last thing you need now."

That's true; but I don't want to deal with it until I have to. "Johanna's going to be here," I tell her, changing the subject. Seeing Johanna will make her feel better, a friendly face in the crowd, even if the circumstances are lousy.

"Who?" she asks, her face blank.

"Johanna Mortimer. Your friend from Boston."

"Oh. Johanna. I didn't make the connection." She pauses. "She's coming? I thought she barely knew your mother."

"She's coming with her mother," I explain. "Her mother and mom were friends."

Maureen looks concerned. "Did you tell her I'm here? About us?"

"I didn't speak with her. She left me an e-mail. She's coming down tomorrow."

"I wish she wasn't," Maureen says.

"Why not?" I asked, surprised. "It helps to have a friend with you at a time like this. I'm not going to be able to be with you that much, I'll have to deal with everyone else. There's going to be hundreds of people coming to the funeral, and then back here afterward."

"Johanna doesn't know anything about us," Maureen says. She's visibly uncomfortable.

"So?"

"It's going to be embarrassing."

"What're you talking about?"

"You and me, Fritz," she exclaims impatiently. "We're lovers. Anyone can look at us and see that."

"So what? We're not hiding anything. Everyone knows that already."

"Johanna doesn't. Her feelings will be hurt. And she'll be angry with me. She liked you, Fritz. She talked about you."

"We were together one time. Love happens, Maureen. She'll forgive you."

She resists my entreaties. "All I'm saying is, you don't need any more tension right now than you already have. Your brother and his wife, the funeral, plus what's going on with Roach." She pauses. "Is he coming to the funeral?"

I hadn't thought about that. "I sure as hell hope not."

"He and your mother were friends, weren't they? He's your next-door neighbor. It would be impolite for him *not* to show up."

"Fuck him. He can't come."

"Why can't he?" she asks. "No one thinks he had anything to do with the fire, or her dying—except you."

"He knows," I say vehemently.

"If he's involved."

"Oh, fuck, are we still beating up on this? He *is* involved, you know he is. Jesus, Maureen, don't you believe that, after all that's gone down?"

"It doesn't matter what I believe, Fritz. It's what can be proven," she points out rationally.

"He isn't coming," I say with finality. "If I have to call him and disinvite him myself, he is not coming to the funeral of the saint he killed, or whose death he's responsible for."

"You'll be opening Pandora's box if you do that," Maureen cautions me.

"So what? This is my mother's funeral. I can decide who I want to come to it, and don't want."

She pulls back. "Do what you want. I'm telling you what I think, that's all."

"Which I appreciate, but that would be too much. Anyway, he isn't coming. I'll take care of that, one way or the other."

We go outside. It's hot and sticky. I pull my T-shirt away from my skin. I know what I want to do, right now. "Let's go see the birds."

Maureen looks at me, wide-eyed. "Are you sure?"

"What else am I supposed to do? Mope around here and feel more sorry for myself than I already do? We're not going to be here much longer, and neither are they."

"Do you think that's wise, considering?"

"I don't give a shit. You said it before—it's my property. I can go anywhere on my property I want, whenever I want, with whoever I want. What's Roach going to do, burn my house down again?"

We drive down to the shell that was my home. It's a skeleton now, burnt shafts sticking up into the sky. I take a quick look-see around.

"Is there anything worth salvaging?" Maureen asks.

The bile is rising in my stomach as I look at the remains. "I don't know. After the funeral I'll come down and sift through the ashes. Maybe there's something." I kick at a rock. It skitters across the dirt. "What the fuck does it matter? It's just stuff, it's not a life. Nothing matters compared to that."

She doesn't say anything in response. She takes my hand and squeezes it. That's the best anyone can do for me right now.

My boat is serviceable—the fire didn't reach my makeshift dock. We get in and I push off, going to the island of the birds, the only refuge I have left now.

When we get there I walk right into the middle of the birds. I don't feel delicate around them—I want to be surrounded by them, enveloped by them. Maureen follows behind, moving tentatively, not wanting to disturb them. She's also nervous about being here.

Fuck Roach, is what I'm thinking. If he's watching, more the better. I turn toward his property and give him the finger.

"Fritz," Maureen says, reproaching me.

"It made me feel better. Look, if he's spying on me, it doesn't matter, and if he isn't, then it doesn't matter either."

I'm sure he has me under surveillance, but I don't think he can see us here. A small note of consolation—in this place, at least, I still have some privacy, some autonomy over my life.

Ollie and the sandhills occupy their usual spot in the low marsh. I stare at Ollie. He seems to be looking at me, but I don't know for sure if he is. I want him to, that's why I'm here. I want to keep the connection for as long as I can.

"Do you think he recognizes me?" I ask Maureen. She should know, she's the expert.

She considers my question. "For his sake I hope not, but birds do bond to people. All animals can. Not as easily in the wild as a pet would, but they do. Whether he's had enough time with you to bond, I don't know. But it looks like it to me." She points at him. He's standing straight and tall, one leg raised. "He's definitely looking at you."

"Are you saying that to make me feel good, or is it true?"

"I can't guarantee it," she says, touching me lightly on my forearm, "but I'd bet money on it. There's a connection between you two, Fritz, I can feel it."

Hearing that, even if it isn't true, makes me feel a little better.

"Pretty soon I'm going to have to contact the proper authorities and let them know he's here," I say, as much for myself as for her. "The time has come. You're going to be leaving, going back to your regular life, and so am I now—leaving. It's time he was taken care of. I don't want to chance him getting shot, once hunting season starts."

"It's for the best," she agrees. She hesitates. "Where are you going to go, when this is over?"

"I don't know yet. I haven't had time to think about it. Everything's happening so fast."

She takes my hand. "You should come with me, Fritz." She squeezes, hard. "You *have* to come with me. There's no other possibility."

She's right. We've come too far now to not go all the way.

"I want to be there for you, Fritz."

"Me, too."

An old life ends, a new one begins. We come from dust and, like my mother, we will all return to it. But what we do in between makes the difference. My mother knew that, which is why she had a great life. I'm just beginning to understand. And I hope, when I get to the place she did, I, too, will have made some kind of difference.

Sam is at the house when we return. He's on the phone with Bill Morton, the pastor. He talks a moment longer, then hangs up, gives Maureen a sour look, but doesn't say anything.

"Will you be speaking at the service?" He looks right through Maureen. "The minister wants to know."

"I hadn't thought about it," I answer. "I don't think I want to."

"I don't, either." He fans himself. "We should keep it short. She would have wanted it that way, no frills. And those old friends of hers'll keel over in the heat if we dawdle." He slumps into an overstuffed chair. "Christ, I can't believe she's gone."

"Yeah," I answered dully. The reality and finality of it is starting to sink in.

"Would you like me to make some iced tea?" Maureen whispers in my ear.

"That would be nice, thanks."

She goes into the kitchen. I sit across from Sam.

"You shouldn't have moved back here," he says.

I flare up. "Don't start in on me, I mean it. I feel as bad about what happened as you do. But I'm not responsible for it." Which is a bald-faced lie. If he really knew what was going on, he'd kill me.

We glare at each other in strained silence. Maureen returns with a pitcher of iced tea and two glasses. She pours one and hands it to Sam. He takes it without thanking her.

"Thanks," I make a point of saying, as she hands me the other glass.

"You're welcome." She looks at Sam for a moment, then turns and leaves the room.

"You don't have to be rude to her," I tell him, irritated by his boorish behavior. "Mother liked her."

"She shouldn't be here," he snaps at me loudly enough for Maureen to overhear. "Only the family should be here."

"What, there's a rule?"

He gets up heavily. "I have work to do. Are you sleeping here tonight?"

"I don't have anyplace else to go, so yes."

He looks in the direction Maureen left. "Is she?"

He's trying to rile me deliberately. I'm not going to bite. "I don't know. She didn't last night."

"She would if you let her. Wild horses couldn't stop her. Harvard professor," he sneers. "Yeah, and I'm Michael Jordan."

I bite my tongue. If I was married to Emily, the original Iron Maiden, I'd be bitter, too. In a couple of days we'll go our separate ways and I won't have to deal with him anymore.

"Are you going to be here for dinner?" I ask, steering the conversation away from his mean-spirited hostility. "Mattie'll want to know."

He shakes his head. "Emily's waiting back at the motel. She's taking mother's death hard. She couldn't bear to be here in the house today."

His wife has never had honest feelings for anyone, including my mother. I don't say that, though. There's a time and place. This isn't it.

Sam leaves. Mattie asks Maureen and me what we want for supper. We pass; neither of us has any appetite. Mattie retires to her room, in the far reaches of the big old house. She's already started inventorying her stuff, deciding what she's going to take and what she's going to leave behind. She can have almost anything here she wants, as far as I'm concerned. My sister will take some of mother's clothes and her jewelry, my brother will take much of the library. The only items I'd like to have are my father's old hickory pigeonhole desk and swivel chair that have been gathering dust in his study since he died—my mother left that room as it had been when the old man was alive. Sam will probably take them, though—primogeniture. I was the afterthought, it will be ever thus.

We watch television, we have a few drinks, some cheese and crackers, we're pretty quiet with each other. Before you know it, the eleven o'clock news is on. My mother's death and the shack burning down is still a story, but not as prominent. In two more days, after the funeral, it will be a nonstory. An event from the past, part of history.

Maureen tidies up the dishes and glasses. "I'd better be going," she says, stacking the dishwasher. "Come with me, come on. Why torment yourself staying here with ghosts?" She takes me by the hand, tries to pull me along toward the front door.

I resist. "I don't want to leave the house alone."

"That's crazy. Besides, Mattie's here."

"It's not the same."

She doesn't argue further. "Okay. Do what you have to do." She puts her hands on my shoulders. "I wish you'd tell me where those pictures are. If anything happens to you—" She stops. "I don't mean it like that."

"I know."

"I want you to be safe, that's all. I want to be able to take care of you, Fritz. I want you to want me to take care of you."

"I know. I will. When this is over."

She leaves. I go back inside. The big dark house feels like a tomb. I lie in my old bed, staring at the ceiling. I don't get much sleep—the memories keep me awake.

The next day goes by in a blur. Sam is in and out, conferring with the funeral director, the minister. Friends of my mother drop in, bringing covered dishes for tomorrow. We hug and kiss, the usual mourning rituals.

Maureen drops in mid-morning to check on me, make sure I'm okay. Sam, hovering nearby, keeps shooting her dirty looks. Emily, also here now, does the same. They're so fucking proprietary, as if they have the right to decide who's here and who isn't. If our mother were still alive, she and Maureen would be chattering away like two magpies.

"I'll come back later," Maureen says, feeling the hostility, "when they're gone. Call me on my cell phone."

After she leaves, I walk the property. Everything is green, lush, there's a smell of growth in the air. It's beautiful here, but there's no future, unless you want to farm, or be a squire. I have no desire to be either.

Too quickly, it's nighttime again. Sam and Emily take off—they'll be back early in the morning. I call Maureen. She comes over immediately.

"You don't look good," she observes. We're sitting in the

living room. The lights are out. "You're not getting any sleep, are you?"

"I will, after tomorrow." I've seen my reflection in the mirror. I look like a raccoon, the bags under my eyes are so black.

"You'd sleep if I was sleeping with you. I'll spend the night here, if you want me to," she offers. "I want to be with you. And you need me to be with you."

I'm shaking. I pull her close to me.

"Trust me, Fritz. We're nothing if we don't trust each other."

My mother is dead because of me. I have to turn this corner. "Be patient, Maureen. Please."

"I have been, you know that. But I have to know it's going to happen."

"It will. I promise."

My bed, barely adequate for me when I was a kid, is absurdly small for the two of us. Arms and legs tangled up all together, bodies pressing against each other. Love, yes; desperation, unquestionably.

I lie with my head on her stomach, on her lean hard thigh, she strokes my wet, sticky hair, fingers twining strands like a woman weaving a quilt, rubbing my shoulders, drawing me to her, her back to me, two spoons. I feel energy leaving my body, a spirit-feeling, evil cares and woes drifting up to the ceiling, soul-phantoms curling out the windows, into the deep, enveloping night.

The ghosts of my parents are in the house with us. I can almost see them, moving from room to room. In my mind I'm moving through the old rooms with them—kitchen, parlor, porches, then outside. I am in here, they are out there. They are leaving, together again.

I come back into my body. Maureen's breath is warm on my face. We fall asleep, grasping each other.

The first thin ribbon of color is beginning to show in the bottom of the sky when I wake up. For a moment I'm disoriented, until I remember where I am.

Maureen isn't here. Her note is propped up on the side table next to my bed, so I won't miss it.

Fritz, darling— I can't be at your side at the funeral this morning, although my heart will be aching that I'm not. But I know there will be more harm than good if I'm there. This is your family's time, and there shouldn't be any discord. I will be with you in spirit, and will say good-bye to your mother later, when the others have gone.

There is, also, another issue, which I fear is deeply dividing us. I can't give my heart and soul to a man who might not be around for the long haul, because of his inability to stop tilting at windmills, a destructive habit that could be fatal. I'm not interested in wearing widow's weeds, not until I'm an old lady with grandchildren. It's time to call this obsession quits, Fritz, and get on with our lives. When you have made the decision to move on with me, in a life clean of regret, looking back, and attempting payback, call me, and I'll come running.

Don't be angry at me for taking what could be construed as the cowardly way out. I wanted to tell you this in person, but I knew you would try to talk me out of it, and I know this is the right thing to do. I hope you understand.

All my love, Maureen.

P.S. If James Roach shows up, either ignore him, or be civil. You'll feel better about yourself, and that's the most important thing.

I crumple the note, toss it in the wastebasket. I understand why she feels obliged to do this, as well as her feelings for my safety, but I hate that I'll have to endure the ordeal of the funeral service without her. We could have worked things out without her running away from them.

But she's right, in the practical, real-world sense: there

would have been tension between her, Sam, and Emily, and that wouldn't be good. Dinah would feel it, too, which would make matters worse. And I also know, in my heart, that I'm not ready to let James Roach walk away from this without trying to bring him down. I owe that to my mother. I owe it to myself.

I can get through today by myself. Later, hopefully, Maureen and I will work everything out and we'll be together again. Because once this is over I'm not going to let her leave me again, or put her in a position where she feels she has to.

The old clapboard church that my parents worshiped in for over sixty years, and that my brother, sister, and I were baptized in, is filled to overflowing. Sam and Emily, Dinah and her husband, Phillip, who's also a doctor—a radiologist—their kids, both young adults (I'm closer in age to my niece and nephew than I am to Dinah, my sibling), sit in the front pew with me, as we receive the mourners who come up the aisle to pay their final respects to mother.

Dinah and I had a private moment at the house before the funeral home limousine carried us here to the church. It was comforting, seeing her.

My big sister has changed noticeably in the four years since I've last seen her. Approaching sixty, she's a woman who's happily given up battling the aging process. She no longer is coloring her graying hair, nor does she seem concerned that her backside and thighs are thickening. She is at peace with herself, and radiates contentment. In that respect, she is her mother's daughter.

"Mother had a wonderful life." She's taking this stoically—she's a doctor, she sees death as the final step in an inevitable cycle. "Better this way than a lingering illness. Ever since she had that seizure last year I was afraid she'd have something more debilitating and wind up a helpless invalid in a nursing home. She'd have hated that. It was her time," Dinah concluded philosophically.

It wasn't mother's time, that's the problem. She wasn't ready to die, death was imposed on her. But I'm not going to clue Dinah in about what's been going on. Let her be at peace with mother's passing.

Johanna and Agatha Mortimer file by to pay their respects. To my surprise, they're accompanied by Ed Flaherty, Roach's friend who I met the time I went out sailing on the yacht; the day Wallace almost killed me. Mrs. Mortimer has her hand on Flaherty's arm for support. She needs it; she's shaking.

"I'm so sorry, Fritz," Johanna whispers as she takes my hand.

"Thank you," I whisper back, thinking of how awkward Maureen would have found this encounter. Maybe her instinct was right, I have to admit.

"We'll talk later," Johanna says before she moves on.

I nod, mutely. Her mother and Flaherty mumble regrets as well. I didn't know Flaherty knew my mother. Mrs. Mortimer looks terrible. Mother's death has hit the old folks hard; they're all wondering which of them will be next.

James Roach is absent; thank God for that. He sent a huge wreath, the biggest one in the church. Typical of him—he's the kind of rich bastard who thinks he can buy anything. If I'd been drinking I'd have kicked the damn thing out the church door. I don't know how I would have reacted if he had shown his face. Punched him out, probably.

Buster isn't here, either, which is a shame, because he really liked my mother, and she felt the same toward him. He called last night, full of regret: he's in the middle of a trial he thought would be over yesterday, but it dragged on, and he can't get off. He sent his love for mother and good feelings for me. We'll have our own private wake later.

The doors are closed, the funeral service begins. The minister's remarks are knowing and loving. He's a youngish man, in his early forties, but he and mother were friends—age was irrelevant to her, she cared about what was in your heart. She was the president of the women's auxilary at the church, so she and Pastor Morton spent time together. He enjoyed her vivaciousness and spunk, and recalls a few memorable incidents that evoke welcome laughter from the assembled mourners, all of whom want to remember mother in a positive, uplifting way.

The service is brief, as we requested. Some prayers, the sermon, a few of mother's favorite hymns, and it's over. Sam, Dinah's husband, Phillip, their son, Jason, and three older men, decades' long friends of mom and dad's (only a few are left, and fewer still are fit enough to carry a heavy box), and I hoist the simple pine coffin onto our shoulders and carry it out of the church and into the hearse. At one point Sam, standing next to me, coughs, and I realize he's been drinking: I smell vodka on his breath. It's a common fallacy that vodka leaves no alcohol trace. Experienced drinkers—I qualify as one—can easily detect it. Sam needs a booze crutch to get through this, I realize sadly.

It's a short drive to the ancient graveyard. Generations of Tullises and Bradshaws, along with Reynoldses, Miltons, Joneses, and other related ancestors, have been laid to rest here for over two hundred and fifty years. The burial, as was the service, is mercifully short, which is a good thing, because it is hot as a greased skillet today, over 100 degrees, with the humidity in the high 90s. Rivulets of water are running down my sides from my armpits. All the men, except the minister, my brother, my brother-in-law, and me, have taken off their coats. Looking around, I see pancake makeup melting and cracking on women's faces, dark stains appearing under dresses and shirtsleeves. Everyone, old folks and not-so-old, beats the air furiously with fold-open fans the funeral home has wisely distributed.

Sam, standing to my right in the row closest to the open grave site, is sweating buckets. His face is flushed crimson; he looks dehydrated. That would be both awful and wonderfully comical—mother's older son, Mr. Uptight, keeling over into her grave. Two old ladies, though, actually do faint, and are carried off to recuperate in the shade of the trees.

Then it is over. The casket is lowered, rose petals are thrown onto it, then handfuls of dirt, as Pastor Morton intones the biblical "ashes to ashes" and the rest of the mournful litany. The assemblage staggers up the hill to their cars.

I lag behind. "Good-bye, mother," I say quietly. My eyes are full with tears. "I'm sorry you had to bear my sins. I can never make it up to you, but I'm going to try."

I hitch a ride to the house with one of the stragglers. By the time I get there the wake is in full progress, mourners walking around with plates of food in one hand and glasses of whiskey or beer in the other. The air-conditioning is blasting away, but it's still hot and muggy with so many people jammed in. The men are in shirtsleeves. Some of the women have shed their uncomfortable heels. I work my way to the bar at the far end of the living room, next to the French doors that open onto the veranda.

Louis, ever faithful, is mixing drinks. He fixes me a tall gin and tonic. "She was the last of her kind," he says sadly, as I nod in mute agreement. He's bearing up stoically, but I know he's hurting inside, as are we all.

I move slowly through the crowd, accepting condolences and wet hugs, listen to old friends tell me what a pistol mother was, how proud she was of me, the usual stuff people say at funerals. There's much conversation about the dreadful nature of mother's dying, how shocked I must have been, and so forth. It was a terrible accident, everyone says that. There is also an undercurrent of something akin to condescension toward me. I was the accidental child, the mistake who didn't quite make it—the one who had to come home and live by his mother's grace because he had problems out in the world beyond the boundaries of our property. It's nothing spoken, of course, but I feel it, the way I'm looked at, the way people turn to each other and talk low after I've moved on. Not a soul among these gathered here thinks, out loud at least, that the fire might have been caused deliberately. It was an old shack, jerry-built, the fire was a result of natural consequences. No one blames me for the fire, but many, I'm sure, hold me responsible.

Johanna Mortimer detaches herself from a group that includes her mother, Ed Flaherty, and my sister and her husband, and comes over to me. "Are you holding up all right?" she asks anxiously. "I mean . . ."

"As best I can, considering."

"I don't know what to say, Fritz."

"You don't have to say anything. I know you feel bad. Everyone does."

She tries to change the conversation to something other than the usual "I'm sorry" pap. "How's the bird-watching going?"

If only she knew. "I'm not getting out much these days."

I don't want to get into birding talk. To avoid the topic, I drain my glass, hold it up. "Refill," I say, turning back toward the bar.

She doesn't have a drink. "I could use one myself."

I can't tell her to bug off. That would be impolite, and even though Maureen has problems with her, I don't.

"Vodka and orange juice, please," Johanna tells Louis. We stand there awkwardly, not knowing what more to say to each other, while he makes our drinks. He hands me mine, begins on hers.

"Where's Harvard's representative from *Hustler* magazine?" a voice I don't want to hear brays from behind us.

I take a deep breath, so that I don't lose control of myself. "Can it, Sam."

He's broken up over this, and he blames me. Not that I'm

blameless, by his lights, but there's a time and place. Our mother's wake, in her house, should be off-limits.

"I thought she and mother were such great buddies," he scoffs. "Doesn't even have the decency to come to her funeral, for Christsakes. You really know how to pick 'em, baby brother."

I've had it. That's the last thing I need, shit from my sloshed brother. I whirl on him. "She didn't come because of how you're acting right now. She stayed away to keep peace in the family. I'll tell her it wouldn't have mattered."

"'Course it didn't. Doesn't matter anyway. You've got her substitute right here."

Johanna's mouth flies open. The people around us start moving away.

"That's all that matters to you, Fritz." He looks at Johanna. "Texas, Maryland, wherever you go, it's women and trouble. You're a champ, Fritz. A champion bird dog."

He's gone too far. I'm going to punch his lights out, right here in our mother's house, right in the middle of our saying good-bye to her.

"You're drunk, Sam." A woman's stern voice: Dinah's. "You're acting disgracefully." She grabs him by the arm. "Everyone's watching you," she whispers roughly in his ear. "If you don't care about how our friends feel, think about mother and how appalled she would be."

He tries to pull away from her. She holds him in a firm grasp. He belches—I can smell the whiskey from five feet away.

Dinah recoils. "You need some air, and a bucketful of coffee. Would you get some strong coffee and bring it outside to my brother?" she asks Louis.

"Right away, Miz Dinah." He scurries off in the direction of the kitchen.

"I'm sorry about this," Dinah says to Johanna.

Johanna is too flummoxed to respond.

Dinah pulls Sam out of the room, onto the back veranda.

People are gaping. I see Emily, white-faced, watching her husband lose it. She stares at him and Dinah for a moment, then turns and runs out of the room.

There is a moment's silence—then it's as if nothing had happened. People go back to talking to each other, sipping their drinks, nibbling their food. Nobody wants to acknowledge such outrageous behavior, especially from Sam, the dutiful son. That kind of fuck-you stuff is supposed to come from me.

This time, I was the good guy. It's a relief.

"Poor man," Johanna remarks, staring out the French doors at Sam and Dinah, who are sitting on a porch swing. Dinah has her arms around Sam, is consoling him. I can see his shoulders are shaking—he's crying.

"We're all stressed," I tell her. "Would you excuse me? I need some air myself."

I go out the front door, the opposite direction from Sam and Dinah. What a mess. I feel like jumping in my car and getting the hell out of here.

A voice cuts into my privacy. "It's a bad time for everyone."

I turn around. Ed Flaherty has come outside. He leans against one of the columns that holds up the heavy slate roof. Taking a pack of unfiltered Camels out of his shirt pocket, he shakes one out, fires it up, holds the pack out to me.

I haven't smoked a cigarette in years, but I reach for one now. He lights it for me. I stand next to him in the shade, a cigarette in one hand, drink in the other. Flaherty's right—it's a fucked day all around.

"I never knew your mother, but everyone says she was a great lady."

"She was." The cigarette smoke burns. I rinse my mouth with gin.

"Agatha Mortimer revered your mother. That's why I'm here, to lend her support. Agatha and I are friends. I've come to know Johanna as well," he goes on. "She's first-class."

"She's a nice woman," I allow.

"Who was your brother referring to, in there? I heard the name . . . *Hustler*?" A curl of a smile crosses his lips.

"A woman I'm working with," I answer, still pissed at Sam for his boorish tastelessness. "Who has nothing to do with *Hustler.* My brother's sick joke."

"From Harvard, then, I take it? I heard the reference."

I shrug.

"I don't mean to pry. I mention it because Johanna Mortimer resides in Boston, in case you didn't know," he offers up. "Perhaps they know each other."

"I doubt it." I don't want Maureen's name dragged into this, even via a disinterested third party. "Boston's a big city."

"The home of the bean and the cod." He picks a stray piece of tobacco off his tongue, flicks it away. "I also came to convey James Roach's condolences. He felt his being here in person might cause discord."

I tense up. "He was right."

"James told me about your meeting," Flaherty goes on. "He expressed himself forcefully, I gather."

"A frank and honest exchange of ideas?" I respond bitingly. "Isn't that how diplomats refer to a meeting when they disagree on everything?"

"I believe so." He grinds his butt out on the sole of his boot, field-strips it, lets the wind carry the shreds away. "James can be blunt. But he isn't what he appears to be."

"What's that supposed to mean?" I don't want to talk about that piece of shit, but Flaherty's sucking me in. He's an old hand, a pro who has one of those underplayed, persuasive manners that make you pay attention.

"Appearances can be deceiving, especially when you're in a delicate position, as James is."

"Our frank and honest exchange went beyond appearances. Way beyond."

He nods. "I can understand your resentment at being dragged to his lair, so to speak, and being chastised. Like a trip to the principal's office. Or in your case, an unpleasant meeting with the dean." He stares at me with calculation under his hooded eyes.

He knows about my past. Not that it matters, but it's disconcerting. Unless he heard it as gossip via old Mrs. Mortimer. That's possible. I can't ascribe every negative comment about me to sinister forces that are out to get me. Sometimes it's mere coincidence. In this instance, though, I don't think so.

"Chastisement doesn't bother me, I'm used to it," I tell him. "Roach threatened me. That puts it in a different category."

"James was making a point. Sometimes one overstates to make a point."

I stamp out my cigarette. The man is overstepping his welcome. "When people start turning up dead, that isn't overstating a point. That's murder. And I don't appreciate that you're bringing this up at my mother's funeral."

He steps back, holds his hands in the air. "I'm sorry. I meant no offense." He pauses. "When you say 'murder,' who are you referring to? You're not intimating you think your mother was murdered, are you?"

"I'm not intimating anything. All I know is, Roach's bodyguard Wallace was killed under weird circumstances, then Roach threatens me, then my mother is found dead in my house . . . you connect the dots. And there's other stuff, too."

His brow furrows. "Such as?"

"Forget it." I can't deal with this now. "Thank you for being here for Mrs. Mortimer. As for Roach, he doesn't need you or anyone standing in for him. He's unwelcome under any and all circumstances. Let's leave it at that, okay?"

He retreats into the house—I hear his boot heels echoing on the marble entryway.

I wonder if Roach put him up to this. I wouldn't put it past the bastard.

It's brutal out. I'm drained. I sit on the front steps. My mouth tastes like asbestos from the cigarette. I have every other vice, I don't need that one. I sip my drink—the ice has melted, so it's weak. A good thing, because I don't want to lose control, like Sam did. I should get some food in my stomach.

In a little while. Right now, I want to sit here and let my mind go blank.

I don't know how long I'm there alone. Five minutes, ten. I start to calm down. I should go inside and get another drink. It doesn't have to be alcoholic, but I need to keep my bodily fluids replenished. People get dehydrated and their brains turn mushy. That's what happened to Sam.

I feel a presence behind me. It's Johanna, I don't have to look to know. "Join me if you want," I invite her without turning around.

She comes down the steps, stands a few paces beside me. "Maybe you need space."

"I've had space."

She sits down. "May I ask you a question?"

"Sure."

"What was your brother talking about? Harvard, and *Hustler* magazine?"

Christ, Sam's vitriolic tongue is going to haunt me all day. "Nothing. He was ranting. He was drunk, in case you didn't notice."

"Everyone noticed. I felt bad for him."

"Don't—he doesn't deserve your sympathy." I run the cold glass around the back of my neck. It doesn't bring any relief. By way of explanation, I tell her, "He thinks I'm responsible for our mother's death. He has to make somebody a scapegoat, so he lashed out at me. It's nothing new."

"But you weren't. It was an accident."

"It's a long story."

"I'm sorry." She reaches over and touches my hand sympathetically, then withdraws. "I shouldn't be intruding."

She means well. Her presence reminds me of a question that's been festering in my brain since she entered the church, and came to a head fifteen minutes ago. "How long have you known Ed Flaherty?"

She brushes some damp strands of hair off her face. "I barely know him at all. He's my mother's friend. Your neighbor James Roach introduced them. Mother's sweet on him," she says with a smile. "Ed told me he met you when you went sailing together, on Roach's boat." She looks at me. "Why do you ask?"

"Curiosity. People don't usually come to funerals when they don't know the deceased."

"He asked to."

"He *asked?*" That doesn't square. "Your mother didn't ask him?"

"No. He wanted to come."

Roach put him up to it, I'm sure of that now. He used his relationship with Mrs. Mortimer as an excuse. And I thought he was an okay guy. I should have figured, him being a friend of Roach's from way back.

She bites on a cuticle. "This might be the wrong question to ask now, but are you involved with someone?"

I turn to her. "Where's this coming from?"

"The way your brother was talking. I know he's drunk, but the way he said it. And my mother told me she'd heard you'd been seen with a woman who isn't from around here." A quick touch to my arm again, another quick pulling away. "I'm sorry. It's none of my business. Especially today."

I'm tired of dodging. It's like trying to find your way out of a maze that has no exits. "Do you know a professor from Harvard named—don't laugh—Maureen O'Hara?"

"Yes," she says slowly, "I know Maureen."

"An ornithologist?"

"She's in the Biology Department. I don't know her specialty. She could be, I guess. Is that who your brother was referring to?" she asks.

I nod. "I've been helping her out. Watching birds."

"That's . . . interesting."

"Why?"

"When you told me you had to go out on some bird-watching trip, when I was here . . ." She hesitates. "That night, at your place? I thought about it later. I thought you were laying a line of bull on me. To get rid of me."

I nod. "I was."

"But then what about . . . ?"

"Helping out your friend?"

"Friend's an overstatement." There's a tone of irritability in her voice. "We know each other. We don't move in the same social circles."

That's unsettling to hear, but understandable. Maureen said they had some issues, serious enough for Maureen to duck out of something she knew was important to me; to both of us.

"She wanted to study birds of the region. She came up with my name." I pause. "I thought she got it from you."

Johanna shakes her head. "She didn't hear about you from—" She stops.

"What?"

"I was at a party in Cambridge, shortly after I came back from here. I mentioned I'd been down, and had met this man . . ." Her face begins to redden. "This nice guy. Actually, I think the words I used were 'sexy' and 'cool,' or something equally silly. Maureen was there. It's the only party I can recall being at in the past year where she was there, too. I didn't talk to her about you, but she might have overheard. Did she say I told her about you?" she asks dubiously.

"More or less," I say offhandedly. It's taking guts for her to open up to me like this. I admire that, but I wish she wasn't, because I can't reciprocate. "It was most likely the way you've described it."

"I wouldn't talk to Maureen O'Hara about my personal life," she says, almost savagely. It's as if she's angry, hearing this.

"Why not?"

"I just wouldn't. Certainly not about a man."

Something weird is going on between her and Maureen. I wish now I had told Johanna not to come today. I stand up. I'm light-headed—for a second I sway on my feet. "I need to put some fluids in my system, get something to eat."

Johanna is slumped over, her legs spread apart, feet splayed out on the steps. "I'm going to sit out here for a while by myself, if you don't mind."

"Why would I mind? Stay here as long as you want."

I go back inside. Whatever's bugging her about Maureen, that's her problem. She and Maureen can duke it out. I have more than enough problems of my own.

Mid-afternoon. The wake's petering out. The last stragglers say their good-byes and leave. No one's left except family. Dinah comes over to me where I'm sitting in our father's favorite wing chair, nursing a ginger ale. I'm done drinking for the day. I'm going to take a few days off, give my liver a breather.

"Talk to your brother," my sister implores me.

"About what?"

"We have to hang together, Fritz. It's just us now."

She takes me by the hand and leads me to the study, where Sam is lying on the couch, a wet dish towel covering his forehead. Emily hovers nearby, wringing her hands.

Sam struggles to sit up. "I made an ass of myself," he proclaims hoarsely to the floor.

I'm not feeling charitable. "Not the first time."

"Fritz." Dinah gives me a big-sister look of reprimand.

Peace in the family. I can handle that, for a short time. "I've done my share of being the jerk, too," I give him grudgingly.

"We'll leave you two to figure this out," Dinah says, casting a "let's-go" eye at Emily.

The women depart. I sit down on the couch next to Sam.

"Why do you have such a hard-on against me?" I ask him. "What have I done to deserve it?"

He looks at me. His eyes are bloodshot, caked drool covers his lips. "You never appreciated what you had."

"That's harsh, isn't it?"

He shakes his head. "You always got away with murder. Whatever you did, however you fucked up, they forgave you. You never paid any dues, Fritz. And you never said 'I'm sorry.' "

"What was I supposed to be sorry for?"

"For not caring. No, that's not it. For not caring about anyone except yourself."

"Well, I care now. I care a lot now."

He blows his nose, a big honk. "What're you going to do?"

"About what?"

"About your house being burned down," he says impatiently. "Where are you going to live, now that mother's not around to support you anymore?"

I shake my head. "I haven't given it a thought yet."

"You'd better." Unsteadily, he gets to his feet. "Because the life that was here, and everything that's connected to it, is over."

Everyone's gone now. I'm alone, except for Louis and Mattie, who are finishing the cleanup. Then they, too, will leave for the rest of the day and night.

I think about what my brother accused me of, my never having paid any dues: I think I have. I'm paying them now. But I understand what he meant. For our family. I didn't make a contribution. No family of my own, no children, no career security, so our mother wouldn't worry about me. I'm rudderless, drifting wherever the stream takes me.

I go outside, aimlessly walk around, come back. This entire situation has been a classic case of what can happen when you do the right thing the wrong way. I got involved. No one wanted me to. Not Buster, not Maureen, not Roach. They all had their own reasons for wanting me to sit this out, but they did warn me, and I didn't heed them. I've gotten involved for selfish reasons, yes, for the thrill of the unknown, the taste of possible danger; but regardless of that, what I have done is what was right, and moral: I was witness to a murder, and I didn't feel the act should go unpunished—whatever that means. But by becoming an involved member of the human tribe, I brought my world down around my ears.

Don't get involved—the modern mantra. I broke it, and now I'm paying more dearly than I could ever have imagined. My mother is dead and other people are dead. It's fucked, this world.

You can dwell on the past but you can't live in it, even if you want to. I don't have a choice now—somehow, some way, I have to see this through to the end. I owe my mother nothing less.

My not-drinking pledge lasted how long? Two hours? I'm nursing a beer, a cold Sierra Nevada. I put beer in the sort-of-drinking category. I'm drinking just the one; at the most I'll have one more.

The phone rings. I don't want to answer it, I want to chill out, do nothing, think nothing. Tomorrow will come soon enough, then I'll do something.

It doesn't stop. The answering machine must have been turned off.

I get up from the comfy Adirondack chair and go inside. The air-conditioning is off, it's hotter inside than outside. The air is heavy in here, the lingering essences of bodies, of drink, food, mourning.

I cradle the phone in my ear. "Hello?" I say, hoping it's Maureen.

No such luck. "How you holding up, Fritz?" Fred asks solicitously.

I knew in my gut Maureen wouldn't call this soon after leaving that note. Nevertheless, I'm disappointed. "I'm holding up."

He hears the fatigue in my voice. "Is this an okay time to talk?"

"What do you want to talk about, Fred?"

"Let's start with the gun that killed Wallace."

"What about it?"

"It's the same gun that killed the counselor. Small-bore gun, .22 caliber."

Now I know why Lieutenant Ricketts asked me if I owned a .22. "How'd you find out about the gun without arousing your cousin's suspicion?"

"I got him talking about the Wallace murder. He's been in close touch with the P.G. police department. They've been comparing notes. I weaseled the info out of him without giving away that you and me are working on this."

"Good man," I praise him.

"There's a second part. Marcus has been checking up on the counselor's history, as part of his investigation. The counselor might not have been an innocent bystander in what happened to him. The getting-murdered part."

"Like how?"

"It may be he was involved in illegal weapons trafficking in years past."

"With Roach?"

"Marcus didn't say, and I didn't press him. Marcus is sharp as they come, but he's a city cop. This is federal stuff, way higher than him." He pauses. "What are you going to do about this, Fritz?"

I lean back. It's a cloudy night, the stars are blanketed. My mind feels like it's spinning out of control.

"I put my mother in the ground today, Fred. Tomorrow's going to come soon enough. Then I'll decide."

19

My father owned an Old Town canoe. He bought it in Maine one summer while on a family vacation (family of four; I wasn't born yet) and had it transported down here. He used to paddle it in the streams and rivers that flowed around and through our property when he was a younger man, before I was born. Sometimes my mother would go for an afternoon's cruise with him. They'd glide along, champagne flutes in hand, like characters in an English country vignette from the Edwardian age.

When I came back to the family manse I hauled the old canoe down from its perch in the rafters of the old garage where it had been stored for decades, recaulked the seams, made it seaworthy. I've only taken it out a few times, preferring the convenience and maneuverability of my little motorboat. Tonight, though, my mode of transportation has to be a craft that's self-propelled, rather than by motor.

The charred remains of my shack loom quiescent in the dark cloudy night, silently chastising me. I stand in front of what used to be the front porch, staring at it. I shouldn't be going where I'm going, but I have to. The birds, until recently my reason for being, are there. As importantly, this burnt-out hulk is a symbol of my life. I have to confront why it was burned down, and along with that, why my mother was killed.

I unstrap the canoe from the roof of my Jeep and carry it to the dock. The air is thickly perfumed with night-flower smells. I have a water bottle with me and some rolls of superfast black and white film in my camera, so I can get an image if there's anything worth shooting.

Lowering the old boat into the green-black water, I climb in and push off. The current, flowing downstream slowly, does most of the work. I paddle easily, concentrating on where I'm going. There's hardly any light; the moon, a few days past new, is obscured by the thick cloud cover, which I know from experience should last all night. The dimness makes the landscape hard to see, but that's what I want—darkness, to conceal my movements. I can almost traverse these waterways blindfolded, so limited light is no problem for me. If the night was cloudless, I wouldn't have the nerve to come down here. I sit low, keeping my head down to avoid accidentally bashing it on one of the low-hanging cypress branches that protrude into the center of the channel.

My little island is so thick with sleeping birds it's almost impossible to walk without stepping on them. I pick my way carefully, wading through the shallow water that separates the two spits of land, making for the marshy area where Ollie and the sandhills are roosting. What majestic and glorious creatures they are! I recall Blake's *Songs of Experience:* his rapturous evocation of the tiger could be applied equally to Ollie.

It's very still. I squat on my haunches and stare at Ollie and his close cousins. From my roosting spot I can't see where I tied up my boat.

Time goes slowly. That's good, I'm not in a speedy mode. I don't know how long I've been here, I didn't wear my watch. It must be very late, after midnight. I swallow the last sips from my water bottle. Even though I've been warned not to I'll come back tomorrow, when the sun is up. I want to take more pictures of the birds to replace the ones I lost, so I'll have negatives, not merely images in my computer, to show that Ollie was here. Otherwise, he won't have existed as part of my life as forcefully. The memory of him, like a bad old print, will fade and fade until someday there will be nothing left.

As I walk back to the canoe and begin untying the line I hear the *whup-whup* sound of helicopters approaching. The two long rows of lights on Roach's landing strip come on in a staggered sequence. Four helicopters loom up in the nighttime sky, flying low over the timber line. Military-style airships, scary-looking machines of death and destruction. They touch down in orderly formation, one after the other. Even before the rotors stop the doors have opened and men are coming out. Bodyguards first, dressed like paratroopers but not in U.S. mufti, different-colored uniforms that I don't recognize. They carry assault weapons. Serious-business expressions. After they come out and spot-check to see that the area's secure, men in civilian garb emerge, a couple from each helicopter. I can't make out any details in their appearance—they're too far away—but I have a strong, immediate reaction: they remind me of the slain diplomat.

They mill around on the runway, each group standing apart from the others.

I'm aware, suddenly, that I haven't drawn a breath in thirty seconds. Now I force myself to, inhale, then slowly exhale. Taking my camera out of the bag, I attach the longest lens I brought, 400 mm.

As I'm beginning to focus on the action, a Range Rover, followed by three Chrysler minivans, approaches from the direction of Roach's house. Roach gets out of the Range Rover. He's dressed casually but elegantly, the picture of the country squire. Two of his bodyguards, the same two men who snatched me from my shack and brought me to his house, flank him. They, too, are armed with heavy-duty weapons. They're dressed in lethal-looking black, the black of SWAT teams, of the SS—if the lights were off, they'd be invisible.

Roach strolls over to the assemblage and greets each group in turn as they stand in the shadows of the behemoth helicopters. Everyone seems edgy except for Roach, who's cool and collected.

I take a quick exposure reading through my spot meter. The light coming off the runway is marginal, but I'm not going to save film now. I focus on the action and begin clicking away.

Roach's equanimity under what feels, even from this distance, like a lot of pressure, seems to be warming up the crowd. They start talking to one another, albeit stiffly. I'd like to be closer, but I don't dare move from my position of hidden cover.

After a few moments of seeing that each group becomes more comfortable with the other (my imprecise take on what's happening, from my distant perspective and my knowledge of Roach's iron-fist-in-silk-glove forcefulness), Roach leads the assemblage to the vehicles. He gets into his Range Rover, the others climb aboard the minivans, and the convoy heads toward his house, out of my line of sight. Their headlights are off, they drive in darkness.

As soon as the cars drive away the runway lights go off, and the entire area goes dark again. Roach didn't want anyone to see these men arrive here, or know that they're here now. And no one does, I'm sure, except me.

I hadn't given conscious thought as to why I felt compelled to come out here tonight, particularly after what I've gone through today, but now I know it wasn't only to see the birds. I was hoping (and dreading) that something like this would happen, something that would force the issue. I climb into my canoe and push off, angling the slender boat downstream, toward Roach's property.

It only takes me a few minutes to get to a place on Roach's side of the stream where I can pull up to the bank, tie my canoe off, and carefully climb ashore, my camera bag slung over my shoulder. I shouldn't be doing what I'm doing, but I can't stop myself: I've gone too far down this path, too much pain and misery have happened for me to walk away from it now; particularly since I've stumbled, through no brilliance of my own, onto this explosive encounter.

If I see anyone, hear anyone, feel anything moving, I'll hightail it out of here faster than Halley's Comet. I can get lost in this swamp like a cottonmouth.

Clambering up the shallow embankment, I find myself a short distance away from the dark runway. The area is quiet—the big machines loom up in the darkness like huge sleeping bugs. Let sleeping bugs and dogs lie should be my motto, but it isn't, not tonight.

After satisfying myself that no one's been left behind to keep watch of the airships, I turn away from the runway and look toward the house, which is about a half-mile away as the crow flies. It's lit on the inside, but I'm too far away to see anything. Carefully, keeping low, listening intently for any out-of-place sounds, I start Indian-walking toward it, one foot quietly placed in front of the other.

The ground under my feet is weeds and scrub grass until I'm about two hundred yards from the house, where the cultivated lawn begins, part of the acres of expanse I saw from inside Roach's house the day I was his captive guest. I feel like the Tom Cruise character in *Eyes Wide Shut,* sneaking into a clandestine, sinister situation that he knows he shouldn't be violating but drawn to it nonetheless by the excitement of what he might find there, and the insane, potentially fatal thrill of possible capture.

I stop and wait. A hot summer wind is starting to come up. It feels good on my face, bracing.

I don't have the guts to get any closer. I'm drenched in my sweat as it is. I'm betting that the security—I'm sure there's an alarm system—is clustered close to the house, that it doesn't extend out this far. The man owns almost a hundred acres. He can't cover it all. The house, the airfield, that's what it would be concentrated on—I hope.

A sound stops me. I freeze, look around, carefully check it out. The noise is that of footsteps crunching on dry grass. Armed guards, patrolling the grounds, midway between me and the house. I squat on my haunches and put a wet finger to the wind—it's blowing in my direction. That's a relief; if they have dogs—I don't see any, but there could be some outside my line of vision—they'd smell me from this distance if I was upwind from them.

Trying not to make a sound, I inch over to a clump of manicured bushes that form a horseshoe fringe around the inner gardens and hide behind them. Peering through an opening in the bushes, I look at the house.

The floor-to-ceiling windows offer me a good view inside. Roach is standing at a table facing the new arrivals, who are seated in comfortable chairs, each small group separated slightly from the other. Roach is talking, the others are listening with intent expressions on their faces.

I take my camera out of the bag, bring it to my eye, adjust the focus. The magnification of the long lens brings my subjects startlingly close. I begin snapping away, making sure I have at least one clear shot of each person in the room.

I complete one cycle and start panning the room again, when I sense something—a subtle movement, borne by the wind. I lower the camera from my eye, trying to feel what it is, like a bird dog on point.

What I intuit, in my churning gut, is that I've been found out. I can't explain why I feel that—the men patrolling the area don't seem to have taken notice of me, but I know it. Maybe there are body-heat detectors that I've tripped, space-age monitors tracking me from above. It doesn't matter how I've been detected; all I do know is that I have to get the fuck out of here, now.

Slowly, carefully, I begin inching away from the house, moving like a crab, crouched low to the ground, trying to steal glimpses over my shoulder to see if I'm being pursued.

I'm not, not yet anyway. I rise up and start running. I can see, in the darkness, the helicopters looming up in front of me, and I'm running for the safety of the water as fast as I can, my breath is coming hard and dry, it's like I'm breathing inside a blast furnace, my chest is tightening, I feel that at any moment I'm going to be nailed, a deer in the headlights.

The sound is deafening, a high, shrill, air-raid-siren shriek. A moment later, the perimeter around Roach's house is lit up like the Christmas tree at Rockefeller Center.

My adrenaline rush kicks in. I'm sprinting full-out now. I hear the crack of a bullet being fired, then another. Instantly, I hit the ground hard, eating dirt, crawling on my hands and knees like a dog. The sharp vegetation tears at my face, body, rips my clothes. Somewhere behind me, I don't know how close, no way I'm going to stop and look, shots are ringing in the night, loud enough to scare anything alive for miles around, as the sentries fire at anything moving—shadows, trees waving in the wind. I don't see birds taking off, it's too dark out, but I hear them, the rush of hundreds of pairs of wings as the birds take to the sky as if sucked up in the vortex of a tornado.

It seems like forever before I get to the river. I slide on my ass down the embankment to the canoe, jump in, push off from the bank, and start paddling upstream against the current as hard and fast as I can.

In the distance behind me, I can see, through the protective canopy of cypress branches, the lights going on back at Roach's airstrip. Then the sound of helicopter engines firing up, the beating of the rotors, followed by the air-sucking *whoosh* as they take to the sky.

I don't stop for a heartbeat, I keep paddling like my life depends on it, which I'm sure it does. It's a crazy maze in here—if you didn't know this patch of water and lowland intimately you could get hopelessly lost. I know these waterways upside down and backward, I've been navigating them every day for months. So even though the sky is almost pitch-black, I know where I'm going. And my pursuers, if there are any, don't. I'm counting on that.

It's quiet and still when I get back to my dock. I pull the canoe onto dry ground, lash it onto the top of my Jeep, and drive back to my mother's house, where I hurriedly store the canoe back in the garage.

There's only one thought in my mind: get out of here. I throw my PowerBook, cameras, and gun into the car. When I get to the road, which is the only connection between our property and Roach's, aside from the water, I pause to check for traffic. Nothing is moving—no headlights approaching, no sounds of cars. Leaving my own lights off, I drive away from there as fast as I can.

I hang out in an all-night trucker's diner until dawn, sitting in the last booth in the back, facing the door, drinking coffee to stay awake, my gun heavy in my pocket. At six-thirty I make a phone call, pay my bill, and leave, checking my rearview mirror with a nervous tic.

Pierce Wilcox is waiting for me at the community college darkroom. He doesn't ask why I called him so early, and I don't volunteer any information. He opens one of the darkrooms for me, then leaves me alone.

I develop the rolls. They come out all right—the light was marginal, but I get images, good enough to make identifications.

Now I have to figure out who these men are, how they're connected to Roach. And to find out how what I witnessed last night is linked to the murdered diplomat, Wallace's killing, and my mother's.

"It's me," I rasp into the telephone.

I made this call knowing I could be setting myself up for an ambush. If Roach knows it was me out there last night—he could have pictures, his spy apparatus is far better than anything I can mount against him—and it filtered down to Buster, our longtime friendship might not be strong enough to withstand the pressures of his job, his career.

"Fritz. I hear the concern in Buster's voice. "How was the funeral? Not too brutal, I hope. I really feel bad I couldn't come."

"We survived." I can't deal with small talk now, not even if it's with the best of intentions. But he sounds genuine, not like he's setting me up. "I need your help," I say bluntly.

Now there's a hesitation. "Is it about what I think it's about?" Even if he's in the dark about what happened last night he still wants to keep as far away from anything having to do with Roach as possible; but I need help that Fred can't provide, and Buster is the one person I know who might be able to give it to me quickly.

"Yes."

Another pause before he continues. "I don't know if that's a good idea. I don't want to get any deeper involved in what you've been doing." He sounds nervous as hell. "You promised me you were going to stop chasing your tail about this."

"I was, but things have changed."

"Like how?"

"I'll tell you when I see you. But Buster . . ."

"What?"

"I need to know I can trust you."

"What's that supposed to mean?" he asks, sounding offended.

"I'm sitting on a powder keg. Several of them. You'll understand when I tell you what they are. But I don't want to talk to you about any of it if you can't keep what I tell you totally confidential."

He doesn't respond immediately.

"If for any reason you can't agree to that," I continue, "tell me, I'll hang up, and this conversation never took place. But I have to be certain, a hundred percent. I know you wouldn't want to betray a lifetime friendship, Buster," I add pointedly, "but you might think you have to, after you hear what I tell you. I don't want to come on like this, but I have to protect myself. So be straight with me."

There's a pause. Then: "You're safe with me, Fritz."

"When can we get together?"

"When can you get here?"

Buster hustles me into his office, embraces me in a bear hug. "I love you, man. You try the hell out of my patience, but I love you."

"Thanks, Buster." I'm gratified by his emotion toward me, but I'm not here to be soothed.

"That's a bitch about your mother," he continues, shaking his head at the pointlessness of it. "Getting killed in a fire.

An old lady should die in her own bed, surrounded by her loved ones."

"The fire didn't kill her."

He gapes at me. "What?"

"She was murdered. The fire was set afterward, to cover it."

He sits up in his black leather office chair. "That's a heavy load, man. You know this for a fact?"

"You mean do I have proof you could take into a courtroom?" I shake my head. "If I did, I'd have already gone to the police with it. But I know."

He shakes his head like he's trying to shake off a nightmare that won't go away. "Are you still beating this drum about Roach? Is that where this is going? You think he had a hand in killing your mother, for Christsakes? That's cold, man." He scowls. "This business with Roach is going to cause a shitpile of heartburn, no matter how it turns out." He stares at me. "How do you know—whatever it is you say you do know?"

"Those pictures I showed you that time? The dead diplomat?"

"Yes?" he says warily.

"There were others." I pause. "Including one of him getting killed. In the act."

Buster groans like he's been pole-axed between the eyes. "You fuck! Why the hell didn't you tell me then?"

"Because I didn't ever think it would get this far."

"That's lame, and you know it," he says angrily. "You should've let me do the thinking, like I asked you to."

"Okay, I know, I knew, whatever," I say ruefully. "But I didn't." I can't deal with recriminations now, I've got plenty of time for that later. "The important thing is, some bastard broke into my place looking for those pictures, my mother showed up unexpectedly, looking for her wayward son who she'd never given up hope on, and she was killed. Then the fire was set as a diversion."

Buster rubs his hands together nervously. "Who knew they were there, those pictures of the Russian being murdered?"

"Nobody. But Roach had to have figured they were. I've been going over all this in my mind. He knew I was taking pictures of his place. He must have thought I had pictures of the murder." I pause. "It all goes back to the very beginning. You remember those first pictures I showed you, the one with the diplomat, on Roach's runway?"

"Yes?" he says slowly, fearful of what other catastrophes I'm going to dump in his lap.

"If you recall, there were two other men in the picture. One I don't know, he's unidentifiable. But the other, I found out his identity."

"Who?" he asks with trepidation.

I lay down an ace. "Wallace. Roach's murdered security man."

"Oh, shit!" he moans.

"Everything comes back to Roach," I tell him passionately. "Everything."

"Did he . . . did whoever broke in get the pictures?"

I shake my head. "That's the tragic, stupid irony of it. They weren't even in my house."

"But somebody thought they were. You think Roach."

"Who else, for Godsakes?"

Buster snaps out of his funk. "Who knows any of these pictures exist, anything you've taken at Roach's place?"

"You, for openers."

"That's . . . true." He gives me a twisted smile. "I knew when I told you to get rid of them that you wouldn't. So— Do you think I could have done it?"

"Don't play the injured party, Buster," I say irritably, "it doesn't fit."

"Thanks for the vote of confidence," he says, only semi-sarcastically. "So who else?"

"What about your senior partner, Roach's old war buddy?"

"Clements?" he responds in surprise. "Why in the world would you think that?"

"Because earlier, when I came to you on this, you said you were going to talk to him and smooth things out for me."

He slaps his forehead with the palm of his hand. "Fuck me. I'd clean forgotten about that." He shakes his head. "I shined it on, because you promised me you were going to leave it alone, and I didn't want to stir the pot if it wasn't going to go any further." He sighs. "I'm sorry, man. I haven't been a hundred percent truthful with you, either."

"It's okay," I tell him. "My hands're a lot dirtier than yours. You were trying to do the right thing."

He gathers himself. "All right. So let's get back to my question: who else knew the pictures existed?"

I think about Maureen. She'd guessed where I'd hidden them, but she didn't know for sure. That she could have been involved in my mother's death is too terrible to contemplate. "No one. But Roach had to have assumed it. He's the logical contender, Buster. Particularly after what I witnessed last night."

I take the manila folder that contains the black and white pictures out of my backpack, fan them out across his desk. He looks at them.

"You took these?"

I nod.

"Roach's property?"

"On his runway and inside his house. Last night."

He literally jerks, hearing that. "Last *night?*" There's terror in his voice now, it's unmistakable. "You're insane, man."

"I know. It was scary as hell."

If he knew about last night, he'd give it away now; I'd be able to tell, I know him too well for him to deceive me. But he doesn't know, I can see it in his blank eyes.

He picks up the photographs. His hands are shaking. "Who are these men?"

"I don't know," I say. "That's why I'm here. I was hoping you could help me find out."

He drops the prints on his desk like they've scalded him. "Like how?"

"You're the only connected person I know besides Roach, and I don't think I can go to him for this information."

"Very funny, Fritz," he says darkly.

"You know the players. It's a tight network, which I don't have access to, like you do."

He rocks in his chair. "I don't know, Fritz. This makes me nervous as hell."

"My mother's dead, damn it," I say, leaning on him hard. "I need to know who killed her. I think finding out who these men are will help." I exhale wearily. "We've been friends over half our lives, Buster, since we were weeny little freshmen. I'm calling in the big one. I don't know anyone else who can help me," I plead.

He sighs. "I can't fight that. Okay." He points to the pictures. "Can I keep these?"

"That's why I brought them." I scoop them up in a pile, hand them to him.

"I'll do what I can," he promises. He's dubious about getting in this deep, but he's stuck.

"That's great, Buster. I really appreciate it."

He gruffly waves off my gratitude. "What happened to your mother pushes this over the line. That makes it family. You'd do the same for me if the situation were reversed." He slides the pictures into the envelope. "What other bombs do you have to drop on me today?"

"Aren't these enough?"

A tight nod. "More than enough."

I get up, stretch. It's a long drive from my place to Washington. My back is stiff. "Actually, though, there is more. And everything keeps leading back to Roach. I think the gun that killed the diplomat was the same weapon used on Wallace."

Buster looks at me in alarm. "Shit, man. This is getting

worse and worse." He cocks a questioning finger at me. "How do you know all this, anyway?"

"I've got my spies out working for me," I say evasively. "I'll tell you something else: the Baltimore cops, the detectives who are working on the counselor's murder from their end, since that's where the body was found, think there could have been linkage between him and an illegal arms-dealing ring, syndicate, however you call it. And James Roach, in case you didn't know, was almost indicted for arms-dealing twenty years ago. So there's synergy there." I lean forward on his desk, resting my weight on my hands. "All roads lead to Roach, Buster."

He shakes his head like a dog trying to shake off a passel of fleas. "This is brutal," he moans. "This is so fucking brutal."

"People are getting killed, Buster. Somebody has to stop this."

"You're trying pretty damn hard."

"He killed my mother. You damn straight I'm trying hard."

He gets up from his desk, walks me to the door. "Take the back elevator. I don't want anyone seeing you here."

"You're a good man, Buster."

"So're you, Fritz. Fucked up, but good."

"I'll take that."

"Be careful," he cautions me yet again. "I mean, be really careful now."

Since I can't promise I will be, I say nothing.

"I'll call you as soon as I find anything out," he promises me. "And I really, truly am sorry about your mother. She was the best." He clenches and unclenches his fist. "We only have one mother," he says, the Irish Catholic in him rising. "You have to take care of your mother."

It's all distilled down to that now. "Or her memory."

Twilight. I should turn some lights on, but I like sitting in the darkness. It matches my mood, how I feel.

I hear a car drive up. It's Maureen. She'd called earlier, said she couldn't not be with me anymore.

I go outside to meet her. She jumps into my arms, holding on to me for dear life.

We fuck our brains out like animals. "Oh, yes!" she cries out, spasming and digging her fingernails into my hair. "I needed that *bad*." She pulls me to her, the length of her body matching mine, head to toe. Lying with her is not snuggling the way I've known it, she isn't the cuddly type, she's too long and lean. And incredibly sexy, feminine, gorgeous, wonderful.

She runs a fingernail along my chest. "I don't want to be away from you anymore, Fritz. We have so little time left before I have to go back to Cambridge. Let's not waste any more of it."

"How much do we have?" I feel an ache starting in my chest.

"Less than two weeks."

"Ouch."

"I know." She runs her finger around my nipple. "You could come with me, you know?"

"Up there?"

"Why not? We've gone over this before, Fritz. There's nothing keeping you here anymore."

She's right. All the reasons I had for being here are gone now—except for Ollie, and he won't be here much longer, either. Thinking of Ollie reminds me that I need to start preparing seriously for his future. I can't put that off any longer.

She rolls over on her side, looks at me. "Either we're going to have a life together, or we aren't."

"I . . . shit, Maureen. I . . ."

She shushes me. "You don't have to talk. Let me talk. I have to say this fast, before I chicken out. I'm not a kid anymore, you know? I'm thirty-five years old. I'm not too old yet for having babies, but I'm not that young, either. When I was younger my mother used to tell me, the days go slow, but the years go fast. I didn't know what she meant then. Now I do. I don't want to wake up on my fortieth birthday never having had a child. Especially now that you've come into my life."

She grabs hold of my hand. "I've been waiting a long time for you, Fritz. My entire life, as it's turned out. I've had opportunities, I'm not modest about who I am, but it was never right. Now it is. I want the whole package—marriage, your kids, a future together. I'm ready to make a total commitment." She lies back. "I already have. Even if you haven't."

I start shaking. "I love you . . ."

"I've scared you, haven't I? Marriage, kids, a house with a white picket fence. That isn't you, is it, Fritz Tullis? You're the wanderer, you like to roam around."

"No, no," I correct her hastily, "I want a family, all that, too."

"With me?"

We're still holding hands, her right, my left. I squeeze hers. She squeezes back.

"If I've ever wanted to," I tell her honestly, "it's with you. It's just . . ."

I can feel her deflating. "So fast," she finishes for me.

"Yeah, that, and—shit, Maureen, my mother just died. I haven't been thinking about us. Not like this."

"I'm sorry," she apologizes. "The timing sucks. But I can't help it, goddamn it, I'm leaving soon. I can't leave without knowing something, even if it's—" She stops herself.

"What?"

"That you can't go all the way with this."

I'm churning in my gut. "I love you, Maureen. The idea of you leaving and us not being together is—shit, impossible."

She's tense—I feel it. "Is that a yes? Are you proposing to me? Hey! I'm a liberated woman. I don't have to wait for you. Marry me!" She pounds on my chest—playfully, but with power. "Say you'll marry me." She grabs my balls. "Or you'll be sorry!"

She starts laughing, almost manically. In a few seconds, though, she's crying, her body wracked with sobs. "Oh, damn it! I didn't want to do this. I fucking did not want to do this, I'm not some grasping woman, shit, I'm sorry."

I cradle her in my arms, holding her tight, like I'm swaddling her. "Listen a minute."

"Oh, shit." She rolls away from me. "This hurts."

I pull her to me. "Let me finish, Maureen! You're not the only one whose emotions are raw. Before you leave—once I'm past the shock of my mom's death, and try to find out how it happened . . ."

She groans. "Oh, Fritz. Please don't go down that rabbit hole anymore. You promised."

"I'm not going to get crazy about it," I say, trying to calm her down. "I just need to know what happened. It won't take long, I swear. Just give me some time, okay, Maureen? What's wrong with a little more time?"

She nods—her crying time is over. "Okay. I'll give you some more time." She laughs—it's a small, rueful laugh. "I don't have a choice, Fritz. When you fall, you fall. And there's not a damn thing in the world you can do about it."

Maureen is staring at me when I wake up, a crooked smile on her face. She kisses me inside the ear. Her breath is warm.

"Maureen . . ." I'm still coming out of sleep.

She puts a finger to my lips. "Don't say anything. I'm with you now, that's all I care about."

She showers while I make coffee, then she makes scrambled eggs and toast while I shower. All very domestic, easy. There's still a gnawing sensation in my brain about her, but right now I'm holding that in abeyance.

"What are you up to today?" I ask, gently prying.

"Get some of my things at the motel for openers. Make some phone calls, trivial stuff. I could be back in a couple of hours. You can take me somewhere I haven't been yet. I love it down here." She smiles. "I love it anywhere you are."

We finish breakfast, do the dishes. She takes off.

Last night was incredible. Not the sex—that was great, but we've had great sex from the beginning—but what we talked about.

A life together.

The phone rings. "This is Fritz," I answer.

"It's Buster, Fritz."

"What's up?"

"I've got some incredible news to lay on you. Can you drive up here this afternoon?"

He sounds wired, like his voice is being filtered through a line of cocaine.

"Today?"

"Yes, today," he says impatiently.

Another round-trip long haul. I'm beginning to hate that drive. But I created all this, so I can't bitch about it. "If I have to."

"You have to. Be in my office at six," he orders me curtly.

"What's this about, Buster?"

"I'll tell you when I see you. Don't dress like a hippie," he adds. "A sports coat and clean slacks wouldn't hurt."

The phone goes dead in my hand. A sports coat? What's the occasion?

Now I have to call Maureen and lay another lie on her. She answers on the first ring. "Fritz?" she says expectantly.

"Hey." Damn, I am sick of lying to her.

"What's up?" she asks innocently.

"I have to see Sam again, this afternoon," I grouse. "Some lease papers or something I need to co-sign. I won't be back till late, I'm afraid."

"Shit." She doesn't hide the disappointment in her voice. "Will you be home tonight?"

"I hope so. I'll call you as soon as I know."

Rush hour is at its peak as I approach Washington. I'm not going to make it to Buster's office remotely on time, so I give him a heads-up on my cell phone.

"Wonderful," he grumbles. "Well, get here as soon as you can."

"Hey, I'm the one stuck in this clusterfuck, not you."

I arrive forty-five minutes late. I park in his building's garage and ride the escalator up to the firm's lobby, where his secretary is impatiently waiting for me. "This way," she commands, her high heels staccatoing across the floor. I follow her as she marches determinedly down the hallway to Buster's office and ushers me in.

Buster, shirtsleeves rolled up, tie slackened, is pacing behind his desk. "You took your sweet time," he grouses as he reaches for his suit coat and tightens the knot on his hundred-dollar silk tie. I'm dressed in a vintage J. Press sports coat, khakis, button-down shirt, plus a tie, since he stipulated I dress like a grown-up.

"You'll do," he allows, checking out my attire. "Call and tell 'em we're on our way," he instructs his secretary. "Ten minutes."

"Where are we going?" I ask. "And who is *them?*"

"Them's who's going to give you the answers to your questions, dodo brain."

We ride the elevator back down and go outside. It's a balmy evening. The streets are bustling with people leaving work for the day, as well as families carrying beach chairs and blankets on their way to a free Marine Corps Band concert at the Lincoln Memorial steps, a few blocks south.

Buster seems uptight about what's in store for us. "We'll grab something to eat later, if you still have an appetite," he says as we briskly weave our way through the crowd. "I suspect you'll want a drink."

That's cheering.

We walk down 23rd Street to Virginia Avenue, then cross the street and head for the State Department building, a massive structure that occupies a full city block. As I realize that this is our destination, butterflies start flying around in my gut. This is where James Roach works.

"What's going on, Buster?" I ask.

He plows ahead toward the main entrance, forcing me into a trot to keep up. I reach out for his arm, almost dragging him to a stop.

"Buster. What're we doing here?" I demand.

He turns to me, almost scowling. "You asked me to do something for you, Fritz. I've done it, okay? It wasn't easy, and it wasn't comfortable, but I did it, because you're my best friend and you're trying to exorcise some strong demons. You want the answers you asked me to get you? Well, you're gonna get 'em." He points to the huge building. "In there."

Both his answer and the attitude he's taken make me more nervous, rather than less. "Who's going to give them to me?"

He tries to give me a reassuring smile; it doesn't come off, his face is stiff. "You're not in any danger, if that's what you're worried about. Nothing's going to happen to you, you're gonna walk out of here with the same number of arms and legs you brought in." He takes a handful of my lapel. "It's time to shit or get off the pot, Fritz."

I brush his hand away. "You didn't answer my question, Buster. Who are we meeting in here?"

"You'll see," he says, continuing to evade giving me a straight answer.

"Not Roach." I'm ready to turn tail and get out of here.

Buster takes another crack at saying what he has to say without telling me what I want to know. "Let me put it this way, Fritz. Roach isn't the problem, okay? So stop obsessing about him. Now come on, we've already kept them waiting over an hour."

I have no recourse but to follow him inside—I've come this far, I have to see it to the finish.

The lobby's almost deserted—it's after seven, most of the personnel have gone home for the day. A uniformed guard sits at the desk near the security gate. He's talking to a man whose back is to us. The guard looks up as we approach, says something, and points.

The man turns to us. He's about our age, dressed in a mid-price-range dark suit. A government lifer, I'm guessing. He strides toward us. "Mr. Reilly?" he asks Buster.

"I'm Buster Reilly," Buster acknowledges.

"And you're Mr. Tullis."

"Yes."

"I'm Kevin Lockhart. They're waiting for you upstairs."

"Who is *they?*" I ask. This is getting spookier by the minute.

Lockhart ignores my question. "Sign in and show ID, please."

We sign in, produce our driver's licenses, pass through the metal detector. Lockhart leads us to a bank of elevators, presses an up button. We wait for the elevator. No one says anything.

We ride to the top floor. Getting off, we follow Lockhart down a long corridor, at the far end of which is a set of double doors. As we approach them, Lockhart stops us. "Wait here." He opens one of the doors and goes inside.

I'm getting more and more nervous by the minute. "This is awfully damn cloak-and-dagger," I tell Buster.

"It's the government, Fritz. That's what they're good at."

Lockhart comes back out. "You can come in."

He stands aside while we enter. Then he closes the door behind us.

We're in a large conference room. The light is low, from soft recessed ceiling fixtures. A long oval rosewood table surrounded by plush upholstered chairs dominates the space.

Two men are standing at the far end, engaged in low conversation. I can't make them out—they're in semishadow, and their backs are to us. As they hear the door closing, they turn in our direction. One of them takes a few steps toward us. I recognize him as the senior partner in Buster's firm who's tight with James Roach.

"Buster," I say softly, not turning my head, "what is going on?"

"Take it easy, Fritz," he answers in a quieter voice than mine, "it's going to be okay."

"It already isn't okay."

Then the other man steps forward.

"Hello, Fritz," he says evenly.

I whirl on Buster. "You motherfucker! You fucking Benedict Arnold!"

Buster's hands fly up in a submissive posture. "I had to do it this way, Fritz." He points to Roach and Clements. "They make the rules."

James Roach takes a few steps toward me. "You're not in danger here, Fritz. No one's going to harm you. But we have to talk to you."

"What about?" I ask defensively. I'm going to kill Buster for this.

"What you've been spying on," he says bluntly. "What you've almost ruined with your amateurish attempts at playing Indiana Jones."

He locks eyes with me for a moment; then he introduces the other man. "This is Rex Clements. Rex is one of my oldest and closest friends. He arranged this meeting, through your friend Buster."

Clements stretches his hand across the table. Reluctantly, I shake it. Then I glare at Buster again, who's preoccupied with his shoes.

"So much for confidentiality and trust, right, Buster?"

"You asked me to help you, Fritz," he comes back defensively.

"You fucked me, man."

Roach intercedes. "Calm down, Fritz. Don't blame Buster for this. He had no choice."

I don't buy that. Buster had a choice. He chose to cover his ass, at the expense of mine.

Roach motions toward the table. "Sit down."

I slouch into a chair. Buster puts what he hopes is a comforting hand on my shoulder. I shrug it off. "It's gonna be okay," he tries to assure me. His voice rings hollow.

I shake my head. I don't want to hear this. I don't want to be here.

He gives up on trying to make it okay, because he knows he can't. "I'll be waiting downstairs," he tells me.

I hear the door closing behind him.

Roach and Clements sit down opposite me. I stare balefully at my nemesis. I'm pissed enough that I'm not as scared as I'd have thought I'd be.

"Let's cut through the crap, okay?" I say to Roach. "You shanghaied me into a meeting before, over at your place. Now you've done it again. What do you want from me this time?"

Roach stares at me with lizard eyes. He picks up a large-clasp envelope that's resting on the table, takes some pictures out, spreads them in front of me. I stare at them. They're pictures of me taken with an infrared lens the other night, when I spied on the clandestine gathering at his property.

My instinct about being under observation was right. I start to shake.

"It goes without saying I'd have security," Roach says. "You were under observation from the time you got close enough to my residence to take these." He flicks a finger at the pictures.

This is scary. "Then why didn't you—"

"Do something about it? Like kill you? My people came

close, didn't they? They could have, if I'd wanted them to, but they were under orders not to. That's why you got away, Fritz. That's why you're here now."

I am so far out of my league it's pathetic. He's ten steps ahead of me, without breaking a sweat.

"There's already been too much killing, don't you think?" he continues. "But that isn't the reason I didn't pursue you, Fritz. I let you go because what I was doing there, what I've been working my heart and soul on for the past two years, was more important than exposing one small-time snoop. As it was, my guests panicked and our meeting was aborted. I assume you saw them leaving, while you were making your great escape."

I mutely look down at the table.

"It took me two days on the phone, around the clock, to put Humpty-Dumpty back together again," he tells me harshly. "It was only this morning that I finally convinced the last faction that they weren't in danger, that our work hadn't been fatally compromised, and that they, personally, had not been identified." He glances at Clements, then turns back to me. "I knew I could take care of this with you on this later on down the line." He pauses. "And there was another factor."

"What's that?" I ask edgily.

"You saved young Joe's life, on my yacht. I owed you one for that." He looks at me unblinkingly. "The books are even now. I don't owe you anymore."

So much for my thinking I'd get away with spying on him without repercussions. I was the rat in the maze and he was playing with me, running me any way he wanted. And by telling me that debt has been paid, he's also telling me that if there's a next time, I won't be let off the hook.

"You as a person don't concern me, Fritz," he tells me with frosty condescension. "But what you're doing does—a lot." He slides another set of pictures over the table to me. I don't have to look at them to know what they are—the photos I shot at his farm.

"You trespassed on my property, which is against the law. You asked your friend Mr. Reilly to find out who these men are, and what their business is with me. And how this meeting you photographed—another unlawful act, I might add—ties in to everything that's been happening."

My stomach is churning. "Yes. I did."

"You thought it was something illegal, didn't you?" he asks, his voice dripping venom. He taps a finger on the pictures. "You don't have a clue as to who these people are, do you?"

I shake my head. "If I did, I wouldn't have had to come to Buster for help, would I?"

"I don't know how your crazy mind works," he answers. "But since you want to know so badly, I'm going to tell you."

He points to the first picture. "This man is the Israeli prime minister's most trusted lieutenant."

I feel like the floor's going to open and swallow me up. *Oh shit, what have you gotten into now, you idiot?* is the only thought that comes into my mind.

His finger moves to the next picture. "The man next to him is the Palestinian delegate to the U.N." He waggles his finger between the two photos. "These two men are never seen together," he informs me solemnly. "Never," he repeats for emphasis. Then he indicates the other photos. "The Russian deputy prime minister, and the Syrian assistant foreign minister."

He sits back in his chair and stares at me. "Do you know how dangerous it would be for these men if it ever got out they were meeting with each other, especially clandestinely?" He leans in to me. "They'd be dead in less than twenty-four hours."

My head is spinning. "You've lost me."

"That's the problem," Roach says coldly. "You don't understand the ramifications of this. So let me explain."

He taps a manicured finger on the table. "What you have been doing with your senseless, destructive meddling could jeopardize our national security, Fritz. Not only that, it could ruin our international credibility. If these pictures ever got out, they could scuttle a process that our government, and their governments"—he indicates the pictures sitting on the table in front of me—"have been painstakingly laboring on for years, under the most secret of circumstances. That I have been *personally* devoting my life to for years," he goes on. "Including the morning of the day we first met, at your mother's house," he says, his voice dripping with ridicule. "When you were clumsily pumping me for information."

So he's known about my nosing into his business all along. I haven't fooled him for a minute.

"I . . ."

"Don't say anything," he orders me. "Shut your mouth and listen." His voice rises in anger. "That's why I inveigled bringing you here. To try to finally convince you to stop your reckless, dangerous conduct."

"How was I to know that?"

"Jesus Christ, Fritz!" he thunders. "I asked you, in what I thought was a polite, civilized way, to keep clear of this, when I brought you to my place. I warned you. *Didn't I?*"

"Jim." Clements is trying to calm Roach down.

Roach shrugs him off. "Then why in the world didn't you do what I told you?" he rails at me. "You didn't think I was serious? You don't think I'd cut your legs off at the knees if I had to? For Godsakes, you fool, who in the world do you think you're dealing with?"

Something snaps inside me. I've had enough of being intimidated. Screw being on the defensive. "I knew who I was dealing with. At least, I thought I did."

"Who?"

"The man who killed my mother. Or had her killed, same difference."

He stares at me as if I've completely lost it. "That's the reason?" he asks incredulously.

"What other would I have?"

Roach shakes his head in disbelief. He looks shell-shocked.

"If it wasn't you who killed her, then who was it? And who killed Wallace? And that Russian diplomat, who was also murdered on your property," I press on. "It all leads to you. You're the common denominator."

He sits back, staring at me intently. "How do you know about the Russian?" he asks me. For the first time, his voice has a hint of panic in it. "Where did you get that information?"

"Are you denying it?"

For a moment, no one says a word. Roach looks at Clements, then at me. "You know a lot, don't you."

"I know a lot of things you don't know I know," I respond.

"I'm not going to get into that Russian diplomat situation," he says curtly. "It's a separate issue, that isn't connected to this one. Which, again, you should be steering very clear of." He stares at the photos for a moment. Then he looks up at me. "I don't know who's behind these killings," he says. His internal fires are banked now, he's the calm, in-control statesman again. "What I can tell you, unequivocally, is that it isn't me. I haven't killed anyone, or had anyone killed." He paused. "But even if I did, Fritz, I wouldn't tell you. What we're doing is more important to the total picture than your mother, or Wallace, or any single individual—including *you.*" He sits back. "That may be cold, my friend, but it's reality."

"Your reality, not mine," I throw back at him. "And I'm not your friend."

He shakes his head, gathers up the photographs, puts them back in the envelope. "This ends here," he orders me. "Everything. Or there will be very dire consequences for you. Do you understand?"

I stare back at him; then I nod.

"As does any involvement you have with me. *Any.* Are we completely clear on that also?"

"Yes," I tell him in a lifeless voice. "We're clear."

Buster and I walk back to his office in silence, take the elevator down to the garage. I'm shaking, as much with anger as from nerves.

"I'm sorry I had to lie to you, Fritz," Buster apologizes for at least the tenth time. The poor bastard looked like he'd had his blood drained when we met up, back down in the lobby. I felt like punching his sorry ass out when I first saw him there, waiting for me, but he looked so woebegone I had to let my anger go.

"It was the only way Roach would do it," he says, trying to justify what he knows was shitty behavior. "You want to play ball with flamethrowers like Roach, you have to play by their rules."

I don't want to deal with this now. "It's okay," I say woodenly. "The message was more important than the way it was delivered."

"I warned you, didn't I?" His voice has risen an octave, like he's a teenager whose balls haven't dropped yet. "The first time you brought this time bomb to me, not to be reckless about this. Didn't I?"

I nod.

"I wish to hell you had taken my advice, one time."

"I guess I wish I had, too."

We've reached my car. He offers his hand. "Still friends?"

I hesitate—then I take it. "Yes, Buster. We'll always be friends. But don't ever fuck me over like that again."

"I won't," he promises. "So now what?" he asks anxiously.

"Nothing. I found out what I wanted to know." My laugh is forced, brittle. "Way more."

"Where're you going now?"

I check my watch. It's after eight. "Home. Where else?"

"You want to grab a drink? I know I could use one."

I shake my head. "I'll pass. It's a long drive, and I'm beat."

"Be careful, man," he cautions me. "Call me if you need anything. Anything," he repeats.

I do want a drink—I need one badly—but I don't want to be with Buster, not now. His heart was in the right place when he threw me into that lion's den, I grudgingly admit to myself, but he should have given me advance warning. It's my decision if I want to meet with Roach, not Buster's or anyone else's.

I cruise a few blocks, luck out in finding a parking spot on the street, and go into the Old Ebbits Bar & Grill, where I sit at the end of the bar and order a double Johnnie Walker Black, neat. A popular watering hole, the restaurant is crowded with Washingtonians of a certain stripe, male and female—lawyers, congressional aides, lobbyists. Power suits and slick haircuts are de rigueur. Buster would be at home here. I'm not.

I knock half the drink back in one swallow, then let my mind ruminate on the meeting I just had with Roach—more an inquisition than a meeting. Roach gave a great performance—he has a splendid Sir Laurence Olivierish air about him—but whether he spoke the truth or not is still up in the air as far as I'm concerned. I instinctively haven't trusted the man since the first time I met him, and my feelings in that regard haven't changed. If anything, they've hardened. I don't doubt who his nocturnal visitors were, or why they were there. I don't even care, that's not the point. What's important is that I still feel, in my gut, that he was involved in the murders, including my mother's. As good as his newest dog and pony show was, he didn't change my mind about that, not by a long shot. But it's beginning to sink in that I'll never be able to prove it.

Still, what he said was very heavy, with ominous consequences for me. I'm already under suspicion by the Prince Georges cops for Wallace's murder—how much, I don't know, but Ricketts hasn't forgotten me, I'm sure of that. I don't want to find myself in a position where I'm also accused of jeopardizing an important and fragile government operation.

It's after eleven by the time I get home. I called Maureen from the road, told her I was going to be very late, that I'd call her in the morning. She was disappointed, but she knows how stressed I am, so she didn't push. Still in my clothes, I fall into bed and thirty seconds later I'm asleep.

Maureen comes over early the following morning. She looks better than ever—appealing, vulnerable, real. We hug for a long time. I cling to her. When we break, she looks at me peculiarly.

"You seem different, Fritz. More *here.*"

I can't tell her about my meeting with Roach, so I tell her how I'm feeling about her. "I'm getting rid of the shit in my life, and keeping the sweet stuff." I take her face in my hands. "You're the sweet stuff."

"Finally," she says with relief. "You know how worried I've been about you over this, Fritz. I don't want to spend the rest of my life with someone I have to be scared for all the time. I want the sweet stuff, too." She hugs me. "Thank God," she whispers in my ear. "That you're going to be with me, after all."

We stay put in the afternoon heat, then at twilight we go down to bird island. The light is perfect—soft, diffused twilight. I shoot a couple rolls of film. Maureen watches me observing Ollie. She's more interested in me now than she is in him.

"When are you going to do the right thing about this bird?" she asks.

"Soon. You're the expert, I'll let you make the arrangements."

Thinking about Ollie having to leave makes me reflect again on my own situation. As Maureen and everyone else has pointed out, there's no reason for me to be here anymore. I'm going to have to get serious about looking for a job. I've never had to before; they've always come to me. I don't know what it's like to be a supplicant. I'm not going to like it. I'm better at being pursued than being the hunter.

That's going to be a big issue—where I find a job. If I got something across the country, I couldn't take it, unless I was willing to let Maureen go.

I can't do that.

I scrounge around in the refrigerator to see if there's anything I can cook for dinner. Maureen's on her cell phone, checking messages. I find a stash of Mattie's chicken pot pies in the freezer, pop two in the microwave.

"Damn." Maureen's frowning at her telephone.

"What's the matter?"

"I have to go to Boston. There's a situation I can't fix over the phone."

Now I'm the one who's upset about the other's departing. "When?"

"Tomorrow morning. I'll drive up to BWI and catch the shuttle."

"For how long?"

"Not long, although I may have to stay over a night or two. God, I hope not. I so do not want to be there." She slings an arm around my shoulders, gives me a kiss. "I want to be here. Nowhere else."

We go to bed early, make love, sleep like babies, get up early, make love again. She has to go back to her motel and grab some things for her trip, so she leaves without eating breakfast.

After Maureen leaves, I call Fred and fill him in on what's been going on in my life—stumbling into the top secret gathering at Roach's compound, then my being blindsided by Roach at the State Department.

"So now what?" Fred asks.

"I've drilled a lot of dry holes, Fred. I think it's time to pack it in."

"It's your life." He sounds disappointed—he's been living the excitement of all this vicariously, through me.

"You can live in the past," I tell him, "or you can look to the future. It's time for me to start thinking about where I'm going, not where I've been."

The call comes from out of the blue. "Fritz?"

"Yes?" I say tentatively. I'm jumpy about all unsolicited calls these days.

"It's Ted Kelston. How are you? It took me a while to track you down."

I relax. "This is my mother's line." I don't go into the details. "I'm hanging in, Ted. How long has it been?"

"Five years, at least. I don't think we've seen each other since the tenth-year class reunion, have we?"

"No, I don't think so. What's happening with you?"

"I'm the vice-provost of the University of Massachusetts."

I break out in a big smile. "No kidding! That's great. Since when?"

"A year ago last June."

"Congratulations," I tell him sincerely. "Well done."

"Thanks."

Ted Kelston and I were classmates at Yale. He's one of the

nicest men I've ever known, and certainly one of the most courageous. He was born with severe birth defects—he's a hunchback, a dwarf, his eyesight is 20/400 (at best). He could have gone through life with an angry chip on his shoulder, but he didn't—he's more positive and optimistic than anyone has a right to be, regardless of his afflictions. A sports fanatic, he couldn't play regular sports like the rest of us so he found his own particular, wonderful niche—he became the coxswain for the crew. He won three letters, and went on to a Rhodes scholarship. After he came back from Oxford he got his doctorate in university administration, married a terrific woman, and has had a great all-around life. Whenever I used to feel sorry for myself I'd look at Ted and I'd pull out of my funk—how can you indulge your self-pity when this guy, who had every reason to, never did?

"So what's happening with you?" he asks. "Job-wise?"

Ahh. "I'm unemployed at the moment, Ted."

"I heard about your situation," he says with diplomatic understatement.

"It was my own damn fault, so I can't complain."

"Well, we all make mistakes. I've made my share, and then some."

I doubt that, but it's nice of him to say it.

"Something's come up," he says, getting to the point. "Which might work out really well for you."

"What's that?"

"There's an unexpected opening in our History Department. One of our professors died suddenly last week."

"That's too bad."

"It was. He was a decent guy, and a good teacher. But it's left us in a quandary. We have to fill his spot, and we have to do it right away."

"That's why you called?" I ask. This is a shock.

"We need a professor in the American history section for the fall semester. That's less than a month away. I immediately thought of you."

I start tingling. "Jesus." I have to ask the obvious question. "What about my problems at UT?"

"We discussed it internally. You learned your lesson, I assume."

"Oh, yeah. Absolutely."

"Fine," he says, dismissing the issue. "What's in the past is back then. I have to worry about the present. The people down in Austin gave you raves, by the way."

"That's decent of them." If I had another job they could stop paying me off, an incentive to be charitable.

"Are you interested?" he asks. "And available?"

"Of course I'm interested. And definitely available."

"Good," he says briskly. "It's going to be a fast process. We're only going to interview a few candidates. With your record you've got a good shot, particularly since I'm going to be pushing for you."

"That's great, Ted. I don't know how to thank you."

"Can the false modesty, you jerk. If you get it, you'll do a great job. That'll be more than enough thanks. UT's loss would be our gain. Can you come up tonight, so you can meet with the selection committee tomorrow morning?"

"Sure."

"Make your own travel arrangements, and we'll reimburse you," he directs me. "This is a good school, Fritz. We're moving up the academic ladder, we need all the talented faculty we can find. You could be a good fit. You'll like the people here, and I'm sure they'll love you. It could be a great opportunity for you, and for us as well."

We briefly discuss logistics, then we ring off.

I book an afternoon flight to Boston from Washington. It's too bad Ted didn't call earlier—Maureen and I could have flown up together. I'm on cloud nine. A chance to start my career up again, with one of my best friends in my corner? It's almost too good to be true. And Amherst, the town in which the university's located, is less than a two-hour drive from Harvard.

A resurrection in my life's work, and a future with Maureen. For the first time in a long time, I begin to believe that I'm going to turn it all around.

My interview at UMass goes well. I'm charming, informed, they're impressed with my résumé. Ted and I have lunch afterward at the faculty club—he's so giddy he almost breaks out into a jig.

"I'm only one voice, Fritz," he cautions me, "but that was a knockout." He holds up his hand—his fingers are crossed.

"When will I know?"

"We have two more candidates to see tomorrow and the next day. It could be as soon as the end of the week. Beginning of next week, for sure." He pumps my hand. "I have a good feeling about this, Fritz."

"I'll light a candle," I tell him.

"You're Catholic now?"

"I want to cover all the bases."

He'll call me as soon as he knows anything. He doesn't want to build my hopes up too high, but it wouldn't hurt to start making preparations to move.

I'm euphoric—I'm going to be in the academic life again, it's practically signed, sealed, and delivered—Ted wouldn't be so confident if there was much doubt. Until I got there, walked the campus, talked to the faculty interview team, saw the summer school students walking to class, throwing Frisbees, eating their lunches on the grounds, I'd forgotten how much I love teaching, and how much I've missed it.

My flight back to Washington isn't until seven tonight—I have plenty of time to get back to Boston. Earlier, I'd thought about calling Maureen, but I didn't want to raise false expectations, in case this falls through.

As I approach Boston on I-90 east, I make a snap decision. Screw playing games, Maureen deserves to know about this. God knows she's been through the wars with me—she should share in my good fortune. It will be hers, too. Instead of driving straight through to Logan Airport and sitting in the terminal for a couple of hours with nothing to do, I detour off the freeway, and head toward Cambridge.

It's a beautiful late-summer New England day. Scullers are out on the Charles River, both men's and women's crews. When I was rowing for Yale we came up here every year to compete against Harvard. We never won.

I cross over the Larz Anderson Bridge and drive up John F. Kennedy Street to Harvard Square. Luckily, I find a parking spot on Church Street, not far from the entrance to the yard. If I'm here for more than two hours I'll eat the ticket.

A thought occurs to me—what if she isn't in? I activate my cell phone and get the Harvard Biology Department telephone number from the operator, punch it in.

"Dr. O'Hara's office, please," I say when the phone's answered.

"One moment."

A ten-second hold—then the same Boston-accented woman's voice that I spoke to the last time I called comes on the line.

"Dr. O'Hara's office."

"Is Dr. O'Hara in?"

"She's in a meeting," the woman informs me curtly. "She can't be disturbed."

"How late is she going to be in her office today?" I ask.

"Until five. Perhaps later. Who is this, please?"

I hang up. I want this to be a surprise.

The Biology Department is at the far end of the campus from the main gate. Summer school is still in session. Students of all ages, including adults, up to octogenarians, take courses here. They spend two or three weeks attending classes in urban development and Renaissance art, so that for the rest of their lives they can say they went to Harvard.

I approach Maureen's building, go inside, and look up her office location on the hallway directory: the third floor. Taking the polished marble steps two at a time, I walk down a long hallway and open the door that has her name stenciled on it.

The woman whose desk placard identifies her as Mildred Rabwin, Maureen's assistant, is a middle-aged, skinny, lank-haired woman, dressed in an old-fashioned shirtwaist dress. She has no chest or hips, but there's a discernible fuzz on her upper lip. She looks up as I enter.

I glance toward the door behind her, Maureen's personal office. The door is closed. "Good afternoon," I greet Ms. Rabwin with a friendly smile. "Is Dr. O'Hara in?"

She looks me up and down. I'm dressed properly—sports coat, slacks, white button-down shirt, rep tie. The picture of respectability.

"Who are you?"

I smile. "The love of her life."

She gives me a very strange look. "Just a moment." She gets up from her desk and goes into Maureen's office, closing the door behind her before I can get a peek in.

Maureen's going to fall on her ass when she sees me. And when she hears about my interview, she'll be beside herself.

Rabwin comes out. "You may go in," she instructs me.

I take a beat to gather myself. Then I walk through the door.

The woman I'm looking at is stocky, in her late middle age, with straight gunmetal gray hair cut almost crew-cut short. She stands up from behind her desk as I enter. She's wearing a baggy man's golf shirt and jeans. No makeup, no personal adornments of any kind.

I've seen pictures of Gertrude Stein. This woman could be Gertrude Stein's sister; or daughter, if Gertrude Stein had ever had children. Which she didn't, of course.

I take a moment to compose myself—I'm in a state of shock. "You're Dr. O'Hara? Dr. Maureen O'Hara?"

She gives me a quizzical, penetrating look. "Who else would I be? The better question is, who are you, where are you from, and what do you want?"

"My name is Fritz Tullis."

I pause. There's no reaction.

"I'm residing in southern Maryland presently, but I've been living in Austin, Texas, for the past few years. I'm a professor at the University of Texas, presently on sabbatical."

A faint smile crosses her lips. "Are you?" she asks. If I wanted to, I could think she was mocking me. I choose not to think that.

"If you want to verify my credentials, I'll give you some numbers to call."

She shakes her head. "That won't be necessary. What you do doesn't matter to me, one way or the other. What does matter to me is what you're pulling here. What do you want from me, Mr. Tullis. Or is it Dr.?"

"Dr. is for students, not colleagues, as far as I'm concerned," I say, forcing a smile—I need this woman's help. "But yes, I'm a card-carrying Ph.D. I'm also an avid bird-watcher, which is what I want to talk to you about."

Her eyebrows go up. "Yes?"

"The stretch of Maryland where I'm staying is a great birding area. I've been doing some fieldwork."

Now I have her interest. "In what, specifically?"

"Sandhill cranes."

She frowns. "In the wild?"

I nod.

"I didn't know there were any sandhill cranes in that region," she says with authority, "aside from the breeding flock at the Patuxent Wildlife Refuge."

"Mine are a lost flock," I explain. "My assumption is that whoever was leading them was accidentally killed near this site and they settled in, before I found them." I pause. "It's a very remote area. No one except me knows of their existence."

"I see," she says slowly. "Are you working with anyone? Professionally?" She motions me to take a seat, which I do. She sits back down at her desk.

"Not exactly," I hedge. "It's family property, where these cranes are. My family. And I don't let anyone near the place."

I have her attention now. "You want to keep the birds to yourself," she says with a knowing smile.

"That's right, Dr. O'Hara." I pause. "With one exception."

"Who is that?" she asks.

I give her a good, long look. "Until I walked in here, I thought it was you."

She frowns. "I don't understand."

"That makes two of us."

I reach into my inside jacket pocket for my wallet and take out a picture of Maureen, one that I took when we were out watching the birds and I snapped some off without her being aware I was doing it. I hand it across the desk.

"Do you recognize this woman?"

She looks at the picture for a moment, shakes her head. "No, I don't. Should I?"

"I don't know."

"You're talking in circles, Dr. Tullis. What's going on?"

"This woman has been impersonating you."

"Impersonating me?" she says in alarm.

"Yes. She's been bird-watching with me for over a month now. She told me she was you." I pause—a tremendous sadness washes over me. "Until now, I believed her."

She gives me a savvy look. "That's why you're here. To find out who the real Maureen O'Hara is. Aside from the movie actress, that is. A cross I've had to bear my entire life," she says with bitterness.

"You don't get mistaken for her?" I ask, in a feeble attempt to lighten my mood, which is as dark as the far side of the moon.

"Look at me, Dr. Tullis," she scolds me. "Do I look like a sex symbol?"

I don't reply.

She stares at the picture again. "I don't recognize this woman at all." She hands it back to me. "What's her game?"

"I don't know."

"Access?" she surmises. "To your private birding area?"

"That's what I thought. But I don't know if that's the real reason." I pause. "I don't think it is," I say more definitively.

She gives me a funny, almost compassionate look. "Are you and she involved?"

I shake my head. "Not anymore."

Dr. O'Hara walks me out of the building. "It's a lucky coincidence you caught me here today in my office," she says. "This is my first day back in the country in over two months. I've been on a field trip all summer and I wasn't due back for another couple of weeks. A remote area, in the Andes," she goes on. "One of my team took sick and we had to leave early. Otherwise, you wouldn't have found out. As soon as you did," she adds.

Somehow, I don't feel lucky.

"Good luck at finding out who my impersonator is."

"I don't know if I want to find out," I tell her honestly.

"If you ever allow a real ornithologist to have a gander at those birds, I'd appreciate being considered." She hands me her card. I pocket it.

"I'm going to do that. I have some details to take care of first, but I'll give you a call. You'll be surprised at what's down there."

I haven't brought Ollie up. She'll go batshit when she sees him. Any real ornithologist would.

"Thanks for your time," I say. "Sorry to have bothered you."

"It wasn't a bother," she assures me.

We shake hands, say good-bye. "Good luck," she says, as she turns away from me and goes back into the building.

I walk across the campus. I have no faith in anything anymore. Maureen was the one person I thought I could count on. She was going to be my future. And now I've found that she, and what we had, was an illusion, a dream.

No, not a dream: a nightmare.

I drive straight to Maureen's motel from the airport. The curtains to her room are drawn shut. There's no response when I knock on the door. I'm not surprised—I knew she wouldn't be there.

I didn't expect her to be, but I'm still disappointed. I'm also hurt, and most strongly, I'm angry, angry as hell. What in the world was all this about? Who is she, and what's her game?

Once again, a woman I loved has played me for a sucker. I thought I'd learned my lesson. Obviously, I haven't.

I hope this isn't too late."

Johanna Mortimer shakes her head. She's wearing a thin nightgown with an old-fashioned chenille robe over it, which I assume is her mother's. Without any makeup on she looks very young, sweetly vulnerable. "I stay up late. It's the only time I have to myself when I'm down here. My mother clings to me like a baby possum. She hardly sees me anymore, since we live so far from each other, and she's getting on, I don't know how long . . ."

There's a delicate unease between us, as her words, and their import, hang in the air above our heads.

"I shouldn't have brought it up that way," she apologizes.

"It's all right."

I'd called her from my car, asked if I could come by on my way home. She had no problem with that. It didn't matter when I arrived.

"I'm sorry to have intruded on your private time. I could have seen you tomorrow."

She puts a hand on mine. "I'm glad you did."

This is a hell of a nice woman. You always underappreciate the nice ones. We're sitting in her mother's front parlor. It's an antebellum house, three stories of brick and weather-bleached wood on the outskirts of downtown Jamestown, an old district of fine old houses. Presidents Jackson, Polk, and Grant slept in some of the houses in this neighborhood. So did the legendary Robert E. Lee, when he was still a Union officer.

Mrs. Mortimer has been asleep for hours. An atomic explosion directly overhead might awaken her; nothing short of that would do the trick, Johanna informs me. It's her not-so-subtle way of saying we can get cozy, if we want to.

She doesn't know about Maureen—I don't mean the aging lesbian professor from Harvard, whom she does know—but my Maureen. Whoever she really is.

"I saw Maureen O'Hara this morning."

She stiffens. "She's still down here?"

"No. I was in Cambridge, on business. I stopped in her office. Listen, when I told you I'd been helping her do her bird-watching thing?"

She nods warily.

"It was only a couple of times. We don't have a lot in common."

She looks at me. "That's all? A couple of times?"

"Yes. Why?"

"I don't know. The way you put it before it was like . . . never mind."

"She's not exactly my type."

"I guess not."

We're going in the wrong direction. "You don't care for her, obviously."

Johanna stiffens. "Maureen's predatory. She hit on me once. It was an ugly scene. I try to avoid her, but I have many gay and lesbian friends, so we run across each other occasionally. If we're at the same gathering I try to stay on the opposite side of the room."

"Well, I won't be seeing her anymore, so you don't have to worry about bumping into her when we're together."

That was the right thing to say. She loosens up, moves closer to me.

Without being obvious, I keep a safe distance. I don't want to throw cold water on her hopes for tonight, but I'm not here for romance.

I take the picture of Maureen out of my pocket. "Have you ever come across this woman?"

She reaches behind me and twists the switch on the lamp, so the bulb comes up brighter. She takes the picture of Maureen from me, studies it for a moment. Her face clouds. "Yes, I've seen her."

"Where?" I don't want to seem too excited, but it's hard not to be.

"In Boston. Not long after I'd come back from being down here, the first time I met you."

"Had you ever met her before?"

"No." My questions are obviously disturbing to her. "Why do you ask? Do *you* know her?"

"Not really." I pause. "Do you remember her name?"

Johanna shakes her head. "No. Shoot, this is embarrassing."

"Why?"

"Because I talked to her about you."

"About *me?*"

She nods. "This woman"—she taps the picture—"approached me at a party. She asked if I knew someone named Fritz Tullis. I was surprised, since I'd just met you. I told her I did. She seemed excited about that."

"Did she say why?" I ask. I feel a vein involuntarily vibrating in my neck.

"She said she'd heard you were into bird-watching, that you were a good photographer and took pictures of birds on your property. She told me she was a professional ornithologist who was interested in studying bird life in the Chesapeake Bay area."

Johanna pauses. "She pumped me a lot about you," she tells me, shaking her head. "You must think I'm a ditz."

"Not at all." I'm breaking into a sweat, listening to this. "I think you're a damn nice woman, actually."

"You do? After I've told you that?"

"It's no big deal," I say, not wanting her to know that it is. "So—you and this woman got into a conversation about me?"

She nods. "It was more like an interrogation, now that I think back on it. She asked me a bunch of questions about you. Where you lived, your photography, whatever I'd mentioned." Her face reddens. "I was a little tipsy. I ran my mouth about you more than I should have. Particularly to a stranger." She frowns. "Why do you have her picture?"

"She came to see me."

"She did?" Johanna asks, distressed.

"Yes. She showed up at my place one day, asking if I'd take her bird-watching. She told me what she'd told you—that she was an ornithologist from Boston."

"Did you take her out to see birds?" Johanna probes. The unspoken question is, did you do anything else with her.

"One time, that day," I say breezily. "I shot some film, as I always do, and this picture of her showed up on the roll, when I developed it. I guess she saw what she wanted," I add, "because I haven't seen her since." Casually: "It's a small world, isn't it?"

"It can be," she agrees.

It's clear she's upset that she may have caused a problem for me, and by doing so, hurt her chances for any kind of ongoing relationship with me.

"Hey, it's nothing," I hearten her. "By the way—do you remember if you mentioned that James Roach was at my mother's party, that night we met?" I try not to sound desperate.

She thinks back. "Yes, I did. That was a big deal, meeting an assistant secretary of state, particularly in a remote location like here. Why do you ask?"

"Just curious. I'm like a cat that way."

"Which curiosity killed. That's the saying, anyway."

"I've heard that," I tell her. "Which is why I'm always careful."

We say our good nights at her front door. "I'll call you," I tell her. "I'm tying up some loose ends, so it might be a few days. Are you going to be down here for a while?"

"Until the end of the week, at least. I might stay longer." If I have motivation to do so goes unspoken.

I regard her for a moment. "Can I ask you a question? It's personal."

"That's okay," she says encouragingly. She wants to get personal.

"I know I'm a reasonably attractive guy, but there's plenty of attractive men in Boston. So why me?"

She smiles. "That is pretty personal."

"You don't have to answer. Forget I asked." I start to go.

She puts a hand on my arm, stopping me.

"I don't mind answering." She moistens her lips. "It isn't true there are that many attractive men around, at least not that many who interest me. And you are a man, a real man."

She pauses. "But there's a lot of boy in you, too, Fritz. It's like you're not quite fully grown up. There's still a part of you that's a reckless adolescent." She smiles. "And that is a turn-on."

She's telling me something about myself that she means as a compliment. But it isn't, not entirely. I can't say I'm thrilled that she said it, but it's something I need to hear.

She kisses me on the cheek. "I'm glad you called and came by, Fritz."

"So am I, Johanna," I say, concealing my heavy heart. "So am I."

Sleep isn't going to come tonight. Maureen's deceit is a vise around my heart. Who is she? And why has she been lying to me?

What's her motive? The stealing of another's identity to get close to me is her most flagrant violation, but there are others—her mysterious disappearances at critical moments; the times she's suddenly been called away on business, or had to visit a friend, such as the night Wallace was killed. There's a pattern, it seems to fit.

The accordian folder Fred brought over the night after my mother was killed, which has all the paperwork detailing the companies Roach was involved in two decades ago, sits on the desk in my mother's study. I have nothing else to do now—I'll take one last look through it before I throw it all away.

The material is tedious, complicated, and boring. Although Roach is no longer part of the equation, I turn to the section Fred highlighted, because Roach's name is the only thing in this shitpile I know. All the deals he was involved in transpired fifteen or more years ago, before he put his holdings in trust. He unquestionably had been a heavy player in the arms game. But there's nothing to indicate he still is, or has been for over a decade.

The words on the pages are blurring into each other. Time to pack it in. I start to put the files back into the folder, when something resonates in the back of my brain.

I leaf back through the document, look at it more carefully. And there, buried among a dozen other names, is a name that screams at me from the page.

I should have thought about this possibility sooner, the signs were all there.

I begin poring through the documents again. This time, I pay closer attention.

Maxwell Simmons, in pajamas and bathrobe, opens his front door and ushers me inside. It's still early in the morning. I broke every speed limit in two states to get here as fast as I could. I'm bedraggled—I haven't showered, shaved, or changed my clothes. I'm sure I don't smell delightful, either.

"I'm sorry I woke you," I apologize. I'd called him at four in the morning.

Simmons doesn't comment on my appearance. "It's all right," he says graciously.

He offers me a cup of black coffee. "Anything in it?"

"Black's fine, thanks."

I wouldn't mind a shot of Maker's Mark to spice it up, but he's a decorous old gent, he'd think badly of me. His blind dog wanders into the room, settling at his master's feet. Simmons reaches down and scratches behind the dog's ears. "You sounded agitated over the phone, Mr. Tullis. Almost feverish."

My hands are shaking. Excitement, lack of sleep, adrenaline. I put the cup down so I don't spill coffee on myself, hand him one of the documents I've been poring over.

"You didn't tell me about this." I point to a section I've highlighted.

His bushy eyebrows go up, forming an inverted V. "We talked about Roach. You didn't ask about anyone or anything else."

"I didn't know to. All I knew was Roach."

He shrugs. "I don't feel obligated to do your work for you, Mr. Tullis. I've already gone deeper into this than I should have by meeting with you." He sighs. "I thought I'd buried my feelings about all of this years ago. But when you came to see me, the possibility that Roach might finally get his just reward overcame my qualms about being involved, however indirectly."

"Well, sir," I tell him, settling in, "let's talk about all of this now. So that maybe, at long last, he will."

The thermometer on the facade of the brick courthouse reads 97 degrees in the shade, and the humidity is equally brutal. This is no climate you want to be outside in. The dogs on the street lie on their sides in the shade, panting feverishly, their long pink tongues caked white with sweat.

I park my car across the square from the First Bank of Jamestown. Even though the air-conditioning is turned up full blast, my skin is clammy as an eel's and my mouth feels like it's stuffed with socks. I take a moment to compose myself; then I get out of the car, walk across the street, and enter the bank, where I head for the safe deposit section, sign in, and take my box to a cubicle.

I brought a photographer's loupe with me to view the transparencies. I spread them and the enhancements out on the flat table, each image side by side, examining them carefully under the magnifier.

And there it is. I look closer, to be absolutely, one hundred percent positive.

I'm positive.

The shades are still drawn at Maureen's motel room. As before, I knock on her door. There's no response. I didn't expect one.

I scan the area. No guests coming or going, and it looks like the cleaning ladies have finished tidying up the rooms along this row. I try the door; maybe I can force it.

But I don't have to. The maid must have forgotten to lock it. Maybe this is a portent, that all my luck isn't going to be bad. Looking around once again to make sure no one's watching, I step inside, quickly shutting it behind me.

The room is dark. I turn on the dim overhead light, hurriedly pull open drawers in the small chest, rummaging among her underwear, other garments. I check the bathroom, the medicine cabinet. I even get on my hands and knees and look under the bed, which hasn't been dusted for who knows how long. Nothing.

Some clothes are hanging neatly in her closet—dresses she'd worn to my mother's house for dinner, shorts and jeans from when we went to observe the birds. Her shoes are lined up against the back wall. Running shoes, dress sandals, low heels. At the far end, lying on their sides, laces askew, are her custom-made hiking boots. I pick them up, heft them. They're almost as big as my Nikes.

I tense as I hear a car pull up outside. A door slams, some footsteps, then a room door down the breezeway opens and closes. My hands are wet—I'm sweating. I have the same premonition of impending calamity I had the night I snuck onto Roach's property.

There's one more place to check—the most obvious one, which I've saved for last. I open the drawer of the small corner desk, quickly rummage through it. Inside I find a dog-eared Gideon Bible, some motel stationery, assorted blank postcards featuring local attractions—Amish buggies, quilts, old bridges, fishing boats in a harbor.

Under the Bible there's another, smaller book. I pick it up. It's Maureen's notebook, the one she's been writing in since the first day we went birding. I open it, holding the pages up to the light filtering through the door. There's no mistaking Maureen's handwriting. It's the same precise penmanship that informed me she wouldn't be coming to my mother's funeral.

Quickly, I riffle through it. As I'd suspected, there's nothing in it about birds, because this isn't about them. It's all about me, everything I've done and told her since she and I met—my comings and goings (particularly as regards my suspicions about Roach), the pictures I've taken of his property since she's met me, what I know about the murders, especially what I've hidden from the police. Nothing about her, nothing that tells me who she really is. The most depressing thing is that there's not one entry about her and me on a personal level. To read this, one would never know we'd had any kind of romantic or emotional relationship.

I flip to the back of the notebook and see an entry with today's date. Unlike the other entries, which are neat, precise, and detailed, this one was simply and hastily printed, in big, block letters:

"MEET ROACH AT BOAT. TEN O'CLOCK TONIGHT. AVOID FRITZ!"

I walk to my car, activate my cell phone, and call Fred.

"Hey, Fritz. What's going on?"

"Call your cousin. I know who the killer is." My voice is surprisingly calm, considering.

Fred isn't calm at all—he's jumping out of his pants. "Who is it? How did you figure it out?"

"I'll tell you all about it when I see you. When can you guys get down here?"

"I'll check with Marcus. Damn, Fritz, this is incredible!"

"Call me back. I'll wait to hear from you."

He gets back to me in less than five minutes.

"Marcus can get down here in four or five hours. He has to bring the local cops with him, since this is their jurisdiction. And he's gonna bring the Prince Georges County Police, too, because of Wallace. Where do you want to meet?"

I want the final dénouement to be on my family's property. That's where it all started, and it's fitting that's where it should end.

"My mother's house. But Fred . . . not this afternoon. I have something I have to take care of first."

"Okay," he says. "When?" I can hear the impatience in his voice.

"Tonight. After . . ." I calculate quickly. "After eleven."

"Eleven it is. We'll be there."

My parents' house bakes in the afternoon sun. I pull up in front and sit for a moment, staring at it. When my mother and father lived here there was a quality of aliveness. Now it's an inanimate structure, a collection of rooms.

Generations of Tullises have lived in this house. That's over now. I'm holding the fort until the hammer comes down.

What a job it's going to be to pack it all up. The furniture and furnishings are old-fashioned, out of style, almost nothing Sam or Dinah or I will want to keep. We've already split up the items that had emotional value—Dinah got my mother's china, silver, and jewelry, Sam took my father's collection of antique watches, I dibbed my dad's old desk and chair, and the three of us divided some paintings, family albums, other special heirlooms. The rest goes on the auctioneer's block.

To the northeast, large, ominous gray thunderheads are gathering. By evening we should have a heavy downpour; perhaps a full-blown storm. Then, once it passes, the air will be light and breezy, sweet with the fragrances released from the trees, the green grass, the rich, loamy earth.

I've come to love it here—I didn't appreciate this place

when I was younger, I took everything for granted. I'll never take anything for granted again.

I park my car out of sight in the garage, close the door, enter the house through the mud room off the kitchen. Immediately, I can feel the change, it's palpable. I've been in this house when no one was here, but this is a different kind of emptiness, it's like oxygen being sucked out of a bell jar. This is a home that no longer has a soul. As has my mother's, it's departed to another place, never to return. An inanimate shell, a collection of wood, brick, glass, mortar. Nothing more.

Moving through the house, I close the windows, pulling the shades. I leave all the lights off as well. Anyone snooping around would think the house was empty. That's how I want it.

The hours crawl by. I could really use a beer, but alcohol in any amount, even one beer, would be stupid and dangerous. I need a clear head. I have more than enough conclusive evidence now to go to the police, which is what I promised Fred I'd do, what Buster would urge me to do, what I know I should do, not only because it's the right thing to do, but more important, for me, because it's in my best interest, my best interest being my self-preservation. Turn everything I've learned over to the professionals and remove myself from danger.

But I'm torn, because of the unresolved business with Maureen, or whoever she really is. That entry in her daytimer really threw me for a loop. Why is she meeting with Roach? What's their relationship? What else has been going on with her that I don't know about? And how does that connect to all these murders? My need to find out the answers to these questions is more important to me than anything else, even my own safety.

I started this. I have to finish it. I can't help it.

I check the ancient hand-wind clock on the mantel. Eight, straight up. I peer out a kitchen window through a crack in the blinds. Sunset is approaching fast, made darker and more sudden by the low-hanging clouds. Off in the distance, about five miles, I hear thunder, feel the rumble. In an hour, maybe less, heavy rain will begin falling all around here. I'm counting on that.

Eight-thirty. The thunder is getting closer, less than a mile away now. I've been sitting in the gloom, trying to find as much inner calm as I can, given the perilous circumstances. Now it's time I go. Checking outside one more time to make sure no one's snuck up on me unawares, I leave by the back door, open the garage, strap the canoe to my Jeep, and slowly, with the lights out, drive down to the burnt-out hulk that was my own home. I take the canoe off the Jeep, slide it into the water, climb in, and start paddling.

The rain dances across the water toward me, swaying like a wet, glassy hula skirt in the high, accompanying winds. Its force is of almost tropical storm intensity, immediately dousing me, the raindrops smashing down like wet BBs.

For once in my life I'm glad I'm being drenched. Not only will the storm provide valuable cover, it should also discourage surveillance. I've come equipped not only for weather, but for stealth. I pull on midnight blue foul-weather pants and jacket over my T-shirt and shorts, cover my backpack with a black garbage bag. That backpack's been everywhere with me, I'm not about to leave it behind now. I kneel in the center of the slender canoe, silently paddling downstream, toward Roach's dock.

Around one more bend in the narrow river, under a majestic stand of cypress tree roots that hang way out overhead, forming a ghostly canopy, the edge of Roach's property comes into view. No illumination anywhere—no ambient light coming from his house, nothing from his landing strip, a quarter-mile downstream. No lights on his dock, nor on his boat, which is bobbing in the rain-fed swells.

Normally, this yacht, shimmering in the darkness, would be a thing of beauty, a vision to behold. But not now. Now it's a land mine I have to negotiate, without blowing myself up. From the cover of the dense foliage, I survey the area. I assume there are sensors and hidden cameras guarding the place, as there were when I trespassed here last time, but I don't see any real live people. I don't know how far afield Roach's security extends—not this far from his house, I hope. The pictures that were taken of me were closer in; until I reached a certain point on his perimeter, about two hundred yards from the house, I think I had been undetected. The dock is a considerably greater distance than that from the house. And tonight, with this storm blowing like crazy, the security's likely to be lax—guys working for wages, no matter how professional they're supposed to be, aren't going to stand around outside in weather like this, getting wetter and more miserable by the minute. They're going to be inside where it's warm and cozy, counting on the alarm system to cover their backs. They'll hop to when Roach comes down here, but not before. An important element in my favor.

I look at the yacht through my binocs, a hand over the lens to keep the rain off. Nothing at all is moving—it's like a ghost ship. Of course, according to the note she'd left to herself, the meeting isn't scheduled for another hour. When Roach and whoever he brings with him do arrive they'll have plenty of security, that's a given. But the appointment is still an hour from now.

As I stare at the boat some more I'm forced to think of another possibility that's been dancing around the back of my mind: that the note in her daytimer is bogus. She figured (or hoped) I would find it and wanted to throw me off her trail. Hiding it in plain sight was pretty blatant, now that I've had time to think about it.

If Maureen isn't here, I'm doubly fucked. I have to confront her, for my own sanity. And for closure. I'm risking my life to do it, but I can't help it. This experience has devastated me like none I've ever had, or ever want to have again. I know I've been set up, but how elaborately? Frailty, thy name is woman. Duplicity or shamelessness is what the bard really meant. Yet who am I to cast a stone at her, to quote another impeccable authority? I've been lying to her, to myself, to the world for years.

The recent events in my life are payback for my own dishonesty. Big-time.

I fidget around in my canoe, watching and listening. Check my watch. Five after nine. Maybe there's something on the boat that will help me find the answers I'm looking for about Maureen. I've got an hour before they show up—if they come at all.

I scan the area again. No guards anywhere that I can see, no one's gone on or come off the yacht. I'm cramping, hunkering down in the little boat. The rain, falling harder than ever, is wearing me down. I'm irritable, nervous, antsy. I can't wait here for another hour.

Screw it—I'm going over there now. I'll look into the belly of the beast, find out what I can, and I'm gone. I'll confront Maureen at a time and place when it's safer.

Getting to the yacht from where I'm hiding will take only a couple of minutes, but it will be the most dangerous part. It's pitch-black out and the conditions are shit, but I'll be exposed. If I'm wrong—if Roach's security is alert and does extend this far—I'm a dead duck.

Mine not to reason why anymore. I untie my boat line from the tree, and push off.

My canoe glides quietly across the choppy water. I'm hunched down low, my oar slipping in and out of the water without a sound, my head swiveling back and forth, eyes looking everywhere—on shore, on the boat, behind me.

A hundred yards and closing. Seventy-five. Fifty. My shoulders and arms are aching, not from exertion, but from anxiety. And then I'm alongside the silent, dark vessel, on the side facing away from the dock and the rest of the property, out of sight from land, protected by the bulk of the sailboat.

I take a moment to catch my breath, then press an ear to the ship's hull, listening intently. But I don't hear a sound except that of the rain, which is still coming down hard, the heavy drops pounding the surf and the ship's deck.

Get in, find whatever I can, get the hell out. I secure my

boat line onto the yacht, slip my pack onto my back, and moving as quietly as I can, I hoist myself aboard.

The deck is slippery. I'm wearing running shoes instead of deck shoes, so I walk carefully. As I approach the closed hatch, an absurd thought hits me—what if the cabin door is locked, and I can't get in? All this stress for nothing.

My luck's still holding. The hatch cover slides open effortlessly. I climb in, pulling it shut behind me—and as soon as I do I enter into a world of total darkness, not a streak of light showing from anywhere, inside or out. The normal claustrophobic, almost overpowering fear that everyone has of being entombed nearly takes my breath away, the feeling is so suffocating.

I force myself to stand absolutely still, to steady myself. It isn't easy; I can't even hear my own breathing, my heart's pounding so hard in my ears. I'm really fighting, in this pitch-blackness, not to have a full-on panic attack.

It takes a few moments for my pulse rate to come back down to a level approaching normal. And when it does, I realize that I am not alone.

There's a moment of silence. I can hear someone else's breathing, along with mine. "You found it, didn't you?" Maureen says to me out of the gloom, in a monotone that's devoid of emotion.

A few low lights come on inside the cabin. She's sitting at the saloon table less than five feet from me, staring at me through lifeless eyes. She looks terrible—there are bruises on her cheekbones and neck, her hair is all awry, she's deathly pale. And she's been crying, there's caked makeup under her eyes.

I grab the edge of the table to steady myself—I'm trembling so bad I can hardly stand. "Of course I found it. You set me up perfectly. But you're an hour early," I blurt—I'm not thinking straight, I'm way too freaked out. "You're not supposed to be here until ten."

"Oh, Fritz, you damn fool! You shouldn't have come," she wails.

I don't know whether to shit or go blind. I stare at her, transfixed. Then I hear another body shifting. And I know.

"She's right, Fritz." The low, harsh, voice comes from behind me. "You shouldn't have come."

I turn slowly. Ed Flaherty, wearing a worn slicker, a pair of seaman's pants, and those stupid trademark cowboy boots of his, is standing behind me. He has a weapon in his hand, an automatic that looks as big as a cannon. It's pointed right at my gut.

"Put your bag down," he orders me, pointing to the table with his gun.

I carefully slip my day pack from my shoulders and lay it on the table. "That was your writing in her daytimer, wasn't it?"

He bares his teeth in a lupine smile. "I figured you'd take the bait, if you found it. Which I set up pretty good, don't you think?" He taps his temple. "Lots of book smarts, but not enough street smarts. You're too damn predictable, Fritz. You want to play in this game, you've gotta zig when the other guy thinks you're gonna zag."

I turn accusatorily to Maureen. "I'm sorry, Fritz," she says despondently. "I was hoping you wouldn't fall for it. That you'd see through it."

Of course I do, now, I think, kicking myself. A blind man could have read this in Braille from a mile away, after I figured out the mystery of the photographs. But I was too hell-bent on my vendetta to see clearly. "You know me pretty well, Maureen. Or whatever your name really is. I always act first and think later. When it comes to you, anyway."

"Which is why you're in shit up to your eyebrows," Flaherty says.

"Where's your partner in crime?" I ask heatedly. "Is he going to make his grand appearance at the appointed hour? Is he even showing up at all? Or is he going to leave the dirty work to you again, as usual?"

"Who's that you're talking about?" Flaherty asks me coyly.

The prick has to play games with me. "Roach, who else?"

Flaherty smiles. "Jim?" He shakes his head. "He's not involved in this."

"Yeah, right," I reply bitterly. "His security coincidentally vanishes, you're on his boat, but he's not involved. Mr. Clean Hands. I've got enough street smarts to see through that one."

"Don't worry about Jim Roach," he warns me. "You've got enough to worry about, with you and her. So shut your mouth about Roach."

He motions toward the hatch door with the gun. "We're gonna take a cruise, the three of us. A nighttime cruise on the ghost ship *Helena*. You—" he points to me—"go up top, cast us off, and take the boat out into the Bay. I'll stay down here with the lady, where it's warm and cozy."

"Don't do it, Fritz," Maureen says sharply.

"Hey!" He takes a menacing step toward her. "Shut the fuck up."

"*You* shut the fuck up," she spits at him.

Flaherty's face reddens. Then he rakes the side of the gun across her face, a hard *whamp* that sounds like a coconut being cracked open by a hammer.

"You bastard!" she cries out, her body convulsing in pain.

Reflexively, I start to lunge at him, but he pivots and points the gun at me again, inches from my face, freezing me. "Don't be a hero, ace. You don't have the chops for it." He backs off, trains the gun on Maureen. "Do it," he orders me.

"Fritz . . ." She's whimpering now. Her face is ballooning where Flaherty coldcocked her. Her cheekbone could be broken—he hit her hard enough.

"Whatever you say," I tell Flaherty. "But don't hit her again."

He's cold: "That's up to her."

"Don't provoke him anymore, Maureen," I plead with her. "Please."

"You think it's going to matter?" She glares at him. She

doesn't back down, I'll give her that. Not always the best attribute in a situation like this.

"Just don't," I plead with her. This disaster could spiral completely out of control. "It's not going to help anything. I'll do whatever you ask," I promise Flaherty. "But stay cool, okay? Let's everybody try to stay cool."

"I am cool," he says hotly. "Tell her."

In response, she turns away.

I have to tamp this down. "Where are we heading?" I ask.

"We'll worry about that once we're out there," he replies.

I go up top. It's still raining, but not as hard as it had been earlier. I walk across the deck to the railing where the boat's tied off, stop and look back to the cabin opening. From this angle I can't see them, which means they can't see me either. I turn and stare in the opposite direction. Nothing's visible, 360 degrees—no lights, no bodies, nothing. Even the birds, bullfrogs, and crickets are silent. It's spooky, the quiet is so pervasive. It's as if the place has been evacuated, which makes sense—that we're isolated is not an accident.

My mind is swirling with conflicting emotions. Maybe, I think for a fleeting moment, all this is the most elaborate hoax that's ever been played. Maybe Flaherty and Maureen are in cahoots, trying to make it look like . . . What?

Get a grip, Fritz. Think how insane your logic has become. That's the stupidest idea I've had yet. That was no love tap Flaherty laid on her. He could have split her skull open.

It wouldn't be hard to cut and run in this darkness and weather. Get away from here, call the cops, leave Maureen to whatever fate Flaherty has planned for her. This was never my battle until I idiotically decided to get involved, which turned out to be a tragic mistake. Several tragic mistakes.

None of that matters now. Maureen and I have a history, which is undeniable. There are a handful of turning points in your life when you think you have a choice, and then find out you simply don't.

I cast away the lines that secure the yacht to the dock, push off, and jump aboard. Carefully walking along the slippery deck to the rear of the cockpit, I turn the key in the ignition. The big diesel turns over. I thrust the throttle forward and begin to navigate the yacht through the narrow shoals that lead to the Bay.

In less than ten minutes we're in open water. I stand at the helm, staring straight ahead, wondering what's in store next.

"How're we doing?"

I look over—Flaherty's at the top of the stairs in the hatchway, his lank white hair plastered to his head from the rain.

"I don't know. You tell me."

"Turn on the autopilot to the present course and come over here."

I reach down and set the autopilot, cross to the doorway. Flaherty has a navigational chart in his hand. "Here," he points. "We're close to this place, aren't we?"

I look at the chart. His finger is on Cloudshead Island, a small rocky outcropping in the middle of the Bay. It's uninhabited, the terrain is too steep and cramped.

"Yes," I tell him. "We're close."

"Take us there."

"I'll have to plot our course. I can't do it up here, I need the compass."

"Fine."

Leaving the yacht on autopilot, I follow him below. Maureen's eye is almost swollen shut, like a fighter's. She looks up at me with her good eye as I enter the saloon. "I know," she says with bite. "I look beautiful."

I don't answer. I have to try to keep a steady head. I sit down at the nav table, lay the chart out, and plot our course. Flaherty sits opposite me, near Maureen. I adjust the GPS. The boat turns slightly.

I turn on the radar. "I'm better off watching from down here. That way I can see if anything's in our path, on this," I say, tapping the screen.

"Whatever," he answers laconically. "Just get us there in one piece."

I turn to Maureen. "Are you thirsty? Want some water?"

She starts to say no, then changes her mind. "Yes, please. Thanks."

I open the refrigerator, take out a bottle of Evian, open it, hand it to her. She takes a long, thirsty swallow.

"How about putting some ice on that?" I ask, pointing to her eye.

"Leave off the Florence Nightingale shtick," Flaherty rasps. "This isn't a floating hospital."

"I'll be all right," Maureen tells me, glaring at him with her good eye. She holds the cold bottle to her face.

"Lighten up," I beseech Flaherty. "You're holding a lethal weapon on us. You're in control."

He grunts, then turns to the radar screen. "Is that where we're going?" he points. "Looks like we're close."

I nod. "A few minutes."

"When we get there, drop anchor near shore, then come back down." He points his gun at Maureen to make sure I get the message.

We're all on edge. I concentrate on the radar. The blip that's the island is getting closer to our track. A few minutes later, when we're on top of it, I go up on deck. The rain is slackening off. I feed out the chain until I feel the anchor hit bottom and set. Then I tie the line off, make sure it's secure, and go below again. Flaherty motions me to sit down, next to Maureen. Then he gives me a penetrating look.

"One thing I've got to know. When did you figure out it was me?"

I look at Maureen for a moment, then turn back to him. "Not until today," I admit.

He stares at me in astonishment. "It sure as hell took you long enough," he rebukes me. "But then again, you weren't looking for me, were you?"

"Not until recently, no."

My second meeting with old Mr. Simmons had clarified what I'd discovered in the documents. Roach and Flaherty had been a great one-two punch for decades: Roach the front man, the smooth talker, the con artist who could sell oil to the Arabs, Flaherty the behind-the-scenes operative who did the heavy lifting, the murders and the necessary brutal acts.

"But around 1987," I had told Simmons, "Flaherty dropped out. It's like he disappeared, or retired."

"Flaherty disappeared, all right," Simmons had answered tersely. "He disappeared into the Maryland prison system. He killed a rival," the old man had explained. "He'd killed before and gotten away with it, but this time he finally got nailed. He was given a sentence of fifteen to twenty-five at the Maryland House of Correction state prison."

That fit. I'd computed the time in my head. Flaherty was active in Rampart Industries, the skeleton corporation he and Roach had set up to cover their nasty business, until at least 1986. Even if he'd done the minimum amount of his sentence, he hadn't been out of prison for long.

"Flaherty is back on the street," I had informed the old man.

"You know that for a fact?" he'd asked anxiously. He was still fearful of repercussions, after all these years.

"Yes," I'd said. "But Roach isn't in the arms trade anymore. I've checked him out. He's clean now."

Of course, I was wrong, and he'd vigorously corrected me. "James Roach is a greedy pig. I wouldn't believe James Roach was clean if he stood before me buck naked. If Ed Flaherty is out of prison he's without a doubt back to his old tricks, and he and Roach are the closest you can come to being Siamese twins. Knowing Roach, he's using his position to benefit himself, and Flaherty."

The old man, tired, had leaned back in his chair. "The Roachs and Flahertys of this world steamroller everything in their path. The meek don't inherit the earth, Mr. Tullis," he'd sadly informed me. "They get buried under it."

Once I clarified their relationship, and found the evidence in the photographs, it all fell into place.

Our captor nods at my day pack. "What's in there? Dirty pictures?"

I glance over, but don't answer.

"You saw that Russian bastard get murdered on Roach's runway, didn't you? And you took pictures of it." He looks at my day pack again. "They're in there, aren't they?"

My lack of response is confirmation enough.

"Take 'em out," he orders me.

I look at Maureen, look back at Flaherty, take a deep breath. Then I open my pack, reach in, look at Flaherty yet again. He's staring at me intensely. I hesitate a moment; then I remove the manila envelope that's on top of my computer, which contains the two photographs of Putov being murdered.

I hand them to Flaherty. He opens the envelope, takes out the pictures, looks from one to the other. For a moment he seems confused. "You can't see my face. That could be anybody." He's talking more to himself than to us. "What the . . ." He looks at the pictures again. Then he sees what I'd found, earlier this morning.

"My *boots?*" He moans, stares at the pictures yet again, as if he's seeing a ghost come to life. "Ah, fucking vanity! It'll bite you in the ass every time." He strokes the supple ostrich skin coverings of his cowboy boots with the fingers of his free hand. "The first thing I did when I got out of prison was have these made. Cost me three thousand dollars, and they're worth ten times that to me. Buying these boots made me feel like a man again instead of a caged animal, which is what I was all those years."

He looks at the pictures some more. "Talk about for the want of a nail!" He wags an accusatory finger in my face. "That day we went out on this boat and I saw you with your camera—I had my suspicions about you already, before I'd even met you, but that iced it, before we halfway finished the cruise. Not that I knew you had pictures of me, but that you might. I had to assume that you did." He touches his large proboscis. "In my line of work you develop a smell for shit. I could smell it on you right away."

I think back to that day, remembering him questioning me. I'd thought Roach was the one interested in my photography, when it was Flaherty all along.

He's right. A street-smart pro would have known where to look. I didn't—which is why I'm here now, with Maureen. And speculating about her true identity, and what her real game is.

Flaherty's way ahead of me. "You're wondering about her, aren't you? What she's doing in all this."

I turn to her. She holds my look, I'll give her that. "Yes."

"Go ahead," he directs her. "Tell him."

"I had to deceive you, Fritz," she says. "But I never thought things would become as they have between us."

"What does that mean, for Godsakes?" I cry out. This is all too bizarre, too terrible.

Flaherty takes a small leather case out of his side jacket pocket, flips it to me. I open it. It's a badge.

"You're a *cop?*" I say in utter disbelief.

She almost chokes over her answer. "Yes."

I fell in love with a cop. How pathetic.

"And this"—Flaherty brandishes the automatic in his hand—"is her gun. Glock .40. Cop special."

I look at Maureen. She's shaking her head, like she's trying to shake this all away.

"You shouldn't have come here tonight," Flaherty admonishes me. "You were warned not to, how many times? But you couldn't restrain yourself, could you? You had to be Arnold fucking Schwarzenegger, saving the damsel in distress." He glances over at her. "Lucky for me you're so gallant, because she was the key to snaring you."

He runs his hand along the barrel of the gun like he's stroking a woman's leg. "Jim made her as a cop that night the three of you met up at your mother's house," he explains. "He'd met her years before. She was hoping he wouldn't remember her, but he did."

I think back to that night. Maureen had seemed particularly

nervous and concerned about meeting Roach in the flesh. Now I know why.

"He put me on to her," Flaherty goes on, "and I've been shadowing her since then. Yesterday, I made my move. I got the jump on her at her motel, when she came back to change clothes. Even cops let their guard down sometimes, especially when they're in their bra and panties." He leers at her. "Oh, man, was she pissed, especially me taking her gun away from her. She cussed me out some kind of fierce, hurt my feelings."

"Fuck you, you son of a bitch," she snaps at him.

"See what I'm saying? She's a spitfire, ain't she? I had to knock her around some to quiet her down, but in the end, you don't fuck with this." He brandishes her gun. "Anyway, once I got her under control, I put the note in her book, and brought her here." He smiles crookedly. "I knew you wouldn't be able to resist coming after her. Only love can break your heart," he sing-songs. "Or in this case, kill you."

I groan inwardly. He's right about that.

He cocks an eye at me. "What was it someone said about dying, in some movie? 'It is a good day to die.' I can't remember what movie that was, but it's a good line. Except the guy who wrote it had never actually died himself, personally. It's never a good day to die, not when you don't want to."

"Little Big Man," I tell him.

"What?"

"Little Big Man. Dustin Hoffman said it in *Little Big Man."*

"That's the one where he plays the hundred-year-old Indian?"

"Yes."

"Sounds like a fucking Indian, that stoic shit."

As I listen to him I'm hearing the rain falling outside as well. It's coming down lighter now, slackening off. If the storm had come through an hour earlier, I wouldn't have had the guts to come out, I wouldn't be on this boat. I wouldn't be here at all. And Maureen would be alone with him.

I wish I knew more about her. I may never know, not the way this is going.

"That first time we went sailing together," I ask him. "When Wallace almost killed me. That wasn't an accident, was it?"

Flaherty shakes his head scornfully. "Taking a shot at you on the boat like that. Amateur night in Dixie, the whole fucking affair. And the man called himself a professional," he spits out disdainfully. "Shit, my sainted grandmother was more professional than him. Only thing that clumsy attempt did was arouse your suspicions more and make it harder for me to kill you without it looking deliberate. Which is why I've been biding my time, until now."

He gives me a sharp look. "Near-death experience, a man remembers that. Most men, they'd have shied away from this like it was a live hand grenade." He stares balefully at me. "But even after that close brush, you had to push it, and push it. Why?" he asks, bewildered. "What was in it for you?"

My explanation is more for me than for him. "Someone had been murdered, and I knew about it. I didn't think that should be buried under the rug. It's wrong."

Flaherty shakes his head in stunned disbelief. "A man with a conscience? Jesus, I didn't think they existed anymore. That can be dangerous to your health."

"I know that now," I say morosely. I think back to the very beginning. "Why did you kill that diplomat on Roach's runway?" I ask. "Wasn't that taking a big chance?"

"Of course it was," he agrees. "Otherwise, we wouldn't be sitting here now, would we? But it was the only way I could get the little shit alone," he says. "He thought we were going to meet with Jim." He smiles. "Wasn't he surprised when he found out Jim wasn't there."

He gives me a vicious look. "After I had to kill that little prick I was in for the whole enchilada, one or a dozen, what's the difference? Wallace couldn't keep his cool. You saw how he fucked up on Jim's yacht, and that ugly scene with you at your mother's house. Once I heard about that I knew he couldn't be trusted to keep it under wraps, that he'd crack under pressure." He laughs. "Asshole was taking a dump when I nailed him, did you know that? Caught him with his pants down. For real."

"I can understand Wallace," I press. "But why my mother? She had nothing to do with anything."

"That was an accident," he answers darkly. "Killing old ladies is not something I like to do. You left me no choice."

"*I* left you no choice?" That enrages me. "What the hell does that mean?"

"I needed those pictures. I figured they were in your shack."

"So you went in looking for them," I say tightly, "and she was there."

He nods grimly. "I had headaches over that for days." He almost sounds remorseful—almost. "And then to top it off, the damn things weren't even there. You'd taken them out." He sighs, as if trying to will away a bad memory.

As he's recounting this I realize something doesn't make sense. "You said you were suspicious of me *before* we ever met? What in the world could you mean by that?"

"I got lucky," he tells me with a big grin. His teeth are stained brown—must be the hard water in prison. "Shortly before our sailing adventure—misadventure for you—Jim got an invitation to Agatha Mortimer's house for dinner. She'd hit on him at your mother's house, that night they met. Which is why he brought me along with him to dinner that night. He knew the old dame would make a play for him, and that I could step in and be a satisfactory replacement. Jim gets his hard-ons from power, not pussy. Me, though, I like the ladies." His smile broadens. "Agatha and I have been seeing each other since then. She's not bad in the sack for an old broad, and she lets me smoke cigars in her house, which is more than any of my ex-wives ever did."

He gets serious again. "Her daughter was there that evening, and the conversation got around to Fritz Tullis. As soon as she told us where you live and about your photography setup and all that shit, the bells went off in my head."

This is where deceitfulness can lead you. All the way to your grave.

"So that's how it got started," he concludes. "If you had been a gentleman and taken Miss Mortimer home to mama that night, instead of hustling her back to your place, shtupping her, and showing off for her, we wouldn't be here. Life's funny that way, isn't it?"

"Hysterical," I reply dully.

"What do women see in this jerk, anyway?" he asks Maureen. "Can't you tell he's a loser, through and through? Particularly you, you're a professional. What's your excuse for acting so lame?"

She looks at him, then at me. "I fell in love."

My heart drops all the way to my toes. Then why did you lie to me? I lied, too, I admit it; but my lies were small, self-centered, childish. Yours were monumental. And ruinous.

Flaherty points to my day pack. "You have other pictures of me and Putov, don't you?"

I nod.

"Take them out."

I hesitate. "What happens after I give them to you?"

"I'll give you three guesses," he taunts me. "The first two don't count."

"You're going to kill us."

"You're finally learning. Too late, unfortunately."

"But then you'll be stuck in the middle of the Bay with two dead bodies," I say, pointing out the obvious. "How're you going to explain that away?"

He gives me a withering look. "Stop trying my patience at this late stage, for Christsakes. I'm not a novice at this, in case you've forgotten. I'll drop the dinghy over the side, motor back. No one'll ever have a clue."

He gets up, towering over us. "I'll tell you how this is going to play out, a theory the cops'll jump on, because they'll want to, it'll solve a multitude of problems for them in one neat package. You found out that the woman you loved is a cop herself, on your trail for killing the Russian guy—you and him were doing some smuggling deal or whatever, using your secluded access to the Bay. And you've had a hard-on for Jim Roach for no good reason, you've been stalking him for months, even when you were warned to lay off. That's well documented. You're enraged at both Roach and your cop lover, especially after your mother's death, and you snapped. You came looking for Jim, but she beat you to the punch. Unfortunately for her, you managed to kill her as she was killing you."

He smiles wide. "It'll be an easy call. The Prince Georges County cops already have you pegged as a suspect in Wallace's murder—and when they find your dead bodies, they'll also discover a little gift for them, in your backpack."

He reaches into his pocket and takes out another pistol, holds it up for my inspection. It's small, the size of a toy gun. "Know what this is?" he taunts me.

I stare at the little weapon. What goes around comes around, in spades. "The gun you used to kill Putov and Wallace."

The bastard's right—it's all going to tie together. He's had everything worked out from the beginning. Silently, I curse myself for ever having thought I could play in his league.

"And that's all she wrote," Flaherty says, almost gleefully. "It's time to put this show to bed." He moves toward my pack.

"That's all right," I sigh in resignation. "I'll get you the pictures." I start to open the flap—then I pause. "You don't have to kill us, do you? Once you have the pictures, there's no evidence to link you to those murders. And I'm sure James Roach could come up with ironclad alibis for you."

He shakes his head. "You know too much. And she's a cop. I can't leave a cop alive."

I look at her for a moment, then back to him. "So kill her and let me go."

They both stare at me, dumbfounded. Then Flaherty laughs. "You're a prince," he says. "A real stand-up guy."

Maureen is beside herself. *"You fucker!"* she screams at me.

I wheel around to face her. "You got me into this. Why should I have to die because of you? Wasn't my mother enough?" I turn back to Flaherty. "I can't hurt you. You know that."

He's grinning like a shit-eating dog, watching the two of us go at it. "What do you think?" he asks her jovially. "Should I take lover boy up on his offer?"

"Go fuck yourself, asshole. The both of you," she cries. She's a mess, her eye all mashed in, tears running down her cheeks.

Flaherty looks at me. "I don't know," he says wickedly, for Maureen's benefit. He wants to see her suffer as much as possible, until the very end.

That's it for me, though. All the lies, the deceit, the dishonesty—it's over. It's awfully late in the game, but I'm going out the right way.

"Hey," I say to her softly. I can't be anything but dead-serious anymore, not with her and me, not even when my life's flashing in my brain like a movie being projected at a thousand frames a second. "Come on, Maureen. You know me better than that." I bend down and put my hand on her head, a final benediction of forgiveness. "I'm not going to abandon you, for Godsakes. We're in this together. I fell in love with you, too, remember?"

She's sobbing uncontrollably, big, heavy gulps. "Then why did you . . . ?"

"To know, for sure, how low he'd go. I knew, but I wanted to hear it from his mouth. Now I have." I straighten up, get to my feet. "Okay," I say to Flaherty, finally admitting defeat. "You win."

I reach in to get the remaining pictures. Maureen's gun is in his fist, pointing at my gut. His finger is on the trigger, relaxed but ready. I slide my hand down to the bottom of the pack.

My entire arm feels like I've stuck it in a blast furnace as the explosion shreds my pack. Flaherty's mouth opens with an expression of shock and surprise—but it's a fast reaction, a hundredth of a second, before he collapses backward onto the floor, his shirt front pooling blood like a strike from an oil gusher.

Maureen is screaming. She can't stop.

I kneel down next to Flaherty, my gun in my hand. His eyes are vacant. I must have hit a main artery—blood is pouring out of him onto the yacht's expensive wood floor.

"You were right," I tell the lifeless body. "It was a good day to die." Then the nausea hits me, and I puke my guts out—all over the floor, and all over the corpse.

I weigh anchor. We motor back across the Bay. Maureen, her face swollen up like an overripe cantaloupe, sits on deck shivering in the rain. She spends the time on her cell phone, making calls. I don't listen—it's over for me, this part of it. We don't say anything to each other; we're too numb and wiped out. And fearful of each other, the chasm that's between us.

By the time we sight Roach's property, the rain has stopped. Overhead, the sky is still cloudy, but the moon and a few stars fight through the overcast. Under any other circumstances I'd take that to be a hopeful sign, but I don't have much hope left.

The dock is ablaze with light. Cars are stacked behind each other. Several have red and blue lights flashing on their roofs. People are milling about, looking and pointing at us as we approach.

I cut the engine as we glide into the dock. Federal agents wearing black windbreakers grab the lines and secure the boat. Right behind them, a team of medics come on deck and approach Maureen. She shakes them off impatiently. The agents talk low to Maureen; then they and several others follow her below. I hear gasps and fulminations.

I stand off to the side, watching. Fred and Marcus are coming toward us, along with some Prince Georges County police officers, and a contingent of local King James cops. Fred gives me a "what's going on" look as they board. I shake my head, move away to the other side of the deck, as far from everyone as possible.

Fred and Marcus fight their way down into the ship's cabin. Mabel Ricketts, the no-nonsense detective from the P.G. County police department, carefully maneuvers in low heels across the slippery deck, grasping on to the boat's lifelines for support. "What the hell's going on?" she demands brusquely.

"Check it out," I answer dully, pointing my thumb toward the hatchway.

She looks at me sourly, follows the others inside. It's getting awfully cramped down there, especially with the strong puke smell.

Then it quiets down. Maureen is doing most of the talking. I don't pay attention.

After a few minutes, all the county and state cops, except Fred and Marcus, troop out from the boat's cabin, stumbling over each other in their haste to escape the death scene. Some have handkerchiefs over their mouths to ward off the smell. Ricketts, one of the last out, glares at me with open hostility.

"You're a regular Typhoid Mary, ain't you, Tullis?" she dry-spits. "If I had my way, I'd bring you up on charges of obstructing justice." She sloshes her way across the deck and gingerly climbs down onto the dock.

The Prince Georges and King James contingents get in their cars and take off. A short while later, Fred and Marcus come up from below. Marcus walks over to me. He's angry, too.

"I'm out of it. You should've brought me in earlier," he rebukes me. "You and my cousin had a deal."

I'm too wasted to say anything.

"This is federal. I'm superseded." He cracks his knuckles. His hands are big—he could palm a basketball like it was a grapefruit. "You had no idea what the fuck you were into, did you?"

I shake my head no.

"You're a lucky sonofabitch, I hope you know that," he says. "By rights you should be the dead motherfucker in there, instead of that dead motherfucker."

I get his point, but I don't feel lucky. I just killed a man. He deserved killing, but that doesn't make me feel better.

Marcus puts one of his meathooks on my shoulder. "I thought I was ahead of the pack, but they caught up to me," he says resignedly. "It's okay. I'll get my promotion anyway, she'll see to that. I just won't get the glory." His face tightens. "No one will. Including you. This didn't happen," he says, his voice low.

"What didn't happen?"

"None of it." He cocks his head toward the cabin. "She'll explain."

His anger toward me has abated, now that he's vented his spleen. He puts out a hand. I take it.

"I'm sorry about your mother, man. Be thankful you aren't joining her."

He walks away from me. I look at Fred, who's been watching us but staying out of it. He and Marcus walk the length of the dock, get into his car, and drive away.

Shortly after Fred and Marcus leave, two of the federal agents emerge from below with a lumpy body bag slung over their shoulders. They strap the body into the back of one of the vans, drive away.

The noise of an incoming helicopter cuts through the sounds around the boat. I look up as it banks for a landing, disappearing behind the low hills at the other end of the property. A few moments later, a black Range Rover arrives from the direction of the tarmac. James Roach gets out of the passenger side. He's wearing a raincoat over a tuxedo—he must have been summoned here from some fancy diplomatic function. A couple of bodyguards emerge from the backseat, flank him tightly.

Roach says something to one of the remaining cops on duty. The officer nods, points toward the boat. Roach turns and looks. And sees me, standing on the deck like a beacon, staring at him.

Although we're fifty yards from each other, I can see the fear in his face. For a moment, we're locked into each other. Then he braces himself, walks down the deck to the boat, and jumps aboard. Even though he's wearing patent leather pumps with slick soles he strides manfully across the wet surface over to me.

"You've overstepped your boundaries for the last time," he tells me in anger. "I'm going to have you arrested and see that the book is thrown at you."

I almost laugh in his face. "Jesus Christ, man, is that all you can come up with at this late date? The best defense is a strong offense? Like back there at the State Department, with your phony scare tactics of the collapse of civilization because I shot a lousy roll of film?" I shake my head. "Nice try, but no cigar this time."

"You still don't know who you're fucking with, do you?"

I hold my ground. "Oh, yes. I know exactly who I'm fucking with."

He's trying to put up a good front, not only for me, but for the rest of those who are here, Maureen and the other federal cops, as well as everyone who's going to be involved in this, up and down the line—but a blind man could see through his transparent facade. This fucker is scared shitless. As well he should be. If nothing else positive comes out of this disaster, this bastard is going down.

"We'll see how this plays out," he says tightly.

"You're fucking-aye right we'll see. You really are a one-eyed jack, you son of a bitch, but I can see the other side of your face now. And so can everyone else."

He glares at me once more, trying one last time to break me

by the force of his will. But this time, I don't back down—I'm standing toe-to-toe against him. Tonight I've found a strength I didn't know I had. And despite all the horrors that have gone down, I have to feel good about that.

Roach feels it—it overwhelms him. He turns away, walks off the boat, and goes back to his car, where he immediately gets on his cell phone.

For the moment, I'm alone on the deck. A wave of exhaustion hits me, a release of the tension that's built up all these fearful hours. I sag, grabbing a shroud for support.

I've had enough for tonight. I cross over to the side of the yacht where my canoe is still where I tied it up. I climb over the edge of the deck, lower myself into the little boat, untie my line, and begin paddling away. In less than a minute I'm back in the shelter and safety of the swamp.

My mother's house feels more like a tomb than ever. After I brush my teeth and gargle with mouthwash to try and get rid of the barf taste, I grab a cold six-pack from the refrigerator and take it outside, where I sit on the front porch under the wide awning. I drink one brew straightaway, in four long gulps. It helps, but not enough. I crack the second one.

The phone rings several times, but I don't answer it. It's probably Maureen, but I don't want to talk to anyone now, especially her. I want to be alone, to wallow in my sorrow and self-pity. I've earned it.

Some time later—I'm unaware how long, I haven't moved from my spot, but it must be several hours later, I've gone through the entire six-pack plus a couple belts of bourbon—a car comes up my road, throwing bits of oyster shell and fresh mud. It's a government car, a beige Ford Taurus. It stops in front. Maureen gets out. A large bandage covers her battered eye and cheek. She stands there, feet spread apart, looking up at me with her working eye.

"We have to talk, Fritz. You can't avoid me."

"What about?"

"Everything," she says firmly. "I know you're angry as hell with me right now, but we have to talk. Can we go inside?"

I'm too weak to resist. "Come on."

She reaches into the car and grabs a bulky briefcase, then walks up the porch steps and lets herself into the house. I follow her into the living room and sit down on one of the old down-filled couches. Maureen pulls off her wet shoes, sits opposite me.

The tension between us is excruciating. "You want to talk, Maureen—or whoever you really are—go ahead, talk."

She fidgets in her seat, takes another moment to compose herself. "You might not believe this," she begins, "but I was going to come clean yesterday. Tell you who I am for real, everything."

I shrug. "Easy to say now."

"It's true. Except Flaherty got the jump on me." Her face contorts into a scowl. "I let my guard down. I was thinking about you, instead of my business. It almost got both of us killed." She looks at me. "I'm sorry."

I stare at her. "For openers, who are you?"

My bluntness catches her up. She hesitates for a moment before answering. "Well, I'm not Maureen O'Hara. Nor am I a professor at Harvard. I'm not a professor anywhere."

"I already know that. I met the real professor."

"When?" she asks in surprise.

"Yesterday." I glance at the clock on the mantel. It's way past midnight. "Technically, the day before that." *Christ, yesterday seems like a century ago.*

"In Boston?"

I nod.

"You went there to check up on me? I thought you trusted me." She actually sounds hurt, as if I did her an injustice.

That's a joke. But it isn't funny now.

"I did trust you. I had a job interview at a college nearby," I explain. "I thought I'd drop in and surprise you." My laugh is hollow. "Guess who the surprise was on."

She grimaces. "I *told* them I shouldn't use a real person's name," she laments. "But they insisted, in case you decided to check up on me. Which backfired, as I was afraid it would."

"Who's *they?* And who are you, for real? If you know how to be real."

"I know how to be real," she answers. "But I couldn't be, in this situation."

She rearranges herself on the couch. She's having a hard time with this. I'm glad. Why should I be the only one to suffer?

She clears her throat. "My name is Vanessa Gardner. I'm originally from Chicago. I went to Southern Illinois University, got my degree in criminology, then went to Northwestern Law School. Now I live in Alexandria, Virginia."

She looks away for a moment, then brings her eyes back to meet mine. "I'm a special agent with the Justice Department. In plain words, a cop. As Flaherty told you."

"Don't remind me. Married, too, no doubt."

"No, I'm single. That part wasn't a lie."

"The only one, I'll bet."

"Not the only one. But that's for later." She sounds like she's in pain. I know I am. "I used you, Fritz. I hated doing it, especially after I got to know you. But I had to. It's my job."

"Fucking over people."

She doesn't flinch. "Sometimes that can't be avoided."

I look away in disgust.

"Do you want to know what happened, and why?"

"Does it matter?"

"I think it does." She hesitates. "It matters to me."

I'm in heavy denial. "I wish this could all go away. I wish I could wake up and find this was all a bad dream."

"Me, too. You don't know how much I wish that."

I sigh wearily, lean back. God, I'm exhausted. "Go ahead," I tell her.

Outside, the sky is awash with stars, now that the rain's passed. Through the open windows I can smell the heavy summer fragrances, powerful after a cleansing rain. Under different circumstances, there's no other place I'd rather be, and no other person I'd rather be with. But that was in my old life.

She begins her story.

"The Justice Department had been keeping tabs on Flaherty while he was still in prison. We were sure he was doing business from inside, but we could never get enough physical evidence to do anything about it. After he was released, we intensified our surveillance. We were pretty sure he was working on something big, and that it was coming fast. But we still didn't have the real goods on him."

She takes a photograph from her briefcase, hands it to me: Putov, the murdered Russian diplomat.

"Is he familiar to you? Was," she corrects herself.

"Don't play games with me. You know he is."

She flushes. "As I assume you also know, he was a top-ranking diplomat in the Russian delegation to this country. What you don't know is that he was also a key figure in one of the Russian Mafias. Russia's totally corrupt, no matter what nice propaganda you read in the papers, from our side or theirs. Everything's for sale, and everybody can be bought. Up to and including jet airplanes, submarines, even enriched plutonium."

She shifts position again—I've never seen her ill at ease like this. I hope it's not only because of the deception; I'd like to think there's some feeling involved. But I don't know; it's probably wishful thinking. Despite everything, I can't help feeling like this—you can't turn love on and off like a spigot. I'm sure she's also in considerable pain, from the beatings Flaherty gave her.

"We became aware of Putov's criminal connections a long time ago," she goes on, "and we'd been shadowing him. It took over a year of hard work, but we were finally putting the pieces of the puzzle together. We knew that Putov and Flaherty had done business with each other before Flaherty went to jail. Never directly, always through third parties, which is how it's almost always done. It's a closed shop, what they do, particularly at their level—people only do business with people they do business with, and if you're not inside the business, you're out of luck. Flaherty was one of the people who does business."

She pauses, then continues. "As soon as Flaherty got out, he and Putov set up a new deal. Putov was involved in arming a clandestine rebel faction that was comprised of Russian hardliners who wanted to return to the old ways. Real Neanderthals," she says with a scowl. "You'd be surprised how many old-liners, even today, still think Communism is better. Give them their quart of vodka and they're happy."

She glances at the photograph. "Flaherty had the money connections from all over the world, and Putov had the buyers. It was a deal made in heaven—their kind of heaven. For Flaherty, it was one last big payoff, after all those years he spent in jail. He was going to go out in a blaze of glory."

She shifts in her chair again. "We had a tap on Putov's phone," she continues. "We had to be careful, because he had diplomatic immunity, so we couldn't mess with him too much, and our relations with the Russians haven't been very good the past few years."

She brings her hand to her battered face, winces at the touch.

"Do you want something for that?" I ask.

She shakes me off. "Later, after I've told you everything." She sits back. "Our surveillance paid off. We learned about when he and Flaherty were going to do this deal. But we couldn't make a move on them until it actually went down. We had to catch them in the act. So we were watching and waiting."

"Then what possibly could have gone wrong?" I ask caustically—this sounds like one more government fuckup, such as the ones I've been living with.

Before she answers, I get up and walk over to the sideboard, pour myself a generous shot of bourbon. I don't offer her a drink. I take a sip. It goes down like liquid fire.

"What happened was," she says, pressing on doggedly, ignoring my rantings, "at the last minute Putov decided to cut Flaherty out. No honor among thieves, the usual old story. But Flaherty got wise, and the deal was iced. Which left Flaherty crazed—he knew that would have been the scheme of a lifetime for him. So he was out for blood."

"Putov's."

She nods. "For a while, everything was flat-line. Then Flaherty, who as you know all too well was a crafty son of a bitch, got back in touch with Putov, told him he wanted to construct another deal, that he would make it worth more for Putov, bygones would be bygones. Business takes precedence over personal egos, he reminded Putov. Putov thought it over, and agreed to move forward with it. Nothing motivates more than greed to people like them."

She rubs one bare foot against the other, tucks both of them under her. I sip my drink, listening.

"Except Putov didn't trust Flaherty, for good reason. He was scared he'd run out his string and would be busted, with no payoff and heavy jail time. So, being the double-crossing little bastard that he was, he came to us, offered to work undercover. He'd set it up so there would be hard evidence against Flaherty, and he'd walk him right to us. In exchange, we'd wink at his transgressions. He could go back to Russia or anywhere he wanted and retire on his dividends."

She clenches her teeth, shaking her head in frustration. "It wasn't perfect—if we had Putov and Flaherty both it would have put a huge hole in the Russian underworld's operations in this country, and we'd have Flaherty, too. But it was still a good deal. Their transaction would be in the toilet, Putov would be out of our hair, and Flaherty would rot in jail for the rest of his life."

She massages her temples. I'm tempted to get up and do it for her; but I resist the impulse.

"We agreed to let Putov work undercover for us," she goes on. "It was risky, but we didn't think we had a choice. We had him under close watch." She exhales, a deep sigh. "Unfortunately, we underestimated Flaherty."

"You lost track of Putov."

She nods. "Flaherty spirited him away from us." She shrugs her shoulders. "Mistakes happen. We aren't perfect."

"No shit."

She ignores my gibe. "Flaherty lured Putov to Roach's farm on the pretext that they had to include Roach in what they were doing. Putov would have bought into Roach's being involved—he knew Flaherty and Roach had been partners, and assumed they still were. It was a crafty move on Flaherty's part. He never intended to do a deal with Putov—he just wanted to kill him, for fucking up the other deal. He had other people like Putov he could do his business with." She sighs. "By the time we figured it out, Putov was a stiff in a Baltimore slum, and Flaherty couldn't be tied to his murder."

"That must've been embarrassing," I say sarcastically.

"It was a disaster, I'm not going to sugarcoat it. There was a lot of yelling and fingerpointing. The agent who was running Putov was terminated."

"He was *killed?*"

She shakes her head. "Fired. We don't kill people for screwing up. This isn't Russia." She pauses; then she gives me a nervous look. "Are you sure you want to hear the rest of this? It isn't pretty."

"Yes," I say resolutely. "I want to hear the whole story. All the unvarnished, sordid details. Leave nothing out. I almost got killed over this, in case you've forgotten. I deserve to know everything."

She draws her legs further up under her, unsuccessfully trying to get comfortable. "As I said, the Justice Department was pretty sure Roach's farm was the killing ground and that Flaherty, if not the actual trigger, was behind it. One thing we knew for sure—the murder wasn't a street crime, and it hadn't gone down in Baltimore."

"So did the cops," I tell her. "That cop from Baltimore, Marcus DeWilde? He's been working this from the day it happened."

"We knew all about that," she says almost dismissively. "They thought they had an exclusive, but they didn't. But what *we* didn't have, what *nobody* had, was incontrovertible proof that the murder had taken place on Roach's property, and that Flaherty was involved. And we didn't know how to get it."

And then, she tells me, they caught a break. They found out about a local resident named Fritz Tullis. He lived close by Roach's farm, and he had taken photographs in the area. The dossier and psychological profile they hastily compiled on him informed them that he was an impetuous risk-taker who thought he was smarter and cleverer than everybody else. And most important, for this specific situation, his romantic history meant an attractive woman should be able to institute a relationship with him, and then exploit it.

"We know everything about you, Fritz," she tells me, her face flushing. "From the day you were born, until this very moment. More than you can remember yourself." She pauses. "Given your situation, we assumed that if you did know anything, you'd try to be a hero and solve it. And we could piggyback on your effort."

I think back to my late-night session with Jack, the photo wiz at the Anacostia lab. He'd told me the same thing as an abstraction—nobody's life is private anymore—but it went right over my head. I wasn't thinking about myself then. Now I realize I should have known I'd be the one under the microscope once I got in Roach's face.

They had me pegged, all right. Johanna called it—there's still a lot of the reckless adolescent in me. The boy, not fully the man. I feel like a jackass, an utter fool. "So they sent you to be Mata Hari."

She nods heavily. "We'd been keeping tabs on James Roach as well. At the beginning it was more for our comfort level than anything else, because his friendship with his ex-partner had bad karma written all over it. So we knew about Johanna Mortimer and your—" She catches herself.

"One-night stand?" I say in self-flagellating anger.

"Your evening together," she answers tactfully. Having said that, she turns away. "That's when they brought me in," she says, still not looking at me.

This is beyond embarrassment, chagrin, mortification. Samson was a rock of self-control compared to me.

She was dispatched to Boston, where she bushwacked Johanna Mortimer and pried every detail about me out of Johanna that she could. Then she came down here, and the game began in earnest.

"How did you know enough about birds?" I ask, ruminating on all the things that happened, from our first encounter on my front porch until now. "You faked it pretty good."

"I wasn't faking it," she says. "I'm a bird-watcher, for real. That's one of the reasons why I was chosen. Do you remember that story I told you, about hiking in the Alps?"

I nod mutely. I'm numb, listening to this.

"That was true. Except I wasn't the leader, I was just part of the group."

I think back to that sailing excursion on Roach's boat, when he busted me for lying to Johanna. He knew the truth about me. As did Maureen's people.

Maureen. That isn't even her name. Her name is Vanessa. Nothing wrong with Vanessa, it's an okay name, but I don't know Vanessa Gardner. Maureen O'Hara, real or fake, I know intimately. But as I've painfully found out, I don't know her well.

Fuck me—I don't know her at all.

My glass is empty. I don't recall finishing my drink, but I

must have. I pour myself another one. I doubt I'll stop until the bottle's empty.

"Will you get me one, too?" she asks.

"Aren't you on the job?" I ask petulantly.

"Screw the job. This is me and you. Please."

I make another drink, hand it to her. She takes a long swallow.

"The government will do anything to get its man, is that how the game's played?" I ask with bitter invective. "Including federal agents fucking potential witnesses? Shit, you didn't even know I had the damn pictures when we became lovers. And you smoked your share of my weed, too. What's the deal, it's okay to break the law if the end justifies the means? Up to and including murder? What's off-limits? Anything?"

She blanches. "Not murder. And not sex. My job was to engage you, not sleep with you."

I'm getting sick, listening to this. "You *used* me. You fucking *used* me."

She hangs her head. "I know. I hate it."

"Didn't stop you, though."

"It was my *job,* damn it! These were big stakes. *You* made the decision to play at this level, Fritz. If you're going to do that, you have to play by our rules. And our rules can be cutthroat and vicious."

She's nailed me, and I don't like it. "If your people thought I had photos of the murder, why didn't you come out and ask me?"

"We didn't know if you had anything. It became clear to me early on that you probably did, but I didn't know conclusively until you told me."

"So why didn't you say something then?"

"I *did,*" she says fiercely. "Many times, if you'll recall. Not directly, but as straight as I could. Then when I found out, I begged you to take what you had to the police. You wouldn't. I pleaded with you to drop this. You wouldn't do that, either—you had to solve this by yourself. The Lone Ranger. You had good intentions, Fritz, but you didn't have a clue." She pauses for breath. "You solved it, I'll give you that. Unfortunately, people got killed because you were an obstinate . . . never mind."

"Asshole? I plead guilty." A wave of profound, sad emotion washes over me. "My mother died because of my stupid recklessness. I'll never forgive myself for that."

She reaches across the table, puts her hand on mine, and squeezes it. "No, Fritz. Your mother died because Ed Flaherty killed her. Just as he killed Wallace and Putov. Flaherty was a killing machine. Mary got caught in the cross fire. If it hadn't been her, it would have been you. And Flaherty would have gotten away with it. He'd be alive, a free man."

She clutches my hand tighter. "It tore me up when I saw her body," she says, her voice thick with regret. "I was ready to pack it in. But it was too late by then. I had to stick with this, if for no other reason than to bring retribution to her killer."

I pull my hand away. "What about Roach?" I ask. "How does he figure in this?"

She answers my question with one of her own. "Why do you think he bought his farm? He's a city man, not a farmer." She thinks back a moment. "That night he showed up at your mother's house, I was afraid he'd recognized me—I'd met him at a reception, about three years earlier. My hair was different then, shorter. There were a hundred people at that party. I didn't think he'd remember." She looks bleak. "But as we know now, he did, and tipped Flaherty."

It all makes sense. "What's going to happen to Roach? Is he going to finesse this, like he's done everything else in his life?" That would tear it, if that fucker walked away from this unscathed.

"I can't answer that," she says. "I think—I hope—I'm sure going to try to nail him—but his situation will be handled at a much higher level than I normally operate on. It's a fuzzy area. For instance, those really were diplomats he was meeting with secretly that you photographed—he was telling the truth about that. But he was involved with Flaherty—he had no choice, Flaherty took a big fall for him back then, as you found out. Roach was grateful for that, but more important, Flaherty had a sword he could dangle over Roach's head, which Roach knew he'd use if he bailed on Flaherty. At the least, we know that Roach not only supported Flaherty financially, but that he turned a blind eye when Flaherty wanted to use his property, like the day he and Putov landed on the runway. And tonight as well. It's no coincidence that none of Roach's security people were around."

Exactly what I'd thought.

She sighs. "Bottom line, though, the only thing that matters is do my superiors think Roach was involved deeply enough to do something about it? The truth is, they don't want to know. He's a powerful man. He has powerful friends. But this time, thanks in no small part to you, I don't think they're going to be able to avoid it. The elephant in the room is too big to ignore anymore."

She regards me with her good eye. "Can we forget Roach now? He's going to be dealt with, one way or the other. He's not our problem anymore. What I want to know is, what about me, Fritz? When did you start doubting me?"

I think back to the first time I laid eyes on her. God, what a sight that was. "From the beginning, as I think back on it," I tell her honestly. "The way you showed up seemed bizarre, for openers. Then when we made our deal—a real ornithologist wouldn't have allowed Ollie to stay out there in the wild, where any number of bad things could have happened to him. Regardless of personal gain, it was too dangerous for such an endangered species. She would have had him captured that very day, transported to the proper place for him. You never even mentioned the possibility of doing that."

She nods seriously, listening.

"But I let all of those inconsistencies go, because I fell for you." I crunch some ice cubes in my mouth. "Later, though, you did things that forced me to start doubting you again."

"Like not coming to the funeral."

"That, of course, but there were other incidents, too." I pause—this hurts, badly. "Even with those iffy situations, I believed you, because I wanted to. I shouldn't have, all the signs said not to, but you owned me."

"It was reciprocal."

I shake my head. Even if it's true, I can't handle it. I drain my drink, place the glass on the table. "Near the end, I even thought you might have been the killer. Or involved with whoever was."

She stares at me, wide-eyed. "How could you think something so horrible as that?"

"Don't play the wounded party," I rail at her. "It's logical, damn it! Look at the evidence, your deceptions, your convenient disappearances. It fits."

She nods wearily—it makes sense, she can't deny it. "I was aching to tell you the truth. But I couldn't."

I can't look at her. "You have no idea how devastating my meeting the real Maureen O'Hara was. And then what's happened tonight. I had a gun to my head. I could have been *killed!* We both could have. What if I hadn't had my own gun in my pack, and the luck and guts to use it? I saved *your* life, for Christsakes!"

She starts crying. "I know you did. I'm the professional, and you had to be the one to save us." The tears are coming fast now. "Do you think I wanted you to be in that position? I love you! If you believe nothing else I ever tell you, you must believe that!"

I explode. "*Love?* Who are you kidding, Maureen, Vanessa, whatever your name is. I was the Judas goat, is that it? Lead the flock to slaughter, and probably die in the process?" I'm shouting so loud now they can probably hear me clear back to Jamestown. "There was no other way? What if I hadn't had my gun? What's one more dead ex-professor?"

I think back on my meeting with Roach at the State Department. He'd told me the truth, at least: *What we're doing is more important to the total picture than any single individual—including you. That may be cold, but it's reality.*

She looks up, to tell me that wasn't so. Then she turns her head from me, because she can't.

"All that shit about you wanting to marry me!" I rail on. "What if I'd taken you up on it? What would you have done then? Oh, I changed my mind, I have to wash my hair tonight, I don't want to miss *Sex and the City*? What excuse would you have used when the judge asked for identification? You would have had to come up with a doozy, since you were never Maureen O'Hara in the first place!"

"It was never going to come to that."

"Don't be so damn sure. I wanted to. I thought about it, a lot."

"I know you did," she says. "I still do. But there was no chance you'd take me up on it until this was all over."

"How can you say that? I was in love with you. You don't doubt that, do you?"

"No, I don't doubt that." She hesitates. "In the end, though, you wouldn't have gone through with it."

"That's bullshit."

She shakes her head. "The time before, in Texas, with the married woman? What was her name?"

"Marnie." God, that seems like light-years away. I barely remember what Marnie looks like anymore; the details that make the difference.

"Marnie," she repeats softly. "What if Marnie had said she was going to leave her husband, marry you, the whole shebang? What would you have done?"

"Marry her, what else?"

"I don't think so, Fritz," Maureen says knowingly. "You don't go for women you can have, you go for women you can't have, it's part of who you are, your boyish charm. A rich married woman, almost a decade older—be honest with yourself, that's as close to safe as there is in the real world. If that woman had said yes you would have run like hell, and later on convinced yourself it was she who kiboshed it, not you." She puts a hand on mine. "Even with me, and I really do love you, it was going to be hard, but I was hoping I could change that." She pauses, a long time. "Despite everything, I still do."

I don't want to hear this, not now. It's too close to the bone. I've had more emotional truth than I can handle.

The morning sun is on the horizon. She stands at her car. "You can't talk about this with anyone," she instructs me firmly, as Marcus had told me she would. "Any of it."

"The cops are in on the fix?" I ask in disgust.

She nods soberly. "Everyone who knows is. Whatever comes out of this, with Roach or anyone else, it'll be handled inside the necessary agencies. No one outside of those who need to know will ever see, hear, or feel anything."

"A conspiracy of silence. Our government at work."

She doesn't respond.

"Fine with me." I kick at the crushed oyster shells under my feet. "I wish none of it had ever happened. It's done nothing but fuck my life up, completely."

She looks away from me, looks back. "What about us?"

"There is no us," I tell her curtly.

"There was. There still is."

"There was Fritz Tullis and Maureen O'Hara. There is no Fritz Tullis and Vanessa Gardner. I don't know anyone named Vanessa Gardner."

"But she knows you, better than anyone," she answers stoutly. "And she loves you. Whether you want her to or not."

"That's your problem."

"Yes. It's my problem." She stares at me with that one sad eye. "So I guess this is—good-bye?"

"Good-bye," I say flatly. I don't hug her, I don't shake her hand. I look at her. That's all.

She looks at me once more, opens the door of her car. But she can't let this go—she turns to me. "Goddamn it, Fritz. It can't end like this! Not like this!" She grabs my shoulders with both hands. "It was a job, yes. That's how it started. But I didn't sleep with you because it was a job. I could've done what I needed to do without doing that. I could've held you off, made excuses, diddled you around. I became your lover because I fell in love with you, and I'm still in love with you. It doesn't matter what my name is, what matters is how I feel. And how you feel."

"I can't," I tell her. "I can't handle this. It's too much."

She takes a step back. "I understand. But when you get some feeling back, think about how it felt to know I'd be here, in your kitchen at dinnertime, or in your bed at the end of the day. Think about what that was like, for both of us. Then call me, if you want to."

She hands me a business card. Looking at it, I'm reminded of what we've lost. But I don't say anything. There's nothing I can tell her at this moment that would have any truth to it.

She stares at me one last time; then she gets in her government car and drives away. I watch until she's gone. Then, feeling very alone, I go back inside.

I've been sleepwalking through these past few days. The only times I've been out of the house have been to visit the birds. The first day I came I shot a roll of film. Since then, I've left my camera at the house. I find a shady out-of-the-way spot, sit quietly, and watch.

As adolescents grow and fill out, so do birds. Ollie has matured from when I first saw him. His immature reddish brown feathers are now almost entirely white. He is no longer a boy-bird. He's a man.

I'm weaning myself from him. It's hard—he's been momentous in my life, the hub around which most of my daily routine rotated. It's because of him, my fascination with him, that all the terrible events of the past two months happened.

But I'm leaving here, and so must he.

Buster drives down to see me. We sit in old rockers on the front porch, sweaty Mason jars of iced tea in our hands. It's muggier than usual today—hopefully, we'll get showers by nightfall.

Buster looks around. "It's damn nice down here. You aren't staying though, are you."

I shake my head. "Time to move on."

"You did a good thing, Fritz," he commends me.

"What the hell are you talking about? People are dead because of me, including my mother. What good is that?"

"Okay, you did the *right* thing," he amends. "You saw an injustice committed, and you did something about it."

"I fucked things up, is what I did."

He shakes his head. "Not intentionally. *I* fucked things up, by being asleep at the switch. Roach. And your girlfriend, the Justice Department chick." (I'd told him about Vanessa—formerly, and always to me, Maureen.) "All of us. We did the *expedient* thing, the save-your-own-ass thing. You were the only one in this who risked what he didn't have to. You stood up and were counted."

"For whatever that's worth."

"Plenty, in my book."

"That's nice of you to say, but it doesn't bring those lives back."

"No," he agrees somberly, "it doesn't."

"What about Roach?" I ask. "Is he going to pay any price at all for his role in this?"

"Oh, yeah," Buster replies. "To what extent yet, I don't know. But I will let you in on a secret. He's leaving the State Department. It's going to be announced in a few days. The usual 'to pursue private interests' crap, which everyone knows is bullshit. They shitcanned the fucker, they can't get rid of him soon enough, his stink's contaminated the whole department. And the truth is going to come out, no two ways about it. Bob Woodward and Chris Matthews and all those other media freaks won't let it lie fallow, it's too juicy."

"But what about criminal charges? He's guilty, Buster. He's as guilty of those murders as Flaherty was."

"I don't know how that's going to go. It's a gray area, secondhand, indirect. Will he ever go to trial, or to jail? Maybe, but more likely not." He leans forward, refills his iced tea jar. "But here's the important thing, Fritz. The man's life will end in disgrace. He's going to be shunned by everyone and everything he cares about. For someone whose ego is his entire life, that's unbearable." He pauses. "I wouldn't be surprised if he killed himself over it."

"Give me the gun and I'll spare him the trouble."

"No, no," he tells me, smiling. "You've done all the killing you're ever going to do in this lifetime."

Amen to that, I think.

He stretches his legs out on the old wood planking. "I've taken a leave from the firm, so I can figure out whether I want to stay with that den of thieves or not. Right now, my attitude is fuck 'em all."

That's a surprise, but not entirely. An incident like what happened to me, and by reflection to Buster, could shake up your world. If it didn't, you're brain-dead.

"What do you think you'll do?" I ask.

"I'll probably go back—they don't want to lose me, they'll pay me a bundle to stay, I'm a valuable commodity. And let's face it, it's where the action is. But I've got to tell you—a part of me wants to find a situation where I only have to deal with moral ambiguities, not political ones, which come with the territory at a firm like ours."

"You might be happier. Knowing you, though, you'd miss the action."

"We'll see. I'm not in a hurry. What about you? Are you going to be happy?"

I look out onto the great, green expanse of my mother's front yard, the tall, graceful ashes and birches, at her flower beds that are starting to go to seed because they aren't being cared for anymore. I can understand why she and my father never left, never wanted to.

"I hope so," I tell him honestly. "If I can ever figure out how."

Sam and I walk the property with the live-wire real estate agent who's going to sell it for us.

"This is a wonderful place," she says energetically. "One of the few remaining intact estates." She makes some notes in her PalmPilot. "Are you insisting on selling it to an individual who will keep it in one parcel, or would you be willing to sell to a developer? I know it has sentimental value, but you could get quite a bit more from a developer."

"We want the money," Sam says bluntly. "None of us live here anymore, and with both our parents gone, we won't be coming back." He looks over his shoulder at me as he tells her that.

"Get as much as you can," I agree with him.

"Nothing lasts forever," she chirps. "The house will have to remain," she informs us. "It's historical. If a developer buys this, they'll use it as their sales office. It's a charming place. Is anyone living in it now? I'd like to start showing it as soon as possible."

Sam glances at me. "It'll be vacated by the end of the week."

"Great." She's all business. "You're going to make a bundle off this," she promises us. "This area is becoming increasingly popular with the Washington and Baltimore crowd. In ten years it's going to be like Solomons Island."

"It already is too damn popular," Sam says brusquely, shooting me a meaningful glance that sails right over her head. "That's why we aren't hanging on to it." He checks his watch. "Got to run. Fritz'll finish the paperwork with you."

He shakes hands with her, gets into his car, takes off. The agent and I walk up the front steps.

"Busy man," she notes. "What about you? You seem more laid-back. Are you on vacation?"

"You could put it that way. I'm going back to work in a couple of weeks."

She takes in the view from the porch. "It must have been a super life when you boys and your sister were growing up. Like Huckleberry Finn and Tom Sawyer."

"It was idyllic," I reply, with no irony in my voice. "But that's in the past."

"Tell me about it. You can't live in the past," she advises sagely. "It'll drive you nuts if you try."

The real Maureen O'Hara's breath is taken away when she sees Ollie and the sandhills. It's early morning, the birds have just come to the ground from their roost.

"This is amazing," she marvels.

The sandhills in and of themselves are exciting to see, but Ollie's the main attraction, of course. To her he's the lost tribes of Israel, miraculously found.

"How long have you been observing them?" she asks critically. She isn't looking at me, her eyes are riveted on Ollie.

"Since the middle of April," I admit.

"Wow! That's a long time for them to have gone undetected," she exclaims. She calculates in her head. "You don't recall when they arrived, do you?" This is the scientist speaking—she wants to know as much about this phenomenal situation as she can.

I shrug. "No. They'd already settled in when I started coming down here."

"So from the beginning of spring, would be likely," she declares. "On their northern migration." She shakes her head in disbelief. "It's a miracle no one else saw them."

Someone else did.

"We're about as isolated here as you can get for hundreds of miles around," I explain. "A quirk of geography." And my own stubborn tenacity, which led to so many catastrophes, far beyond the concealing of one endangered bird.

I'd called her a few days ago and invited her to come down

to the property. I played it cagey—I didn't want to tell her I had a wayward whooping crane living on my property with some equally lost sandhills, because I knew she'd bring the troops in faster than butter melts in a hot skillet, a scenario I wanted to avoid at all costs. I came at her sideways, informing her that through a series of extraordinary circumstances an extremely rare and exotic bird had come to live here, adding that this bird's being on my property had been the springboard for all the deception regarding her name and position.

I also made her promise that if I delivered the goods she would take no action regarding my special bird for a couple of days—she could look, but neither she nor anyone else could touch. It's going to be a bitch, all the changes about to come down: moving away, selling the property, letting go of Ollie. I knew I'd need time to adjust, emotionally.

She'd hemmed and hawed, but finally agreed to come down on my terms, as I'd guessed she would; the situation regarding the theft of her identity was weird and unsettling enough to motivate her.

I had a particular reason for calling Ms. O'Hara. I wanted her to be involved in overseeing Ollie's transfer to wherever it is he's going to be taken and relocated. Under normal circumstances I would have contacted the people at Patuxent—they're the experts in the field, and they're here in my own backyard, so to speak—but it seemed fitting that someone named Maureen O'Hara would do it, even if she's not the one I'd hoped for.

She'll work with the Patuxent scientists, of course. They'll be blown away when they discover that a whooper has been living here in the wild, virtually under their noses. That's part of the beauty and wonder of nature—that the most bizarre and extreme situations can, and sometimes do, happen.

She's almost trembling with excitement, she's so mesmerized by Ollie. "You should have reported this immediately," she scolds me. "These birds are so extremely fragile. Every one of them is irreplaceable. God forbid if anything had happened to him. You're lucky nothing did."

I know that, and I do feel badly about it. But like so much of what's happened these past couple of months, that's water under the bridge. The only thing that matters now is Ollie's safety and survival.

She agrees to honor our arrangement, but only for two days. Then she'll bring in the team that will capture the cranes. It'll be an intricate and hairy situation. The specialists will be dressed in crane costumes, playing crane songs on tapes, all that crazy stuff, so as not to imprint humans on the birds as adult leaders. The whole operation will be a complicated and extremely delicate undertaking.

Assuming everything goes okay, the sandhills will most likely be placed with an existing mature sandhill flock. Ollie will be separated from his brothers and sisters, the only family he's really ever known, and transported separately to the whooping crane flock that winters in Texas, where hopefully he will bond with his own kind. If that proves to be unsuccessful, he'll be sent to Florida or to the International Crane Foundation in Baraboo, Wisconsin, where captive whooping cranes are also being bred.

Ms. O'Hara hopes Ollie will make it in the wild—he wasn't raised as a captive bird. But like everything else in life, there are no guarantees.

The house already feels empty, even though the furniture's still in it. The real-estate agent didn't want us to clear it out—it will sell better this way.

I'm done packing. What I'm taking with me is being shipped up to Amherst, Massachusetts. The rest will go into storage. I start teaching at UMass next week. Ted Kelston found a nice apartment for me, near the campus. I'm looking forward to my new job and life, but I'm saddened to be leaving here, too.

Earlier this afternoon I spoke to Maureen/Vanessa over the phone, the first time we had talked at any length since judgment day at Roach's. She had called me before, but I couldn't handle hearing her voice for more than a few moments. This time, I was able to.

She was excited about my going back to teaching, although she knew I'd gotten the job, I had managed to tell her that much about what was going on with me. "It's a great new start for you, Fritz." I could hear her happiness for me coming over the line. It felt genuine. It felt good, too.

"We'll see," I told her cautiously. I'm on my own twelve-step program—I'm taking life a day at a time.

Then she hit me with her own news. "I'm being transferred."

"Oh? Where to?"

"Boston."

Boston? Jesus. "Is that a good move for you?" I ask warily.

"We'll see. I requested it. It's the closest posting to Amherst I could get. I'll be there by mid-November."

"Maureen," I stammered. "I mean Vanessa . . ."

"It's okay," she said. I could almost hear the smile in her voice over my stumbling. "I'll answer to anything you want to call me." She paused. "As long as you call me."

"Ah, look . . ."

"Listen to me, Fritz. What we had . . . what we still have . . . is way too special and important to walk away from. I couldn't do it, even if I wanted to, which I don't. And I don't think you do, either."

I didn't answer. What she was saying is true, but dealing with it is another matter.

In the end, we made a date to get together during my Thanksgiving break. "I'll call you next week after I get situated, give you my address and phone number," I promised her. "Maybe we'll do Thanksgiving up there. A Grandma Moses New England Thanksgiving."

"A New England Thanksgiving sounds wonderful," she responded eagerly.

That's three months away. If we still have feeling for each other then, we'll see if we can make a fresh start. I make no promises, to myself or to her.

Maybe we still have a chance—like she said, when you fall, you fall, and you can't do a damn thing about it.

I leave tomorrow at dawn, heading north to my new home. A few hours after I depart, Professor Maureen O'Hara and her team will be on the job. I won't be with them. What's done is done, I'm moving on, for real this time.

For the last time, I go down to the island to see the birds.

The sun is about to go down. Most of the birds are preparing to roost for the night, but Ollie and the sandhills are still active, restless. I think they know they're going to be leaving. I don't know why I believe that. Wishful thinking, I guess—that I've made that strong a psychic connection with them, especially Ollie.

I've brought a camera with me. This will be the last film of him I'll ever shoot here.

I go through most of the roll, saving a few exposures. Then I wade into the middle of the marshy water, where they're feeding. I'm part of the landscape now. I'm not going to harm them, and they can sense it. I stop when I'm about thirty feet from the cranes—the closest I've ever gotten to them.

"Good-bye, Ollie," I say softly. "I'm going to miss you."

I know I'm projecting, but I swear his hard marble eye fastens on me. Steady, unblinking. He begins strutting, his wings rising and falling. The others start up, dancing and calling out.

"Gar-oo-oo!" the sandhills trumpet. Ollie responds with his own mighty song. Their dancing becomes faster, more frenzied.

The spirit of their joy and freedom grabs hold of me. I begin dancing around with them, flapping my arms up and down like wings, crying out my own improvised song: *"Aye aye aye aye aye!"*

The birds seem baffled by my craziness. I don't care. For the first time in a long time, longer than I can remember, I feel as free as a bird.

Off to the southwest, the sun is falling into the Bay. I stop dancing and bring my camera to my eye, framing on Ollie.

With a great rush of wings, the cranes take flight. I track Ollie through the lens, shooting off the remaining frames on the roll. As I watch reverentially, the birds, Ollie most magnificently, circle overhead, soaring higher and higher, getting smaller and smaller in the distance.

And then they're gone.

ACKNOWLEDGMENTS

This is, as noted at the front of the book, a work of fiction. All of the characters and some of the most important locations exist only in my imagination and on these pages.

In particular, the unique situation regarding the whooping crane, as depicted here, is extraordinarily unusual and unlikely—the odds of this combination of circumstances actually occurring in nature are probably higher than one in a million. But what I have written is technically possible—whooping cranes commonly congregate with sandhills in the wild, and migratory birds are sometimes, for a great many reasons, found in locations far from their natural habitats. That is part of the incredible beauty and variety of nature, and why the events that I have created in this novel are, although highly unlikely, within the realm of possibility.

I am extremely grateful to Robin W. Doughty, Professor of Geography at the University of Texas in Austin, author of *Return of the Whooping Crane* (University of Texas Press), for his gracious assistance regarding whooping cranes. He has patiently read and critiqued the material about the whooping crane scenario that I created, answered my questions about birds and cranes, no matter how strange or naive, and sent me extensive and sympathetic notes and corrections. Any factual errors are mine, and in no way reflect upon his expertise.

Ernest Willoughby, Ph.D., Professor of Biology (emeritus) at St. Mary's College of Maryland in St. Mary's County, Maryland, took me bird-watching in southern Maryland, and was very helpful in matters having to do with birding in that region.

The Websites of Operation Migration, the Patuxent Wildlife Research Center, and The International Crane Foundation were useful in aspects of crane life and migration. The people who work at the Aransas National Wildlife Refuge, which I have visited and where I observed whooping cranes in the wild, were also helpful.

Sergeants Lyle Long and John Rhodes of the St. Mary's County, Maryland, Sheriff's Department, assisted me with local law-enforcement rules, regulations, and methods of operation.

The St. Mary's County Chamber of Commerce helped me regarding local customs and life in the southern Maryland area of the western shore of the Chesapeake Bay.

Stephen Harrigan escorted me around Austin, Texas, particularly the University of Texas. He also read and corrected the sections in this book about the university, as well as those sections that take place in the Hill Country of Texas.

Stephen Semple, the photography teacher at the Cate School in Carpinteria, California, assisted me in the areas of photography and computer-imaging information.

William A. Graham advised me in matters regarding sailing, big fancy sailboats, and custom-made shotguns.

Lynn McLaren, Licensed Investigator, helped with the nuts and bolts and protocols of private detective work.

Carol Warner read this book numerous times and gave me wonderful notes, particularly regarding style and grammar.

Susannah Freedman came up with the title.

Bob Lescher, my agent, was a great cheerleader, and also, as he always does, had many helpful comments about the manuscript during all stages of its development.

Lastly—I am very appreciative of the support given me by all the people at Warner Books, particularly Larry Kirshbaum and Jaime Raab. I am looking forward to a long and fruitful relationship with them. My editor, Maggie Crawford, painstakingly went through several drafts of this work with me, chapter by chapter, page by page, paragraph by paragraph, line by line, word by word, to make sure that I was as true to my vision as I could be, and that this book was as good as I could write it. That is the best gift an editor can give an author, and for that, as well as her commitment to the book and to me as a writer, I am deeply thankful.